CONFLICT OF DUTY

A LEGAL THRILLER

JAMES CHANDLER

SEVERN RIVER
PUBLISHING

Severn River Publishing
www.SevernRiverBooks.com

This is a work of fiction. Names, characters, businesses, places, events and incidents are either the products of the author's imagination or used in a fictitious manner. Any resemblance to actual persons, living or dead, or actual events is purely coincidental.

ISBN: 978-1-64875-587-3 (Paperback)

ALSO BY JAMES CHANDLER

Sam Johnstone Legal Thrillers

Misjudged

One and Done

False Evidence

Capital Justice

The Truthful Witness

Conflict of Duty

Course of Conduct

Smith and Bauer Legal Thrillers

Justice Bites

Never miss a new release!

Sign up to receive exclusive updates from author James Chandler.

severnriverbooks.com

For the staff and attorneys of the Wyoming State Bar, wherever you are. Thank you for doing what you do, and for doing it so well.

PROLOGUE

The Tri-Basin Divide is among North America's lesser-known geographic phenomena, probably due to its location high atop the Wyoming Range in the western part of the state. To the east is the Wind River Range; to the north, the Tetons and Yellowstone Park—each of which is well known and draws hordes of tourists. In between, and among the ancient peaks, lies a fly fisherman's paradise, for atop the divide along the comparatively smallish range are the headwaters of streams that flow north and west to the Snake River, then the Columbia River, then the Pacific Ocean; south to the Gulf of California via the Colorado River; and also south—this time to the Green River and ultimately the Great Basin. Each drainage hosts native cutthroat trout (the Snake River, the Colorado, and the Bonneville, respectively), which, combined with the Yellowstone cutthroat native to the Missouri River's headwaters to the east, comprise the fish sought by anglers hoping to accomplish Wyoming's "Cutt-Slam," the catching (and, preferably, releasing) of each of these wily trout species.

In search of trout before the late spring runoff commenced, Sam Johnstone began his day just before four a.m., when he climbed into his old truck and drove east into the foothills from the flatland camping spot where he'd spent the previous evening. Because the snow was still measured in feet at higher elevations, he was confined to fishing the foothills. But he'd had a good day, and by noon, he had landed both a Snake River and a Bonneville cutthroat; thereafter, he'd driven one hundred and fifty miles around the range searching unsuccessfully for a willing Colorado variant. He'd caught dozens of fish, but all were non-native (rainbow and brook trout). By mid-afternoon, he called it a day and drove into a small town on the east side of the range. A full tank and a gas station hotdog later, he saw a combination coffee shop and bakery that appealed to the sweet tooth he'd developed since he stopped drinking.

Now, he sat contentedly in the late April afternoon sun, enjoying the sounds of spring: children playing in the town square, dogs barking, and the occasional motorcycle motoring by. For an instant, he recalled the events of the weeks prior—a grueling trial that culminated in his client and mentor Preston Daniels being convicted of voluntary manslaughter. Daniels was a retired district court judge and sometimes cohort of Sam's. Sam had defended him—unsuccessfully, as it turned out—on a charge of killing his wife, who had died of an overdose. While the jury had acquitted Daniels of second-degree murder, they returned a guilty verdict on the lesser-included charge of volun-tary manslaughter. Daniels had been sentenced to serve a stint in the county jail followed by several years of probation and refused Sam's offer of help with an appeal. Losing was hard on the now-sober Sam, and this trip was his effort to put the recent loss behind him without resorting to booze and pills.

He'd ordered a cup of hot water and a bear claw, which garnered him a brief but questioning side eye from the gum-chewing teenager staffing the counter. He had taken his water and donut outside and sat at one of two tables adorning the sidewalk in front of the place. Reaching into his pocket, he retrieved a tea bag filled with an expensive variety of green tea. Since getting sober, he'd substituted green tea and candy for the vodka and hydrocodone he had favored for years. Aware he was being observed, he carefully lowered the bag into the water, looked at his watch, and made a mental note of the time needed to steep.

"That looks like quite the operation." She was at an adjoining table, about his age, stunningly attractive, well-tanned and by the looks of the ring on her right hand, well cared for.

"It's not bad," Sam replied. "I carry my stash with me wherever I go."

She showed straight, white teeth. "And where do you go?"

"Generally, wherever I want."

"And you take your stash with you?"

"I do," Sam admitted. "I'm a bit of a tea snob."

"I'm surprised," she said, looking him up and down. "You don't look snobbish."

"Selectively," he explained. "Everyone gets to be a snob about three things. Any more than that, and you're just a frigging jerk."

She had a wonderful laugh. "Just visiting?"

"Doing a little fishing. Nice country. Nice town."

"It is," she agreed. She blew the steam off a coffee concoction of some sort, then indicated his cup. "You do realize you're cutting into my profit there, sport."

Sam looked at his cup, then her. "Your place?" He gestured toward the storefront.

"Yes." She put her cup down. "My husband and I loved this town. When he got sick, I promised I would put his ashes in the river near here at a favorite spot of ours. So when he died, I came to do that. I came in here that morning and there was a "For Sale" sign on the window. So, I bought the place." She shrugged as if that explained it all.

Sam took a bite of the donut. "I'm sorry."

"The donut's that bad?" she teased.

Sam laughed. "No, that your husband died."

She stood and moved to his table, then sat and offered a hand. "Mickey Lindstrom." Seeing that Sam was taken aback, she added, "Nothing like you're thinking."

He was thinking that she didn't have an Adam's apple. "It's an unusual name."

"Technically, it's Michelle, but I was always a bit of a tomboy," she explained. "And you are?"

"Sam Johnstone—and no, it's not short for Samantha."

She measured him with large blue eyes. "You wouldn't make much of a woman—not with those legs," she joked. "What is that?" She indicated the bulge above his knee. "Some kind of brace?"

Sam smiled wanly. "No, it's some kind of leg." He knocked on the prosthetic device that replaced the leg he'd lost in Afghanistan.

"Oh my God . . . I—I am so sorry," she said bleakly. "I didn't know."

"Of course you didn't," he replied. "You couldn't."

Her face was coloring. "I had no right—"

"Forget about it," he said. "You couldn't know. I lost it a long time ago in a place far away."

"Oh no! You're a veteran?" she cried, standing as if to leave. "Now I feel doubly embarrassed!"

"Mickey," he said, struggling to use her nickname. "It's okay, really. I've learned to cope." He lifted the bag from the tea and placed it on a napkin. "Join me. Really."

"Can I buy you a drink?" she asked. "I really feel like I need to make it up to you."

He considered the offer. The thought of sitting in the warm afternoon sun with a gorgeous woman and catching a nice buzz was tempting. For years, day drinking had been a favorite pastime. "I don't drink anymore," he said apologetically.

She covered her mouth with a hand. "Wow. I'm striking out left and right. Could this get more awkward?"

"I'd take a piece of pie as a peace offering."

"At this time of day?" She laughed. "And on top of the bear claw?"

He shrugged. "Better for me than vodka."

"I'll be right back," she said, and stood. "What kind?"

"Surprise me."

"À la mode?" she offered.

Sam laughed. "I'll pass." He patted his stomach. "Too fat."

"We're going to have to disagree about that," she said.

He watched as she walked into her business, briefly considering how she might be in bed, then turned his attention to his phone. The Veterans Administration had been pestering him with daily if not hourly reminders of next week's counseling session with Bob Martinez ("VA Bob," Sam called him). He was accepting the appointment and electronically promising to make it for the umpteenth time when Mickey returned with two pieces of pie—one à la mode.

She placed the two generous slices on the table, then seated herself. She raised a flute containing what appeared to be a mimosa. "To new friends."

He toasted with his tea, feeling a little foolish. Perhaps just one drink wouldn't hurt. "What's mine?"

"Mixed berry."

"What if I don't like berry pie?"

"You will," she assured him. She carefully cut a small piece of her pie with her fork. "You said you don't drink *anymore*. Can I assume there was an issue?"

He watched her scoop the small portion and a dab of ice cream, put the mixture in her mouth, and chew carefully while he thought about his answer. "Just my lifelong inability to deal with life on life's terms, is all."

"You're very brave," she observed.

He wasn't sure what she meant by that. "Not really. I was forced into recovery. Like just about everyone." She had a small dab of ice cream on her upper lip. He considered what to do and decided to tell her. "You've got a little ice cream—"

"How embarrassing," she said quickly. "My gosh, you must think I'm a mess!" She giggled.

Nice laugh. "Not at all."

"I thought people had to be ready to get sober, or recover, or whatever."

"Nobody's really ready," Sam replied. "People get sober because they want the judge or their wife or husband, or their boss or their kids—or all of the above—off their ass. Some of us find out in the process of getting people off our back that it's a better way to live, is all."

"Interesting." She took another bite, eating carefully but with obvious enthusiasm. "This is good. I tried a new recipe for the crust."

Sam cut a piece of his own pie with a fork, admiring the flaky crust disintegrating with only a slight touch. "That is wonderful," he said, wishing it were apple.

"You sound surprised."

"Yeah, well, I've eaten cooking by attractive women before; a lot of it was terrible."

She smiled again. "Do you miss it?" she asked.

"My leg, or the booze?" It was gratuitous, and her smile disappeared.

"I'm sorry. Not sure why I thought that would be funny. I'll talk with my VA guy about it next week," he promised. "I do," he replied at last, in reference to the boozing. "It's funny; your mind plays tricks on you. Asks you to recall just the good times—and there were a lot of them. I've got to remind myself on occasion that there were a lot of bad times, as well. I want to leave it all behind, take the rearview off the truck so I can only see ahead of me, all that kind of stuff, but better that I keep aware of mistakes and . . . Damn, I'm sorry."

"It's fine."

"Not really. I don't need to be peeing on your foot and complaining—"

She had her mouth full, and covered it with a hand. "You've got an interesting vocabulary."

"Comes with the job."

"What job is that?"

"Now? Lawyer," he said, and awaited the inevitable reaction.

"And before that?"

"Soldier."

"That doesn't surprise me at all. You have the look."

"Is that good or bad?"

"Oh, that's good," she assured him. "So, that's how . . ." She indicated his leg with a fork.

"It is."

She put down her fork. "You're a hero."

"No," he corrected her. "Jenkins, Fish, and Jones were heroes."

"Who were they?"

"Three of the five men I lost the day I lost my leg."

"I—I don't know what to say," she said. She turned her attention to her pie, then washed a bite down with the mimosa. "Does this bother you?" She raised her glass.

"No," he said. "I look at my inability to drink as akin to an allergy. Some people are allergic to peanut butter. I'm allergic to booze."

She smiled in understanding. "Your men. Is that why you drank?"

Why was he telling her all this? "I had convinced myself it was," Sam replied. "But the real reason I drank is because I'm an alcoholic. I had plenty of reasons to drink before my men were killed, plenty of reasons to drink after, and I have plenty of reasons to drink now."

"But you're better now?"

"In some ways. I'll always be an addict and an alcoholic."

"Addict?"

"Oh, yeah," he said. "I'm addicted to everything, sooner or later. Percocet, hydrocodone, tobacco, coffee, chocolate—if I try it, I'll likely get addicted to it. It's how I'm wired."

"My gosh!"

"Addiction's a bitch." He shrugged. "Right now, I'm just looking for new ways to get gone, as they say. Fishing is one way—a healthy way—for me to cope without substances. What about you, Mickey?"

"Nothing so exotic." She shrugged. "I was a bit of a tomboy. Ran long distance. Accepted a scholarship to Southern California. Got there and decided that running dozens of miles per week while everyone else was partying was insane, so I dropped out."

She certainly had the legs for it. "And then?"

"Waited tables, did some modeling, and even had a couple of non-speaking, uncredited roles in movies no one has seen. Was about ready to go back to school when I met my husband-to-be. He was a wealth manager or something—I never really understood. But he could work from anywhere—even before the pandemic. We got tired of California and we'd vacationed in Jackson and had driven through here a time or two. When we decided to leave the rat race we purchased a place outside of town here and were going to build a house. He was so excited." She was examining the empty glass in her hand. "You mind if I have another?" she asked. "Slow day."

"Not at all."

When she returned with another drink, he put down his phone.

"Anything interesting?"

"Not as interesting as you," he assured her. "Just my secretary telling me about clients."

She blushed. "Anyway, we had just moved here. His cancer was in remission, he was doing really well, and he was out bicycling and got killed by a hit-and-run driver."

"Oh my gosh."

"Yeah. And they never found the guy. Well, I assume it's a guy—"

"I'm sorry."

"I've been so . . . angry. He fought to get well and then, well, some asshole . . ." She drank deeply, then looked squarely at Sam. "You're a lawyer—would you represent him?"

"Who?"

"The man who killed my husband."

"No."

"Why not?"

"Because I know you."

"What if you didn't?" she asked.

"Then I might."

"How could you do that? How can anyone represent someone who does something like that?"

How to explain? "Well, he's got rights. And everyone makes crappy decisions—it's just that some turn out worse than others."

"I don't know how lawyers do it—representing guilty people."

"Well, I don't determine who is guilty or not guilty," he began. "That's a job for the jury, unless my client decides to change his plea and admits."

"It's all a game."

"Well, to some degree. But our criminal justice system, if nothing else, staves off the fanatics and irrationally judgmental—you know, the people who run for office and serve in government," he joked, trying to lighten the mood.

She didn't smile. "Is there anyone you wouldn't represent?"

This was getting heavy. "Oh, sure."

"Like?"

He sighed. It was worth another try. "Well, for starters, the guy who is on his phone when the light turns green," Sam replied. "I mean, I have high hopes." Encouraged by her smile, he continued. "Anyone with three or more bumper stickers."

She laughed. "Even if you agree with them?"

"Especially if I agree with them," he said. "Then I'd know how screwed up they were. Men with flat bills on their baseball hats, any male over twelve wearing open-toe shoes anywhere other than the beach or the pool, dudes sporting a man bun."

"What about a mullet?"

"That's a Montana mudflap," he corrected. "I actually had one of those when I was a kid."

She was sipping her mimosa and almost spilled it. "Stop it."

"I did," he insisted. "Anyone wearing a mask in their car by themselves. People who eat fast food burgers on airplanes."

"Really?"

"Oh, yeah. That's death penalty stuff there," he replied. "You got beads in your beard and you aren't David Allan Coe? You're out."

"Oh, I hate that, too."

"Pipes coming out the bed of your El Camino? White dude with dreadlocks? Can't help you."

"You've got a long list!"

"Sadly. Add student body presidents, people with a 4.0 grade point average, and anyone out to change the world." He made a face as if deep in thought. "Come to think of it, it's a wonder I have any clients at all."

"Whew!" she said. "Glad I'm not on that list!"

He feigned a stern look. "Does your coffee order include the words 'soy' or 'sprinkles?'"

"No."

"Do you order your steak well done?"

"No way!"

"You might be okay."

She wiped carefully at a corner of an eye. "You're ruining my mascara," she said. "But really, is there anyone?"

Back to the subject at hand. "Well, I've done some murder trials, so I guess not—that's as bad as it gets, right?"

"Well, just about. Child rapists—or rapists in general?"

"That'd be tough," he acknowledged. "I don't know; I've never been asked."

"Drug dealers?"

"Depends."

"On what?"

"Well, there are two kinds of drug dealers," he explained. "One is your basic user who is divvying the stuff up and selling to his user buddies so he can feed his own habit at a reduced cost. Most of those people are basically harmless. It's not much different than sharing a bowl or a joint with a friend or giving them a can of beer out of a case."

She nodded understanding and agreement. "And the other?"

"The other is your more classic dealer—some guy making his living from other people's difficulties. Those guys and gals . . . well, there's a special place in hell for them."

She finished the second mimosa. "What are you doing tonight?"

He looked at his watch. "I'm not sure. I've got a seven-hour drive, and I work tomorrow."

"Can you take a day off?"

He had to try not to be too eager. "I own the business." He shrugged. "They can live without me for a day, I suppose."

"You cut into my profit margin," she said, indicating the tea. "It's only fair I return the favor and cost you a day's billing. Here." She stood and handed him a piece of paper with her address written in a distinctly feminine hand. "It's about ten minutes out of town. I'm going to do some shopping. Do you like salmon?"

"Pacific salmon, yeah." Seeing her raised eyebrow, he explained, "Fish snob. Atlantic salmon is flavorless."

"You're cute, but you could prove insufferable," she said as she turned. "See you at six."

1

Days later, Sam was back in Custer at the local jail, waiting impatiently while the jail staff retrieved Daniels, who was technically still a client. The clock was ticking on a possible appeal, and they needed to make some decisions soon. More importantly, he wanted to get a look at the older man. A judge housed in a local jail was obviously at risk; Sam was determined to keep eyes on his client, friend, and mentor. When Daniels was finally led into the attorney-client room, Sam was taken aback. He had already lost significant weight, and his face was showing signs of the sallow complexion that long-term inmates sport.

"How are you doing?" Sam asked, attempting to sound upbeat.

"That bad, huh?" Daniels replied. When Sam didn't respond, he continued. "You've got a lot of talents, Sam, but don't take up poker. You look sadder than a Sunday morning steel guitar."

Sam smiled wanly, then they spent several minutes catching up before he cleared his throat and got to the point. "I, uh . . . well, I was thinking we could appeal on the grounds that—"

"No."

"But—"

"No. I won't have it. Won't support it. End of discussion."

Big surprise. Sam studied Daniels until it was time to move on. "So . . . are they treating you okay?" he asked.

"Yeah. They're keeping me in isolation in Booking, so they've got round-the-clock eyes on me. The good news is, I'm plenty safe. The bad news is, I'm awake all night. Between the drunks, tweakers, and mad-at-the-worlds, this place is a zoo at night." He put a hand to his mouth and coughed deeply. "Must be coming down with something."

"Take care of yourself," Sam advised. "I've been thinking. Do you want me to petition to have you transferred to another jail? I mean, you gotta know most of these folks."

"No, I don't," Daniels said. Seeing Sam's disapproval, he shook his head. "Seriously, I'd be more afraid to attend a school picnic or a Rotary Club meeting—I've presided over divorces and custody battles for a lot of those folks. That's what pisses people off. These guys, well, most of 'em know they screwed up. Besides, here in Custer I know the staff. I'm catching up on my reading and getting stuff done. Which reminds me, you get my will done?"

"Not yet. Working on it. Listen, Judge—"

"Press."

"Press, I just want to say that I'm sorry."

"For what?"

"For you being here."

"Bullshit. You gave me a defense—a good one. The jury didn't see it my way. That's how the system works."

"How can you still believe in the system when it failed you?"

"The system didn't fail me; it simply didn't give me the result I wanted. Big difference. The State brought a case, I defended against it, the jury made its decision. The system worked *exactly* as designed. I can't condemn the system because I didn't get the result I wanted. What kind of person would I be if I did that?"

A normal one. "But—"

"No system that depends on human beings is going to return the right result one hundred percent of the time. Good grief; if I start pissing and moaning about the system, I might as well exchange my jail cell for a dorm room. I believe in the system; that's what makes me different from some law school professor who hasn't been inside a courtroom since his eighth-grade field trip. And you know what?"

The old man was on a roll now. "I'm afraid to ask."

"That professor doesn't have a better idea. He says that because the system doesn't work perfectly, we should discard it and simply do nothing. Well, how's that working out?"

Oh, boy. "Well, I think that's a matter for debate."

They heard the knock at the door. "We're out of time," Daniels said. "And don't you have someone to bill outrageously?"

Sam smiled and stood, then shook his mentor's hand. "Take care of yourself."

That evening, Sam took a booth in the back of the Longbranch Saloon and looked around to see who he knew, and to ensure he had a plan in case things went wrong. Unconsciously, he touched the small revolver he was carrying concealed in a holster inside his waistband. It didn't hurt to be prepared, especially where booze was involved. He'd arrived back in Custer after two days and nights with Mickey and was still thinking of her when he returned to his office to see a frowning Cassie waiting impatiently. In his defense, he'd called her and told her his return would be delayed.

The first words out of his mouth to her that morning comprised a lie. "Car trouble."

"Right." Her hands were on her wide hips. "Blonde or brunette?" When he didn't answer, she continued. "You've got clients stacked up like cordwood. It's amazing I was able to get them all rescheduled."

"Amazing. Give me a minute," Sam said. "Did you make coffee?"

"Not my job," she began. When his eyes narrowed, she added, "But yeah."

Sam nodded, walked to the office's small galley kitchen, and poured himself a cup. He sipped appreciatively with his eyes closed and tried not to think of Mickey as he walked the short hallway. On his desk were stacks of documents awaiting his review and signature. He had paged Cassie. "Who's batting lead-off?"

"Mrs. Schumer."

"Aw, crap-on-a-cracker! What now?" he had whined. As a child, Eva Beck had been raised and schooled in what was then West Germany. But she married an American lieutenant named Jack Schumer in 1965 and accompanied him through the entirety of his career, including seventeen moves in twenty-six years. When he retired, they moved to a family ranch south of Custer, where they scratched out a living until his death. Sam had met Jack shortly before his death, and now helped Eva solely from a sense of duty. Eva's habit, Sam had learned, was to instigate trouble in the family, and to then amend her will accordingly. Sam had warned her on a couple of occasions that this couldn't continue.

"She says this is the last time," Cassie had said.

"Okay. Bring her on back," he had instructed, then shook a couple of aspirin into his hand. When Cassie opened his office door and showed Eva in, Sam stood and took her hand. "Mrs. Schumer, always good to see you. How can I help?" he asked, ignoring Cassie's mocking of him.

From there, the day had gone slowly downhill, culminating with his visit to see Daniels, so when Cathy Schmidt had called and asked if he was up for a late dinner, he had readily accepted. Now, feeling unaccountably guilty about Mickey, he gazed about the saloon. Somewhere, he had read the place had been on Yellowstone Avenue in downtown Custer for more than a century. Featuring a bar that ran from the front door to the back, it hosted thirsty patrons from Custer's various walks of life (who sat toward the front), as well as tourists (who generally preferred the repurposed saddles near the back door that served as seats). The ceiling was covered with bills of various denominations featuring the donors' signatures and the occasional pithy quote. The walls were adorned with tin beer signs and pictures of customers and staff celebrating everything from New Year's to Halloween. Owner/bartender Gino Smith had operated the place for twenty years or so, Sam knew, and like any good small-town proprietor, he had his finger on the pulse of what went on in town.

"You finally back?" he asked Sam.

"How'd you know I was out of town?"

"It's my business to know," Gino said. "How was the water? Catch any fish?"

"Still down, but starting to color," Sam said. "Caught a few."

Gino nodded. "I figured. Always wanted to get over there myself. But running this place . . . well, you know." He shook his head and then looked around the bar. "What'll you have?"

"Diet cola."

"And for the lady? Moscato?"

"Not sure."

"All right, I'll be back."

Sam was looking at his phone when Cathy took the seat across from him. She was tall and blonde and had played college basketball as an undergraduate. Divorced and with an active twelve-year-old clone of a daughter, she had been a prosecutor when Sam moved to town—a good one. But the arrival of county attorney Grant Lee had soured her on the prosecutor's office, and Sam had helped her get established in private practice.

"Welcome back," she said, settling in.

"Thanks. I didn't order a drink for you," Sam said. "Wasn't sure."

"That's fine," she said. "Lemme take a look at the wine list." When Gino approached, she was ready. "I'll just have a carafe of the house white," she said. Gino nodded and left. "Probably opening the box right now," she joked when he was gone, showing even white teeth.

Sam smiled. "How's Kayla?"

"She's doing well," Cathy said. "Still focused on basketball, although she wants a smartphone for Christmas."

"What is she—twelve?"

"Thirteen. Her dad's all for it, of course, but he has no clue. All he knows is it will make it easier for him to get ahold of her when he wants to talk to her in between dating bimbos." When Sam didn't respond, she continued. "That sounded bitter, didn't it?"

He laughed. "Like dandelion tea."

"Yeah, well, he missed another child support payment," she said. "It's not the money, you know? I'm okay there. But it pisses me off that he can fail to comply with a court order and avoid any kind of repercussion."

"It's that damned legal system."

Gino delivered her carafe and poured her a glass. "I'll drink to that," she said, and they touched glasses.

"So what did I miss?" Sam asked.

"Hold on," she said. "I want to hear about your fishing trip. What'd you do?"

Sam thought briefly of his encounter with Mickey. "Spent my time stalking the wily cutthroat."

"Catch any?"

"A few." Sam eagerly powered up his phone and for the next few minutes showed her pictures of the different species of cutthroat he had caught and—just as important—the country he had seen. "I was kind of hoping to catch a grayling as well, but it didn't happen," he concluded.

"Poor you," she said. "Did you do anything other than fish?"

A vision of Mickey in bed interposed itself, and he was attempting to respond when she continued, "Didn't you do any pub crawls in Jackson, dancing or . . ." Apparently realizing what she was saying, her face fell. "Sam, I'm sorry, I didn't mean to—"

It was common for people—even friends—to think that he might do things differently in the absence of the left leg he'd lost in Afghanistan. "I did not," he replied, adding, "Cathy, it's fine. I fished, hit some taverns for bar food, and when I was in the small towns having my daily gas station hotdog, I watched girls in crop tops and fell in love a thousand times."

"Love, or lust?"

Again, he thought of Mickey. "I'm never sure. So what did I miss?" he asked, changing the subject.

"Not much. As you might imagine, the two major topics of conversation were Judge Daniels and Grant Lee."

Sam nodded. Lee was embroiled in an epic small-town scandal stemming from his having shot and killed a woman named Misty Layton at a local convenience store. As it happened, Cathy had previously defended Misty on drug charges. Lee was claiming self-defense, and the investigation was ongoing. A fine trial attorney, Lee had skills that were rivaled only by his high opinion of himself. "From what I hear, Miller is all over this one and it is only a matter of time."

Ashley Miller was a detective with the Custer PD. "She needs to be careful," Sam opined.

Gino appeared and they ordered—sirloin for him and a filet for her.

"Sirloin?" she scoffed. "That's like eating the sole of a boot."

"It's a lean cut. Gotta keep my girlish figure—and half the price of your filet."

"I'm expensive to keep around," she said, and poured herself another glass from the carafe. "Will you give me a ride if I need it?"

"Of course." Sam looked at his watch. Thirteen months since his last drink.

"The whole thing with Lee is a disaster," she said.

"Has Julie opened up?" Sam asked. Julie Spence had been a home health aide for Daniels and his wife and had testified for Daniels during his trial. Unfortunately, Julie had a significant criminal history, and Lee pounced on it and destroyed her credibility on the stand. Karma being what it is, Julie had been in the store when Lee shot Misty but was claiming she hadn't seen anything. While no one really believed her, at the time Sam had left to go fishing nothing had been discovered to discredit Julie's story.

"Not that I know of."

"Lee must be coming out of his skin," Sam mused. "He burned Julie on the stand and then the tables turn and . . . wow. I think I'd be heading for the hills."

"He's so arrogant he's still in the office every day, bringing charges against other people. It'd be funny if someone hadn't died." Cathy leaned forward in the booth, closing the distance between them. "So, I'm going to tell you something, but I need you to keep it under your hat. Promise?" When Sam made a show of silently zipping his lips, she continued. "A couple of the members of the county commission have contacted me."

The implication was clear. "Will Lee resign?"

"I doubt it, but they are going to lean on him."

"Well, they can do what they want, but it takes the Attorney General to get rid of him."

"I know, but the pressure's on, and the commissioners have already asked me if I'm interested."

Sam sat back in his chair and looked closely at her. "Are you?"

"I am."

If Cathy got the job it would kill anything between them. Of course, there was Mickey now—maybe. Long-distance relationships were tough. "You'd make a great county attorney," Sam said. They sat quietly while Gino served them. When he was gone, Sam continued, "You've got the practical experience, knowledge of the community, and the smarts."

"You're too kind," she said, pouring the last of the wine into her glass. "Will you give me a ride? I think I might have another. Kayla is at home right now. She's got a big school project due tomorrow. I'm giving her some space to get it done."

"Of course," Sam said, contemplating yet again his decision to stop drinking. If only he could have a couple and call it good, like "normal" people. But he was one drink, one bad decision, away from trouble.

"But no funny business," Cathy said as she sliced off a hunk of filet and dipped it in a puddle of bottled steak sauce.

"I wouldn't think of it," Sam said, trying not to think of it. "I still can't believe you put that crap on a thirty-dollar steak," he joked, pointing and shaking his head in disgust. "Some cow gave her all for that piece of beef."

"Much appreciated." Cathy covered her mouth with a hand. "Kayla says I'm a distraction."

"I agree," Sam said, debating whether to ask her out before it was too late. Then he remembered Mickey.

2

Aiden Cates had finished law school one year prior and had taken the only job he was offered, working for Lee as a deputy county attorney. Like a lot of would-be lawyers, he'd gone to law school with dreams of grandeur—in his case, a professed desire to be an environmental lawyer (whatever that was). But upon graduation, the reality of being a graduate of unimpressive class standing from a law school of no renown quickly set in, and he was forced to either adjust his goal or find a job as a barista while he floated resumes. When Lee (at the time the newly elected county attorney) had called, Cates had taken the job on the spot. To his surprise, the work was interesting, the pay and benefits decent, and the people nice enough. He was getting plenty of time in court, and in the short time he'd been in town he had already sat first chair in several trials and assisted Lee on several more—this while his peers in large urban law firms were carrying binders and overseeing Artificial Intelligence-facilitated discovery.

Lee's subsequent involvement in a recent shooting was unsettling, to say the least. Cates had no doubt that Lee's version—that he'd shot the woman in self-defense—was true, but with charges possible he was concerned for his own future. So when Lee had called this morning's meeting out of the blue, Cates had quaffed a handful of antacids before grabbing pen and paper and rushing down the hall to the boss's corner office. Now, Cates sat quietly across from William "Buck" Lucas, Custer's chief of police, trying to catch his breath and calm his nerves. Detectives Ashley Miller and Punch Polson (who was detailed to the Wyoming Division of Criminal Investigation) arrived together shortly thereafter. When the chief finally took a seat, Lee looked at the assembled group and asked without preamble, "On the Hayes matter. Where are we?"

Rebel Hayes was a seventeen-year-old who had died days earlier of a suspected overdose in a dingy motel in the company of two adult men. Like the rest of the country, Custer had seen an uptick in the number of opioid-related overdoses and deaths of late.

Miller was the first to speak, shaking her head. "We don't have enough to bump up Trent Gustafson's charges, if that's what you're asking."

Gustafson was a young man long suspected of bringing drugs from Colorado to Custer. Everyone in the room knew that DCI was investigating him for just that, and that Gustafson had been in the motel room with Rebel shortly before her death. Years prior, he had been associated with Ronnie Norquist, who was convicted of murdering Kaiden Miles after Sam's client, Davonte Blair, was acquitted. It was whiteboard complicated, but drug interactions always were.

"Of course that's what I'm asking! A girl died. My phone's been ringing off the hook. We need to do something, and we need to do it now!"

Lucas stepped to the defense of his detective. "Grant, this is going to be a tough one. Sure, the girl died, but we've got another guy—Clayton Pierce is his name—who overdosed as well, and Gustafson isn't saying shit. We are still waiting on the toxicology; we've got to give the lab time to get that right. But even when we get that, we are going to be up against it to try and prove anything beyond possession—maybe possession with intent to distribute."

Lee snorted derisively. "Possession? We get the guy on possession and he'll walk away with a straight probation sentence. With possession, he gets maybe three to five. I want drug-induced homicide."

Wyoming, like many states, had recently adopted a statute criminalizing the provision of drugs to another which resulted in the death of the user. In Wyoming's case, the statute applied only if the decedent was a minor and the accused was an adult at least four years older than the decedent.

When no one else spoke, Punch figured it was time to chime in. "That's a tough get. The statute says—"

"I know what the statute says," Lee interrupted.

"Then you know we need to be able to show her death resulted solely from her use of the drugs."

"She had a needle in her arm!"

Punch sighed. "We," he began, indicating the members of law enforcement in the room, "knew her. She was young, but she'd been doing drugs for a while. Probably learned it from her dad. So her toxicology will probably come back as polypharmacological or whatever—she'll have all kinds of stuff in her system. Then we'll have to see what the docs say. Proving that she died from the drugs in that syringe is the key."

Miller appreciated the support. "And even if we can do that, we'll have to show that Gustafson and/or Pierce knew that the drug they were giving the girl was fentanyl."

"Leave the proving to me," Lee snapped. "You just get me enough that I can get it in front of a jury, and we'll be fine."

Cates had been doing some reading. "And then we've got to have 'but-for' causation. A simple contributory effect to death is not sufficient to create criminal liability. That's *Burrage*," he said, referring to a Supreme Court ruling in a case arising in a state with a similar statute that it wasn't enough for law enforcement to show contributory causation.

"I know the case," Lee said. "What's your point?"

Cates' face reddened. "My point is that even if we get a conviction, it's likely to be overturned unless the toxicology shows that her use of whatever was in that syringe—even assuming it was fentanyl—was the *sole* cause of her death. Have you talked with the coroner?"

Lee shook his head dismissively. "No, and I don't have any reason to. The coroner is an elected official; I probably know more about toxicology, death, et cetera than he does." He looked around the room for confirmation. When nobody spoke, he continued. "Drug overdoses in this country are now one of the leading causes of death of our young people. I can't do anything anywhere else, but here in Custer, I'm going to stop it and I'm going to stop it now!" He banged the desktop with a fist. "And I would do that whether I had the Mr. Hayeses of the world beating on my door or not.

For too long, we looked at overdoses as death by misadventure. We treated ODs as unintentional accidents involving no violation of law or criminal negligence. And what happened? Well, we've seen a steep increase in the number of deaths."

"I hear you," Lucas said. "I've got the same duty to the taxpayers as you have. But we're not going to move forward with charges until and unless we have evidence that one or both of those idiots knew what the drug was, provided the drug to her, that she took the drugs provided, and that that's what killed her. Until then, we're going to continue to investigate."

Lee studied Lucas for a long moment, then shifted his eyes to Miller and then Polson. These people were weak. "Well, my expectation is that you will step on the gas and get the proof that you need so that I can do my job, which is protecting this community. I consider this an urgent task. Apparently, I'm the only one in this office who feels that way."

"Don't you play that shit with me!" Lucas barked as he stood to his full height. "I've been protecting and serving the people of this community since before your mama was wiping your butt." He leaned forward and put both hands on Lee's desk to emphasize his point. "And I'll be doing that long after your ass is back in whatever gated community you crawled out of."

"Buck," Punch began.

"Shut up, Detective."

"Buck—"

Lucas was pointing now. "We will bring the charges if and when we are convinced that we have enough evidence to prove them—and not before."

"It's my job to advise you with respect to what evidence it's going to take," Lee replied quietly. "And I don't think it's going to take a lot. We've got a dead girl on our hands and a pissed-off father."

"I know that—I had a protest in front of my headquarters yesterday. But I'm not going to charge someone simply because he was the last person who was with the girl before she croaked." Lucas huffed before straightening again. "And thanks for your opinion, Counselor, but I'm not so sure you're even gonna be here."

Lee's eyes narrowed. "I think that'll do it," he said. "This meeting is over."

"Let's go," Lucas said to Miller and Punch. "We've got investigations to undertake," he added, emphasizing the plural.

Minutes later, Punch and Miller were seated in Lucas' office when the still-flushed Lucas looked at them. "What do you think toxicology is going to show?"

"Not entirely sure," Miller admitted. "If what her friends are telling us is true, we will find THC, heroin, methamphetamine, and maybe cocaine."

"Booze?" Lucas asked.

"Oh, hell yes. I didn't even think to add that."

"Well," Lucas said, thinking aloud, "it could be dicey. Heroin, meth, and booze are all agents of overdose. Determining that she didn't die from alcohol poisoning is perfunctory, but the rest will be more difficult to rule out. But when you get the toxicology report we ought to know one way or the other."

"I don't think it's going to be that easy," Punch offered. "Even if we find that fentanyl killed her, that doesn't mean Gustafson or Pierce gave it to her."

"Who else could have?"

"Hell, I don't know. But I do know that we're going to want the answer to that question before we move forward," Punch replied. He looked at his watch.

"Lee and his people can deal with that," Lucas replied. "If some defense attorney wants to stand up there and point to the Invisible Man as the source of those drugs, let him. I would love for that to be their defense." His eyes met Miller's and Punch's. "Lean on Pierce—he'll give you what you need. Now, on another subject—you can go, Punch—Miller, what've you got on the shooting?" Punch departed. When the door closed behind him, Lucas looked to Miller. "Well?"

"We've got just about everything we need. We've got a confession—he says he shot her. We've got ballistics—it was his gun that fired the round that killed her."

For a variety of reasons, matching weapons and expended rounds was no longer considered scientifically infallible. "Not conclusive anymore," Lucas observed.

"Right, but it adds to the picture," she acknowledged. "We've got the medical examiner's and coroner's reports, which show that she died of a gunshot wound at about the time the call came in."

"So we've got everything but motive. Did they know each other—aside from the court case, I mean?"

"Doubtful."

"What's that mean? Haven't you checked?"

"Well, he says they didn't know each other and we have no indication they did."

"Not good enough; chase that rabbit down the hole," he directed.

Miller was biting her lip. "So, let me ask you this," she began. "Let's say we're ready to take this to the county attorney. How does that work?"

"I called one of my buddies down in Cheyenne. He said that if Lee won't resign, they're going to have to appoint a special prosecutor. Someone independent."

"Oh, thank goodness. I was afraid that Cates kid would have to handle it."

"No. It'll have to be a pro. They'll find someone," Lucas assured her. "But you've got to get going. Between not bringing charges on Lee and not bringing drug-induced homicide against Gustafson or Pierce, we're about to get raked over the coals here. Let me know when you are ready. We're gonna run this by Chief Sprague over in Jefferson County—I want to be able to tell the press we had another set of eyes on it. But hurry up. I'm not gonna be checking parking meters on Yellowstone Avenue by myself."

3

That afternoon Miller watched in disgust as Gustafson dumped spoonful after spoonful of sugar into the Styrofoam cup. "A little coffee with your sugar there, stud?" She was hoping to get information from him before he lawyered up.

"I've just never really gotten into the stuff," Gustafson explained, stirring the mixture with a plastic spoon.

She waited impatiently while he finished stirring, sipped carefully from the cup, then placed it on the laminate tabletop in front of himself. "You know why I'm here?" she asked at last.

"Well, yeah. You people are saying I had something to do with drugs and that dead chick. You're trying to get me to cop to it."

"Her name was Rebel Hayes. She was seventeen," Miller said curtly. "And yeah, *something*. We know you've been hauling weed, then meth, and now fentanyl from Fort Collins here to Custer. It was all fun and games until that little girl died. Now, your tit is in a wringer." She placed a photo of Rebel and Clay entering Gustafson's room on the table where he could see it.

Gustafson looked at the photographs with a practiced air of nonchalance. "Big deal." He shrugged. "I'll tell you the same thing now that I told you when you and your people were beating the shit out of me outside that hotel. I'm not saying a damned thing without my attorney present."

"You and I both know that didn't happen," Miller countered. "You ran like a mailman from a pit bull. And fortunately, we have dash and vest cams to back us up. But hey, it's your right to keep quiet. Might even be a good idea. I'm just trying to clear some things up; thought maybe if we got some information, we could all get on with our lives. I could get the county attorney to talk with the judge and maybe we could drop the charges. But hey, if you want to wait until your attorney gets here, that's cool, too."

"Straight up," Gustafson said, jutting his chin defiantly. He picked up his cup.

"Good enough." Trying not to laugh at Gustafson's tough-guy pose, she stood to leave. She couldn't help herself, and openly appraised the young man. "Start doing push-ups."

"What's that?" Gustafson asked, carefully replacing the cup.

"Start doing push-ups," Miller repeated. "You don't want to go to prison with pipe-cleaner arms like those. Seriously."

"Bullshit. Even if you could somehow get me convicted on these charges, I'm not going to do any time," Gustafson countered. "It's posses-sion; no one does time for possession. You know it; I know it."

"Yeah, well, guess what? When that little girl died, your shit got weak. The county attorney is dead-set on amending your charges to add drug-induced homicide."

"Excuse me?" Gustafson asked.

"Oh yeah. And that fella you were with? Clay? He says he watched you give that little princess the drugs that killed her." It wasn't true, but there was no prohibition against lying to a defendant. "That's called drug-induced homicide and it can get you twenty."

"That's a lie!" Gustafson said, standing.

She shrugged. "The way I look at it, it was either you or him that gave her whatever killed her. You've clammed up, which you have every right to do. I respect that. But he's flapping his lips like a camel chewing bubble gum—and he swears it was you."

"That old bastard doesn't know anything! He's full of—"

"Don't know what to tell you, except maybe don't get too comfortable."

She made a show of appraising Gustafson again. "Military presses are real good for the upper body, too," she added before turning to leave. She pressed a button on the small recorder she was carrying to stop the recording. "Interview terminated, nine-twenty a.m. Wait here, Mr. Gustafson, I'll get a jailer to take you back."

While Gustafson had been uncooperative, Julie Spence was downright bitchy an hour later when Miller went to see her about the shooting of Misty Layton. Miller stood with her hands on her hips in the parking lot of the store on Teton Avenue where Layton had been shot. It had reopened earlier in the day after having been closed since the shooting. A sign reading, "Caution. Cleanup in Progress—Floors May be Wet," remained in place.

She entered and immediately observed Julie stacking cups near the coffee station. "Julie Spence?" Miller asked. "Don't know if you remember me, but I'm Detective Miller with the police."

Julie nodded her understanding, then turned her attention back to stacking cups. "Is there a problem?"

"I just wanted to follow up with you about the events of a couple weeks ago."

"I already told you people everything I saw or heard."

"Well, that's kind of why I'm here," Miller explained. "There seems to be a substantial difference between your version of events and that of Mr. Lee."

"Well, maybe you better believe him, 'cause I didn't see anything."

Miller looked steadily at Julie's back. Might as well say it. "Well, if I do that, I'll probably have to take you into custody, because he is saying you must have hidden evidence." She watched as Julie's back stiffened.

"Well, he's full of shit."

"I thought you said I needed to believe him? What's it gonna be?"

Julie stopped stacking and now turned to face Miller. "Can you give me five minutes? I've gotta get the coffee re-stocked, and then it will be my break time."

"Sure," Miller said. "I'll wait in my car." She turned and went outside, taking a seat in the aging sedan. Seeing Julie step outside, Miller waved her into the car.

"Can I smoke?" Julie asked.

"No," Miller said. Seeing Julie's face, she explained, "State car."

"Of course," Julie said sourly. "What do you want to know?"

"Well, just give me your version of what happened."

"I already—"

"Humor me, would you?"

"So, I was kind of in the hallway to the bathroom, and I heard some guy say, 'Hello?' or something. Misty had told me to clean the restroom floors and she was going to take a smoke break—she did that all the time. So my thinking was she needed to put out her cigarette and help the guy, right?" Without waiting for a response, Julie continued. "So I'm mopping or whatever and I can hear Misty and the dude talking, so I figure she's got a handle on it."

"And then?"

"So, it gets loud, and I hear him say something like, 'I don't want any trouble.' Then I heard her yelling something at him about her endangering children. Then he said, 'Stop!' and then I heard a shot."

"Did you see who fired it?"

"Nope. I came into the store and then I asked what happened. He said Misty came at him with a knife and asked me if I knew CPR."

"What happened next?"

"Well, he asked me to do CPR while he stepped outside to call 9-1-1."

"Did you?"

"Well, yeah, kinda. I mean, I don't really know CPR."

"Okay, what then?"

"Well, she was dead, so I just kinda went back around to the bathroom and waited. Cops got here and I told 'em she was dead. I told one of them her name. He told me to lock the door, so I told him I didn't see nothing, just like I told you. Then he had me wait in my car. He came out and the next thing I knew that Lee guy was yelling in my face. I went downtown and gave 'em a statement," she concluded, looking at her phone. "I got like two minutes."

Miller had been taking notes and mentally comparing them to Julie's initial report. "So, you never saw a knife?"

"No."

"You didn't remove or hide or do anything with a knife?"

"I just told you I never saw one."

"And the thumb drive to the video system?"

"You'd have to talk with . . . . well, Misty would remove it whenever she went to smoke. I told the cops that."

"Any idea where it might be?"

"Wasn't on her?" Julie asked.

"If it was, I wouldn't be asking you about it, now would I?" Miller asked sharply, before softening. "He was hard on you in court and—"

"He ruined my life!"

"I know," Miller agreed. "Look, he did some stuff. But if you saw something, you have a duty to—"

"Duty? To who?"

"Well, to everyone, I guess. The system only works—"

"The system doesn't work!"

"—if everyone tells the truth."

"The last time I told the truth, what'd it get me? This!" She gestured around the dingy store. "This is what it got me. Well, no thank you." She dug in a pocket and retrieved a cigarette. "I gotta burn one—my break's almost over."

"Okay, well, if you think of something that might help, let me know, okay?"

"Sure thing," Julie said. She exited the vehicle, then lit her heater and walked to a spot near the front door, where a one-gallon coffee can partially filled with sand served as the smokers' area.

Miller was drinking iced tea from an enormous plastic cup when Lucas knocked on her cubicle. "Got a minute?" he asked.

"Of course."

"Come see me," he said. When she entered his office, he closed the door. "Sit," he commanded, and moved ponderously behind his desk and sat. "How did it go?"

"Not good. She says she didn't see anything."

"What do you think?"

"I think she is lying her little ass off."

"Why?"

"You watched Daniels' trial. Lee ripped her to shreds. He ruined her, or so she says. I'm not so sure her own choices hadn't already done that, but whatever."

"If she doesn't come across—"

"We've got a dead woman and a county attorney who admits to killing her, but says it was in self-defense."

"No video?"

"None."

"What about adjacent businesses?"

"Nothing yet. Degrees of cooperation vary," Miller said. "I've still got a warrant or two with Lee's office. We'll get the warrants served and see if we have any luck."

"The knife?"

"If there was one, she had to have taken it."

"Damn it! How?"

"Baker was first on the scene. He did what he could, and he used Julie to help him secure the scene. But because he had already gotten a confession of sorts, he didn't think to search Julie before he sent her out the door."

"You searched the surrounding area?"

"Of course."

"Her route home?"

"Yes."

Lucas shook his head. "Damn."

"I know. She could have driven five miles in any direction and been in the middle of nowhere."

"Can you appeal to her conscience?"

"After what Lee did to her? She was a truthful witness, and for her trouble she lost everything. At least that's how she looks at it."

"She's getting even, then?"

"Sounds about right."

Lucas looked at Miller. She'd been a good hire—even better than he'd expected, and she'd been impressive during her interview. "What do you think happened?"

"My gut says Lee's telling the truth. Misty Layton had lost access to her grandkid. She was blaming Lee. And Julie was fired from a job she liked after her history came out in the trial. Lee's story makes a lot of sense, and he doesn't seem like the kind of guy to go around shooting people—hell, if he did that, he wouldn't have anyone to sneer at."

Despite himself, Lucas laughed. "He is one uppity prick," he agreed. "Well, I don't have to tell you the pressure's on. We either need to charge him or clear him, and I want Sprague looking at it first."

"I know."

"The city council and county commissioners are getting antsy," he added. "The last thing they want is to have Custer make an appearance on one of those unsolved crimes shows. Now, speaking of high visibility, where are we on Gustafson and Pierce? We need to get those two to trial as soon as possible, before Hayes has folks outside the station with pitchforks. You can prep Punch for the preliminary hearing—hearsay is allowed with no limitation, right?" He looked pointedly at his watch. When she stood, he continued, "I got a meeting with the chamber of commerce. Check in with me later, okay?"

"Right, boss," she said as she turned for the door.

"Miller."

She turned to face him. "Yes, sir?"

"You're doing a great job."

"Thanks. I—"

"Close the door, will you? I gotta make some notes."

4

Sam opened the door of his refrigerator, smelled the milk, and grimaced. There was only one egg, and the bacon looked rancid. Before closing the door, he looked briefly at a lone longneck bottle of beer. "Morning, soldier," he said. It was the last of a twelve-pack he had drunk (along with a pint of vodka) on the evening of his last drink. Alcoholics in recovery debate being around booze early in recovery. For Sam, the beer served as a reminder.

He looked at his watch and decided he had time to run down to the Lasso Café for a bite before starting the day. Ten minutes later, he entered the small café and saw Punch sitting alone in a booth. Punch had served four years in the army and Sam had always liked him. Since Punch's detail to DCI, they hadn't seen much of each other.

"Mind if I join you?" Sam asked.

"Sit." Punch indicated the booth's other bench. "How are you?"

"I'm warm and dry and no one is shooting at me." The waitress appeared and poured his coffee. "Thank you." Sam sipped appreciatively, then put the cup down. "I'll have a short stack and one over easy." He looked to Punch. "You?"

"She got it already," he said.

Sam nodded. "So, what's up in your world?"

"Christ, I'm busier than a first-grader trying to give two puppies a bath. Chasing down this fentanyl is kicking my ass."

"What's the issue?" Sam asked. "Can't be that hard; seems like you grab a couple of users by the short and curlies and they'll cough up their dealer."

"You'd think," Punch replied. "But every user is a dealer; everyone's cutting it to get their own on the cheap. I can't seem to get above the level of brothers-in-law and the-guy-I-met-at-a-bar, source-wise. And I can't get a solid handle on who is bringing the crap into town."

"It's Gustafson, right?"

"Well, yeah. Among others. But aside from your guy Pierce, no one will rat his ass out." Punch blew on the surface of his cup to cool the contents. "Seems like as things relate to Gustafson, people get a case of sudden-onset specific memory loss syndrome."

Sam nodded knowingly. His client, Clay Pierce, had agreed weeks prior to testify against Gustafson in return for a lighter sentence. "Clay will hold up, I think."

"Yeah, well, we'll see if Cathy will do the deal. With new charges, who knows?" Punch replied. "So, you've had it rough lately. How are you?"

"I'm okay," Sam said truthfully. No reason to snivel.

"Well, don't kick your own ass over Daniels. You did what you could. Don't get bent too far out of shape. Hey, you still sober?"

"Yep. Little over a year now."

"That's great!"

"Yes and no. The world is an ugly place for a sober man."

When the food arrived, they ate silently for a few minutes until Punch put down his fork. "This Lee thing. Holy crap!"

"It's ugly."

"That dude is so uptight it would take an M-1 to pull a needle out of his ass," Punch said.

Sam laughed at the image of an Abrams tank in that role. "I know. He's impossible. Just a nightmare to deal with on stuff."

Punch indicated his understanding. "Well, he's done now, I would think."

"You'd think so," Sam agreed. "I mean, innocent until proven guilty and all, but if I were facing charges, how could I bring cases against others with my own foot in a snare? That's a special level of audacity. But no charges yet, right?"

"Not that I've heard. I know I'd be doing things by the book," Punch said. "There's gotta be conflicts of interest out the ass, right?"

"I would think so," Sam agreed. "They'll have to bring in a special prosecutor, for one thing."

"Hey, maybe they'll call you! You can come over to the side of God and country!" He laughed.

Sam joined the laughter. "I don't think so."

"I'd pay money to watch that trial. Just think: you prosecuting Lee." When Sam merely smiled, Punch showed concern. "You sure you're okay, Counselor?"

"I'm good," Sam assured him.

"You say so." He shoveled a piece of omelet into his mouth.

"It's just, you know, second-guessing myself, I guess."

"Speaking from experience, I can tell you there is no future in that," Punch said, unironically. "I've spent a good portion of my life doing just that, and that'll get you drinkin' again, if nothing else will," he added, pointing at Sam with a fork.

"I know." Sam turned the cup in his hands. "Speaking of futures, I've been thinking it might be time to move on."

"Seriously? You've built yourself quite a practice already. Lotta older attorneys in town—hell, in five years they'll all be retired and you'll own this place."

"I know," Sam said. "You're probably right. I could build a great practice here, hire a couple of associates . . . But sometimes I feel like it's time to hit the road. Maybe it's the soldier thing—new job, new post around the corner all the time."

"Maybe," Punch agreed, but he was looking at Sam doubtfully. "You sure you don't just have your tail in a knot? I mean, it ain't been the best what with Veronica and now the judge, an' all."

Veronica Simmons had been a sometimes girlfriend of Sam's before she left town. "I said I'm okay," Sam snapped.

"Hey, Counselor." A chagrined Punch held up a hand in a halting gesture. "Not trying to get outta my lane here. Just concerned, is all."

Why was he so edgy? "I'm sorry," Sam said.

"I get it." Punch reached for the check. "On me."

"Sure?" Sam asked.

"You bet," Punch said, then looked pointedly at his watch and donned a weathered cowboy hat. "I'm on the taxpayers' clock. Finish your coffee. And take care of yourself."

5

To facilitate interagency collaboration, Lucas had allowed Punch to keep a desk in a cubicle in police headquarters while he was detailed to DCI. Now, following his breakfast with Sam, Punch was in the tiny space attempting to access the assigned computer. Frustrated after several unsuccessful attempts, he slapped his desk's surface viciously. "Damn it!"

"What is it?" asked a young cop—Punch couldn't recall her name.

"I can't get this freaking computer to run. Keeps telling me to enter some kind of code."

"Did you enter the security code?"

"Did I what? It puts my PIN in automatically—I got it saved."

She smiled tolerantly. "You're not supposed to do that—it's a security violation," she said. "Since you were here last, we added another layer of security. We've now got what's called triple-factor security."

"Meaning what—the IT department can prevent *three* guys like me from doing their jobs?" he asked sourly. "I can see it now: bad guys running wild while we all sit at our computers trying to remember our freaking security credentials."

"Meaning less chance of compromise," the young officer explained as she pecked at the keyboard.

"Compromise? Christ, what're you talking about? I just wanna check my email!"

"There," she said, straightening. "Try it now."

"My password?"

"No, your user ID."

"What's that?"

"I don't know. It's private. You should know."

"I don't."

She looked at him, then leaned over and keyboarded. When nothing happened, she keyboarded again. She looked at him, then held up an index finger as if she had it. She typed one more time. "Bingo!" she said. "It's 'Sergeant.' Now enter your password," she instructed, pushing the keyboard back to him.

"I can't remem—"

"You are always talking about your family. What's your wife's first name and the date of her birth?"

"Rhonda; the twelfth."

She again pecked at the keyboard. "I think I got it. Bazinga!" she said when the screen opened. When he looked at her curiously, she wrote, *Sergeant* and *Rhonda#12*.

"Not very original," she scolded.

"Meh, what can I say?" He shrugged. "I gotta write that down." When she rolled her eyes and departed for her space, he hunted and pecked until he accessed a copy of the investigation into the death of Rebel Leigh Hayes, the seventeen-year-old he had found dead in a room at the Horseshoe Motel.

He had been on stakeout, eating a sandwich that Rhonda had made him, when Gustafson stepped from the motel room and looked quickly in the direction of where Miller had been pretending to have car trouble. Seeing her, Gustafson had (as anticipated) headed in the other direction toward his car, where he'd been intercepted by Officer Ron Baker, who used an arm bar to push the much smaller Gustafson up against the door of a room until Miller arrived and the pair quickly cuffed him. By the time Punch arrived on scene, Baker was completing his advisal of rights. "Do you understand?"

"Kiss my ass," Gustafson had replied.

Miller had previously obtained a warrant to search the room, so after Baker hauled Gustafson off, Punch and Miller walked quickly to the door, assuming the room's remaining occupants—Clayton Pierce and an unknown young woman—were ridding the room of evidence. Time was at a premium. Punch had knocked loudly. "Clay? This is the police. We have a warrant. Open the door, please." Hearing nothing, Punch had continued pounding while Miller cupped her hands and peered in the window.

"I can see a foot! Looks like he's on his back on the bed." Punch pounded on the door again. "He isn't moving," she said.

Punch tried the door and, finding it unlocked, drew his weapon. He and Miller entered the room, where they located Clay in coronary distress and —on the floor in a pile—an unresponsive teenage girl with a needle in her arm and blood seeping from her mouth and nose.

Punch sat back in the small cubicle and recalled the evening had only gotten worse when he accompanied Miller to the girl's home, where her burly, bearded father, Wrangler Hayes, seemingly tagged all five stages of grief in one half-hour.

Now, days later, Punch could still hear Hayes' cries of grief. He began typing, updating his investigation notes.

"What do you think, Punch?" It was Buck Lucas.

"I think Gustafson oughta be given the same sort of consideration he gave Rebel Hayes," Punch answered.

"Punch!" Lucas scolded. "You can't say shit like that!"

"Why not?" Punch asked. "It's true."

"You know damned well why," Lucas whispered, eyeing the cubicles in the squad room. "Don't say stuff like that out loud. The last thing we need is one of these prairie dogs going to the press and repeating that. Come on down to my office. We need to talk."

When the two men entered Lucas' office, Punch was surprised to see Lee standing in the corner. He nodded his recognition and received the same in return.

"Now," Lucas continued. "Whatcha got?"

"Honestly, it's not great," Punch said. "You've got a dead girl and two guys in jail. As you know, this isn't even my jurisdiction; I'm just trying to help out. My boss at DCI finds out I'm briefing you before him and—"

"Your secret's safe with us," Lucas said quickly.

"I know," Punch said uncertainly. "I'm going to see if I can squeeze the one—he's a veteran. Sam Johnstone is his lawyer. We had a deal before this."

"What about the other guy . . . Gustafson? He's the one we want anyway, right?"

"He's not gonna say anything. Miller's moving ahead, but I'm still not comfortable we've got enough on drug-induced homicide," Punch lamented.

Lee smirked. "You've got him in possession of a felony amount of fentanyl, and you've got a dead kid with a needle in her arm and fentanyl in her system," he observed. "I can get a jury to connect the dots."

"Well, there's Pierce," Punch argued. "Gustafson points at Pierce; Pierce points at Gustafson. I'd feel better if we waited until we get Sam's client in here to make a statement."

"Pierce is a loser," Lee replied. "And the fact that Johnstone is representing him tells me the guy is likely a sick puppy."

"What the hell does that mean?" Punch asked. "And are you even allowed to—"

"Punch, stay on topic," Lucas ordered.

Lee ignored Lucas' comment. "Detective Polson, I haven't been charged with anything. I am still the elected county attorney."

"Yeah, well, good for you."

"Punch," Lucas began. "We're all on the same team here. Let's focus on what we can agree on, and that's doing what we can to put Gustafson's ass in a sling."

"I'm just saying that if I were Miller, I wouldn't bring the charges yet."

Lucas exchanged a look with Lee. "You've got a lot more experience. Why don't you put together an affidavit of probable cause?" Lee suggested. "I'll take a look at it, and if I think we can make a run at it, we'll do it."

"I don't know that we've got enough," Punch argued. "I'd like to bust him as much as anyone, but if we can't prove it—"

"We'll dump the charge in return for him pleading guilty to felony possession," Lee said.

Punch was surprised that Lee had said the quiet part out loud. "So you're saying to bring a charge knowing we can't prove it?"

"We do it all the time."

"*We* don't," Punch replied. "Is that even ethical?"

Lucas' face was reddening. "Punch—"

"As a practical matter, we never know whether we can prove something," Lee responded calmly. "How about you leave the legal ethics to me and focus on getting that affidavit prepared, huh?"

Lucas knew that would do it. Before Punch could reply, he intervened. "Punch, head on back. I'll be down to see you in a minute."

Punch was already on his feet. "Right."

"Pierce and Gustafson are both being arraigned today," Lucas said. "Let's amend the charges and get an information including drug-induced homicide to the judge before court." This meant that Punch would have to draft an amended affidavit of probable cause and get it to the county attorney's office in time for them to review, prepare, and deliver the amended documents to Downs' office for her signature. Time was already running short. "Any issues, let me know."

"I'll do it," Punch said. "But I don't like it and I ain't signing it."

6

While Punch was hammering at his keyboard, Sam was looking around the small, cinder-block room while awaiting Pierce's arrival. According to law enforcement, Clayton "Clay" Pierce had been at the Horseshoe Motel with Gustafson and a minor female before she died. Clay had apparently over-dosed for the umpteenth time as well, and after a brief visit to the hospital, he had called Sam, asking for another chance. Sam had made his way to the detention center, debating whether to take this on. He'd been working with Clay for months but saw little progress. Addiction was a grind, but sooner or later an addict had to say no. To this point, he'd seen no evidence Clay was inclined to do so. He looked up sharply when he heard the key in the door and watched as the jailer led Clay to the small table and chained him to the center post.

"Twenty minutes," the jailer told Sam.

Sam nodded and turned his attention to Clay. "What the hell is the matter with you?" he asked as the door shut behind the jailer.

"What?"

"*What?*" Sam mocked. "I mean just what I said—what is your major malfunction? How in the hell is it that you can literally die, then turn around days later and go back and do it again?"

"Hey, man, I don't need this—"

"You called me!"

"Yeah, but not to give me shit."

"What did you think was going to happen?" Sam asked. "Standing ovation?"

"No, but a little understanding—"

"What I understand—and what you apparently don't—is that you are not the victim here! There's a dead girl on a slab here in town, and you made the decision to somehow be in a room with her and the biggest drug dealer this side of Denver."

Clay looked at his chained hands. "Look, I used bad judgment and got too high and—"

"Bullshit," Sam said. "Bad judgment is buying a one-hundred-dollar bottle of champagne for a stripper when she says she likes you."

Despite himself, Clay cracked a brief smile before sobering in the face of Sam's continuing glare. "Sam, I was hurting. I figured I'd just get a little tweak on—you know."

He did know. "But it never works out like that, does it?"

"No," Clay admitted.

"Then you need to quit!"

"I—I'm trying," Clay insisted. "I need treatment."

Ah, using addiction as a shield. "How many times have you been?"

"A couple."

"Something you didn't understand?"

"Sam, stop givin' me shit, okay? Besides, I ain't hurtin' no one but me."

"That's because you already ran everyone off," Sam pointed out. "And I'll remind you, a young woman died."

"Not because of anything I did!"

"You were there! How in the hell do you end up hanging out with a seventeen-year-old girl in the first place?"

"It's complicated," Clay said.

"Try me."

"Well, she's exonerated, I think you call it."

"Emancipated?"

"I guess," Clay said. "I think her dad had neglected her, or something. Or maybe perped her—I dunno. Anyway, Rebel was—"

"Rebel?"

"That's her name. Or was."

"Christ, you name your kid Rebel, and you wonder why she's in trouble. . ."

"I don't think her dad wonders about much."

"Yeah?"

"Well, yeah. I mean, she was there picking up some stuff for *him* and . . . well, she and I did a blue and the next thing I knew the cops was all over me."

"You took drugs with that kid?"

"Sam, I'm sorry. I relapsed."

"It isn't a relapse if it's just another day using between pauses," Sam countered. "That's just irregular use."

Clay looked at the ceiling and took a deep breath to compose himself. "Sam, I'm asking for your help."

"Who had the blue?"

"I can't remember. I—"

"Think!"

"I can't recall—really!"

Sam watched Clay closely. This was a really good time for his client to remember that he didn't give the drug to the kid, and he was half-tempted to advise Clay of that. "You'd better think hard," Sam said, leaving it at that. "And for your information, I've got other people to help, people who in some cases will actually listen and heed my advice. Some of 'em will even pay me." Seeing the hurt in Clay's eyes, he backed off. "Clay, I've been there and—"

"Oh, I know, Sam—you've told me twenty times how you managed to break the habit and get things under control."

"Well?"

"Well, maybe I'm not perfect like you."

"That's me," Sam snapped. "Mr. Perfect." He eyed Clay suspiciously. "You still high?"

"Do I look high?" Clay asked, then answered his own question. "I'm fine. I just need out."

"Well, nothing we can do about that until you make your initial appearance."

"When's that?"

"Should be this afternoon, one-thirty."

"Sam, you'll help me, won'tcha?"

Sam gathered his materials and stood. "I'll do a limited appearance and argue bond for you. After that, you're on your own unless you get a job and come up with some money to pay my fee. The handouts are over." He walked to the door and knocked on it. "I've got some clients to see."

"Thanks, Sam," Clay said. "You won't regret this. I promise."

"Every time someone tells me that I end up getting my foot stomped."

"Not this time, Sam. I want to get my life back on track."

7

That afternoon Sam stood with a courtroom full of people as Judge Melissa Downs entered the courtroom. Downs was the circuit (lower) trial court judge in this part of the state. She had taken the bench a couple of years prior following the suicide of her predecessor, Jonathon Howard. In Sam's opinion, she was turning into a fine trial judge: steady, predictable, and inclined to accept deals hammered out by defense attorneys and prosecutors. Because she'd been a trial attorney before her appointment, she understood the challenges attorneys faced and made allowances where reasonable, but held the line when necessary.

"Mr. Johnstone, who are you representing?" she asked after opening court. Her habit was to take defendants who were represented by counsel first.

Sam stood. Because he knew her practice, he had already seated himself at the defendant's table, joined by Clay. "Your Honor, I filed moments ago a limited entry of appearance on behalf of Mr. Pierce."

Under Wyoming's rules of criminal appearance, an attorney appearing on behalf of a client was in for the long run unless—as Sam had done—he or she filed a limited entry in writing. That too was questionable, as some read the rules to preclude a limited appearance in criminal matters.

Fortunately, Downs did not. She nodded and began to make notes as she spoke. "Will Mr. Pierce waive an advisal of rights and a verbatim reading of the allegations?"

"He will, Your Honor," Sam said. Because Clay was charged with misdemeanors, the judge could accept Sam's assurances the defendant knew what was going on, and pass on the time-consuming task of advising Clay individually. "I have discussed the charges and his rights with him," Sam added.

"Thank you," she said. Looking at a file in front of her, she continued, "Looks like allegations of use and possession of a controlled substance. How does he plead to the allegations?"

"Not guilty to both," Sam replied.

She made another note. "I've recorded the pleas," she said. "Mr. Pierce, we'll get you a financial affidavit. If you cannot afford Mr. Johnstone's services, then an attorney will be appointed for you—do you understand?"

"I—I'm hoping to hire Sam."

"I understand, but just in case, we'll get you the paperwork to apply for a court-appointed attorney. Let's turn to the issue of bond—Mr. Cates?"

Cates took a deep breath. Earnest but inexperienced, since Lee's incident he had been handling initial appearances and arraignments. "Your Honor, the State would ask that the defendant be held in lieu of ten thousand dollars, cash or commercial surety. The drugs concerned are manifestly dangerous, and he has no ties to the community. He's got a long history of drug and alcohol offenses, and the court should know we continue to investigate his possible involvement in the more serious charge of drug-induced homicide."

Downs and Sam made brief eye contact; pending charges had no place in her consideration. When Cates had seated himself, Downs looked to Sam expectantly. "Mr. Johnstone?"

"Your Honor," Sam said as he stood. "My client is a decorated veteran of the United States Army who has fallen on some hard times. And while it is true that he has some history, the court will note that it has all come following his discharge from service. We acknowledge that he has limited contacts with the community, but it is just as true that he is a man of limited means and lacks the ability to leave. I've seen to it he has made the acquaintance of local veterans. He has a place to stay. Most importantly, the charges are use and possession," he concluded.

"Fair enough. I'm going to order as follows," she began, and outlined the terms of Clay's release on his own recognizance, including prohibitions against using drugs or alcohol, random drug testing at least three times per week, and a curfew. "Any questions?"

"No, ma'am," Sam said. "May I be excused?" When Downs had agreed to his release, Sam leaned over to Clay. "Come see me when you get out," he said as he nodded to court security.

When Sam was gone, Downs advised the remaining half-dozen defendants of their rights. She had reviewed each defendant's charges before court and knew that among them today she would see an older man in on his ninth charge of possession—a record that somehow included six convictions from Colorado *since* that state's legalization of weed. He would be followed by a woman who had been caught with a gram of methamphetamine in the local halfway house, a truck driver who had tried to avoid the port of entry and was subsequently arrested for driving while under the influence and with an open container (a bottle of whiskey on the seat next to him), and a Custer College freshman who had flipped out after dropping acid in the dorm and was eventually charged with being under the influence of a controlled substance.

She had each defendant come forward, where she advised them of the charges they faced, the elements of each, and the maximum possible penalty they faced in case of conviction. She took pleas from those charged with misdemeanors and sentenced those who pleaded guilty to brief periods in jail and imposed fines, court costs, and statutory fees.

At last, she looked to the remaining defendant. "Mr. Gustafson, would you please step to the podium?"

When Gustafson had nonchalantly made his way to the podium, Downs asked if he had understood his rights. "Do you have any questions?"

"No, ma'am."

"Mr. Gustafson, you're here pursuant to a warrant signed by this court earlier today. The warrant contains three counts. Count one alleges that on or about the tenth day of April, here in Custer County, you possessed more than three grams of fentanyl in pill form. If you were adjudicated guilty of that you'd face up to seven years in prison and a fine of up to fifteen thousand dollars. Do you understand?"

Gustafson stood stock still at the podium and stared at Downs. "I do, ma'am."

"Count two alleges that on or about the tenth day of April, here in Custer County, you possessed with intent to distribute fentanyl in pill form. This is another felony, punishable by twenty years in prison and up to twenty thousand dollars in fines. Do you understand that one?"

"Yes, ma'am."

"And finally, count three alleges that on or about the tenth day of April, again in Custer County, you committed drug-induced homicide by providing a minor at least four years younger than yourself a drug that resulted in her death. This is another felony, punishable by not more than twenty years in the state penitentiary. Do you understand?"

"Yes, ma'am."

"Mr. Gustafson," she continued, "it looks like you are facing up to forty-seven years in prison and up to thirty-five thousand dollars in fines. Are you going to hire your own attorney or apply for the public defender?"

"I'm going to try and hire *him*," he said, indicating the door through which Sam had exited.

Unlikely. Sam would certainly have a conflict. But it wasn't her place to tell the defendant that. "Get to it, then," she ordered. "If that isn't working out, you'd best get someone else lined up, because your preliminary hearing will be in ten days. Now, are you employed outside the home?"

"Not right now."

"How do you support yourself?"

"A little of this, a little of that," Gustafson said, then turned to acknowledge the laughter in the courtroom from the few remaining spectators.

Downs' brows knitted. "You understand that employment is deemed an indicator of the likelihood of you showing up to future court hearings? It might behoove you to take my questions seriously, Mr. Gustafson." She then asked a series of questions designed to assist her in determining whether Gustafson posed a danger to the community. Completing her questioning, she looked to Cates. "Mr. Cates, what is the State's recommendation?"

Cates stood and rubbed his face. "Judge, Mr. Gustafson has few if any ties to the community. These are serious charges. We're asking he be held on twenty-five thousand dollars cash."

Not an unreasonable request. She had been thinking ten thousand per count, cash. "Mr. Gustafson, anything you'd like me to know?"

"Well, yeah, Judge. I'm not guilty of this, and I'll make any hearing you set."

"Thank you," Downs said. "Having heard the recommendation of the parties, I will set your terms and release as follows: You'll be held in lieu of twenty-five thousand dollars, cash only. If you do get out, you'll follow these rules." She proceeded to explain the terms for Gustafson to live by, including that he not leave the state, test regularly for drugs, meet with his attorney once per week, and not use, consume, possess, or be in the presence of illegal controlled substances. "Mr. Gustafson, any questions?"

"Well, so I gotta pay twenty-five thousand dollars to get out? No bail bondsman, or whatever?"

"Right."

"And I can't leave?"

"Right again."

"So where am I gonna stay?"

"Somewhere with no drugs?" Downs replied levelly.

Gustafson watched her closely. When he knew she wasn't joking, he spoke. "I understand, ma'am. No questions."

"Thank you, Mr. Gustafson. We'll be adjourned." She stood and departed quickly.

When she was gone, court security approached, and Gustafson was immediately escorted out of the courtroom en route to the attached holding cells. "So, how do I pay that?" he asked the court security officers accompanying him.

"Step one: get twenty-five thousand dollars," said the younger officer. He rolled his eyes while his female supervisor laughed at his joke.

"I've got it," Gustafson said quickly.

"Sure you do, pal," the supervisor said.

As Gustafson was led away, Cates watched as Gustafson passed behind another man who Cates knew to be Rebel's father, Wrangler Hayes. Cates noted the grieving man never took his eyes off Gustafson.

Two hours later, Gustafson signed an inventory sheet, acknowledging the return of his wallet, shoes, a pocketknife, and a baseball cap adorned with a Colorado Rockies logo. As he left the detention center, he was accosted by a blonde woman holding a spiral notebook and a phone.

"Mr. Gustafson, my name is Sarah Penrose," she said, sticking the phone near his mouth. "I'm a reporter for the *Custer Bugle*. Can I ask you a few questions?"

"Of course," Gustafson said, stopping and running a hand through his hair before replacing his hat.

"Did you sell the drugs that killed Rebel Hayes?"

"Of course not!" Gustafson replied. "You don't mess around, do you?"

"The police tell me they have little doubt that you sold her the drugs," she pressed, ignoring his question.

"Yeah, well, their record in this town ain't so good, is it? I don't know anything about any drugs."

"What will you do now?"

"Follow the terms of my bond. Hire a lawyer. Get something to eat, then find a place to rack out." Seeing his car had been parked as prearranged, he walked toward it. "They've got the wrong guy."

Penrose remained at his side. "According to law enforcement, the only people in that motel room were you, the deceased, and a Clayton Pierce."

"That right?" Gustafson asked, now at the door of his coupe.

"That's what they say," Penrose replied quickly. "So, if you were the only ones in the room, and if you didn't sell Miss Hayes the drugs, it must have been Mr. Pierce—is that right?"

"You'll have to ask him," Gustafson said as he closed the door.

"I will!" Sarah assured him as he drove off quickly. "You can bet on it." Turning, she saw Wrangler Hayes watching them. "Mr. Hayes! Can I get your reaction to the bond?" she asked, approaching him.

Hayes focused on Gustafson's car while replying. "I ain't got nothin' to say. I'm gonna let my actions do the talking."

8

Lee had summoned Cates with a terse email: *Come see me. I need to give you some guidance.* Cates had entered seconds later, eager to please. He had that going for him, if nothing else. Well, that and loyalty. That was good. When the young lawyer was seated nervously across the desk from him, Lee sipped from a cup that read "World's Greatest Lawyer" and took a deep breath.

"What do you think, boss?" Cates asked.

"I think these yokel nitwits can't find their ass with either hand!" Lee snarled. "For Christ's sake, they ought to be able to figure out in about five minutes I didn't shoot that woman purposely! Why the hell would I? I didn't even know her—I cannot know every defendant who appears in my court! It was obviously self-defense! How hard could it be?"

"Well, they've got Miller on it and—"

"She's a novice," Lee complained. "A rookie. Damned affirmative action appointment."

"People tell me she is a capable investigator," Cates countered. "A real bulldog."

"Oh, they do, do they? Who? Who said that?"

"Well, I don't want to get into that—"

"Because you're full of shit," Lee snapped. "No one said that, and you know it. Tell you what: if I oversaw the investigation we'da already had a team covering every highway out of town. We'da had a search already conducted of every drainage ditch in the area, and Cavalry Creek would have divers popping their heads outta the water, maybe scaring the crap out of tourists! Instead, we've got one inexperienced investigator asking Julie Spence what happened, and begging local business owners to show her their video. Well, that ain't gonna cut it. I'm going to go see Buck Lucas and—"

"Boss, you can't get involved!" Cates reminded Lee. "You've got to stay well out of the way on this one!"

"And allow myself to get railroaded?"

"Of course not. That's why I'm here: to help you."

This wet-behind-the-ears nobody was going to help him? Surely these morons would wake up and get their crap together. All they had to do was find the knife and the cloud hovering over him would lift, allowing him to get back to the business of seeing to justice! He sat back in his chair and, clasping his hands behind his head, recalled making a turn into the parking lot of a convenience store located on Teton Avenue. While filling the tank, he decided to buy a drink of some sort. As he approached the entrance, he encountered a heavy, pink-haired woman who appeared vaguely familiar sitting on a plastic chair next to a coffee can. She pulled on a cigarette and eyed him suspiciously with one eye, the other closed to avoid the smoke. They exchanged greetings and he got what he needed and approached the register. No one was there, so he pantomimed through the glass, asking for help. The woman sighed heavily and entered the store, walked slowly behind the counter, and rang up his items, stink-eyeing him the entire time.

"You don't recognize me, do you?" the woman had finally asked. She then blamed him for her possibly losing custody of her grandson—the lives these people led!

Immediately recognizing a possible situation, he had asked her to leave him be. But she wouldn't. Eventually she approached him and drew a knife. He recalled drawing the pistol and pulling the trigger. But this time, nothing happened, and she closed on him, drawing the knife back while he frantically squeezed the trigger. When her hand began to move forward, he closed his eyes in terror, opening them only when nothing happened.

The textured, off-white drop ceiling was a welcome sight. Cates' wide eyes were less so. "S-Sorry. Got to remembering what happened, you know," Lee stammered. He used the corner of a paper towel to wipe perspiration from his forehead. "Anything else?"

"Well, you had called me in to give me some guidance. What do you want me to do?"

Lee took a deep breath and held it for a moment to steady his heartbeat. When would this nightmare be over? These people would have to understand there was nothing he could do; it was a clear case of self-defense. Once that Spence woman came clean, everything would begin to fall into place, and the scandal would be behind him.

"Let me think on it," Lee replied at last. "I'll get back with you later."

"O-Okay," Cates said uncertainly.

"Close the door behind you."

9

On a late April afternoon, Sam was drinking coffee while looking at his calendar for the day. He was dreading an afternoon appointment—a woman he had twice represented after she drove under the influence had been arrested on yet another charge of driving under the influence, this time with her kids in the car. He had done what he could and had previously gotten her favorable deals, but she had failed to follow up with treatment, and her addiction—predictably—had gotten the better of her yet again. Because in Wyoming a third conviction required a minimum thirty-day stay in jail or treatment, things were coming to a head. The best place for her right now was jail, of course (she didn't have the skills or ability to stay sober), but she had people enabling and making excuses for her, and someone had posted a bond, freeing her from jail temporarily.

The good news was that having the children in the car had drawn the attention of the Department of Family Services, so for at least a little while the children would be cared for in an alcohol-free environment. An alcoholic client in denial ("I just had one too many—everyone does"); an enabling family ("she's a good mom"); and a court system that provided for graduated (and well-earned) sanctions made defense attorneys' roles as *counselors* difficult, and he was considering how to handle his client at the afternoon meeting when Cassie paged him.

"Sam, there is a man here who wants to speak with you."

Something in her tone was odd—strained, maybe? Trouble?

"I'll be right there," Sam said. Touching his revolver to assure himself it was in his shoulder holster, he donned his jacket and made his way down the hallway. "Can I help you?" he asked the large man in his waiting room.

"Yeah, you can stop representing the guy who killed my daughter!" the man barked.

Sam recognized Wrangler Hayes and stole a quick look at Cassie, silently instructing her to remain where she was. "Couple of things," he began, edging between Hayes and Cassie's desk. "First, I'm representing Clay Pierce. He's a veteran, and I'm thinking that like your daughter, he's a victim in all this. He OD'd too, remember?" Seeing no recognition, Sam continued. "Second, my client is only accused of use and possession—"

"He was there! He shouldn'ta been!" Hayes roared. "Ain't no doubt he was part of it!"

"Hold on now," Sam said. "My guy says he was just doing some drugs—getting high, is all."

"Liar!" Hayes yelled. "And why you helpin' him? If not for your client my Rebel would still be alive!" He took a step forward.

Sam put up a hand. "Mr. Hayes, step back. You're crowding me and scaring my assistant."

"And just what are you going to do about it?" Hayes sneered.

"Cassie, walk down to my office and call 9-1-1," Sam said quietly.

"You're a chickenshit," Hayes challenged. "Everyone thinks you're a hero, but I say—"

"Tell them Wrangler Hayes is on the sidewalk in front of my office bleeding heavily," Sam finished as Cassie scurried down the hallway.

Hayes stared at Sam for a long moment. Sam met the grieving man's glare. Eventually, Hayes broke eye contact and turned to the door. "This ain't over," he said, and slipped out.

"Cassie! Never mind!" Sam hollered. He turned and was walking to his office when he heard the front door open. He drew his revolver and returned to the front room.

A skinny, pimply-faced young man was just inside the door, his eyes fixed on Sam's gun. "Whoa, dude! I just got some flowers here!"

"Sorry," Sam said, quickly holstering his weapon. "We had a little trouble."

"Yeah, well, I don't get paid enough for this shit," the man said. He put the flowers on the counter and turned to leave.

"Do I need to sign? Can I give you a tip?" Sam said as the door closed. He was looking at the card when Cassie appeared.

"Well, that was scary," she said. "Whose are those?"

Sam was looking at the card that had come with the flowers. "Mine, I guess."

"Ooooh, pretty!" Cassie said. "Here, I've got a vase in the back. I'll put them in some water. These from your new girlfriend?"

Sam smirked. "Cassie—"

"Don't deny it, Sam. Whoever she is, she made you two days late to work. Must be somethin' there."

After she took the flowers to the small kitchen, he walked to his office, dropped the card on his desk, and took a seat. He started to type, then looked again at the card. "Don't forget me," was all it said.

He smiled at the memory of her touch. Fat chance.

10

While Sam was dealing with a distraught father, Punch was nearing Chugwater, Wyoming, headed south in his state car en route to Cheyenne when his phone rang. It was his supervisor at DCI. "That didn't take long," he said aloud as he pushed at the car's touchscreen to take the call. "Polson."

The irritation in Mitch Packard's voice was immediately obvious. "I thought we agreed that you were going to wait until I gave you the go-ahead?" he stormed, referring to a meeting he and Punch had attended several weeks prior. "I came away from our meeting with the under-standing that you understood where we, uh, stood."

A lot of standing ongoing. "It was the city's deal," Punch explained. "They asked for a little assistance. As you know, we have a memorandum of understanding that says we can help each other out. Well, an opportunity presented itself—"

"There are no opportunities where you failing to follow orders is concerned, damn it!"

"Mitch, a girl died. Besides, I didn't sign the MOU—someone in Cheyenne did."

"Don't quibble with me! I've seen the affidavit of probable cause, and I can tell you wrote it! And you were postured to arrest before it went down,"

Mitch countered. "You were in the process of busting his balls—finding the dead girl was a bonus. Of sorts. Damn it, Punch, I've got the Wyoming Attorney General's office all up in my grill, as well as the feds wondering why we moved! According to them, we just wasted years of work."

"It's a solid bust!" Punch argued. He pulled over to the side of the interstate to maintain the good signal he had; Wyoming was notorious for dead spots. "We've got a dead girl and the county attorney—his name is Lee—says he can pinch him. Tell the feds and the AG if they want to come here to Custer and answer to the public, be my guest."

Packard was silent for a moment; Punch could tell he was looking at a screen. "Punch, this isn't good."

"Look, tell them it was an interagency decision to arrest, led by the Custer PD. All I did was assist local law enforcement on short notice and in the interest of public safety. They got him for felony possession, possession with intent, and drug-induced homicide. I only wish we could have gotten him sooner."

Packard was silent for a minute. "Your door shut?" he asked at last.

Here it was. "Mitch, I don't have a door. I'm in the state car—the Malibu, headed your way."

"Shit," Packard said. "Pull over."

It was fun while it lasted. "Why?"

"Pull over, damn it!"

"I already am."

"Where are you?"

"North of Chugwater." There was a lengthy silence. Packard was obviously thinking. Punch was looking out the sedan's window at a couple of pronghorn antelope. "Talk," he said.

"Well, as I mentioned, I spoke with my higher," Packard began. "You rattled a lot of cages with the arrest of Gustafson."

"He's one little squirrel, for Christ's sake!"

"I know, Punch. But he was their squirrel, and they are convinced that if you hadn't busted him he would have led them to the bigger fish."

"I think that's a mixed metaphor," Punch observed. "Mitch, they've literally had years to act on the information they have. He can't be that hard to follow and figure out! People are dying up here!"

"I hear you, bud. But they're pissed."

"They'll get over it, or they won't."

"They won't."

"Well, f—"

"Neither will you."

"Meaning?"

"Meaning I've been told to inform you that your assignment with DCI is being curtailed," Packard said. "You might as well turn around and go back."

"Curtailed?"

"Yeah. It's a nice way of saying they are terminating your detail and having you sent back to Custer."

"Breaks my heart," Punch said sourly.

"Look, Punch. You did a great job with us. Turned over a lot of rocks. But the director can't have—"

"I get it, Mitch. No need to explain," Punch said. "How does it work?"

"Not sure. Let me get with the human resources bubbas, but in the meantime drop the car off and turn in your keys, then lie low—okay? I'm going to send you an order that will essentially say that you are no longer detailed to us, meaning you don't have DCI authority to act in any way."

"Got it."

Again, there was silence on the line. "Hey, Punch, I just want you to know that I appreciate everything you've done, and everything you've tried to do," Packard said at last. "Including this. I just wish you had waited. I can't—"

"I got it, Mitch. I can't expect you to stick your neck out."

"Well, it's not that, it's—"

It was exactly that. "I appreciate your support," Punch said, not appreciating the lack of support at all. "Send me the docs; in the meantime, I'll go talk with the chief and find out if I'm gonna be cleaning porta-potties at the qualification range, or what."

When Packard rang off, Punch drove the car to the next exit, turned around, and headed back toward Custer and an uncertain future.

11

Twenty-four hours later, Punch was cleaning out his desk at DCI's Custer office when his phone rang. It was reception. "Hey, Punch? That Gustafson guy is here. He's asking for you."

He had no authority; Packard had made that clear. On the other hand, why not? "Okay," Punch said. "I'll be right there." He'd have to be careful, he reminded himself. First question was whether Gustafson had an attorney.

When he got to the lobby of the little DCI station, he saw Gustafson on his phone in one of the chairs. He approached him and made his presence known.

"Gotta go," Gustafson said. "Cops are here."

"What's up?" Punch asked without preamble. "How'd you get out?"

"I posted the money," Gustafson explained. He looked around the lobby. "Is there somewhere we can talk?"

"You got an attorney?"

"Not yet."

"We can talk, then, I suppose," Punch said. He led the way to an interview room behind the locked doors. Through a window he could see other agents milling about near his soon-to-be vacated cubicle. When the door had closed behind them, he looked to Gustafson, who took a chair.

"So, you know these charges are crap. You can't prove that stuff was mine, or that I was intending to deal," Gustafson began. "Let alone that I gave her the stuff. No jury is going to buy that."

"Who are you trying to convince?" Punch asked. "Me or you? I was just helping out—call it interagency coordination. Miller is a solid investigator, and she generally doesn't make arrests without proof. In any event, that's for the attorneys and judges—and eventually, the jury—to figure out. Sounds like the Custer PD is just doing its job—bringing charges where they see violations of the law." He stood.

Gustafson stared hard at Punch. "I might have something for you."

"I'm no longer with DCI," Punch said quickly, indicating the window. "See my box? It's got all my stuff in it. Unless you've got another box, you don't have anything I need."

"I might have some information," Gustafson insisted. "Stuff that could help you right a wrong—you're all about right and wrong, aren't you?"

Punch ignored the jibe. Druggies always ratted each other out. "What do you have?"

"Well, first I'm gonna need something from you."

"There's a surprise," Punch said.

"You want to insult me, or do you want to hear what I've got to say?"

"I'm kinda okay with a little of both," Punch replied. He watched Gustafson pout before continuing. "What do you have?" he asked impatiently. "I've got to get to my new job polishing parking meters."

"What?"

"Never mind. What do you have?"

"I have information on one of your old cases."

"Wanna narrow it down a bit? I've been a cop for a minute or two." Punch saw Gustafson measuring him carefully before saying anything.

"Kaiden Miles."

Kaiden Miles was a young man who had been murdered a few years back on the Custer College campus. Punch had arrested a prominent athlete named Davonte Blair for the murder. Blair was defended by Sam Johnstone and acquitted after a witness, Ronnie Norquist, took the stand and confessed to the killing. "What about him?"

"Ronnie didn't do it."

Punch shrugged. "He said he did."

"I'm telling you, he didn't do it," Gustafson insisted. "He was a stooge."

"How so?"

"That's all you get unless I get some kind of deal."

"You have to know I don't have that kind of twist," Punch said, shaking his head. "In fact, I'm on double-secret probation as we speak."

"Huh? Well, I know you know the people who do."

"Just out of curiosity, what do you want?"

"Everything dropped."

Punch shook his head. "Okay, so this isn't how it works. What you need is an audience with the county attorney. You and your attorney go and tell him what you've got and he agrees—or doesn't—to do the deal. But here's the deal: you will almost certainly have to agree to testify."

"Won't need any testimony."

"I seriously doubt that. You think people are simply going to take your word for it?"

"I don't know," Gustafson said. "What I do know is that if I don't talk, no one will, and you'll have the wrong kid in jail forever."

Punch considered what he was hearing. Gustafson's testimony wouldn't be worth squat, and neither would Ronnie's—recanted testimony was notoriously unreliable. But it wasn't his call.

"I'll do this much," he said at last. "I'll run this by Miller and she can take it up the cop chain to Grant Lee—he's the county attorney—and we'll see if he wants to hear what you've got. But don't get too excited," Punch cautioned. "Lee has voters to answer to, and they are pissed off because of kids dying from that stuff you sell."

"I didn't have anything to do with that!" Gustafson argued.

"Yeah, right," Punch replied sarcastically. "She just happened to accompany Pierce into your motel room and just happened to use fentanyl sometime later, and just happened to croak while you were there. That about right?"

"Well, that and there was another person in that room."

"Pierce? You want me to believe he had the wherewithal to sell her the shit? Be real," Punch said. "That guy can't get out of his own way. Besides, he beat you to the punch. He's already rolled you under the bus."

Gustafson's eyes widened for just a second before returning to the practiced, half-lidded look of nonchalance. "You morons won't find out shit about Ronnie unless you start looking into it, now will you?"

"You need an attorney. Have them take your story to Miller. Maybe she'll listen," Punch replied.

"I'm gonna hire Johnstone."

"He won't do it."

"Why not?"

"Well, I'm no legal scholar, but he already represents Pierce. That'd be a conflict of duty."

"Then he can dump him. I want Johnstone. I won't come across without him, meaning Ronnie will rot in prison because you got the wrong guy."

"I told you: I've got no twist with the county attorney, and I certainly can't tell Sam what to do. But I'll make a call."

After Gustafson departed, Punch reflected on the visit and what his investigation years earlier had revealed. While Davonte had been his initial suspect and had become his prime suspect after everyone else was eliminated, Punch had looked at the possibility of others being involved or even committing the crime. One working theory was that Miles—who was known to deal drugs—had failed to make payment on a shipment after he'd been stiffed by Davonte and had gotten killed by *his* supplier, who was probably Gustafson. Gustafson had been a suspect early on, but he had an alibi: he and Ronnie Norquist each claimed to have spent the night with the other. Punch had operated off that being true until Ronnie confessed.

Punch removed a pencil from a bullet-shaped holder and tapped it against what used to be his desk. Gustafson was telling him Norquist didn't do it. He wouldn't do anything to take the heat off Ronnie if it would turn attention to himself, so if Ronnie didn't do it, and if Gustafson didn't do it, then it could only be Davonte, and he couldn't be charged again.

It was too damned convenient. He left the interview room, left his keys to the office, retrieved his box, and carried it to his car.

The courthouse was only a few blocks from the police station, but because he and Rhonda had Kenneth Jr.'s high school band concert to attend, Punch decided to drive. He was surprised to find a spot right in front, parked, and quickly made his way to the clerk of court's office, where he asked to see the Blair trial transcript.

"You wanna check it out or look at it here?" the clerk asked, clearly hoping Punch would choose the latter.

"I'll just look at it right there, if that's okay with you," he said, pointing at a wooden table a few feet away.

She nodded and indicated he should follow her. He complied and they walked into a room filled with movable file cabinets the size of library racks. She pointed at a row of thick green file folders labeled *State v. Blair*. "Knock yourself out," she said. "I'll be at my desk if you need anything."

Punch groaned at the thought of reviewing the thousands of pages, but in a moment of clarity pulled the last two files, opened each, and reviewed the index. Ronnie had testified near the end of the trial; his testimony was contained in the last few pages of one and the remainder of the other. Punch returned to the small, bare table and began to read.

He'd been present throughout the trial, and as he recalled, Sam had called Ronnie to the stand—ostensibly to corroborate testimony regarding Blair's whereabouts at the crucial time. Instead, Ronnie had admitted that a watch cap found on a bed in a room he shared with Miles—and long thought to belong to Miles—had been his. DNA identification had earlier shown his DNA as well as that of the victim on the cap. Everyone assumed it was Kaiden's cap, until Sam began questioning Ronnie on the stand.

Punch remembered Ronnie getting tearful, then beginning to shake. Like everyone there that day, he would never forget the admission: "It was an accident!" Ronnie had shouted. "I didn't mean to!" he had added from behind his hands. Sam had stood quietly, watching and from time to time looking at each juror in turn. When Ronnie looked up and wailed, "Kaiden was going to call the police! That would ruin everything!" Sam ceased his questioning.

As Ronnie would later explain it, Blair had promised Ronnie money and access when he got to the NBA. Kaiden threatening to make noise over Blair's refusal to pay for drugs delivered would "ruin everything!" Ronnie testified he and Kaiden had struggled and that Kaiden had been injured, whereupon Ronnie invented a ruse to get Kaiden alone, after which they again fought. "He was going to tell the cops all about Davonte," Ronnie had said. "He turned around on me and I grabbed a snow shovel that was on the sidewalk and . . . uh . . . hit him."

As Punch finished reading, he turned the page and flipped the file over. Could it have all been a lie? He was present when Ronnie later entered a plea. Daniels had coaxed an admission from Ronnie that was detailed and consistent in every way with the evidence and with his confession on the witness stand during Blair's trial. But would the young man really have agreed to go to prison for someone else based on a promise? Was he that naïve?

According to Punch's watch, he was late. Rhonda was gonna be madder than a mule chewing on a bumblebee, but he needed to talk with Sam.

12

Although Sam had always liked and respected Punch, he was cautious when Cassie buzzed him to tell him the detective wanted some of his time. "Did he say what it's about?" Sam asked her.

"Just said it's personal and he's in a hurry."

Maybe Punch and his wife Rhonda needed a will or something. Cops had the same legal problems as everyone else—and because the job was so dangerous, a pressing need to get matters in order.

When both Sam and Punch had declined Cassie's offer of coffee, she closed Sam's office door behind her. "How are things?" Sam asked.

"If they were any better, I'd hang myself," Punch replied. "Maybe ventilate my own skull."

"Yeesh," Sam replied, genuinely concerned. He sat up in his chair. "Any particular reason, or just the usual life-on-the-line-for-an-ungrateful-public stuff?"

"DCI let me go a couple days ago," Punch said simply.

"Damn," Sam said. "Gustafson?"

"How'd you know?"

"I didn't know; I figured. For whatever reason, they've let him have free rein for some time," Sam observed. "You and Miller busting him probably upset their game."

"*Game* is right," Punch agreed bitterly. "They kept telling me they were trying to catch Mr. Big. I'm like, 'How much bigger you want?' This guy is selling shit that's killing people left and right!"

"So, what now?" Sam asked. "The city needs you."

"Don't know about that, but thanks, Sam," Punch replied. "I'm back on the force—just unsure in what capacity, so I really don't know." He held up crossed fingers. "The chief is looking to see if I can get my old position back, but that would require the city to fund another detective's position. Otherwise, I could be checking for perverts in the city park's restrooms until a job opens up."

"You'd be good at that," Sam offered with a smile. When Punch didn't react, he turned serious. "Given the numbers that the courts are seeing, seems like they could use another good hand."

"Dunno," Punch replied. He looked at his watch. "I'm just trying to stay loose and not step on my own foot here anytime soon. Which brings me to today."

"Yeah?"

Punch looked left and right as if someone were watching. "We're not having this conversation, okay?"

"What conversation?"

Punch nodded. "Gustafson says he wants to hire you."

Sam shook his head. "Not enough money in the world. Besides, I have a conflict of duty. I represent Clay."

"Yeah, well, there may be a complication."

Not on Sam's end. "Like how?"

"Like Gustafson says he's got information showing that Ronnie Norquist didn't kill Kaiden Miles."

Sam stood and walked to his window. "He's full of shit."

Punch spoke to Sam's back. "Yeah, well . . . didn't you think it was all a little too convenient at the time?"

Sam turned quickly to face Punch. "I represented Davonte. It's not that I didn't care, but my duty was to my client," he explained. "And if you'll recall, Ronnie gave a full confession on the stand, and then—I'm told—said the same thing when he pleaded guilty in front of Daniels. What's this got to do with you?"

"I want you to represent him."

Sam turned from the window. "You're the first cop ever to try and arrange counsel for a drug dealer."

"Because Gustafson says he has information, and he will only come across if *you* represent him," Punch said. "I need to know what he knows about Ronnie's case."

"I can't, Punch. Clay is charged with use and possession arising from the same events."

"I know, but those are pissant charges. Maybe we can get Lee to drop them. Or maybe you can plead him out," Punch added hopefully.

"Ethics rules don't differentiate between the big and little matters," Sam observed. "And even if he pleads, I'm still out. The attorney-client relationship never ends."

"Could you get a waiver?"

"Unlikely."

Punch looked at his watch again. "Why?"

"Clay would be an idiot to waive. What if he waived and then Gustafson tried to throw him under the bus?" Sam explained. "And why are you believing anything Gustafson says?"

"He's trying to get your old partner's son out of prison!"

"No, he's trying to get his own ass out of a crack. He *says* he has information."

"Well, yeah. But what if he does?"

"I don't think I'm the right guy," Sam interrupted. "Did you tell him you'd speak with me?"

"No."

"Good," Sam said. He softened. "Look, I'm always flattered when someone wants to hire me, but in this case, I'm conflicted."

"I know," Punch agreed. "But something doesn't feel right."

"Well, maybe it's because you're hearing it from Gustafson. Dude is an accomplished manipulator—he talks folks into selling poison for him."

"He is," Punch agreed, standing. "But I don't want to walk around for the rest of my career—life, really—thinking we got the wrong guy in prison."

"Ronnie confessed!" Sam reminded him. "I'll grant you that on occasion an innocent person might take a deal. But Ronnie confessed and then pleaded out cold. Innocent people don't do that. I mean, if we had a statement or something, things might be different."

"I know, Sam. But I just got a bad feeling about this one." He stood and crossed the room, then took Sam's hand. "Thanks for your time. I gotta get to a band concert or you're gonna be defending Rhonda on charges of kicking my ass."

Sam smiled. "No sweat."

Sam spent an hour researching using an online system, but he couldn't find what he needed, so he turned to the wall of musty law books he'd purchased from the estate sale after Judge Holmes' suicide. For the most part, they served as an expensive substitute for wallpaper, but occasionally he would find something in a book that for whatever reason he'd overlooked on legal online search engines. Not today. The law was clear: he had a conflict of duty. Best stay the hell out of it. Ronnie had confessed; it had surprised Sam, too.

Water under the bridge.

13

The next morning Sam was looking at a mental evaluation he had asked Downs to order on a client of his who had been charged with criminal trespass. The seventy-three-year-old man was a Marine Corps veteran who had been referred to Sam by another former client. Sam had spent only a few minutes with John Hadley before determining his client was guilty as charged but unfit for trial. He'd filed the appropriate motion, waited the intervening month, and was now reviewing the doctor's evaluation. Hadley, it appeared, was suffering from post-traumatic stress disorder, unspecified schizophrenia spectrum disorder, generalized anxiety disorder, as well as diabetes, high blood pressure, and incontinence. What Custer needed was a program to deal with people who—but for their mental illness—wouldn't be involved with the criminal justice system. He looked up when Cassie knocked.

"What's up?"

"Call for you. Won't give his name." She shrugged. "Oh, I read that," she said, pointing to the evaluation in Sam's hand. "Looks like John is a little cray-cray," she opined, circling with an index finger near her temple.

"He doesn't know whether to wave or wind his watch," Sam agreed. He normally wouldn't accept a call from someone who wouldn't give Cassie a name. What the hell. "File this, please, and send the call through." He was making a note when his phone rang. "This is Sam."

"Sam, my name is Trent Gustafson. I don't know if you remember me."

Sam remembered him being a pencil-necked drug dealer. "I know who you are." Was Punch behind this?

"So, I am sure that you are aware that I was arrested on bogus charges."

"I saw you in court."

"I wanna talk with you about representing me."

"That's not going to happen; it would be a clear case of conflict of duty."

"I don't understand."

Sam considered his answer. He had made an appearance; the fact that he was representing Clay was no secret. "I already represent Clay Pierce," he explained. "He was, as you know, on scene with you when you were arrested."

"What did they charge him with?"

"You were there."

"Yeah, well, I wasn't listening real close."

Big surprise. One of the great legal fictions was that defendants listened, understood, or paid attention to anything in court except bail amounts and sentence lengths. Most were uninterested in their own constitutional rights, let alone anything going on with someone else. The only thing that mattered to them was how long they would be cooped up.

"He's charged with possession and use of a controlled substance," Sam replied.

"Yeah, well, that's bogus," Gustafson said. "It was his shit what killed her, man. They're trying to hang felony possession, possession with intent, and drug-induced homicide on me. That's deep shit. Any idiot can defend him. I need your help."

He was going to try and pin it on Clay. What he didn't know, of course, was that Clay was Confidential Informant No. 1 and had earlier agreed to roll on *him*. "I hear you, but as I mentioned, I already have a client. I can recommend someone else for you," Sam offered.

"I don't want anybody else," Gustafson said. "I don't think there's anybody else in this pissant town who knows what the hell he is doing."

"Well, I'm not going to be able to help." Sam began to hang up.

"How much is he paying you?"

"None of your business."

"I can make you a wealthy man."

"Too late," Sam said. "My accrued wealth lies in the rich, varied tapestry of clients I serve."

"Huh?"

"I can't take your case. Changing clients is called 'client hopping,' and it's not allowed, either. So that's two reasons I can't take your case. Thanks for calling."

"You always follow the rules?"

"I do when my license is at stake. Anything else?" he asked, only half-listening.

"Yeah, one thing: what would happen if the charges against your client were dropped? That would change things, wouldn't it?"

"Not really," Sam said, signing a motion. "An attorney's duty to a client doesn't end with representation. It goes on forever. So, I'd still owe him a duty of confidentiality and loyalty."

"Forever?"

Yes, forever. "Until the client dies." There was a continuing duty even then, but it was too much to explain now. Sam was looking at another file as he spoke. "Thanks for calling," he concluded. "Goodbye."

Cassie arrived within seconds of his hanging up. She stood in his doorway with her hands on her broad hips like she always did when she had bad news. "Mrs. Schumer is here again. Another fight with her son."

14

Penrose was in her office reading the online comments for the article she had written on Gustafson's initial appearance. The story had only been up for an hour and had already garnered significant discussion. Even better, the largest newspaper in the state had called and asked her to buttress her piece for publication tomorrow.

"Fentanyl, a dead kid . . . If this gets picked up by the wire services, it might go viral!"

"I'm pleased for you." It was Bill Gordon, the owner and publisher of the *Custer Bugle*, a newspaper (and now, web publisher) that had been in his family for decades. "Where are you taking this?" Circulation was dropping monthly; the last thing he needed was his writer stirring up trouble. Just report the news.

"I've got an interview with Wrangler Hayes," she said. "Reaction of the victim's father."

That might work out okay. "He's done some stuff, if he's the guy I'm thinking of."

"Oh, yeah," she said. "He's got a record as long as your arm, and an attitude to go with it."

"Must be killing him to be rooting for the cops and the county attorney's office."

She snorted. "I'm not sure he's on their side. From what I'm told, he's been a pain in their butt since Minute One."

"Well, before you go and get all teary-eyed when you're interviewing him, make sure he actually knew her."

"What do you mean? He was her father!"

"Biologically," Gordon allowed. "But that doesn't mean he knew her. We got a lot of people that had kids for no better reason than one too many hard iced teas after a Maroon 5 concert."

"I'll look into it." She laughed.

"Seriously, there is an ongoing epidemic of over-grieving," he continued. "Used to be your parent or whatever died, you felt bad and moved on. Now, there's an entire industry that sees to it you don't get over it, and I'm convinced it's because of guilt people carry over their crappy relationships—"

"Get off my lawn!" Penrose said.

Gordon laughed, chagrined. "I guess you're right. I'm getting curmudgeonly and starting to yell at clouds. Just . . . be careful and don't lionize this guy until you know he's worth it."

"You see the comments?" Penrose asked.

"I'm monitoring them," he said. "Volume's good, but the tone . . . Gustafson will be lucky not to catch a bullet."

"Maybe it would be better if he did," she said. "Selling that crap to kids."

"I don't want to see that on the pages of my paper," he warned. "Play it down the middle of the fairway."

"You and your old-fashioned ideas about journalism."

"What can I say? I'll admit my refusal to change. And I'll ask you to respect that. Now, how about Grant Lee?"

"Nada."

"You talk with him?"

She had. "Um . . . Yeah. Same old stuff—self-defense, yada, yada."

What are the commissioners saying?"

"Nothing publicly."

"That's smart. But off the record?"

"I think he's a dead man walking."

15

Sean O'Hanlon put down the local newspaper. He was sitting on his usual stool in the Longbranch. A hometown hero, except for one year at the University of Wyoming—where he'd quickly discovered his all-Wyoming high school quarterback credentials meant little—he'd spent his entire life in Custer. And like many top athletes, he had little interest in education, so after three semesters he brought an out-of-state cheerleader home, married her, and went to work. Now, he unbuttoned the cuffs on his discount retailer dress shirt, rolled them halfway up his pale forearms, looked at his drinking buddies, and shook his head sadly. "Can you believe that crap?" he said, shaking his head in disbelief. "The judge set a cash bond and the drug-dealing little shit paid it."

"All them judges are on the take," replied John Drake, who owned a dry cleaning store just down from the bank where O'Hanlon served as chief loan officer. He looked at Gino and made a circular motion with his finger, indicating they were ready for another round.

"Even Downs?" asked Steve Dodge, the youngest member of the trio. Dodge was the franchiser/owner of several sandwich shops in the county.

"Oh, hell yeah," Drake said. "It's a conspiracy. They're all in on it."

"All about who ya know," O'Hanlon agreed. He took a long pull at his beer and looked at his watch. The senior vice president he answered to was out of town this week. He'd be okay to have another.

Dodge was watching the older men and decided now was the time to disclose what he knew. The dead girl had worked for him at one of his shops, and her dad had recently come in and demanded her last paycheck. "Well, all I know is that Wrangler Hayes has said if he gets his hands on the perp, he's dead meat."

"Dude is probably better off in prison," Drake agreed. "Wrangler don't play."

"He was middle linebacker on our team my junior year," O'Hanlon said. "We'da won state, too, but coach wouldn't give me the okay to pass."

Dodge accepted a small tumbler of whiskey from Gino. "I just don't get it."

"I know, right?" O'Hanlon said. "The dude was a moron in coaching shorts with a whistle in his—"

Dodge looked at O'Hanlon levelly. "I'm talking about judges," he said.

"It's all political," Drake said. "Judges are under pressure to not put people in jail. Public says it's cruel and too expensive."

"Yeah, well, the people sayin' that ain't getting their places robbed or cars broken into. You seen the way some of those folks live?"

"Right?" O'Hanlon added. "Jail is expensive, but that's just the cost of doin' business. Maybe if those folks down in Cheyenne would get out and around the state a little bit, they'd see how the other half lives."

"We were puttin' people in jail for two hundred years and it worked!" Drake said. "Didn't have a bunch of weirdos running around beatin' people, shootin' 'em or whatever."

"I'll drink to that!" Dodge said, offering a toast.

O'Hanlon joined in the toast, but drank sourly. "Yeah, but we're all enlightened now."

"People are the same," Drake offered. "I'll tell you what, though. Judge Howard woulda set a bond that would have busted that little drug dealer's chops. The dude wouldn't have seen the light of day." Howard had spent time in this bar until his scandal-induced suicide a couple of years prior.

"I miss that old bastard," O'Hanlon offered.

"Me, too," Drake echoed. "He was a damned good man."

"Right up until he got tangled up with Emily Smith," Dodge said, referring to an attorney who had been murdered years prior. Following her death, the public learned that she and Howard had been involved.

Drake agreed. "He wasn't the only one!"

O'Hanlon spun his glass between his thick hands. "And now, Howard's dead, Daniels is in jail, and we got all new judges," he said.

"Lots of changes going on," Dodge said, because he thought that was what he should say.

O'Hanlon checked his watch. "And none of them for the better," he lamented. He had a board of county commissioners meeting in a few hours.

Drake looked at his watch as well. "Man, I would not want to be Press Daniels. Can you imagine being a judge in jail?" He shook his head. "Boy better be watching his back."

"His ass, you mean," Dodge said.

The men laughed together. "I've got time," O'Hanlon said. He finished his drink, wiped his mouth, and ordered another round.

16

Days earlier, following his release from jail, Gustafson had driven to a nearby extended stay hotel and paid cash for a two-week residence in advance. The girl at the front desk was someone he had seen around, an occasional customer who today was slightly stoned and clearly in awe of Gustafson's apparent wealth. She smacked her gum and twirled a strand of blue hair with a tattooed finger. "Gus, is there anything else I can get you?"

"I think that'll do it."

"I could bring you a receipt," she added. "Later, maybe?"

He ignored the offer. Now, having been rejected by Sam, he was in his room, raw and angry. He ordered pizza delivery from Justin Ward, a long-time customer he could be sure would add a little "something extra." While he waited, he looked at his phone, educating himself on attorney conflicts. According to what he read, in Wyoming attorneys had a continuing duty to former clients but only insofar as their representation of the new client was averse to the interests of the former client. Moreover, it seemed that aside from Sam's decision to disqualify himself, an objection would have to be brought by the former client.

He put down his phone and stepped to the window, pulled the shade to the right and peered carefully out, looking for Ward—or anyone watching his room. Seeing nothing, he took a seat on the double bed, his thoughts returning to his situation. Bottom line: Sam could represent him if Clay didn't object and if Clay's interests weren't adversely affected.

Until the client dies.

He was weighing an idea when there was a knock at the door. Looking through the peephole, he saw Ward pacing back and forth in the hallway. He unlocked the door and opened it quickly, then reached out and tugged Ward's sleeve, yanking him inside. "What are you doing showing up to my place tweaking?"

Ward handed the pizza box to Gustafson. "Wh-What are you talking about, man?"

"You heard me. Damn it, JW, you can't be bringing me shit when you're tweaking! You're all dinged up!" Gustafson put the box on the small table in the room and fiddled with the lid while he spoke. "Gonna get both of us run in, you dumb—where's the shit?" he asked, having stepped back and pointed at the box.

Ward reached into his pocket. "S-Sorry, man. It's been a long day," he said as he handed a vape pen to Gustafson. "My ol' lady's pissed 'cause I spent the rent money she gave me on some solid crystal."

Gustafson took the pen and hefted it in his hand, then shook it lightly. Seemed full. "Not smart."

"Yeah, well, she took the stuff and I ain't seen her in two days—how's that?"

"She ain't smart, either."

Ward looked at Gustafson as if he might take offense to the dealer insulting his baby momma, but apparently thought better of it. "So, Gus, I heard you got hung up, man," he said, looking pointedly at the vape.

"Nothing I can't deal with," Gustafson said. He inhaled from the vape and held it at arm's length, appraising it, fully aware that Ward was watching him like a child watching a parent eat a candy bar.

"Bet that," Ward agreed. "You been outsmartin' them dumb cops for as long as I can remember."

"Right," Gustafson said. "Sit down, JW." He handed Ward the pen. "Go ahead," he encouraged him. When Ward had hit the pen and closed his eyes, Gustafson continued. "So, I was looking at my books the other day. Seems you are a little behind."

Ward's eyes were now wide open. "I—I know, man, but I've got a plan." He handed the pen back to Gustafson.

"Yeah?"

"Oh yeah, Gus. Trust me. I just need a little time."

"Right," Gustafson said. "The problem is, JW, most of your plans don't turn out good, so I'm gonna help you." He again offered the pen to Ward, who shook his head. "Really? Okay. More for me," he said, and inhaled deeply. A minute later, he exhaled. "See, JW, you and me are gonna do a deal."

"Wh-What's that?"

"It's okay, JW," Gustafson said, eyeing the man carefully. "What are you afraid of?"

"I—I dunno, man. I don't wanna get in trouble. My probation officer has basically said that one more mistake and I'm gonna catch another revocation. Last time, the judge said that was it."

"You're not going to get in trouble," Gustafson assured him. "I just need you to do me a favor. I need you to get a little something, and then I'm gonna have you deliver it to a friend. I want to surprise him."

"That's all?"

"That's it."

"And in return?" Ward asked, licking his lips nervously.

Gustafson smiled wickedly. "I'm not going to have my other friends bust your balls."

Ward swallowed hard. "O-Okay, but what if I can't get what you need, or if I can't—"

"You can," Gustafson said. "You will."

"But what if I can't?" Ward was sniveling now.

"Then my friends will come and see you. I thought I made that clear?"

"Gus, I'll try! Really, I will. But I can't guarantee—"

"Just listen for a minute, JW." Gustafson explained what he needed and when, and then handed the pen to Ward, who this time accepted and inhaled deeply. "You can do that, can't you? You know who he is, right?"

"Okay," Ward said, trying to speak while holding his breath. "Yeah. But I'm gonna need some money."

"Then you better start delivering pizzas," Gustafson said, taking the pen back and showing Ward to the door. "You'll figure it out, JW. I have great confidence in you. Maybe work a little extra or whatever. Now go. And don't forget about my friends," he said, closing the door behind Ward. He then sat on the bed and thought for a minute before dialing the front desk on the room phone. "It's Gus. You still wanna deliver that receipt?"

17

On the first of May, Sam was plugging away on a brief in a civil matter when Cassie buzzed him. "Your appointment is here."

Sam looked at his watch and sighed. Never enough time. He directed her to seat the man in the small conference room. He stopped and got a cup of coffee on the way. When Sam entered, the man turned, holding one of the relics of Sam's service in his small, delicate hand. "What's this?" he asked, brandishing the item.

Stepping into his conference room, Sam took the man's proffered hand and felt an instant dislike for him. Short, pencil-thin, dressed in black, and with a ferret-like face featuring a mustache waxed so that the ends curled upward, he had tiny, even teeth resembling those of a child. The entire effect was such that Sam half expected the man to leave his conference room and tie an unsuspecting damsel to the nearby railroad tracks.

"It's a piece of metal that means something to me," Sam replied.

"I figured that. From what?"

"From the up-armored HMMWV I was riding in when I got blown up."

"My dad was in the Army. Germany, I think."

"Great," Sam said. He stared at the little man until the signal was received. When the relic was put back and they were both seated, Sam looked at the notes Cassie had made him and continued, "How can I help you, Mr. Edison?"

"I got arrested. It was bullshit!"

It always was. "Yeah? What happened?"

"The bastards tased me!"

"Really?"

"Yeah, and I wasn't doin' nothin'."

That would be unusual—and unlawful. Few cops would risk losing their job to get their jollies tasing some poor slob. "Tell me more."

"So, it was a Saturday and the weather was nice. I was mowing my lawn and listening to music at my own house. But someone said it was too loud. I tol' 'em to kiss my ass and they got mad and tol' me to stop and I said I ain't stoppin', so they started callin' me names."

"And?"

Edison put a hand to his mustache and twirled it. Sam looked away to hide his smirk. "They said I was just bein' obnoxious and—"

"Were you?"

"I was just listening to my stuff and they call the cops!"

"All right," Sam said. "The cops showed up and then what?"

"Then they walked onto my grass!"

"So?"

"So they can't do that!"

"Actually, they can if they are investigating a crime," Sam corrected.

"Weren't no crime."

Sam was quickly tiring of Edison. "Breach of peace," Sam explained. "So, you told them to get off your land." He was steering him back to the subject at hand. "Then what?"

"They wouldn't leave! Kept tellin' me to lower my voice and to stop swearin' and shit. So, I tol' 'em to leave."

"And they didn't."

"Hell no! They said they was gonna arrest me for interference with a peace officer!"

"Did they take you into custody?"

"They tried. Had three of 'em tryin' to break my arms."

Sam made a note and nodded. "The vest cameras will tell us a lot. We will be able to verify your version of events that way. Did you resist arrest?"

Edison stared at Sam blankly. "No. I tol' 'em to let go of me!"

"Then what happened?"

"Then they tased my ass! I want to sue 'em. Will you take my case on a continuance, or whatever?"

"I think you mean contingency basis—and no."

"Why not?"

"Because I don't like to lose, and your case is a stone-cold loser."

"But they trespassed onto my property and tased me! They can't do that!"

Sam sighed heavily. "Mr. Edison, were you drinking that night?"

"Well, a little. Maybe like a six-pack," Edison replied. "An' a coupla shots—you know. It was a Saturday an' all."

"So, what happened was this: you got drunk, played your music too loud, got in an argument with your neighbors, and when the cops showed up you argued with them, cursed them, resisted arrest, and eventually got tased. That about right?"

"Look at this cut on my face! I got that when they tased me!"

"Mr. Edison, I really don't think I'm going to be able to help you beyond working to negotiate a plea. You got any kind of criminal history? I might be able to get the State to drop the interference charge if you'll plead to breach of peace or public intox."

"I ain't pleadin' to shit. I'm a law-abiding citizen."

Sam stood and walked to his office door. "Then we can't do business. Cassie out front will give you the names of someone who might be willing and able to help you."

"How much? It's all about money with you guys, isn't it?"

Sam turned from his door. "You got drunk and your mouth outweighed your ass. Now, you're feeling hurt and humiliated—and you should, by the way—and you're looking to get even somehow. Well, I'm not your big brother. Thanks for stopping by."

"You—"

"Mr. Edison, please leave, or I'll escort you out."

"Folks were telling me you were different. But you're just another—"

"Goodbye, Mr. Edison. I won't ask you again."

A few minutes later, Sam was in his office looking at a file when Cassie buzzed him. "Sam, you have an email on the office account."

And? "That's what we pay 'em for."

"This is personal."

"Okay," Sam said. "I'll take a look at it." He pulled up the office email and saw immediately the message to which Cassie was referring. The subject line was "Personal For Sam Johnstone."

He opened it and read: "Dear Sam, I'm sending this because you haven't responded to any of my phone calls or texts. I hope nothing is wrong. I enjoyed our time together and I'm looking forward to seeing you again. Please respond so I don't have to take drastic measures. Mickey."

Drastic measures—what the hell? Sam reached for his phone and reviewed the history quickly. No recent phone calls, no voicemails, no texts that hadn't been returned. Did she have the right number? He sent her a quick email, giving her his number, and tried to return his attention to the file. He'd been thinking about her every day. She was gorgeous, single, a splendid lover, and fun to be with. He didn't want to blow this one. He could call the business. What the hell was the name? How many coffee shop/bakeries could there be in a town that size?

He snatched at his phone when it rang, even though the caller ID read "Unknown."

"This is Sam."

"Sam! So good to hear your voice!" Mickey said.

"And yours. Listen, I'm so sorry about the missed calls. I haven't been getting any, no voicemails or—"

"Oh, don't worry about that," she said. "I made that up."

That was bizarre. "Why?"

"I figured it would get your attention, and it worked!" she said brightly.

"I guess it did," he said. Why didn't she just call? "So, how've you been?"

"Lonely."

"Uh, me too."

"Want to do something about that?" she asked.

"Uh, yeah. What do you have in mind?"

"Oh, you know the answer to that," she teased. "The question is where?"

He might be able to find a stream en route. "I can head that way again."

"Are you trying to keep me a secret?"

Maybe. "Of course not," he said lamely. "I'm just thinking it's not safe for a woman to drive across Wyoming—"

"How very paternalistically twentieth century of you," she said. Perhaps realizing he was taken aback, she continued, "I'm teasing, Sam. I think it's quaint."

"Well, I—"

"When are you thinking?" she asked.

"I've been trying to catch up since my last trip over. Let me look at my calendar and clear it with Cassie and—"

"Who is Cassie?"

"My legal assistant."

"What does she have to do with it?"

"She runs the office."

"And your schedule?"

"Well, yeah," Sam admitted. "Kinda."

"We need to fix that."

We? And she didn't know Cassie. "Okay, I'll get to work on that," he said. "Anyway, I'll get back with you."

"You've got my number," she said. "Use it."

18

The county was governed by a five-person board of county commissioners, each of whom was elected on a partisan ballot to a four-year term. To ensure some degree of continuity in government, the terms of the commissioners were staggered three and two. In contrast to more urban areas, where the job paid well, commissioners in Custer were not professional politicians but generally businesspeople in the twilight of their careers. This year, two of the commissioners would be on the ballot. While neither had announced his candidacy, each understood the eyes of the few voters concerned with off-cycle elections would be upon him, and each wanted to ensure no missteps were made.

O'Hanlon was one of those commissioners. Nearing the end of his first term, he was on the lookout for an issue that could bring his name to the forefront. Accordingly, when Lee was named as the suspect in the killing of Misty Layton, he had his cause. "We gotta suspend him," he told the board chair, Allison Criss, during a pre-board meeting lunch.

"I hear you," she said, placing an index finger against her lips as if to quiet a child. She was a retired physician, had been on the board for several terms, and was a stickler for the rules. "But we can't have that discussion right now," she cautioned. "That is official business, and the Open Meetings

Act prohibits our discussing it except during a public meeting or in an executive conference."

"Ridiculous," said Commissioner Gary Burroughs. "The guy has to go. You see this?" he asked, pointing to the local newspaper. "We got a guy who is about to get charged with murder still serving as our county attorney!"

"It's obscene. We've gotta be a laughingstock around the state," Gene Tyson replied. Tyson had owned a shoe store in town until the discount chains had moved in and put him out of business. "He needs to go."

"We have to do this correctly, and by that I mean not informally," Criss replied. The brussels sprouts in her salad were overcooked, and she was pushing them around her bowl with the tine of a fork. "The first thing we need to do is speak with our attorney. Someone needs to move for an executive session when the issue of personnel comes up."

"Got it," Tyson said.

"Whatever." O'Hanlon took a huge bite out of a sandwich. "I'm gonna move to bounce him. We can't have a suspected murderer—"

"He hasn't even been charged yet!" Criss interrupted. "And that's not how it works, anyway."

"You've looked at it?"

"Well, of course," she replied. "The first thing is, we'd have to get a legal complaint prepared and signed by the Attorney General. It gets filed in district court." She found a soft sprout and ate it greedily.

"Then what?"

"Then he files an answer, then it gets set for trial. Maybe a jury, maybe not. Depends on what he and the people ask for."

"How long?"

"Thirty days after the answer."

"Then we need to get started!" O'Hanlon replied. "He poses a danger to the community in his current position and he's a distraction to boot."

"We gotta be careful, though, right?" Burroughs cautioned. "I mean, I want him out as much as the next guy, but he's got the right to due process or whatever you call it."

O'Hanlon was now tearing at a small bag of corn chips. "I'm gonna ask him to come to the meeting and demand his resignation, is what I'm gonna do," he vowed.

"And if he refuses?" Criss asked.

"Simple. We fire his ass," Burroughs said. "We're a right-to-work state. We can fire him for any reason or no reason at all." He popped an entire chip into his mouth.

"Wrong," Criss countered. "He's an elected official. Besides, I think the public has a right to expect us to provide people with due process."

"What the public wants is for us to do the right thing," O'Hanlon replied. "They are tired of politicians and judges lying and cheating in a two-tiered justice system."

"Spare me the national talking points, Sean. We're talking about Custer here," Criss said. "And we will have no more discussion of this matter prior to the meeting convening."

"Now you're censoring our speech!" Smith said.

"No, I'm enforcing the law," Criss said. "And if you continue to discuss this matter, I will bring it up as a violation of the Open Meetings Act at tonight's meeting," she added, stabbing viciously at the arugula greens in her salad.

19

The next morning, Lee was in his office reviewing charging documents when one of his many new office employees appeared in his doorway. "Mr. Lee, it's a lady named Sarah from the *Bugle*, I think? She wants an interview."

"Thank you," he said. "Please tell her I am unavailable at present. I'll call her when I get a minute."

"She said you'd say that. She said to tell you she is on deadline and that she is running a story about your impending resignation with or without your comments."

"My *what*?" Lee asked. He sighed. Damned small-town rumors. "Send her back."

Moments later, Penrose took a seat without being asked. "You don't mind if I record our conversation, do you?"

"Of course not."

She made a production out of withdrawing a small recorder from her purse, placing it on his desk, and thumbing the "on" button. She looked at him and began without preamble. "So, I'm sure you know the commissioners have voted to ask for your resignation."

He didn't know but was not surprised. "I am aware."

She saw him flinch. Good. "Your reaction?"

"I have no intention of resigning," he said. "I was elected to do a job, and I intend to do that job."

"I'm told charges are pending in the shooting you were involved in."

"I don't know who told you that, and I'm not going to comment on that except to say that I continue to stress my legal and factual innocence."

"But surely there is a conflict of interest?" she asked. "I mean, you are the county attorney and make all charging decisions on felonies."

"It can be worked around," he explained. "If and when—*if*, I stress— charges are passed over from law enforcement, then I will ensure that we obtain the services of a special prosecutor to look into them."

"My sources tell me the commissioners are seeking your *immediate* removal."

"I can't speak to that," Lee said. "What I can say is that there is a process in place for the removal of elected officials in Wyoming, and thankfully it doesn't directly involve the board of county commissioners. I say thankfully for good reason: they are politicians."

"So you won't consider resigning?"

"Not as of this moment."

"But you're not saying you wouldn't if conditions were—"

"Just as I always have, I will put the people of Custer first. And I will do that despite anything the commissioners might say or do to undermine me. I have a job to do, and I intend to do it. Perhaps by doing so I can set an example for . . . others."

Penrose leaned forward and snapped off her phone. "I think I've got what I need."

"Glad to be of help," Lee replied. "See yourself out?"

"I know the way."

As soon as she had cleared the room, he picked up his office phone and started to dial. Then, thinking better of it, he cradled the office phone, removed his personal cell phone from his vest pocket, punched a programmed number, and waited.

When she answered, he spoke quickly. "We need to talk."

20

Sam lifted his glass of club soda. "Cheers!" he offered self-consciously.

"Your health." Cathy clinked glasses with Sam and drank deeply. "It doesn't seem real," she said, referring to her appointment by the county commissioners to the job of interim county attorney. The past couple of weeks had been a whirlwind beginning shortly after a story featuring disparaging remarks made by Lee regarding the county commission had appeared in the *Bugle*. Within days, the commissioners had called a special meeting, withdrawn into executive session to discuss a personnel matter, and then called upon Lee to resign. He had resisted for a time, but under threat of a complaint filed by the state's Attorney General and the specter of a mass resignation by his attorneys and staff, he finally succumbed to the pressure and submitted his resignation, effective immediately. The commissioners accepted the resignation later that day and soon thereafter had appointed Cathy.

Sam recalled his experiences taking command of platoons and companies. "Oh, it's real. And it will get *real* real when you walk into your office Monday morning and see nine smiling faces—"

"Ten," she corrected.

"—Ten smiling faces all looking at you and saying, 'What now, boss?'" He laughed.

She drank again. "It is going to be a challenge, for sure."

"Who is swearing you in?"

"Judge Downs, first thing tomorrow morning."

"Very cool."

"It'll be short and sweet," she said. "You are invited, by the way."

"I'll be there." Because she seemed doubtful, he decided to pump her up a bit. "You are more than up to it. That's why you were selected. You'll do great."

She smiled wryly. "Sam, I was selected—on an interim basis, mind you —because I was the only person dumb enough to not run for the hills when they inquired."

"That's one way to look at it," he countered. "But maybe no one else expressed interest because they knew you had?"

"You are sweet."

"That's me. Sam the Sweetheart."

She drank again, then put down her glass and looked steadily at him before starting to speak. "Sam, I . . . ." Then she seemed to lose her train of thought.

Here it came. He waited expectantly. "What?"

"I . . . really like you, but—"

"You are breaking up with me?" he joked. "We haven't even slept together. This hasn't happened since the eighth grade. Women usually at least wait until we've slept together to dump me." He smiled at his attempt at humor.

She didn't return the smile. "Don't make this harder than it has to be," she said. "I have to break this off, don't I?"

"I'm not sure what *this* is," he replied. On the other hand, no reason to feel bad about Mickey now.

"You know what I mean. I'm sorry. I don't like it either. But you and I both know if I take this job we can't continue to see each other. It wouldn't be right."

"If seeing you is wrong, I don't wanna be right," he said, trying to keep it light.

She knitted her brows. "I've thought about it a lot and I just don't see how we could be together. Even if I swore myself off every case you are on, well, it would still *look* bad."

"We could sneak around behind everyone's back," Sam offered. "That always adds to the fun."

She shook her head. "We'd get caught. People always do."

"Not if we were at my buddy's cabin in the Bighorns." He had a brief, lascivious vision of snow and a fireplace before she brought him out of his reverie.

"Sam, I—"

She was hurting. "Cathy, I get it. It's okay. Honestly, I don't want to think about it. Let's just enjoy tonight."

"Okay," she agreed. "But no funny stuff."

"I wouldn't think of it," he said, thinking of it.

Then he thought of Mickey and stopped thinking of it.

The next afternoon, as Cathy pushed the last number on the office phone, she recognized her antiperspirant had failed. Thankfully, the day was almost over. "Dylan Roberts, please," Cathy said when his receptionist answered. "I'm Cathy Schmidt. I'm the new county attorney over in Custer."

"I'll see if he is available."

Cathy looked at the boxes on her floor while she waited for Dylan to answer. It had been a long time. She and her ex had gone to law school with Roberts. He was the smartest guy in the class and not afraid to let anyone know it. Despite that, he was engaging and generally fun to be around. In fact, before Cathy and her ex had become an item, she had spent some time with Roberts—including a spring break trip to Hawaii. When her marriage hit the rocks, Roberts had been one of the first to call, offering her both a job and what seemed to be heartfelt condolences. Since then, he had offered her a job on several occasions.

"Cathy, long time no hear!"

It had been less than a month. "Right."

"So, have you decided to accept my offer?" After news of Lee's involvement in a shooting, Roberts had offered her a job for the fourth time.

"Not exactly."

"No? I'm surprised," he said. "That place must be in an uproar . . . Hey, this isn't a negotiating tactic, is it? I mean, it's a pretty good offer, and Jefferson County ain't Custer."

"You obviously haven't heard."

"Heard what?" he asked, alarmed. "Are you okay?"

"I'm fine," she assured him. "Grant Lee resigned under pressure. The board of county commissioners has appointed me."

"Permanently?"

"Not as of yet," she said. "As of now, it's only an interim appointment."

"Be careful," he advised. "These jobs . . . well, commissioners can be fickle. Is that what you called to tell me?"

"Well, that and to ask you a favor."

"Of course," he said. "How can I help?"

Cathy sat quietly, debating the next step. She could probably find someone else. Given their history, it was dangerous—he was dangerous, in a way. On the other hand, he was without a doubt the best prosecutor she knew, and that was what it was going to take. "Well, I'm obviously going to have some serious conflicts."

"I'd be happy to help," he said. "I'm looking forward to working with you again. I always enjoyed that . . . and stuff."

"I know, but it's a big ask."

"Anything," he said again.

"I need a special prosecutor."

Roberts read the papers. "Lee's case?"

"I can't very well do it myself, can I?" she asked rhetorically. "And there will be others, of course."

"No, I don't suppose you can," he agreed. "Have they arrested him yet?"

"No."

"Are they close? I've got a major tax case coming down the line. It's complex to the point that I'll have to try it myself."

Of course he would. "Not that I know of. I took the oath this morning; it's not like law enforcement has got me on speed dial yet. And I've put up a wall." A *wall* was a technique to partition one attorney from knowledge of a case being handled by another attorney in the same office.

"Good idea," he said approvingly. "Any decent deputy attorneys?"

"Lots of potential," she said, with Cates in mind. "My chief deputy is Mike Shepherd. You might remember him; I think he was a year ahead of us in law school."

"Big, heavy guy?"

He was that. And useless. "Yeah."

Roberts was quiet for a moment, calculating. "Will your commissioners cough up expenses for me to bring over one of my folks?"

"I think they'll do whatever they have to do," she said. "I made it clear I'll have some conflicts. I just need to be able to assure them you'll keep costs down."

"My folks will vouch for my being a tightwad," he said. "What kind of timeline are we on?"

"No idea, but if you have interest, you probably ought to touch base with the investigating officer."

"Who is my point of contact?"

"Well, to begin with, the chief of police. His name is Buck Lucas. Been here forever."

"Great name for a police chief in a place like Custer. Either that, or an outside linebacker for the Denver Broncos."

"Trust me when I tell you he looks the part of either. Straight out of Central Casting."

There was silence on the line for a moment. "It's good to hear from you," Roberts said. "Even if you are rejecting my offer."

"For all the right reasons."

"True. Listen, maybe we can have dinner when I get over there to scout things out?"

It wasn't unexpected, but she stiffened. "Your wife is okay with that?"

"We . . . Well, we're not really a thing."

"Meaning?"

"Meaning we're getting a divorce," he said. "We've just kind of grown apart. Should be final any day now."

"I'm sorry."

"I guess I am, too. You know, I always thought I'd marry once and be with a woman for life, but here I am, twice divorced, paying child support all over the place, and eating in front of my television."

"Pretty picture."

"Yeah, well. The good news is, we will be working together again."

"Yeah," she said.

"And seeing each other again."

"Sure," she said, remembering nights long past. "Dylan, I gotta go. I'll be in touch."

"Looking forward to it."

She rang off and looked at the boxes of personal items on the floor. She needed to focus if she was going to get moved in anytime soon.

21

Punch rubbed his eyes, then looked up and tried to focus on the tile ceiling. After Sam said a "statement" would be good, Punch had gotten to thinking, and he'd awakened early and been in before six a.m. After downloading all jail phone calls featuring either Gustafson, Davonte, or Ronnie, he had settled in and spent the past few hours listening to conversations that were alternately banal, blasphemous, or profane, beginning when Davonte was in custody. Having finished those, he was listening to Ronnie Norquist talking to his mother. It was uncomfortable and embarrassing—Jeannie's pain was palpable—and Punch was looking at his watch, about to call it a day, when he heard Ronnie and Davonte.

"Davonte! Man, I am glad to see you. I've been waiting for days! Thanks for coming to see me. What's going on? How is getting me a lawyer going?"

"Just wanted to stop in and tell you I'm leavin' town, little man," Punch heard Davonte say. "Wanted to remind you that the way to succeed in jail is to keep your mouth shut."

"What do you mean?"

"I mean I got to go. Just reminding you there are certain subjects that, you know, are off-limits. Shit no one needs to know about."

"Davonte, you know you can count on me. I mean, we're friends, right? I got rid of . . . the thing . . . and testified just like you said."

"You done good. That acting stuff—you're good at it, I'll say that. But you just remember to keep quiet. Because if you was to forget, well, then my other friends—the ones probably watching you right now—they might take offense. You know what I'm sayin'?"

Punch could hear Ronnie swallowing hard. "I understand," Ronnie said. "I helped you and—"

"And I'm gonna help you, man. Just as soon as I get drafted and get my boys here taken care of. Right now, those are my priorities—you know what I'm sayin'?"

"But we're friends! You said if we did this, then when you got off, you'd square me away at my trial! You said you'd testify for me and be in the clear because of double jeopardy or whatever you learned in Sam's class! You said if we did it this way, no one could prove anything against either of us!"

Punch could hear the desperation in Ronnie's voice.

"Well, I'm gonna be busy here for a while. You know, the draft—things like that. Don't know I'll be back this way." Punch could hear a chair; Davonte must have stood. "Now, you just go on back to your cell and think about what I said. I gotta get ready to fly out east to meet with my agent."

Ronnie was pleading now. "Davonte! After you get drafted, you'll hire me a lawyer—that's what you said, right? I'll need you to testify or I'll get convicted! You got my back, right? Then I'll get through school and be your agent, just like we agreed, right? Davonte!"

Punch sat back in his chair and shook his head. "I'll be damned. That's a world-class double-cross."

Punch watched Cathy closely while she listened to audio of the jail call between Ronnie and Davonte. He had a lot of respect for her. As a prosecutor, she'd been Grade A—fair, but tough if necessary. He was pleased that she had been appointed county attorney while the fiasco involving Lee got sorted out.

"I hear you, Punch," Cathy said after the video was complete. "But this doesn't mean that Ronnie didn't do it. It just means that maybe Davonte was a little more involved than we knew."

"Okay, well, I've got something to add."

"What's that?"

"Trent Gustafson wants to do a deal," Punch said. "Now that his ass is in a crack over the death of that young gal, he's telling me he's got information that could spring Ronnie, but he'll only cough it up if we do him a solid on his cases. It all fits!"

"What's he got?"

"I don't know, exactly," Punch said. "He won't cough anything up without a deal. But it's got to be related—don't you think?"

"I don't know. I *do* know Gustafson is dealing fentanyl. I'm not doing anything until and unless he pukes up something useful. Right now, we've got a guy who says he did it in prison, and a guy pending dope-dealing charges—who just happens to have been the guy in prison's dealer—saying his client didn't do it, but refusing to say who did. Can you see why I don't want to poke at this mousetrap?"

"Very colorful."

Cathy ignored him. "Besides, even if he has some information, what do we do with that? Davonte is untouchable." Because Davonte had been tried and acquitted of Kaiden Miles' murder, double jeopardy precluded his being tried again.

"I'm thinking maybe we can right a wrong and get an innocent man out of prison."

"Well, again, I don't know how innocent Norquist is," she said. "He confessed. What I do know is that what this call shows is a guy in jail saying he's willing to take one for the team to protect Davonte. But from what, exactly, we don't know. Was it the killing? Was it just covering up Davonte being somehow involved? Was Davonte an accessory before or after the fact? A co-conspirator? We don't know. And that," she said, indicating the thumb drive, "doesn't clear it up for me."

"I'm going to keep looking," Punch said. "Sooner or later, if there's something there, one of these weasels will cough it up like a cat with a hairball."

"I think you should."

"So would you consider a deal?"

"Maybe," she said. "But he's going to have to testify, and he's going to have to testify to more than what he heard. He'll have to rat out whoever *did* do it, and my money's on Davonte." She tapped a pen against her desktop. "And just to bolster things, I wouldn't even consider a deal unless Gustafson coughs up an affidavit with his attorney present before he testifies, just in case he conveniently gets run over by a coal train or something."

"You're hard."

"Damn right. Somebody's daughter died because of the shit he sells. And keep in mind, that's just the one we know about. How many sons and daughters bit the big one because of him? And, I might add, if he says what I think he is going to say, then he most definitely interfered with the investigation into Miles' death and thereby obstructed justice. It isn't like he is some kind of hero for coming forward."

"Understood."

"And I'll tell you what else," she said as he stood to leave.

"What's that?"

"If Gustafson says what you think he is gonna say, and if it's true, Kaiden's mom and Ronnie's mom are both gonna want a piece of our asses. We'd best be ready."

Punch was nodding in agreement before she finished her thought. "I know," he said.

When he left, Cathy sat quietly, tossing a baseball-sized foam ball made to replicate a basketball. At last, she stood and shot it one-handed at a toy backboard and basketball rim attached to her door. When it banked in, she stuck a fist in the air. "And the crowd goes wild!"

22

Sam was reviewing a brief he had drafted for an upcoming hearing when Cassie buzzed him. He removed the readers he'd begun wearing in the last few months and rubbed his eyes. This was the fourth call in the past hour. "Yes," he asked testily.

"Sam, it's Mr. Gustafson."

Something he didn't understand? "Please tell him I'm busy."

"Sam, it might be best if you see him. He seems . . . upset."

"I'd be upset if my stuff was killing people, too," Sam snapped before catching himself. His sponsor would advise him to pray for the man rather than condemn him. "I'm sorry, Cassie. Put him in the conference room and give him some water."

When she rang off, he made some cryptic notes and took some deep breaths. The exercise in self-control failed, and after retrieving a bottle of sparkling water for himself, he stormed through the conference room door, intending to make this short and sweet. "Mr. Gustafson," he began even before he sat down. "I think I told you—"

"Call me Gus. Everyone else does."

Nicknames were reserved for people Sam liked. "Okay, Mr. Gustafson, how can I help you?"

"I already told you, take my case."

"And I already told you I have a conflict."

Gustafson sat back in his chair and swigged water. "I spoke with my Colorado lawyer. He says conflicts can be waived."

"Only by the client," Sam said. "And even if the client waives, I still have an obligation to him."

"He'll waive."

"How do you know?" Sam asked. "And why would he?"

"Because it's the right thing to do." Gustafson drank the rest of the water and stared at Sam impassively.

Sam returned the stare, surprised by Gustafson's nerve. Arrogant little prick. "What do you mean, the right thing to do?"

"It's the right thing. My ass is in a sling, but not because of anything I did," Gustafson explained. "But because of stuff *he* did. It was his."

"Bullshit."

Gustafson shook his head. "I figured you wouldn't believe me."

Sam knew better. "You got that right."

"I have information. Stuff you want. I have sources."

"For the distribution of drugs, yeah."

"I remind you it is only—*only*—an allegation. One I need your help with."

"No."

"What's your hourly rate?"

"Nothing you can afford."

"I might surprise you."

Sam measured the man. He was a twerp, but he had managed to post a high cash bond. "Even if you could, this isn't going to happen. I'm in a position where I only take clients I want."

"How much?"

The money would help. "Not interested," Sam said, and stood.

Gustafson looked up at him. "I'll make you rich." He pulled a pen from a pocket and wrote an enormous number on a piece of paper before passing it to Sam.

He'd drawn on a line of credit last month to pay Cassie. "You aren't serious," Sam said after quickly scanning the paper.

"I don't want to go to jail, Sam."

"Understood. But I know several guys who would be more than happy to defend you for a quarter of that."

"I don't want them. I want you."

"Why?"

"Because you're a winner," Gustafson said. "I like to surround myself with winners."

Sam considered briefly. The money offered was more than he normally made in a year. "I—" he began.

"I'll add twenty-five percent."

The important thing was he might find out if Ronnie really was guilty. "I'm—"

"Nonrefundable."

Might be a one-shot deal. "What if you plead out?"

"I won't. I can't. I can't go to prison, Sam. It's a death sentence for a guy like me." He indicated his slight frame with his small hands. "Around here —on the outside—I control the people around me. In there, the animals rule."

True enough. "Nonrefundable," Sam repeated. It was tempting.

"You keep it all."

"I don't know . . ."

"Sam, I have information I know you want that could free an innocent man—the son of a friend of yours. You don't get that information unless you defend me. Successfully."

"I can't guarantee success," Sam said, shaking his head. "No one can. Anyone who tells you differently is full of it." It was also the best way to get sued for malpractice. "What do you have?" he asked. Punch had alerted him, of course, but best to keep that in confidence.

"It's something you want to know."

"About whom?"

"Ronnie Norquist."

Sam sat back in his chair, trying to feign surprise. He'd lost one of his best friends—Paul Norquist, the man who had brought him to Custer— over his decision to call Paul's son Ronnie as a witness during the Davonte Blair case. "What do you have?"

"He didn't do it."

"He said he did."

"Yeah, well, he didn't."

Paul and Jeannie Norquist had been his best friends. "How do you know?"

"I know," Gustafson said. "I'll tell you, but not until I walk."

Ridiculous. "What if we try the case but the jury votes to convict?"

"Then you keep your money but Ronnie rots in prison."

Drug dealers were manipulative as a matter of course. But what if he did know something? No, that was absurd. "I'll think about it. When is your preliminary hearing?"

"Tomorrow at eleven."

Impossible. "Are you willing to waive?"

"No," Gustafson said. "And I expect you to hold that county attorney bitch's feet to the fire."

Sam felt the hair on the back of his neck rise. More evidence this was a bad idea—like, loss-of-license-to-practice bad. "That's not how it would work with me. I'm not my clients' big brother. You want someone to prove something, you've got the wrong guy."

"She's trying to lock my ass up!"

"That's her job. She's looking for justice for the family of a dead kid." Sam hit the intercom. "Cassie, can you see Mr. Gustafson out?" He looked at Gustafson. "I'm not going to be able to help with the preliminary hearing tomorrow," he said, hoping that would run Gustafson off. When the little man sat and stared at him, he felt compelled to explain. "Even if I was inclined to represent you—and I'm not—I have to get my client's written permission waiving the conflict. Then, I'm going to need to talk with bar counsel to get an advisory opinion on how I could do this deal—assuming we could even do a deal," Sam explained, pointing at Gustafson and then himself. "All that takes time."

"I don't have time!"

"You can ask the judge for a continuance tomorrow. Tell her you want to get an attorney and you're willing to waive your right to a speedy preliminary hearing. Judge Downs will grant your motion."

"Then what?"

"Then look for an attorney," Sam replied. "I can give you some names."

"If I don't walk, your buddy's kid is gonna rot in prison. You want to take that chance?"

Sam ignored Cassie's knock. "How do I know you've got anything that could help?"

"You're just gonna have to trust me."

"Come in," Sam ordered. When Cassie opened the door, Sam indicated her and said, "Yeah, well, I don't know that I can do that. Cassie'll see you out."

He watched as Gustafson reluctantly stood and followed Cassie out. When she returned, she looked pointedly around Sam's office. "Taking him on might be good for us. We need some new stuff around here."

"What's the matter with my stuff?"

"You mean aside from the fact that the hobos living by the tracks would turn their noses up at it?"

"Get out of my office," Sam said, smiling behind his cup as she left.

Thirty seconds later, Cassie was again on the line. "Sam?"

"I'm still here," he replied impatiently. "What do you need?"

"Don't bark at me!" she scolded. "There's a phone call for you from a woman in Bozeman. Something about your dad."

How could this day get worse? "Tell her I'm not available."

"You *are* available."

Sam sighed heavily and thought it over. She might be right, he decided at last. "Hello?"

"Mr. Johnstone, this is Linda Dillon from the Bozeman Regional Medical Center. I think you talked with Dr. Robinson some time back?"

"I did."

"I am with your father," Dillon said. "He wanted you to know that we have completed his move into hospice. He does not have a lot of time left. I think he realizes that, and he has asked for you."

.   .   .

Too little, too late. "I'm sorry," Sam said. "But I am not available right now. I've got a court appearance here shortly. Tell him I'll call him when and if I get a chance." Which was more consideration than he ever gave Sam.

"Mr. Johnstone, I certainly don't mean to be indelicate, but this may well be the last opportunity that you have to speak with him."

When had they spoken last? Before he joined the army? No calls when he was on leave or when he was at Walter Reed getting patched up. Did he even know where Sam was? "Yeah, well, if he asks, tell him I said I hope he's feeling better."

"That's not going to happen."

"I know; he doesn't ask about me."

"No, I mean he's not going to feel better."

Yeah, well . . . It happened to them all. "That's tough."

"Mr. Johnstone, can I say something?"

"Sure. But I have a hearing in five minutes," he lied.

"There are some things you only get one shot at."

Here it was. "People keep telling me that, yeah."

"Saying your final goodbyes to a loved one is one of those things," she continued. "You might want to reconsider."

"I have considered it. I have considered it to no end," Sam said, biting off the words. "This is not the kind of father-son relationship you might imagine. No vacations together or back-slapping coming off the field after the big game. This was a father-son relationship that never existed, because after my mom died, he decided it was more important to drink and chase women than to spend time with me."

"Everyone deals with grief differently. For some people—"

"Look, to be honest, I have enough problems of my own right now."

"Well, I certainly respect that. I just thought you should know. We don't expect that he will make it much longer."

Sam started to hang up, but she caught him with another question. "What is a good mailing address for you, sir? Mr. Johnstone has some materials that he would like you to have. Looks to be family memorabilia. Where should I send it?"

Sam thought briefly about refusing the mailing, but that would probably add to Dillon's troubles. She was only doing her job. "Send it here to my office," he said, and gave her the address. The last thing he needed was a bunch of junk, but he had a dumpster out back that could be put to good use. "And I want to thank you for your efforts . . . I appreciate them. It's just not good timing right now."

23

Days later, during Sam's regularly scheduled visit to the jail, he and Daniels spent twenty minutes catching up. According to Daniels, he was doing well: he was reading, writing, walking, exercising, and generally staying clear of trouble. "There's a couple of guys I sentenced in here who for whatever reason have taken it upon themselves to protect me," he said in response to a question from a worried Sam.

"They, uh, don't expect anything in return, do they?" Sam asked delicately.

"Oh, hell no," Daniels said, shaking his head. "I think it's their idea of community service or something. There's a weird kind of honor code among inmates."

"Well good," Sam said. They covered a variety of topics, from getting someone to take care of Daniels' house to the food in jail. Sam weighed whether to bother Daniels with his own troubles, but finally decided it might give him something else to think about. Besides, no one had a better grasp of legal ethics than Press did. "Can I run something by you?"

"Of course," Daniels said. "I've got all day. Hell, truth be told, I've got most of the coming year!"

Sam didn't laugh. "I'm sorry, Press," he replied. "And I wish you had allowed me to appeal."

"No," Daniels said quickly. "I'm not going to have a bunch of pencil-necked attorneys from Denver or Cheyenne arguing that you, Bridger, or Lee didn't know what you were doing and making Custer out to be what their preconceived notion of us is—if they think of us at all."

"It's not about Custer, Press—it's about you!"

"I made my decision," Daniels said. "What else?" He coughed into his bound hands.

"Seen a doc?" Sam asked.

"What is your question?" Daniels asked, ignoring Sam.

"I've got an issue."

"Several, in fact."

Sam smirked at the wisecrack. "A work issue, smart-ass," he said, then explained his difficulty. "What do you think?"

Daniels stood and stretched. "Seems to me that's about as clear a case of conflict of duty as I've ever seen. Your current client—Pierce—was busted at the same time and same place as this Gustafson guy. I don't know how you could drop one guy and represent the other. You've got to have a career death wish to even consider it."

"Well, at least you don't have strong feelings about it."

"You gotta avoid this whole mess. First reason is your duty to the guy you got now—"

"Pierce—and I did a limited entry."

"I get it, but even with a limited entry you'll have a duty to a former client," Daniels said. "But just as important, you've got a duty to Damian."

"Davonte," Sam corrected.

"Whatever." Daniels shrugged. "You walked him; you can't very well turn around and help Gustafson help Ronnie and thereby put your former client's nuts in a vise."

"But we don't know that he'll implicate Davonte."

"Really? Who else?"

"I don't know. Besides, double jeopardy prevents—"

"I get it, but that's a criminal law thing," Daniels pointed out. "You get Ronnie's testimony on board, and you open Damien—"

"Davonte."

"Whatever. You expose *Davonte* to a wrongful death lawsuit—a big one."

"But an innocent man is in prison!"

"Supposedly," Daniels said doubtfully. "This wouldn't be the first time that friends of a guy doing a long stretch conspired to get him out."

"I know, but—"

"Sam, I took Ronnie's plea, remember? He was unequivocal. That was as straightforward a plea and allocution as I've seen."

Sam was looking at his hands. "I know."

"And you sure as hell fought like you believed your client." When Sam didn't agree, Daniels' eyes narrowed. "Right?" he pressed.

"We had our differences. I never felt like I got the whole story."

"Clients give us enough of the story to ensure we'll take their case, but we never get the full story," Daniels said. "We go with that so the jury can make a factual determination. Once that's done, right or wrong, it's binding on the rest of us."

"An imperfect design," Sam observed.

"Got a better idea?"

"No," Sam admitted. He was about to leave when he remembered Les. "I do have another question. It's personal."

"How can I help?" Daniels asked quickly. He suppressed a cough.

"I've got a situation," Sam said. "But I feel bad coming in here"—he gestured around the jail—"and then peeing on your foot."

"Honestly, it's good to talk with someone not doing time or overseeing those of us who are."

Sam smirked. "I heard from my dad. Well, about my dad, actually."

Daniels' eyebrows rose. "I didn't even know he was alive. You've never discussed him."

"For now," Sam said. "I guess they just moved him into hospice."

"Oh, Sam . . . I'm sorry."

"No need. We weren't close."

"Then fix it!" Daniels urged. "You've got time! Get there now and thank him."

"Thank him? For what?" Sam then spent a full minute explaining his father's faults and shortcomings while Daniels listened closely. When he was done, Daniels leaned forward as Sam had seen him do so many times from the bench.

"Forget all that! You can't change the past, and neither can he. But you can address how you deal with it, and the first step is for both of you to apologize, accept your part in it, and move on."

Sam was incredulous. "My part? I was just a kid! What could I do?"

"Then? Nothing. Now? Forgive. Dump the junk in your trunk and move forward. If you don't do that, I can promise you that you will come to regret it."

"You sound like my sponsor."

"He must be a bright guy," Daniels said without humor. "Now, go apologize for your part in all of it. Let me know how it goes."

24

Sam took a seat across from Cathy and looked at the half-empty boxes strewn around the large office. "Looks like it's coming together," he remarked. Despite Sam's relatively short time in Custer, Cathy was now the third occupant of this very office. Rebecca Nice had been county attorney before Grant Lee forced her out. Karma.

"This is nice."

"I just need some time," she said. "Lee didn't have anything in here, so nothing to toss to the curb, at least." When he smirked, she continued, "How can I help you?"

"My guy Clay? He says he'll take a plea."

"Better be cold. I've got nothing for him."

"Oh, come on," Sam said. "It's possession and use. He's almost as much a victim as—"

"The seventeen-year-old?" she scoffed. "Spare me."

"My client almost died, too." Sam removed his phone from his vest pocket, turned off the sound, and put it on the desk between them. "I think he got played."

"Your client brought a young woman to the scene of her death. Besides, he had a deal in place with Lee before that girl died," she reminded him.

"But look, Pierce pleads to possession and use and I'll cap my recommendation at six months if—and only *if*—he burns Gustafson."

"Six months? That's more than Downs usually gives. What's up with that?"

At that moment, Sam heard dozens of men and women chanting outside Cathy's office. "Justice for Rebel!"

"That," she indicated with a thumb, "is what's up with that. Sam, your guy agrees to testify and I'll take a look at it. But your guy is going to have to do some time. A girl died."

"Clay didn't have anything to do with that!"

She smiled doubtfully. "Sam, he was doing drugs with her—at a minimum. The lab's still looking into everything."

"You mean—"

"Exactly."

"He's a veteran!"

"Okay, so he's a veteran who was doing drugs with a confused seventeen-year-old girl—at a minimum, I say again," she added meaningfully.

"Cathy—"

"He's gonna have to do time—I'm asking for one hundred and eighty days. I'll agree to have the judge waive fines and fees if Pierce gets into treatment and finishes. And unofficially, I want him out of town."

"By sundown?" Sam asked sarcastically. She rolled her eyes, so he changed subjects. It was now or never. "You, uh, wanna go out sometime?"

She looked up from the note she had been making. "Well, Sam Johnstone! What took you so long?"

He squirmed in his chair. "I don't know—I'm shy?"

She laughed. "Right." Then, seeing his discomfort, she turned serious. "We already discussed this."

"We won't talk shop," he promised. He looked at his phone; it was lighting up from a series of texts.

"Right," she said doubtfully, then tilted her head toward his phone. "Go ahead. It's probably your secretary telling you to get back to work."

Sam obligingly picked up his phone and read the text message.

What are you doing?

His attempt at keeping a straight face must have failed.

"Sam, what is it?" Cathy asked.

His phone chimed again. *Are you with someone?* How could she know? He handed his phone to Cathy, who looked at the screen and then at Sam.

"How hot is she?" she asked.

"Molten."

"Well, she's way high on the crazy axis as well, Sam. You'd better be careful," she advised. "Not that it's any of my business, but where'd you meet her?"

"Other side of the state," Sam said. "When I was fishing."

Cathy sipped coffee. "Tell me she's not a stripper, a redhead, or named something like 'Sophie.'"

"She's not."

"Lemme guess. She's tall, blonde, blue-eyed, and sleek like a sports car."

"Am I that shallow?"

"All men are."

"You just described yourself there, lady," he said tentatively.

She looked at him steadily. "Well, you're sweet. And a damned liar." She turned her coffee cup on her desk so the logo faced her. "So are you two a thing, or was this like some kind of hook-up?"

"I'm not sure."

"She appears to be," Cathy said. They both looked at his phone when it chimed yet again. "Aren't you going to get that? I'm dying of curiosity."

He took a deep breath, then picked it up and read: *We need to talk.* He showed it to Cathy.

"Oh wow. You might need an order of protection." When he laughed, she fixed a stern look on him. "I'm serious. And as far as us going out . . . I think this changes things. I'm concerned about her," she said, pointing to Sam's phone. "I don't need some crazy chick in my life because I'm seeing you."

"I'll tell her I'm—"

"Sam, don't forget: I'm concerned about even the *appearance* of impropriety."

"People can think what they want."

"Not that easy," she said. "I'm a public servant now. More importantly,

I'm concerned about the *actual* existence of crazy." She again indicated his phone. "I've got a kid. Let me think this over."

"About Clay, too?"

"All of it."

"Done," he said, and stood. "Open or closed?" he asked, indicating the door.

"Closed. I've got some thinking to do."

25

Sam had just finished with a client charged with endangering her children by using methamphetamine in their presence. She had nothing except a promise from her mother to pay Sam's fees. It was a case he might have passed on, but Cassie said they needed the money. "You need to take whatever comes around for a while," she advised.

"Stay out of my business," he replied.

"I run your business."

"Yeah?"

"Yeah," she repeated. "How much did you make last month?"

"I'm not sure. To the penny, I mean."

"Any idea what you paid in office supplies and utilities?"

This wasn't going well. "Not exactly."

"Your expert fees from that last trial—did you pay those?"

"I get it."

"You should keep an eye on me," she advised. "I could rob you blind and you'd never know it. Speaking of which, Clay Pierce is here for his appointment. You need to get a retainer."

"He's a veteran. I usually don't take—"

"This guy is trouble. Get your money up front or don't expect to get paid. I'm just sayin'. You want him in here?"

"Got it. Send him back."

As soon as Sam saw Clay, he knew his client was high.

"Sam, how you doin', brother?" Clay asked, extending a hand.

"Sit down, Clay. I'm not your brother." Clay's eyes were glassy, his movements exaggerated, and his shoes were untied. "Clay, are you high? Because that would piss me off."

"No, man! I promise!" He crossed his heart with an unclean hand.

"Clay—" Sam began.

"Just a little weed, man."

"It's still a violation of bond!" Sam hissed. "I'm not even your attorney, technically, but I'm working to get you a deal—you blew the one you had. You get busted, you are dead in the water."

"I know, Sam. But sometimes the stress—"

"Spare me," Sam interrupted. "What stress? You don't have a sick kid or a wife with cancer. You don't have a boss on your ass. Hell, you don't even have a job. From where I'm sitting, you are looking pretty good."

"Sam—"

"Zip it," Sam instructed. While Clay sat uncomfortably in his chair, Sam explained the purpose of the meeting. "So, the bottom line is this: I think I can get you a deal." He then outlined the terms and conditions while watching Clay's eyes glaze over as he listened.

"Th-That's a deal?" Clay asked when Sam had concluded. "I might as well throw myself on the mercy of the court."

"With a dead girl out there? Brilliant," Sam said sarcastically. "Better off putting your head in an oven."

Clay was on his feet, clenching and unclenching his fists. "Six months? I can't go to jail, Sam! What else you got?"

"This is as good as it's gonna get, dude. There's a dead kid out there and people want someone to roast for it." He let Clay process that before continuing. "Clay, if you'll agree to get treatment, I could maybe negotiate it down to you doing sixty days and get them to drop the use charge."

"No."

"There is another option," Sam ventured, watching Clay closely.

"Yeah?"

"Agree to testify against Gustafson about that girl's death," Sam said.

"You agree to that, and after that I bet the State will let you walk." Obviously, if Clay took the deal, Sam wouldn't be able to represent Gustafson, and he had a brief vision of dollar bills flying away.

Clay rubbed his hands together and chewed his lip, then walked to Sam's window. He moved the shades and looked out, then sat down again. "You sure?" he asked.

"I haven't offered yet, but I'm pretty sure. They want his ass bad."

"Why haven't you offered?"

"I needed to talk with you first," Sam said. "Squealing on Gustafson might be dangerous."

Clay crossed one leg over the other. "But no jail, huh?"

"I can't promise that yet, but we could make that part of the deal. We'll ask for immunity in return for your testimony. We'll get it all in writing."

"Lemme think about it."

"Think fast."

26

Sam was in his office, watching the sunrise and thinking he needed to get the blinds cleaned, while listening to Davonte's phone ring. When at last his former client picked up half a world away, Sam faked an upbeat greeting. "Davonte, how are you doing? What time is it there?"

"'Bout three," Davonte said. "Waiting on room service. Food here sucks," he added. "Lotta goat."

"How's your game?" Sam asked.

"I'm puttin' up a double-double every night," Davonte said. "For all the good it's doing me."

"Food on the table, traveling foreign countries, and I gotta believe there are some women," Sam said. Or men.

"It's okay, man. But it ain't the show," Davonte replied. "Whatcha need, lawyer man? Momma paid you, right?"

She had indeed. Davonte's mother was a class act. "Of course. But we've had some developments."

There was a long silence before Davonte spoke. "Yeah? What's that got to do with me?"

"Maybe quite a bit. I got a guy here telling me Ronnie didn't do it."

Again, a long silence. "Yeah?"

"Yeah," Sam said. "Says he's got a story to tell."

"Now why would he wanna do that?"

"Because he caught a bust and he's looking at some serious time."

"And you calling me why?"

"Because I'd like to represent him, and I'd like your permission to do so."

"Why you need me?"

"Because I represented you," Sam explained. "I still owe you confidentiality and protection from anything that could negatively impact you."

"If it's up to me, then no."

Sam could hear Davonte inhaling something. "Why not?"

"'Cause he ain't got nothing to say."

"Who?"

"Ronnie."

Getting warmer. "It's not Ronnie."

"Then who is it?" Sam was debating whether he should respond when Davonte continued. "It's gotta be Gus, right? Lemme tell you, that little bitch doesn't know anything."

"He thinks he does."

"He don't."

"He wants to do a deal."

"No."

"Davonte, he's in deep doo-doo and he wants me to represent him. He says Ronnie's innocent. Says he has information, but he won't cough it up unless I represent him."

"Only innocent man I know is me," Davonte said. "Jury said so."

"Right. And you can't be tried twice."

"Double jeopardy or whatever."

Sam could hear Davonte exhaling. Probably a vape. "Exactly." There was civil liability, of course. A discussion for later. Maybe. "Look, Ronnie's dad was my friend. He—"

"Was a dick to me," Davonte snapped.

Sam recalled the strained relationship between Paul Norquist and Davonte. "Even if I agree with you, you know he has to be distraught with his son in prison."

"Better him than me. 'Sides, Ronnie copped to it, right?"

"He did," Sam admitted.

"Then he's where he belongs."

"Davonte, just let me hear Gustafson out," Sam said. "I mean, it could be that you face some civil stuff, but aside from that, no harm's likely coming your way."

"I ain't havin' that," Davonte said quickly. "I got a reputation and a family and the show to think about. Anybody hears this shit and I'll be riding these donkey buses the rest of my life."

"A wrong has been done!"

"Not the way I see it," Davonte replied. "Gus or anyone else says anything, they gonna have my lawyer and my people all up in their grill. Especially Gus. If he starts flapping his soup coolers . . . well, tell him someone will show up to see him."

"Davonte, if you'll just do a limited waiver—"

"No, Sam. No way. Now, I gotta get."

Sam stared at the phone for a long time after Davonte ended the call. Because he had denied Sam's request for a waiver, if Sam took Gustafson as a client and if the information Gustafson claimed to have negatively implicated Davonte in any way, then Sam's involvement would be an ethical violation.

27

Later that morning, Sam was attempting to re-set his password for the third time. After trying and failing again, he pounded his desk.

Cassie paged him, and he braced himself for a scolding. "Not now, Cassie," he said. "I've had about enough of this crap."

"It's Detective Kenneth Polson," she said. "If you want, when you finish speaking with him, I'll come in and re-set your password. I'd rather do that than listen to you squawk."

He started to reply, but she had put Punch on the line. "This is Sam," he said.

"Sam, it's your guy Pierce."

This wasn't a social call. "What's wrong?" Sam asked.

"He overdosed."

"Again?"

"Yeah, and it's not looking real good. We hit him with a couple of doses of naloxone just like the last time, but he's fading."

"Damn it!" Sam said. "What happened?"

"It looks like exactly the same deal as before," Punch said. "He was in a hotel room. Apparently, the housekeeper went in and found him on the floor with a needle in his arm. Looks like he got hooked up with someone and—"

"I'll be right there."

En route, Sam reflected on the ins and outs of addiction, treatment, the criminal justice system, and of course the Veterans Administration. The temptation was to say the system had failed Clay. But in reality, Clay had been to both inpatient and outpatient treatment several times. Sooner or later every addict or alcoholic had a decision to make, or, as an AA old-timer once put it, "When you're ready to change, you'll change."

The Custer Community Hospital emergency department was located on the ground floor of the three-story building. After parking his truck and making his way to the entrance, Sam nodded in recognition at several law enforcement officers with whom he had dealt. Approaching the reception area, he saw Punch talking with the triage nurse. Sensing Sam's presence, Punch turned to face him.

"Sam, he coded on the way in," he said. "I'm sorry."

Sam slapped the counter in anger. "Damn!"

"Sir, please!" It was an elderly nurse. "People are suffering here. Please be respectful of their situations. Leave if you cannot control your emotions."

Sam opened his mouth to speak and then closed it. He turned for the door, then stopped and faced Punch again. "Listen, let's talk later. I'm not up to it right now."

On the way to the office, Sam reflected on his own bad decisions and the good fortune he'd experienced in never encountering anyone aside from bartenders with a serious desire to facilitate or enable his addictions. He fiddled with his phone until he found a Cody Jinks tune on his playlist that fit his mood, then turned up the sound and sang along.

Three hours later, he was dozing fitfully on his office couch after instructing Cassie to cancel all appointments and allowing her to leave for the day after she set the answering machine. He lay in the sun reading from a recovery booklet he kept handy until he had dozed off. In his dream, Ronnie was behind bars, saying nothing, but holding something in his hand. Before he could tell what it was, the bell on the front door alerted him to someone entering the office. Earlier, he had removed the omnipresent revolver from his shoulder holster, and in a panic, he pawed at the coffee table until he found the revolver.

"Sam?"

Recognizing Punch's voice, Sam relaxed, then stood and tucked in his shirt. "I'm back here," he said.

"You look like hell," Punch remarked when he entered Sam's office. "Want me to come back later?"

"No, it's fine. Just doing a little reading." He indicated the booklet on his desk. "Sometimes it helps."

"You don't need to make any excuses for me. After everything you've seen and done . . . well, hey, whatever it takes, right?"

Sam gestured to his chair. "Sit. You want something to drink?" he asked when Punch had settled in.

"I'm good." Punch looked around Sam's office before making eye contact. "I'm here unofficially. I'd appreciate this staying between us."

Sam met the detective's stare. "I don't know if I can agree to that if it affects one of my clients."

"Now, why might you think that?"

"I don't. I said *if*."

"That's why you went to law school and I didn't. My wife says I'm not word conscious or literal. She also says I tend to be cynical."

"You don't sneer enough to be a cynic," Sam observed.

"I'll work on it. I've always tried to meet expectations." Punch glanced at his watch. "Gotta update Buck Lucas soon. I just wanted you to know that we're in the process of discovering what Pierce did in the last 24 hours."

"What are you finding?"

"Bars, convenience stores, the motel—usual stuff."

"Any visitors?"

"We're getting a warrant for the video from local establishments. Bartenders are laying down a pretty good timeline, but they got him alone."

"He had to be with someone."

"If only long enough to do a deal. Guy like this is hard. He's got no electronic footprint, no phone."

Sam appraised Punch. "You're here for a reason." It wasn't a question.

"I am," Punch admitted. "Word is we got some guys in town from Denver. Known dealers."

"And?"

"They may be acquainted with your client."

"Pierce?"

"Gustafson." When Sam didn't respond, Punch continued. "I'm thinking Gustafson might be doing business behind you as a shield."

Sam thought about how to respond. Punch's comment was made in good faith, and he would most likely ask to interview Gustafson. It wasn't fair to Punch to have him chasing Gustafson's tail. "I don't represent Gustafson."

"Oh," Punch replied. "You don't? I figured—"

"I'm looking at it, but we haven't done a deal. Conflict, as I mentioned."

"Even with Pierce dead?"

"Punch, it's only been a matter of hours. I haven't even thought that through."

"So I can talk with him?"

Sam shrugged. "Nothing I can do about it."

"Thanks, Sam. Let's get something to eat one of these days."

"Sounds good," Sam said. "Lock it behind you."

28

Sam watched as Daniels shifted uncomfortably on the hard seat. His hands were chained to the desk—unnecessary, but "policy," or so the guard reasoned. Sam had argued that it wasn't Tom's policy but had gotten only a bored, bureaucratic stare in response. It was a topic for a future conversation with the sheriff.

"What do you think?" Sam asked Daniels after updating the judge on Clay's death as well as his most recent discussions with Gustafson and Davonte.

"I still think you are on thin ice, Sam. The safe play is to refer him to someone else."

"Understood, but—"

"But you don't generally drive down the middle of the road, do you?"

Sam smirked. "I don't want to see an injustice done. And with Clay dead, I mean, things are different now."

"Conveniently."

Ain't that the truth. "I hear you, but—"

"Sam, this thing stinks. You talk with Gustafson and explain the conflict, and then the guy who poses the conflict ends up dead. I think you've got rocks in your head to even consider it, and I'm not talking about legal ethics here. This could be dangerous."

"My question isn't *should* I? It's *can* I—with Clay dead now?"

Daniels shook his head, then leaned forward to scratch his forehead against his chained hands. "All that means is Pierce cannot defend himself. That's all the more reason you need to steer clear of this case. You take Gustafson's case, you're gonna have to throw Clay under the bus, aren't you?"

"Not necessarily."

"How are you going to avoid it? As I understand it, your guy's defense is he didn't bring the shit, so the only defense is the SODDI defense—some other dude did it—right? And the only other dude was your former client, to whom you still owe a duty! You have to see that."

Sam waited while Daniels coughed and drank water. "It could have been a third party."

"Who?"

"I don't know. I don't even care. It's not my job to find out!"

"Give me a break. What are you going to do, stand at the podium and point to a boogie man?" Daniels was attempting to wave his chained hands. "You'll say maybe someone else did it; Cathy will point out no one else was there, and then you'll—what? Say it was some other guy? You know as well as I do the jury will call bullshit on that, so you're going to have to pinch a client to save this one."

"Former client," Sam said quickly.

"To whom you owe a continuing duty of loyalty," Daniels replied just as quickly.

Sam sighed. "The rule says I'm only in conflict if it's reasonably likely he could suffer some sort of adverse consequence," he explained. "He's dead."

"What if the deceased girl's family brings a wrongful death action? Your client's defense might open Clay's estate to a judgment—that's an injury as defined."

"He didn't own squat!"

"Doesn't matter," Daniels replied. "Did he have any insurance?"

"I doubt it. He didn't have the proverbial pot to piss in—I doubt he was faithfully paying premiums."

"Well, you'd better find out," Daniels counseled. "Seems to me like you are putting your ass on the line. Bar counsel is certain to find you knew or should have known of the conflict."

"*If* I take the case; *if* my client rolls on Clay; *if* there is an action brought; *if* there is a judgment; *if* someone complains. That's a lot of ifs."

Daniels looked steadily at Sam. "And *if* they all come to pass, you could lose your license."

Sam looked at his hands. "But *if* I don't take the case, then Gustafson won't say anything. The bastard's got me between a rock and a hard place. If I don't do this, an innocent man could be sitting in prison for the rest of his life."

Daniels shook his head. "First of all, you don't know for a fact that Ronnie is innocent. Second, even if Gustafson does walk, and then gives you the information, it doesn't mean that Ronnie is going to walk. There's a damned good chance it won't change anything."

"I understand that, but Press, he's my friends' son!"

"Ex-friends," Daniels corrected. "Both Paul and Jeannie gave up on you after the trial. And I'll say it again: Ronnie confessed. I was there, remember? And never forget that your client might just be full of it. You're assuming he knows something. You're also assuming that if you tell him to take a hike, he won't go to someone else."

"Well, he will, but he won't tell—"

"Sure he will," Daniels countered. "If he's got that card to play, he's not going to hold it."

"I need to do this," Sam said quietly.

"Aren't you forgetting someone?"

Davonte. "I hear you," Sam said, slumping. "But I've been doing some research that might help."

Daniels clucked disapprovingly. "Do you wake up in the morning and *decide* to step on your own foot, or does it just happen?"

"Hear me out."

"Be quick." Daniels indicated the clock on the wall. "And don't tell me Davonte will waive."

"Oh, hell no," Sam said.

"He shouldn't," Daniels opined. "If I were his attorney, I'd advise him not to."

"Agreed," Sam said. "So, I've been looking at the rules and trying to read them together."

"Always the wisest course," Daniels said approvingly. "The rules are meant to be read in conjunction with one another."

"Right?" Sam nodded, glad that Daniels understood. "So here's what I've come up with: Rule 1.9 says I have a duty to former clients. It says I can't represent another client in the same or substantially similar matter in which that person's interests are materially averse to those of the former client unless I get informed consent, in writing."

"Right. So even if you're okay with Clay—who's dead—you've got an issue with Davonte."

"But what's his interest?"

"Being guilty of murder?"

"He can't be tried!"

"Same deal. Wrongful death—that's a real issue," Daniels pointed out. "Davonte could be exposed to a civil action, like O.J. Might not get his ass thrown in jail, but he damned sure could be sued for everything he owns or could own."

"But here's the thing: the rule also says that I can't reveal or use confidential information relating to the representation of a former client *except as the rules would permit or require with respect to a client.*"

Daniels sat back in his chair and looked at the hung ceiling. "What confidential information do you have from your former clients?"

"I don't know that I have any right now. But that's circumstantial, in any event—right?"

"Well, yeah, but I'm not sure that exception applies," Daniels said. "Let me look at the rule." He reached for the thick tome Sam had brought with him. "Anything helpful in the comments?"

The comments to the rules of professional conduct frequently contained helpful—but not conclusive—interpretations of the sometimes-ambiguous language of the rules themselves. "Not that I saw," Sam replied. He sat quietly until Daniels finished reading.

"Not sure that fits," Daniels said.

"Fair enough," Sam admitted. "But let's take it one step further. Rule 1.6 says

I can reveal confidential information to rectify substantial injury to the financial or property interests of another that resulted from the client's commission of a crime or fraud in furtherance of which the client used the lawyer's services."

"Lemme see the rule," Daniels said. He again read for a moment, tracing the relevant language with a finger and moving his lips. "This seems to apply to situations where the client used a lawyer to facilitate or commit a fraud."

"He did."

"Not a fraud on the court," Daniels said. "I don't read it that way. I think they mean *fraud*. And what's the financial or property interest?"

"Ronnie's freedom."

"I think you're reading the rule too broadly," Daniels cautioned, shaking his head. "And I think you're mixing conflict of duty with the duty to maintain confidentiality. Apples and oranges. You take on Gustafson, and Davonte could find out and seek action against you."

"But he's got to have damages, right?"

"Not necessarily," Daniels countered. "He's only got to show a conflict of duty."

"But to do that he is going to have to say why—and if he does that, he'll be exposing himself to civil liability for Kaiden's death."

Daniels broke into another coughing fit. He indicated a trash can and spat into it when Sam offered it. "Have you done the research? Could he get an injunction?"

"I haven't; I don't know."

"Well, you better find out. Because if he could, he might be able to convince a judge to enter one, and then you'll be caught in the wire while everyone tries to sort this out."

"I'll take a look at it," Sam promised.

Daniels again started coughing. "Chest cold, I guess." He wiped his mouth with a dirty tissue, then sat quietly, measuring Sam. "One more thing."

"What's that?"

"Be prepared to answer some hard questions from Downs and Bridger. They're gonna want to be sure that they don't have to try this case twice."

When Sam merely nodded his understanding, Daniels continued. "You're gonna do this, aren't you?"

"Probably," Sam admitted.

"Why?"

"Because Paul and Jeannie were my friends. They deserve to know—"

"But you don't know what—if anything—this Gustafson has. You could be putting your neck in a noose and find out that little turd doesn't know anything. He might just be blowing smoke up your tailpipe."

"I know, but Ronnie might be sitting in prison because I called him."

"He's only there wrongfully if he lied!"

"I get that, but he was young, immature, and he wouldn't have had the opportunity to lie if I hadn't called him."

"You *had* to call him. You called him to testify about your client's whereabouts at the time," Daniels reminded Sam. "If you hadn't done that, you'd have been committing malpractice."

"Maybe, but my friend's son wouldn't be rotting in prison."

While Sam was speaking, the guard entered the cell. Daniels, ignoring him, asked a final question. "But what happens if it's all a joke, a scheme or whatever for Gustafson to get out of jail?"

"I'll kill the bastard," Sam said. Ignoring the quick turn of the guard toward him, he repeated the threat. "If I represent him and he doesn't come across, he's a dead man."

"Real quick; two more things. One, you put any heat on Davonte, and he's got people."

"Yeah, well, he's made that clear."

"Two, if you start revealing confidential and privileged information— even if you beat an ethical rap—you could be tangled up with this for years, and even if you prevail, your life is going to be difficult. Attorneys won't talk with you; clients won't trust you. You better have Career Plan B in place if you survive an ethical rap."

"Like what?"

"I dunno. Ever wait tables?"

The small town's motel was the old-fashioned kind where cars were parked directly in front of the occupants' front doors. Shaped in a C, it had an algae-covered pool in the center, and an office at one end decorated with carpeting and chairs that were likely in place since the motel's construction shortly after the Second World War. The rooms were small, and featured cinderblock walls on three sides and faux wood paneling behind the plain oaken headboard.

Sam rolled onto his side and admired Mickey, who was lying on her back, staring at the ceiling. They had met at a local steakhouse, then booked a room in the only motel Sam could find with online registration, tumbling onto the bed seconds after the flimsy door closed behind them. Sam barely had enough time to put his phone and wallet on the rickety end table before getting tangled up with her.

"This place must have been something back when Ike was in office," Sam said. He ran a hand over Mickey's flat stomach.

"Who's Ike?"

"He was a president," Sam replied. "Won a war before that."

"Huh," she said. She rolled to face him. "We need to talk."

"Talk."

"I need to know if we are a thing, or not," she said.

"Well, I guess," Sam said. "I mean, here we are." He smiled.

"Sam, I'm serious. I don't sleep with men the first time I meet them, and cheap motels are not my style. But . . . here we are."

"Same here. But we just met and things got a little out of hand, wouldn't you say?" He sat up and reached for his prosthetic leg.

"I need to know that you . . . that we . . . are *something*, you know?" When Sam didn't respond, she touched his back. "That woman . . . Cathy."

He felt a chill up his spine. Was it her touch, or something else? "How do you know about her?" Sam asked.

"People tell me things."

"What people?"

"People who don't want to see me get hurt."

His leg now affixed, Sam stood. "So what does that mean? You're having me followed?"

"I need to know about you."

He felt his pulse rising. "Then freakin' ask me!"

"I'm asking," she said. "Is there someone else?"

"Not right now."

"Is there anyone else you're interested in?"

"Not right now. Give me a second," he said. While he was in the bathroom, he ran a wet washcloth over his face and tried to gather his thoughts. When he exited, she was propped up against the cheap headboard by every pillow in the room with the sheets piled at her waist.

"Ready for round two?" She patted the bed next to her.

"Mickey, I—"

"Shhh," she hushed him. "Don't talk."

"But we need to get some things straight," he insisted.

"Time for that later."

When Sam awakened, he reached for her, but she was gone. His phone and wallet were on the floor.

29

Against Daniels' advice and his own better judgment, Sam decided to take on Gustafson's case and had brought his new client in for a meeting. "I need you to tell me what happened that day."

Gustafson was sitting sideways in a chair in Sam's office, looking at his phone. "I don't really know," he said without making eye contact. "The two of them showed up, did some blues—"

"They showed up together?"

"Yeah."

"Where'd they get them?"

Gustafson merely shrugged.

"What's that mean?"

"Means I don't know, dude," Gustafson said, still focused on his phone.

"I need you to focus here. I need some answers," Sam said tightly. When his client didn't respond, Sam stood, walked around his desk, and slapped Gustafson's hand, sending the phone flying.

"Bitch! You might have broken my phone!"

"Go. Now. I don't represent people who undermine my efforts. I don't have the time or the interest. Get the hell out!"

"What are you talking about? I'm listening!"

"No, and you're not responding."

"I was . . . working."

"You don't have a job, unless we call selling drugs to kids a job," Sam countered. "Now beat it."

Gustafson started to object but then sat back in his chair, considering his next move. "You bounce me, you'll get nothing regarding Ronnie."

"I'm not entirely convinced I'm missing much," Sam replied. "Maybe I'll just tell Cathy Schmidt and Davonte's boys what you told me, and you can sort it all out with them." That got Gustafson's attention, so Sam continued. "From a law enforcement perspective, your involvement in a murder could result in them getting warrants to look into your business affairs for the past couple of years—you know, like bank records, texting, electronic media, stuff like that. And Davonte's family, well, I'm sure they'll appreciate a heads-up if something is coming Davonte's way."

"What do you want?"

"Your cooperation," Sam said. "If I'm gonna defend you, two things are going to happen. One, you're going to help me give you a defense, and two, when this case is over, you're going to cough up everything you've got that could conceivably help Ronnie, or I'm gonna bust your chops."

Gustafson's eyes narrowed. "I'm not used to people talking to me like that."

"And I'm not the usual potato-chip-fingered incel you deal with, who sits on his stoned ass and plays video games all day. This is the last time I'm going to ask. What happened?"

"Sam, I'm telling you I don't know! I didn't give them the stuff. They showed up—"

"From where?"

"I didn't ask," Gustafson answered quickly. "I didn't care, man. Then they borrowed a rig, smashed a blue, and did their thing. Next thing I knew, they both fell out. That's why I was getting out of there!"

Class act. Sam was watching Gustafson carefully. "You didn't sell Clay or that girl any blues?"

"No!"

"I don't mean just then," Sam clarified. "I mean any time."

"Her? Never. Him? It'd been some time."

"How long?"

"I dunno, man! Days . . . weeks, I mean, I had been in Denver for a while, man. Seriously, Sam. I don't know where he got his shit, man!"

"Then why come to your place?"

"For the rig." When it was obvious Sam didn't understand, Gustafson explained. "A guy can walk around with a pill all day and draw no attention, right? But a rig takes some packin' and they were both on paper—subject to search. They knew I might have a rig; that's why they came. These two . . . no plan. He didn't even do a pre-shot."

"Pre-shot?"

"Yeah. Coupla ways to do it. Put the tourniquet on, shoot a little, leave the tourniquet on and see what happens, or just do a small shot and wait to see if it hits you wrong. Prime the pump, you know? Allows you to make sure you didn't get any crazy shit like Carfentanyl."

"What's that?"

"Man, you really don't know anything, do you?" Gustafson then gave a layman's explanation of the various fentanyl analogs. "That's some harsh shit," he concluded.

Sam considered what he'd heard to this point. The State could have a difficult time proving their case for the simple reason that the only people who could testify against Gustafson were dead. On the other hand, if the jury simply *believed* Gustafson was the source, they could decide to solve the problem themselves. Sometimes it happened that way.

Perhaps reading Sam's thoughts, Gustafson spoke up. "They can't prove it was me, can they?"

"It's definitely a challenge," Sam agreed. "But juries are funny. They're composed of ordinary people, and people sometimes want justice."

"What's that mean?"

"It means that sometimes they want someone punished. We've got a dead girl, and now a dead hero. You are all that's left."

"But they gotta follow the law, right? I didn't sell them the drug!"

They were human beings. "Theoretically," Sam replied. "Right now, I want to talk about your testimony in that other matter."

"I told you I'm not testifying unless I walk." Gustafson folded his arms over his skinny chest.

"Yeah? And I won't go through this kabuki dance without some assurance that I'm going to get a return on my investment."

"Look, I don't know a whole lot, okay? And some of what I do know is second-hand."

"From who?"

"Guys in jail or prison with Ronnie who—"

Sam was on his feet. "Are you shitting me? You come here and tell me you got something to trade and it's second-hand inmate gossip?" He walked around his desk toward Gustafson, who stood and practically ran behind his chair. "You better start talking. Now!" Sam commanded.

"Sam, I'm square with you! I know these guys! They ain't stoolies. And I can point you in the right direction, but I'm not going further until and unless I walk."

Sam moved the chair from between them. "Tell me."

"So, Ronnie wanted to be a sports agent. That was what he was going to school for."

"Sports agents don't come from junior colleges in Wyoming," Sam said levelly. "That's Ivy League and maybe Southern California stuff."

"Right? And he knew it. So, him and Davonte, well, they would do this thing where they would talk about Davonte needing an agent when he made it big, and Ronnie being that guy."

"Sitting around vaping or bonging isn't a plan. That's just sophomoric, lit dreams."

"I know, dude. But there was more to it. See, Ronnie had something on Davonte."

"What?"

"I'm not sure, exactly. Anyway, they signed an agreement—had it notarized and everything."

That passed the smell test—lots of non-lawyers thought agreements and contracts had to be notarized to be binding. "And?" Sam asked impatiently.

"And Ronnie would brag about this agreement he had with Davonte. He thought he was going big-time. But then Davonte got arrested, and Ronnie was sadder than Davonte. Davonte kept saying he didn't kill Kaiden."

"I'm listening," Sam said.

"So, all of a sudden Ronnie is saying that he did it. That he killed Kaiden for Davonte."

"And you're telling me this benefits Ronnie how?"

"Because he was desperate to have Davonte out!"

"Nobody admits to murder for someone else," Sam said, shaking his head in disgust.

"Seriously! He was telling us that his dad was a lawyer and that he had no criminal history, so he'd get a minimal sentence. The plan was for Davonte to get drafted, then hire Ronnie a high-priced attorney who would get him out, then when Ronnie got out he'd represent Davonte."

"Says who?" Sam asked. When Gustafson didn't answer, he pressed, "Says who?"

"I—I can't tell you that," Gustafson said. "I do, and you got no reason to stick with me."

Sam sat down. He'd been had. "This is lame. You don't have shit."

"Sam, seriously. I do. I can prove everything I am saying. I've got . . . paper."

"What kind?" Sam asked. When Gustafson didn't answer, he followed up. "Where is it?" Again, no answer. "You'll have to testify, and I've got a feeling that when you do, it is going to implicate a former client of mine."

"I'll do whatever I gotta do, but you gotta walk me first."

"And if the jury doesn't see it our way?"

"They will, 'cause I didn't sell that stuff. And if they don't, Ronnie better get settled in."

Sam watched Gustafson closely before making his decision. "So, here's what you're going to do. You are going to sit down and write out an affidavit of everything you know and how you know it. Cassie is going to notarize it and we are going to place it in a bank deposit box with your *paper* down at the Custer National Bank," he added.

"How do I know you won't take it or read it or whatever?"

"Well, you don't—beforehand. We'll both have access, but because we have to sign the register, I'll know if you pull or replace the document, and you'll know if I'm screwing around, too."

"Okay." Gustafson bit his lip in thought. "So how is she going to notarize it without reading it? She could just read it and tell you what it says."

It was a common misconception. "She does it all the time. The purpose of a notary is for you to prove who you are and that you signed the document," Sam explained. "It has nothing to do with the contents. She won't read it. Hell, you can cover it with a piece of paper. Then you take whatever you've written, put it in an envelope with whatever paper you've got, and seal it with your signature, blood, or whatever."

Gustafson watched Sam doubtfully. "And you won't see what's in it?"

"I will not," Sam replied, shaking his head.

Gustafson brightened. "You trust me."

"Absolutely not," Sam assured him. "I just know that if you cross me, I'm going to waste you. Now, go into the conference room and write that affidavit. Start it out by writing, 'I am Trent Gustafson and the following is true.' Then write everything you know, and how. Now, go."

An hour later, when Gustafson had prepared the document and Cassie had notarized it, Sam finished his thought. "If this isn't what you say it is, I will kill you."

Gustafson looked at an obviously distressed Cassie. "For the record, that's the second time your boss has threatened to kill me."

30

By late May, things were beginning to flow. Cathy had called for a meeting with Miller prior to Gustafson's preliminary hearing. Under Wyoming law, such a hearing was held in felony cases, and was designed to satisfy a judge that there was sufficient evidence for the mythical "reasonable person" to believe a crime had been committed and the defendant committed it. Defense attorneys went into the hearings knowing full well there was a ninety-nine-percent chance the court would transfer ("bind over," in court parlance) the case to the district (higher) court, so a high percentage of preliminary hearings were waived. Sam had tried to buy more time and moved for yet another continuance, which Downs denied.

Cathy was looking through her file as Miller seated herself. "So, there is no doubt it was an overdose," she mused. "Autopsy says that she had a bunch of that stuff in her system. We've got a dead teenager and now a dead witness. Not sure he would have been much help anyway."

"Right," Miller said. "He was out until we pumped him with naloxone."

"Sam's client says he didn't do it," Cathy said as she put the file on a stack of others.

"Of course he does."

"Sam doesn't like to lose. What's he got?"

"I can't imagine. We arrested Gustafson with two hundred tablets of fentanyl in his room, his prints were on the syringe that was still in her arm, he's a known dealer . . . I mean, what else do we need?"

"Well, proof that the drug was intentionally and knowingly possessed by Gustafson, for a start. And proof that he knowingly provided the drug to the kid, and it killed her. Those are the elements of the charges."

"The pills were in a bag in the bedstand of a room he rented!"

"Circumstantial."

"The syringe had his prints on it."

"I like that," Cathy said. "But still, I want to be certain."

"Well, Clay told me it wasn't his," Miller offered. "Before he died."

"Right," Cathy acknowledged. "That may or may not be admissible, but even if it comes in, Sam will show it was a pretty self-serving statement."

"How can he even represent Gustafson? Isn't that a conflict or something?"

It sure looked like it. "Not our concern," Cathy said dismissively. "What else do you have?"

"Gustafson's prints on the baggie of drugs."

"Good. What about e-mail, texts, and other social media?"

"Not yet."

Cathy had been making a note, but fixed a stare on Miller. "What the hell are we waiting on?"

"We never found a phone," Miller explained. "It's hard to imagine a dealer doing business without a phone these days, but we can't find his."

"Service provider?"

"Downs has the warrant."

"How long?"

"Couple of days?"

"You just got it done?"

"We couldn't find a phone; therefore we didn't know which service provider."

"Do 'em all!" Cathy said, immediately regretting her outburst. The law required a nexus between evidence of a crime and the thing to be searched. With no phone, there was no reason to force a service provider to provide information on a suspect's account. "Do the phone he has now," she said. "Sorry for popping off. I'm just . . . pissed."

"We all are."

"Well, keep looking. Sam has to have a defense. He wouldn't sit for the game without having cards to play."

Miller acknowledged her understanding and the two discussed the timeline and discovery matters. "So, are you gonna call Baker?"

"No," Cathy said. "He was about to pee himself just talking about it, so I'll use Punch."

"Good call."

"Anything else?" Cathy asked. When Miller indicated there was not, she changed subjects. "What about Lee?"

"No real change. I've got folks out serving warrants for video, searching the roads between the store and Julie's house . . . we've even been around Custer Lake."

"Nothing?"

"Nada."

"She cannot be that clever."

"Or there's nothing to find."

Exactly what Cathy was afraid of—or would it be worse if his story was backed up? There'd be charges of a coverup—oh, hell. "Okay, well, keep me posted." Cathy looked at her watch and jumped to her feet. "Shit! We're going to be late. Let's go!"

31

While waiting for Gustafson's preliminary hearing to start, Sam sat quietly, looking around him. Downs' first-floor courtroom was approximately half the size of District Court Judge Walton Bridger's second-floor courtroom. Perhaps fifty feet on a side, it was a windowless square dominated by the judge's raised bench, adjacent to which was a witness box. On the other side of that was the jury box. A lectern in almost the exact center of the courtroom was flanked by two library-style tables occupied by Sam and Gustafson on one side, and Cathy and Punch on the other.

Sam removed the items he'd need from his briefcase, then took a deep breath, looked toward the ceiling, and closed his eyes. Behind him, serving to separate the trial's active participants from the audience, was a waist-high divider known as "the bar." Since the mid-twentieth century, all court-rooms in Wyoming contained such a barrier. The rows of seats behind him were filled with observers.

The circuit court was informally known as the "People's Court." In contrast to the district court over which Bridger presided, where the stakes were high and the pace somewhat ponderous, circuit court was fast-paced and wildly unpredictable. Accordingly, judges could be harried and gener-ally impatient.

"Good morning, Circuit Court for the County of Custer, State of

Wyoming, is in session," Downs began. "This is the matter of State of Wyoming v. Trent Gustafson. I note the presence of County Attorney Catherine Schmidt. Mr. Gustafson is here and is represented by Sam Johnstone. We are here for a preliminary hearing." Having called the case, Downs looked to Cathy. "Ms. Schmidt, is the State prepared to proceed?"

"We are, Your Honor."

Satisfied, Downs turned her attention to Sam. "Mr. Johnstone, is your client prepared to proceed here today?"

"Yes, Your Honor," Sam said.

In an earlier meeting, Sam had explained to Gustafson the purpose for and conduct of a preliminary hearing. "Because you are charged with a felony, Wyoming law gives you the right to a preliminary hearing," he had begun. "It's a hearing to determine if there is probable cause to bind you over to district court—the higher court having jurisdiction over felonies—for further proceedings." Gustafson appeared to understand, so Sam continued. "Probable cause means that an ordinary person could reasonably believe that the offense was committed and that you did it. That is a very low standard, so don't get your hopes up," he added in an effort to manage expectations.

"But I didn't do it," Gustafson had said. "Not my stuff."

"I hear you. It's complicated."

"Waste of time," Gustafson had concluded.

Gustafson's reaction wasn't unexpected, and Sam had been ready with a response. "Not entirely. This is our first chance to get a good idea of the strength of the State's evidence. They have to put on a witness, then I will cross-examine the witness."

"Then smoke 'em."

Every client required the same caution. "Trent," Sam had begun, still eschewing the use of his client's nickname. "Remember, I'm not your big brother. I'm your lawyer. There are rules."

"Screw that! I'm innocent!"

"Knock it off!" Sam had ordered. "The best way you can help is by listening to what's going on and helping me. Here's a pad and a pen," he continued, passing Gustafson the materials. "I can't have you talking to me while I'm trying to listen to testimony. So write down your thoughts on what you hear and we'll discuss them."

"What if there isn't time?"

"It's a courtroom," Sam had observed. "There's always time."

"Put me on the stand. Let me talk to the judge. He'll see—"

"No," Sam had interrupted. "This is a hearing for the judge; she doesn't even have to *allow* us to present evidence, even if we wanted to." Which they didn't. "Remember," Sam had concluded, "a lot of this is theater. I need you to go into the courtroom today looking confident and ready to show your innocence."

Now, several hours later, Gustafson was sitting up straight and appeared to be listening closely as Downs asked her questions. "Counsel, before we begin, are there matters preliminary?"

"No, Judge," Cathy replied.

Sam was certain that Cathy had enough evidence to meet the low standard of proof in a preliminary hearing. He would therefore perform as much discovery as the judge would allow him to get away with. "No, Your Honor."

When Downs looked again at Cathy, she was already at the podium. "Your Honor, the State of Wyoming calls Detective Kenneth Polson," she said.

Sam wasn't surprised. Because hearsay was allowed without limitation during the preliminary hearing, the prosecution would sometimes put someone other than the lead officer on the stand to testify, enabling them to protect the testimony of the most critical witness until the trial. After swearing an oath, Punch took the stand.

"Mr. Polson, please state your full legal name for the record," Cathy began.

"Kenneth Polson—but everyone calls me Punch, ma'am. 'Cause of fights as a kid," he added unnecessarily.

"Mr. Polson, are you employed?"

"Yes, ma'am."

"What do you do?"

"I am a detective with the Custer Police Department, assigned to the major crimes unit."

"And how long have you been assigned to the major crimes unit?"

"This time? Maybe a coupla weeks."

"And previously?"

"Oh, maybe six years or so."

"And in between?"

"Wyoming Division of Criminal Investigation."

"What did you do before law enforcement?"

"I started after I got out of the Army. I did a year or so as a detention officer, then went to the law enforcement academy, then out on patrol."

"So, you started as a detention officer at the jail, spent a year or so doing that, then went to the law enforcement academy, then returned to Custer County?"

"That's right. Then I was a patrol officer, and then I made detective, then DCI, then back here."

"Your Honor," Sam said as he stood. "The defendant will stipulate Detective Polson is who he said he is, and that he lost a few fights."

"Mr. Johnstone, please be seated," Downs said. "Ms. Schmidt, I'm going to overrule what sounded like an objection, but please be brief. Given the offered stipulation, I think if you proceed knowing that we all know who Detective Polson is, we'll get through this."

"Thank you, Your Honor," Cathy said. "Were you working on the tenth of April?"

"I was. At the time, I was detailed to DCI."

"And on that date, what were you doing?"

"Helping the Custer PD with a stakeout of a motel room on Yellowstone Avenue."

"Please tell the court what happened."

"We were doing a stakeout of a room in the Horseshoe Motel. I was with Detective Miller and Officer Ron Baker. The defendant here was the object of our surveillance."

"Why were you surveilling him?"

"Suspected him of dealing drugs."

"What kind?"

"All kinds. Meth and fentanyl."

"And what did you do then?"

"We set up and were watching his door. He come outta there like he was shot out of a cannon. He saw Miller and took off, but Baker placed the defendant against the wall—"

"Placed, my ass!" Gustafson hissed.

"Shhh—" Sam scolded. "Write it down," he added, feeling Downs' disapproving glare.

"Then what?" Cathy asked.

"I came up last. I think I told him we had a warrant for his arrest for manufacture and distribution of drugs."

"Then?"

"We looked in the room's window and saw a male's foot."

"What did you do next?"

"The door was unlocked so we effected entry into the room. Observed the suspect, Mr. Pierce."

Cathy briefly smirked at the cop-speak. "You walked in the room and saw Clayton Pierce?"

"Yes, ma'am."

"How'd he appear?"

"Dead."

"*Was* he deceased?"

"No. Well, I didn't know. I didn't think so. We used naloxone on him and he eventually came to."

"Was there anyone else in the room?"

"Yes. The deceased."

"Rebel Hayes?"

"Yes."

"Where was she?"

"On the floor, next to the bed."

"What was her condition?"

"Same as Clay—er, Mr. Pierce. But she didn't respond to the drugs."

"What happened then?"

"We already had EMTs on the way. We tried naloxone and CPR until they arrived. Then they took over and we secured the scene."

"The scene you mentioned—is that in Custer County, Wyoming?"

"Yes."

"Okay, so what happened next?"

"We processed the scene forensically and began our investigation."

"How did you do that?"

"Well, first we blocked off the surrounding areas so only people known to us, like crime scene photographers, forensics people, etc., could get in. Then, we let those folks do their thing. After they had done their job, I went through the scene to see if there was anything I could find out."

"And what did you find out?"

"Well, as I mentioned, she had been found on the floor, unconscious, with a needle in her arm—I'm sorry," he said when he heard the crowd gasp.

Cathy allowed the murmuring to die under Downs' scowl before she continued. "What else?"

"Well, the fingerprint folks went over the whole room, gathering prints. They found quite a few."

"And were you later able to obtain identification of those prints?"

"Most of them, yeah. The ones we found belonging to the defendant were all over."

She interrupted him. "I'm sorry, what do you mean by 'all over?' All over what?"

"All over the room. On the bedposts, in the bathroom, on the bag of fentanyl we found. And on the syringe."

"What syringe?"

"The one in the decedent's arm."

Cathy let that rest before continuing. "When did you identify the fingerprints?"

"I can't recall, exactly."

"Would it help refresh your memory if I showed you your report?"

"It would."

Cathy looked to Downs for guidance. She turned to Sam. "Any objection, Mr. Johnstone?"

"No objection, Judge."

"Your Honor, may I approach the witness?" Cathy inquired, holding a sheaf of papers in her hand.

"You may."

Cathy approached Punch and handed him a copy of his report. While she returned to the podium, he perused it quickly and then looked up at her. "It looks like we got the defendant's fingerprints identified the next day," he said. "We got the others identified a few days later. Some are still unidentified."

"Are you surprised that some weren't identified?"

"No. It was a hotel room. No telling how many people have stayed there."

"So," Cathy began, looking at Sam, who was scribbling on a legal pad. "After the defendant's fingerprints were identified, what did you do?"

"Well, I arrested him on charges of possession and possession with intent to distribute. Then after he was processed, I asked him if he would come and talk with me."

"And did he?"

"Did he what?"

"Talk with you?"

"Well, he came in, but he wouldn't say much. Denied he sold or gave the drugs to the girl."

"Then what?"

"Well, he lawyered up, so I sent him back to the holding cells."

"But you were certain you had the right guy?"

"Oh, yeah."

"Why was that?"

"Well, we already had a match on his fingerprints in the room, on the drugs, and on the needle—that was bad for him. We know he was in the room with both being unconscious, and we know he was trying to hightail it outta there."

"Anything else make him a suspect?" Cathy asked.

"Well, when Mr. Pierce awoke, he denied having anything to do with giving Rebel the drugs."

"Okay. Anything else?"

"Well, like I said, we got a warrant to search the room, and everything we found was consistent with his being a drug dealer of fentanyl."

"When did you get the warrant?"

"When he wouldn't let us search."

"So, you searched Mr. Gustafson's room pursuant to a warrant?"

"Uh, yes. We had a warrant."

"And what did you find?"

"More drugs, a scale, baggies, stuff like that."

"What did you do with the evidence?"

"Bagged it."

"And then what?"

"We kept investigating and eventually we added drug-induced homicide."

"Why the delay?"

"We, uh, needed more information."

Cathy nodded her approval. "Your Honor, may I have a moment?" she asked, wanting the last point to sink in before she yielded the podium.

"Of course," Downs replied, staring down the audience members to ensure silence.

Cathy appeared to consult briefly with her assistant, Aiden Cates, who was sitting second chair. Sam couldn't imagine what kind of help she would get from the neophyte attorney. "Your Honor, the State has no further questions," she said after a brief back-and-forth.

"Mr. Johnstone, care to cross-examine?" Judge Downs asked.

"Your Honor, could I consult briefly with my client?"

"Make it quick."

Sam and Gustafson consulted for a couple of minutes. Sam didn't have a lot of questions to ask. When it came to preliminary hearings, the defense was at a decided disadvantage. There wasn't a lot he could do beyond locking down some key testimony.

"Any cross-examination, Mr. Johnstone?" Downs asked impatiently.

"Yes, Your Honor."

She sighed. "Then get to it, Counsel."

Sam moved to the podium. "Detective Polson, did you know the deceased?"

"No, sir."

"Did you know Clayton Pierce?"

"No, sir."

"Did Mr. Pierce at any time admit to buying drugs from my client?"

"Which one?" Punch asked.

Sam felt his face redden. "Mr. Gustafson."

"No, sir."

"Was my client under the influence of anything when you arrested him?"

"Didn't appear that way."

"Was he in possession of any drugs?"

"On him?"

"Yes. Actual possession."

"No, sir."

"You spoke with Mr. Gustafson?"

"I did."

"Did he admit to dealing drugs?"

"No."

"Did he admit to selling or otherwise providing drugs to the decedent?"

"Of course not."

"Is that a 'no?'"

Now it was Punch's turn to redden. "Yes."

"Any evidence my client forced the decedent to take drugs?"

"No."

"And you were staking out my client's room?"

"Yes, I was a part of that. We had known for a while that your client was dealing—"

"A yes or no is sufficient," Sam interrupted. "And as part of your surveillance, someone was keeping an eye on the room?"

"That's the purpose of surveillance," Punch said.

"Any donut runs?" Sam asked. Two could play this game.

"Of course," Punch replied, playing along. "But someone was always watching the room."

"And that's how you know the decedent and Mr. Pierce arrived together at Mr. Gustafson's room, right?"

"Well, right," Punch said. He could see where this was going. "But—"

"Were they already high?"

"Couldn't tell."

"No reason to believe they weren't?"

"No reason to believe one way or the other."

"And the M.E. said that Rebel Hayes died of a fentanyl overdose?"

"Yes."

"You don't have any direct evidence that my client supplied the drugs, do you?"

"Not really; no video of him giving it to her—and now that everyone except him is dead, I don't expect we'll get any."

"My client rented the room?"

"He did."

"So no surprise that his fingerprints were all over—true?"

"True."

Sam nodded in acknowledgement, then leaned down and whispered in Gustafson's ear. After Gustafson whispered back, he thought for a moment, then returned to the podium. "Judge, I have no further questions for this witness."

"Detective Polson, you may step down," Downs said. "Ms. Schmidt, any other witnesses?"

"No, Your Honor."

Downs looked to Sam.

"Defense will not present," he said simply, then put a hand on the leg of a protesting Gustafson. "Not now."

Downs nodded her approval. "Well then, I'll hear from each of you before I announce my decision."

Cathy stood and addressed the court perfunctorily. "Your Honor, the State has made a sufficient showing that the defendant possessed a felony amount of drugs, and that he provided the drugs to the minor that resulted in her death. We ask the court to bind Mr. Gustafson over to the district court for further proceedings."

Downs nodded, then turned her attention to Sam. "Mr. Johnstone, any response?"

"Briefly, Your Honor."

"That would be appreciated."

"Your Honor, we acknowledge the State has shown probable cause that crimes were committed, but we urge you to find the State has failed to show probable cause that my client committed those crimes. There are too many unanswered questions regarding the so-called evidence. My client, during his interview with Detective Polson, admitted it was his room and that the deceased and her ... companion, I guess, came to his room to get high. But he denied the drugs were his and that he provided the fentanyl to the deceased. There are simply too many gaps in the detective's story at this time." This wasn't relevant; a preliminary hearing didn't weigh the evidence. But it was all he had.

"Thank you both," Downs said, then addressed Gustafson. "Mr. Gustafson, I'm sure Mr. Johnstone discussed this with you, but in this proceeding the State's burden is 'probable cause.' As I mentioned earlier, that just means that an ordinarily reasonable, prudent person could hear the evidence today and find that you committed the crimes. Having heard and considered the evidence presented here today, this court finds that there is probable cause to believe that on or about April tenth, in Custer County, Wyoming, the crimes of felony possession of a controlled substance, of possession with intent to distribute, and of drug-induced homicide were committed, and that you committed them. Mr. Gustafson, your case will be transferred to district court for all further proceedings."

She turned to Cathy. "Ms. Schmidt, are there other matters to be addressed in connection with this defendant?"

"No, Your Honor."

"Mr. Johnstone?"

"No, ma'am."

"Well, if not, we'll be adjourned," she ordered, and quickly left the courtroom.

The crowd filed out, buzzing over the day's events. After his client had departed, Sam sat alone at the defense table, considering his next steps.

Sensing someone behind him, Sam turned in his chair. It was Cathy, accompanied by a man about their age. "Sam, I don't know if you've met Dylan Roberts. He's the county attorney over in Jefferson County. He's agreed to serve as a special prosecutor for me until we can sort out some of these cases where I have a conflict."

Sam stood and measured Roberts quickly, well aware the other man was doing the same. "Good to meet you," Sam said simply.

"Same," Roberts said. "I've heard a lot about you. Cathy speaks very highly of you."

One look at Roberts had Sam convinced the guy could be modeling underwear. "It's a mutual-admiration deal, then."

"I feel the same way about her," Roberts said. "I'm looking forward to working with her again. I anticipate we'll be seeing a lot of each other."

"I imagine we will."

"Right. You should know I pride myself on driving a hard bargain." Roberts smiled, showing two rows of perfectly white teeth. "I know a lot of prosecutors say that, but I live it."

"Good to know," Sam replied levelly.

"You don't believe me."

"I don't really care," Sam responded. "Clients are about emotions. My job is to see to it that the facts applied to the law are presented to the client. I give advice. Your offers—if any—become part of the equation that the client must solve. If they want a trial, I'll try the case."

"And may the best man win?"

Sam shook his head. "I don't measure myself that way."

"How do you measure yourself?"

"I don't. I find that when I do, I always come up short."

Cathy sensed that things were about to take a turn. "Well, you've met. I've done my part. Dylan, why don't we go and take a look at the files I've got for you?"

"Sounds good." Roberts winked at Sam. "I'm always up for that," he added, and followed her out of the courtroom.

When he was alone, Sam looked at his watch. He'd told Gustafson to come by his office later so he could explain upcoming events more fully. But first, he needed to call his sponsor.

32

According to the old-timers, there had been wetter years, but not since the early 1980s. The winter's snowpack had been deep, and was followed by heavy rains throughout May and the first half of June. As a result, the runoff was still significant on high mountain streams, and as Sam crested a ridgeline and got his first look at the small creek, he groaned upon seeing the discoloration. The fish would have to eat, of course, but the high water meant he would have to fish nymphs—not his preferred method—and that he would be restricted to fishing pocket water.

"Gotta hit 'em on the nose," he said aloud, knowing that chilly water would mean the trout metabolism would be slowed. He pulled a small set of binoculars from a vest pocket and scanned the willows lining the creek below, looking for moose. In popular lore, people wrote about encounters with bears, but in the Bighorn Mountains, moose were a bigger threat to fishermen.

Satisfied he wouldn't be stomped, Sam made his way down the rocky slope and was soon streamside. The water was roaring, but to his delight, it wasn't as discolored as it had appeared from above. He sat on a rock, drank water, and strung his rod. When he had affixed a small bead-head nymph to his tippet, he stood, stretched, and gulped clear mountain air. The sky was cloudless royal blue, the hillsides covered in green grass on the tops and the west-facing sides of the slopes. On the east side of the larger slopes, snowdrifts remained.

He was ready.

Sam made his way quickly upstream, hitting pockets of water where he anticipated fish would be resting and feeding. He placed two or three casts in each target area, then moved on. At the two-hour mark, he had caught and released half a dozen small brook trout and a single, surprisingly large rainbow trout. He turned to look downstream to check his progress, then gazed up at the ridge above him. He was about to turn back to the water when he saw a brilliant flash of light in the distance. He'd seen similar flashes half a world and a lifetime away—sunlight reflecting off a glass surface. A lens.

He was being watched. Or worse.

He quickly surveyed the stream for available cover. His best option was a small stand of spruce twenty yards downstream. Walking quickly and changing pace as he went, he made it to the stand and exhaled with relief. He took a prone position and searched the ridgeline until he saw what he was looking for: a lone, camouflage-wearing figure sitting on a rocky outcrop, glassing the streambed and the slope along each side. As Sam watched, the figure exchanged binoculars for a rifle, raised it, and peered through its scope. The gunman slowly traversed the draw from top to bottom, stopping when the barrel was aimed in Sam's direction.

There were two options: wait in place or try moving to a safer position while avoiding detection. He rolled onto his back and weighed the pros and cons while removing the bright red flannel shirt he'd selected that morning. Waiting had never been a strong suit. Was it a hunter? Doubtful; nothing was open this time of year. He could be scouting—but with a rifle? A spotting scope, binoculars, or a rangefinder would all be better options— and a helluva lot easier to carry. Sam made his decision.

Half an hour later, he approached the gunman's perch from the north. From the hillside above the gunman, he could see the end of the rifle barrel slowly traversing the draw. A set of expensive binoculars was positioned on the rocks within easy reach of the gunman, who remained obscured by the rocky outcrop under which he had situated himself.

Drawing his revolver, Sam shrugged off his vest and placed the fly rod and net on the ground next to a large Ponderosa. Moving toward the gunman's position, he risked a quick look back to memorize the location of his cache before commencing his approach. When he was above the gunman and certain the man was alone, Sam spoke.

"What are you doing?"

"Jesus, you scared the shit out of me!" was the high-pitched response. A young man in his late teens or early twenties turned with the rifle in his hand.

"Don't point that in my direction," Sam ordered. "When that happens, I get nervous. When I get nervous, I pull triggers."

"O-Okay," the younger man said. He carefully placed the rifle against a small shrub that had grown in the rocks. "Who are you?"

"I'm the guy you've been glassing."

"What? No, mister, you got it all wrong! I'm hunting!"

"That's what I'm afraid of."

"No! Dude, I'm hunting coyotes!"

"Step on out here where I can see you," Sam ordered, indicating the hillside away from the outcropping. When the pimply-faced youth had complied, Sam relaxed. "Did you see me down there?"

"Well, yeah."

The kid appeared to be telling the truth. He touched his face and avoided eye contact—mannerisms Sam had observed in dozens of young men as they geared up in preparation for an operation. Young men feared death; old men feared failure. "Look, you can't just be . . ."

"What? I got a right—"

"I know," Sam acknowledged. "You just . . . need to be careful."

"Man, you don't own this mountain."

The kid couldn't know. "I know," Sam admitted. "But I thought you were glassing me."

"Maybe you're just paranoid."

"Maybe. Sorry."

Twenty miles down the road and an hour later, Sam decided the kid was probably right.

33

On the first day of July, Bridger was ensconced in his chambers, reviewing the file for his next case. Captioned State v. Gustafson, it was set for arraignment—the legal word for the initial appearance on a felony before the court with jurisdiction to try the case. Two years on the bench had taught him to temper any expectation that things would go as planned. That said, he hoped that Johnstone and Schmidt could get a deal done and quickly, as the last thing he wanted was to preside over a trial involving a dead kid, her grieving parents, and their friends. There was no judicial upside to a case like this; the best he could do was see to it that he only had to try a case once, that any appeal was rejected, and that any sentence imposed kept the uproar to a minimum.

He was straightening a new silk tie in the mirror in his private restroom when his judicial assistant, Mary Perry, knocked on the door to his chambers.

"Everyone is in place, Judge."

"Give me a minute." He took one last look in the mirror, examining himself from both sides. His brief time on the bench had accelerated the graying of what was still—thankfully—a full head of hair. "I'll be out in a second." He smoothed his eyebrows, and after a final look in the mirror, donned his robe. "Okay," he said at last to an awaiting Mary. "Let's do this."

While Bridger was primping, Sam was in the courtroom, seated next to an edgy Gustafson. While his client fidgeted and doodled on the legal pad Sam had provided him, Sam looked around the courtroom, marveling anew at the vision of the men and women of nearly a century past. In the early 1900s, life was uncertain and short. Nonetheless, optimistic people had overseen the design and construction of a courthouse that meant something to its designers and builders. Contemporary courthouses were constructed with an eye toward security and efficiency and were bland structures, what Daniels called "Midcentury Warsaw Ghetto." In contrast, the Custer County courthouse was a study in optimism.

Outside, the red brick exterior was offset by Ionic columns and a large staircase. Inside, one's attention was drawn from the gray marble floors, up the wainscoted walls, to the ornate ceiling fans circulating air for the benefit of the assembled court participants and observers. Bridger's second-floor courtroom was large; Sam estimated it at more than fifty feet wide, and perhaps one hundred feet deep. Double wooden doors afforded entry for two hundred potential spectators who would sit on hard, unmarked pews. Between the bar and the judge's bench were long library tables at which the attorneys and their clients were seated. Next to the judge and facing the back of the courtroom was a single chair with a microphone where witnesses would sit while testifying. On the other side of the judge was a chair for the elected clerk of court. In front of the judge's bench was the court reporter, who was responsible for reporting verbatim everything said during the trial, thereby making a record of the proceeding. In a nod to technological evolution, television screens, computers, and microphones were positioned around the courtroom to facilitate the showing and viewing of exhibits. Beyond that, however, the courtroom likely looked much as it had when construction was completed in 1925.

In Sam's opinion, aside from military parades, little remained in American culture that equaled the pomp and formality of a twenty-first-century American courtroom. He loved it.

At five minutes after the hour, Bridger mounted the steps to his raised bench while Mary closed the door behind him. "Be seated," he said as he took his chair. When all were seated, he looked out over the courtroom and called the case. "District Court for the Twelfth Judicial District of Wyoming is in session. We're on the record. We're here for arraignment in State versus Trent Gustafson. The State is present and represented by Cathy Schmidt; the defendant is present and represented by Sam Johnstone. Ms. Schmidt, is the State prepared to proceed?"

Cathy was on her feet. "We are, Your Honor."

Bridger looked at Sam. "Mr. Johnstone?"

"We are, Judge," Sam began. "And for the record, Mr. Gustafson would waive—"

Bridger had anticipated Sam's offer to waive a reading of the charges and an advisal of rights, an obvious ploy that would never be allowed. "Thank you, Mr. Johnstone, but this is a serious charge—among the most serious on the books, in fact. I want to ensure that Mr. Gustafson has a complete understanding of both the charges and his rights."

"Your Honor, I can assure the court that my client and I have discussed in detail both the charges and—"

"Thank you, Counsel," Bridger interrupted. His face had colored—this wasn't the first time Johnstone had attempted this in a high-profile matter. "I have made my decision." He recited a long list of rights enjoyed by Gustafson, then read into the record the contents of the arrest warrant. Finally, he took Gustafson's pleas.

"Not guilty, Your Honor," Gustafson responded when asked to plea to each charge.

Sam was pleased with his client so far. They'd had a long discussion regarding courtroom decorum and behavior, and up until now, Gustafson had followed Sam's instructions to the letter.

Bridger nodded his approval. "The defendant's pleas have been entered and counsel has been retained." He began to gather materials from his bench. "The court's inclination would be to continue bond on the same terms and conditions. Is there anything further we need to discuss?"

"No, Your Honor," Cathy said.

"No, sir," Sam added.

"Then we'll be adjourned," Bridger said. He stood and quickly departed the courtroom.

Cathy and Sam shook hands. Roberts was with her, and Sam took the offered, soft-as-butter hand. His surprise must have been evident.

"Just seeing how business is done here," Roberts said.

"Anything notable?" Sam asked.

"Not especially. Seems as if you people have the basics down pat."

Sam smiled tightly and turned to Gustafson, who was ready to go. "Hang on a second."

Cathy placed a hand on Roberts' arm. "Dylan has offered to assist in this case," she said. "Any issue with that?"

"The more the merrier," Sam said. Then he indicated his client. "We've gotta run the gauntlet here."

"Good luck!" she said brightly.

"Just keep moving," Sam instructed his client. "I'll do the talking." As he made his way toward the double doors, he observed Rebel Hayes' father in the last row of the courtroom, sitting with a pair of large bearded men in work clothes. Hayes didn't make eye contact with Sam; his focus was fixed on Gustafson as Sam guided him out of the courtroom.

In the hallway, they encountered a small group of reporters. "Mr. Johnstone, what does your client have to say regarding the death of Rebel Hayes?" Sarah Penrose asked.

"My client is saddened by her tragic death," Sam replied. "But he denies any involvement. As you heard, he maintains his innocence, and looks forward to his acquittal following a trial by a jury of his peers."

"So there will not be a plea agreement?" another reporter asked.

"We haven't seen any indications the State is prepared to deal," Sam said. "We'll take this case one step at a time. My hope is that when all the evidence is in and of record, the State will see the futility of continued prosecution."

Satisfied he'd said what needed to be said, Sam put a hand on Gustafson's arm to guide him down the hall and out the back door—his usual method. But when Gustafson didn't move, Sam turned his attention to his client. Seeing him focused on something down the hall, Sam followed his client's gaze and saw Davonte Blair's brother and cousin— Damon and Reggie—leaning against a wall twenty feet away, staring hard. Sam led Gustafson by the two men.

"Good to see ya, Gus," said Damon. "Be safe, man."

Reggie smiled. "Look both ways, brother."

34

An hour later, Cassie appeared at Sam's door, even paler than usual. She came in without knocking and closed the door behind her before stammering, "You're not going to believe who is here."

"Damon and Reggie." When Cassie stared at him blankly, he quickly added, "Saw 'em in the courthouse. What do they want?"

"To meet with you."

"Did you tell them I'm busy?"

"I did."

Screw 'em. On the other hand, the thought of the two men lounging in his waiting area while intimidating Cassie didn't settle well. "No idea what they want?"

"They're not going to tell little ol' me," she replied sarcastically.

True. "Tell them to give me a minute," he said. "I've got an eleven o'clock, right?"

"Yes, with Mrs. Ostland. She wants to start a business making salads."

"In this town?"

"Yes, in this town," Cassie repeated. "We're not that bad, Sam. We've got paved streets, cell phone service, and even the internet."

"I didn't mean it in a bad way. I just meant this is a meat-and-potatoes town."

"I'm not so sure anywhere is that kind of town anymore."

"Give me five minutes." After she'd departed, he positioned two chairs where he wanted the men to sit and opened a desk drawer so that his revolver would be in easy reach. Closing his eyes, he took a deep breath and recited the Serenity Prayer. Feeling better, he leaned forward and pushed the intercom. "Bring 'em on back." He was on his feet when the men entered. On his signal, Cassie closed the door behind them.

"Gentlemen, how can I help you?" He hadn't offered them anything to drink. "I have an eleven o'clock," he informed them.

Damon had seated himself, but Reggie remained on his feet. He walked over to Sam's cabinet and started to reach for an item on display. "I told you last time to keep your mitts off my shit," Sam said sharply. "Nothing's changed."

Reggie turned to face Sam, eyes narrowed, before Damon intervened. "Sit down, Reggie," he said, then turned to Sam. "We got a message from Davonte."

"Yeah?" Sam asked. "My birthday's just around the corner. That it?"

Now Damon's eyes narrowed. "'Fraid not. 'Fraid it's a little more serious than that."

"Yeah?"

"Yeah," Reggie replied, and sat quietly.

Sam looked at his watch. "You've got two minutes. If it's more than fifty words, you probably oughta get started."

"You a real smartass, boy."

"Damn," Sam said, pointing at his watch. "We're already down to one hundred and ten seconds."

Reggie snorted and started to stand, but Damon re-seated him with a sharp look. "Davonte don't like you representin' Gus."

"Yeah?"

"Yeah."

Seconds ticked by. "That it?" Sam asked with more bravado than he felt.

"Naw, he wanted me to tell you that his interests are, uh, *adversarial* to Gus's. Says you'd understand and that you need to find Gus another lawyer."

Sam stood. "Well, fellas, like I said, I've got another appointment.

Thanks for coming by, and thanks for the information. And please tell Davonte I appreciate his continuing interest in my career."

Neither Damon nor Reggie had gotten to his feet; each sat impassively, staring at Sam. He met their stares, feeling his pulse increase and trying not to show his concern. It wasn't fear, exactly—he knew fear. It was more a feeling of dread. "I'll have Cassie show you out," he said, reaching for the intercom.

Damon was up quickly and placed a hand on Sam's. "I know you a hero and all, but my brother don't play."

Sam looked up at Damon. He could smell the garlic on the taller man's breath. "Then you know if you don't take your hand off mine, we're gonna have a problem."

Damon stared hard at Sam, but eventually released his hand. "Make your call, boy. But remember: we watchin' you, and we reporting to Davonte."

"You do that," Sam replied, pushing the button on the intercom. "Cassie, these men are ready to go."

"Do I need to make another appointment?" she asked.

"Oh, no. We got everything cleared up," he assured her. "Put Mrs. Ostland in the conference room and show Reggie and Damon out, please." He hung up.

Damon smiled without mirth. "Just remember what Davonte said."

"How could I possibly forget?" Sam asked. "And tell him I hope things are good in Ankara or wherever."

35

What awakened him, he didn't know. But twelve hours later, Sam looked at the clock. It was 2:05 a.m. In the red glow from the clock, he could see his revolver, still in the shoulder holster. He lay in bed, listening. It wasn't so much a sound as it was a feeling: someone was outside his apartment. Reaching to the other side of the bed, he found his prosthetic leg and slowly, deliberately attached it. He stretched and moved to ensure it was properly affixed, then swung his legs down to the floor, donned a pair of slippers, and stood in the dark. He felt for the pistol, dropped the holster on his bed, and began to walk slowly through his bedroom, paying attention to the shadows and shapes he could see through his drawn shades.

He'd performed this drill a hundred times over the course of the past couple of years. Sometimes it was the wind, sometimes an animal, sometimes a dream. Sometimes nothing at all. He would patrol the inner perimeter of his home, listening at the walls, scarcely breathing, anticipating an unseen enemy attacking in the pre-dawn darkness. Then, finding none, he would spend the remaining hours of darkness watching old movies and trying to get back to sleep.

This time, having patrolled the entire house, he stepped out onto his ground-level back deck, forgetting that his neighbor had installed motion sensors in his backyard following previous incidents involving Sam. Seconds later, Bill opened the sliding glass door. He too was armed.

"Bill, it's me!" Sam said quietly.

"Sam?"

"Yeah."

"What the hell are you doing this time?"

"Uhhh . . . Just looking around."

"See anything?"

"No."

"You need help, Sam."

"I know," Sam replied.

Cursing himself, he re-entered his apartment. He headed for the bedroom, but hesitated and then checked the front door. It was locked, of course, so he unlocked and opened it in a single swift motion. Seeing the small envelope on the welcome mat, he looked around quickly before deciding to chance it. He snaked an arm around the doorframe, exposing as little of himself as possible to a sniper's bullet, then grabbed the envelope and slammed the door shut, cringing at the sound.

Breaking the seal, he extracted a single piece of paper. On it was typewritten, *Nice place.*

He retreated to his kitchen, drank a glass of water, and then got back into bed. It was 2:15 a.m. Sam closed his eyes, took rhythmic breaths, and tried to remember the good times.

———

Several hours later, a crispy-eyed Sam made the videoconference call he had scheduled some ten days earlier. Dr. Miles Sturdevant, Ph.D., M.D. was a retired physician and forensic toxicologist who had worked for the Colorado Department of Health for decades, and now provided expert consultation in criminal cases for a hefty fee. Sam had found him through a referral service and requested today's appointment.

"Mr. Johnstone, how can I help?" Sturdevant asked. It was always difficult to tell on video, but he appeared to be a small man, immaculately groomed, with a full head of silver hair and a matching beard.

"I'm a trial lawyer," Sam began. "I've got a trial coming up in a few months that I need some help with. I'm not sure you *can* help, but I know what I think I need."

"And what is that?"

"I have a client charged with delivering a controlled substance—fentanyl—to a minor who died."

"Uh-huh."

"Right. My client says he didn't do it."

"I'm shocked," Sturdevant dead-panned.

"I'm sure." Sam laughed. "My client was taken into custody after leaving the motel room where the deceased was located."

"That's unfortunate."

Sam liked this guy. "And there was a significant amount of fentanyl found in my client's belongings—the ones he left behind."

"Not good."

You could say that again. "My client says he didn't deliver the drugs."

"Unlikely to be true."

This guy would be good. "There was another guy in the room—he over-dosed as well."

"I hope you obtained a significant retainer," Sturdevant said.

"Of that, you can be sure." Sam smiled. "My client believes the other guy delivered the drugs."

"Of course he does."

"That guy is dead."

"Of course he is."

Sam actually laughed. It was ridiculous. "I've been doing some reading, and in so doing I have come to understand that what is termed 'fentanyl' is not always fentanyl."

"True."

"So, I'd like someone to review the Wyoming state laboratory's analysis of the drugs to see if my guy might be telling the truth. Failing that, maybe I could show that the laboratory didn't or couldn't differentiate or identify the drugs." Seeing the scientist's deadpan stare, Sam continued. "Hell, I'm looking for anything that might help my guy out."

"I understand."

"I just need something so that I might be able to raise some doubt."

"Even with him in the room with two dead people?"

Sam's problem, not his. "I can work through that. Oh, and the guy didn't die then. He overdosed—again—several weeks later."

"So he won't be around to dispute your client's pinning the rap on him," Sturdevant said.

Sam smiled. "You may have missed your calling, Doctor."

"Doubtful. I prefer laboratories to courtrooms."

"But it is possible to determine the difference between different kinds of fentanyl. . . uh . . . I can't remember—"

"Analogs," Dr. Sturdevant said, completing a stumped Sam's question. "Oh, yes. It's a fairly simple process to identify the chemical composition of the controlled substance. In fact, I would hope the State has already done so. That's a fundamental laboratory procedure."

"If they have—"

"It would be a matter of reviewing the laboratory's procedures, documentation, and results."

"And if not?"

"Then it would get expensive. That would require our performing, documenting, and memorializing tests."

"Which may or may not provide the desired results."

"True."

"In either event, I'd need you to testify," Sam observed. "Sometime this winter, in all likelihood."

"How far is Custer from Jackson Hole? I could maybe get a little skiing in?"

"A little over four hundred miles."

"Well, I am available," Dr. Sturdevant replied. He reached into his desk drawer, retrieved a pen, and looked to Sam. "You have my contact information. If you give me yours, I'll send you my CV and a rate sheet. No false modesty here—I'm pricey. However, if your client is of limited means, you might be able to get your point across through effective cross-examination."

"Can we decide later?"

"Certainly. Once I have reviewed the laboratory's methodology and results, I'll be able to make a recommendation."

"Outstanding," Sam replied. "And—"

"Don't put anything in writing until I clear it with you?"

This guy knew his business. "Exactly," Sam agreed. "Thank you."

36

In early September, Sam followed up with his only potential witness. "So, what do you think?" he asked Dr. Sturdevant.

The little man scratched at a sore on his nose, then looked at his finger. "I was helping my wife in the yard and I got scratched by a bush," he said. "But you probably don't care."

"At your hourly rate? I can't afford to." Sam laughed. "And people think attorneys are bad. But did you find anything?"

"Maybe." Sturdevant folded his arms and looked at Sam. "What do you know about fentanyl?"

"Not much," Sam admitted.

"So, let's start with a little Fentanyl 101, shall we?" Then, without waiting for an answer, he commenced a lecture on the drug. "Now, the first thing you need to know is that fentanyl is a synthetic narcotic drug. This isn't like opium or something that grows naturally."

"Okay," Sam said, removing a pen from his pocket to take notes.

"Fentanyl was created as an intravenous surgical analgesic." Seeing Sam's confusion, he explained, "A painkiller. Originally, it was delivered using a needle. But over time scientists and chemists developed patches and lozenges for delivery of the drug to patients."

"I'm with ya," Sam assured Sturdevant.

"The drug is highly lethal and highly addictive, so it was, of course, placed on the FDA's list of controlled substances. It's so lethal, in fact, that kids and pets have overdosed after exposure to patches. Water systems have been contaminated when folks flushed patches down the toilet."

"Yikes!"

Sturdevant smiled. "I haven't even gotten to the bad part yet," he assured Sam. "So, because the drug was listed as a controlled substance, enterprising pseudo-scientists and chemists—usually overseas—soon began creating designer drugs that mimic fentanyl's effects on the user. But because of their different chemical make-up, they can briefly avoid classification as a controlled substance. It's a billion-dollar industry."

"Those are called analogs, right?" Sam asked.

"Exactly." Sturdevant nodded his approval. "Because of their chemical differences from fentanyl, their legality can be in question, and they can avoid some manufacturing restrictions. An added benefit, from the perspective of the user, is that they can be difficult to identify on standard drug tests."

"Ideal from a dealer's perspective," Sam said. "Stuff sells itself."

"Oh, yeah," Sturdevant agreed. "And even more to the retailers' liking, we're now seeing analogs that are astoundingly potent. Carfentanil, one of the most common, is ten thousand times more potent than morphine and one hundred times more potent than fentanyl."

"Wow," Sam said, shaking his head.

"Right? We're talking an amount that wouldn't cover the head of a pin. And it's cheaper than, say, heroin or cocaine, so people cut it into those drugs to increase potency and to lower their overhead. So when fentanyl first came on the scene, we were seeing people thinking they were using one thing—say, hydrocodone—but they get some of that mixed with fentanyl, and boom! We had an epidemic of overdosing."

"People don't know what they're getting," Sam observed.

"Ah, but things have changed. Some do," Dr. Sturdevant corrected. "We now see people seeking out fentanyl and analogs and using them intentionally. That's your Rebel Hayes."

"You think she knew what she was doing? At her age?"

"I would think so," Sturdevant said. "She was shooting it intravenously. That's usually a sign of an experienced user."

"Right. So what does all this mean?"

"Well, the big issue facing law enforcement—one of the issues, I should say—is identifying fentanyl and its analogs. It's not easy. It takes specialized equipment."

"How specialized?"

"Gas chromatography mass spectrometry and liquid chromatography tandem mass spectrometry can identify some regulated fentanyl compounds. Of course, as new analogs appear, we're off to the races again."

Sam stopped taking notes and sat back in his chair. "So, let me ask you this. Scientists can differentiate between batches of fentanyl . . . or analogs?"

"Ideally, yes."

"Or between two regulated—or unregulated—substances, right?"

"Well, yes. I would say we could tell the difference . . . if we checked."

An idea was beginning to form for Sam. Might he have a viable defense? "Did the Wyoming lab check?"

"I can't tell from what I've seen. As a general rule, at the state level, if something field tests as 'fentanyl,' a simple confirmatory test is administered. If that comes back positive, well . . ."

"The state just assumes it is fentanyl?"

"Right. And the reality is, with what we're customarily seeing now—a veritable cocktail of drugs—it takes specialized equipment to differentiate among drug samples."

"Equipment the state lab might not have."

"They may or may not. A lot don't, so states send stuff out for analysis on contract when they think they need to. But remember: since fentanyl is always illicit, for your usual possession or possession with intent charge it doesn't really matter what it is. Most of the research being done isn't being done to identify substances so much as it is to trace sources."

Well, well, well. "Thanks, Doc. Send me your invoice. I'll get it paid and let you know if I need anything else."

Sam rang off, thinking he might have the beginning of a defense. Alternately, he could tell Cathy and perhaps she would drop the charge of drug-induced homicide. But if he did that, he would lose any momentum at trial. No possibility of a home run caused by one or more jurors reasoning, "Well, if they messed that one up, perhaps the other charges are garbage, too."

It was risky. He'd have to sleep on it.

Sam had stopped to pick up some takeout on the way home. As he neared his apartment complex, he was smelling the gyros and recalling a beautiful Australian woman he had spent some time with during a brief rest and relaxation break he'd taken in Crete while on a Middle East tour. He was wondering whatever happened to her when he noticed several people milling about in the parking lot in front of his building. He considered passing by to assess any threat but decided his food would get cold, and the thought of a tepid gyro outweighed any desire to avoid a ruckus. Pulling into the parking lot, he wasn't surprised when his old truck drew the group's attention, and he recognized Hayes. By the time Sam had parked his truck in his assigned spot, it was surrounded by a dozen men.

"Mr. Johnstone," Hayes said.

"Mr. Hayes." Sam nodded. "This is private property. Residents and guests only. I don't recall inviting you—did someone else?"

"I'm here to see you."

Sam grabbed his dinner and locked the truck. "You've seen me," he said. He was checking the distance to his door and a retaining wall when he saw a neighbor's curtains move. Seconds later, his phone rang.

"Sam? It's Bill. What's going on?"

"Unexpected visitors, Bill."

"Want me to call the police?"

"Let me check," Sam replied. He put the phone to his chest. "My neighbor," he said to Hayes. "He wants to know if he should call the police."

"Call whoever you want, boy," Hayes snarled. "We got eyes on you."

"Bill, I think we'll be okay," Sam said, and rang off. He looked at Hayes. "You know I'm just doing my job, right?"

"I know that's what you keep sayin'. You think it's a job, but to me it's a poke in the eye."

"I'm just trying to get home and eat my dinner," Sam replied. "If you and your folks will move, there won't be any issues."

"An' if I don't?"

"My food will get cold."

"You're a real smartass," Hayes replied.

When a couple of Hayes' companions moved in close, Sam turned to place his food on the hood of his truck. He saw the cop car pull into the parking lot, and relief flooded him.

Ron Baker stopped the vehicle and exited quickly. "What's going on?"

"Nothing, Officer," Hayes replied. "We're just making sure that Mr. Johnstone gets home safe, is all."

Baker looked from Hayes to Sam and back. "Mr. Johnstone, is that right?"

"I think it's fair to say that Mr. Hayes is concerned about my welfare," Sam replied. He turned and retrieved his dinner. "But I'd appreciate it if everyone would let me go eat my dinner."

Baker had his cue and quickly dispersed the small crowd. When they were gone, he followed Sam to his door. "You okay, Counselor?"

"I'm good," Sam assured the young cop. "I appreciate you stopping by. It was fortuitous."

"Yeah. Sure." Baker winked and returned to his car.

37

The fishing in the Bighorns was generally poor in late September, but Sam had a clear calendar, and the afternoon found him walking a game trail next to a small stream he'd fished dozens of times. The brook trout had spawned, the aspen had turned and were now past the spectacular yellows, reds, and oranges of autumn. Their leaves joined those of willows and other bushes lining the creek on and under the surface of the stream, making casting tricky and obtaining a proper drift all but impossible.

But he was fishing, and he exulted in the breeze on his face and the sound of water against rock. He picked up a fish here and there and inspected them closely. On most, the brilliant spawning colors had faded, and the chalk-white underbellies were now turning gray as winter or death approached. This stream ran down the middle of a small draw and fed larger streams as part of the Yellowstone and Missouri River drainages. In the early twentieth century, it had served as the source of timber used to make railroad ties. Accordingly, the timber along the stream was second growth, uniform in size and regularly spaced. Nature was not so uniform.

The orange shirt he had purposely selected (bow hunting season for elk was open) reflected in a shallow pool at the end of a long run, so Sam stepped back to keep his reflection off the water. Fish couldn't hear, but they could see—with bald eagles, red-tailed hawks, otters, raccoons, and a litany of other predators always on the hunt, sharp eyesight had evolved in the species. He cast from afar and the fly was eaten by a fish before the rippling had dissipated. The small female was quickly in hand and then released.

The process was repeated until the sun began to set, and he followed his footsteps along the stream almost to his old truck, where he stopped short upon seeing another set of footprints atop his own. He surveyed his surroundings and held his breath to still the rush of adrenaline. The only certainty was that the person was not well-trained and had small feet. But untrained people could be dangerous.

He released a breath and, with a hand on his revolver, made his way to the truck. In the cab, he quickly started the truck and departed, trying not to rush but knowing he was being watched. He saw no one on his way back to the pavement.

While Sam was on stream, Cathy—flanked by Roberts and Lucas—stepped to a small podium that had been hastily placed on the courthouse steps by Jack Fricke and his custodial sidekick, a kid named Michael-something whom everyone referred to as "Frac."

"I will have a brief statement, after which Mr. Roberts and Chief Lucas will answer any questions you may have," Cathy began. "My name is Cathy Schmidt, and I am the county attorney for Custer County, Wyoming. Accompanying me are Chief of Police William Lucas and Dylan Roberts, who is the elected county attorney over in Jefferson County. Mr. Roberts is serving as a special prosecutor for reasons that will be clear momentarily."

She took a deep breath before continuing. "Earlier today, Mr. Roberts signed an affidavit seeking the arrest of Grant Lee, my predecessor as county attorney for Custer County, in connection with the shooting death of Misty Layton." She folded a single piece of paper and placed it in a pocket. "These gentlemen will now take your questions."

Predictably, Sarah Penrose spoke first. "Mr. Roberts, what is the charge?"

"Murder in the second degree."

"Will you seek incarceration, assuming a conviction?"

"That question is premature, of course—we don't even have Mr. Lee in custody—but I can assure you we will treat Mr. Lee the same as we do any other defendant."

"Are you able to prosecute a peer unconditionally?"

"Of course."

"How can the public be assured that you will pursue this vigorously?"

"You'll be free to judge my actions," Roberts replied levelly. "They will speak for themselves. Now, how about we let someone else ask questions. Miss?"

"What accounts for the lengthy delay in bringing charges?" asked a youthful reporter from the *Casper Star*.

Lucas moved to the microphone. "We have been investigating this matter diligently since its occurrence. Our officers, in conjunction with investigators from the sheriff's office and the Wyoming DCI, have worked together."

"What was the hold-up?"

"I'm going to reject your premise that there was any sort of delay. I will say we undertook a careful, considered investigation."

"What was difficult about it? Our understanding is that he admitted to shooting her."

"I don't want to get into the specifics of the investigation, except to say that we wanted to be certain that this matter was charged properly."

Penrose's voice again rose above the chorus. "Would you be that circumspect if the defendant was a member of a minority group or a less notable member of the public?"

Lucas' face colored. "Of course. We—"

A short man with glasses spoke up next. "Some have said that by delaying the bringing of charges you have provided Mr. Lee time in which to formulate a defense."

"Are you kidding me?" Lucas asked. "His defense from the incident onward has been one of self-defense!" As he concluded, Lucas leaned down to hear what the much smaller Roberts was furiously whispering in his ear.

"Follow up? You don't believe him?"

Lucas looked quickly to Roberts, who shrugged. "Isn't it obvious? If we did, we wouldn't have brought charges."

"Where is Mr. Lee now?"

"I don't have that information."

"If he is out of state, will he be extradited?"

Roberts stepped back to the podium. "We hope it won't come to that. We hope Mr. Lee will turn himself in upon learning of the warrant for his arrest."

While the questioning was ongoing, Cathy noticed Julie Spence behind the reporters. For a moment they made solid eye contact, broken when Julie turned and walked off.

"Ladies and gentlemen, I'm sure you understand that we are all busy," she said. "I'm afraid that's all the time we have."

"Will Judge Downs see him, or will she recuse?"

"I don't know," Cathy replied. "Call her chambers. Thank you." Then she led Lucas and Roberts back into the courthouse.

38

Sam was sitting uncomfortably in a small room in Custer's VA clinic, talking with his longtime counselor, Bob Martinez. The session with "VA Bob," as Sam had taken to calling him, had been a grind. Together, they were working through cognitive processing therapy, one session at a time. Between sessions, Sam had "homework" to perform, and he had to promise to use the techniques Bob had given him to deal with life on life's terms. Intentionally reliving wartime experiences was grueling, but Bob had assured Sam the long-term benefits would outweigh the short-term pain. Nevertheless, things hadn't gone well today, primarily because Sam had not practiced the techniques or performed the exercises suggested by Martinez.

At last, Bob looked at Sam expectantly. "Something on your mind?"

"Big trial."

"I read about that."

"And a woman who is . . . weird."

"Scary weird?"

"Yeah."

When Sam didn't expound, Martinez prompted him. "And?"

"My dad is sick," Sam said, changing subjects. When Bob didn't respond, he continued. "I know I should feel bad about it, but I don't, really."

"Ah, there's the issue," Bob said. "We've talked about this before. You're gonna feel how you feel. No reason to feel guilty. But aside from not feeling bad, how are you feeling?"

"Honestly, I don't know how to feel. On the one hand, he will be dead real soon, and I can't say that I'm gonna miss him, because I never really knew him well at all. On the other hand, I suppose that I might have done more to get to know him."

"What do you mean?" Martinez asked.

"Well, over the last couple of months he tried to contact me," Sam explained. He was on his feet and pacing. "But only because he was sick, you know what I'm saying? I mean, where the hell was he the rest of my life? What right does he have to come into my life and expect me to feel sorry for him when he's sick and dying?" Sam looked to Bob for answers.

Bob didn't give answers—it wasn't his job. "Do you think he felt like he had a right to ask, or do you think he was just reaching out?"

"I don't know. All I know is he reached out and I couldn't see reaching back, so I didn't," Sam said. "And can't you ever just answer a question?"

"Not my job," Bob said. "Anyway, are you okay with that?"

"Shouldn't I be?"

"Sam, I'm not judging you. I'm asking how you feel about it. That's what's important. If you are okay with it, then things will be fine. On the other hand, if you are feeling conflicted, then we can expect to have some issues moving forward."

"What kind of issues?"

"Well, in your case, I would worry about you relapsing with booze, drugs, or both."

Sam laughed derisively. "I haven't had a drink in almost eighteen months," he boasted.

"I know," Martinez said. "And that's one hell of an accomplishment. But you must remember that addiction is a cunning and baffling disease, and that we are all one day, one hour, or one minute away from a relapse. All it takes is one bad decision and everything we've worked for goes right down the drain. If it was anything easier than that, I would be out of a job."

"I know," Sam said. "And I appreciate everything you've done for me, but I think I've got a pretty good handle on things now."

"Dangerous words. Do those inventories daily and keep an eye on how you feel," Martinez said. "I'm available 24/7/365. You know that."

Sam sat quietly, trying to decide whether to broach the subject. If not with Bob, then who? "His nurse at hospice sent me a box of his stuff," he said.

"What was in it?"

"I don't know," Sam said. "I haven't had the balls to open it yet."

"What are you afraid of?" Martinez asked.

"I'm not sure," Sam admitted. "I just know that I haven't wanted to open it."

"You will, when the time is right. Be careful. Make sure you are in a positive frame of mind. We all have secrets, and it sounds like your father had them as well," Martinez explained. "It's more than likely that you will discover some things you might not want to know when you open that box. Could be a Panera Box."

"Pandora," Sam corrected.

"What?"

"It was Pandora's Box—that's the allegory you're thinking about."

Martinez laughed. "What can I say? I wasn't a literature major."

Sam was smiling as he left the VA clinic. He always felt better when he spent some time with VA Bob. He approached his truck and nodded in the direction of a short man sitting on a Harley-Davidson in the adjacent spot smoking a cigarette. He was wearing camouflage pants, a black T-shirt, a leather jacket, and reflective aviator sunglasses. His hair was tied back in a ponytail.

Sam got in his truck and exhaled when it started on the first try. He didn't expect trouble, and it wasn't unusual for men in this town to eyeball him closely when he was wearing a suit. It wasn't standard VA attire, after all. But there was something about this guy.

As Sam backed out, the little man stared unflinchingly at him. He was unaccountably irked. "What's your claim to fame, dude?" he wondered as he drove to his office.

39

As the trial approached, Gustafson's behavior became increasingly erratic, and word on the street was he had started trafficking in drugs again. If that wasn't enough, Cassie, courthouse staff, and just about everyone else Sam knew mentioned having seen Gustafson and his posse in the Longbranch or on the town at some point. In Custer, the pool of eligible voters was small to begin with, and Sam was increasingly concerned about potential jurors having knowledge of his client's shenanigans.

All that aside, trial preparation was not going well. While Cathy didn't have a ton of direct evidence, Sam had almost nothing factually in his client's favor, and it was becoming increasingly apparent he would have to try the case solely by poking holes in the State's story. He could show gaps in the State's theory, of course—for example, no one could testify to having seen his client sell or provide fentanyl to anyone, let alone to Rebel. But jurors had common sense, and Cathy would appeal to that. Under Wyoming law, a jury could convict given only circumstantial evidence, but a lack of direct evidence was also reason for a jury to acquit. And while Custer juries were renowned for holding the State to its burden of proof, simply playing defense was not Sam's preferred method of trying cases.

As he studied the State's case from his perspective, and his case from the State's perspective, one thing had become abundantly clear: he could not afford to put Gustafson on the stand, as the few positive aspects of his character were far outweighed by the negatives.

On a November evening just days before trial, Sam stopped by the jail to see Daniels. "How are things?" Sam asked.

"Not bad. I'm certainly catching up on my reading. Have you ever read *Anatomy of a Murder*?" Daniels asked. When Sam indicated he had not, Daniels continued. "I think you'd like it. It was written by a prosecutor who was later appointed to the Michigan Supreme Court. His name was John Voelker, but he wrote under the pen name Robert Traver. I read the book when I was an undergraduate; it inspired me to go to law school. They made it into a movie starring Jimmy Stewart and George C. Scott."

Seeing Sam's lack of recognition, Daniels asked, "You don't have any idea who I'm talking about, do you?"

He looked pretty good. "Not really," Sam admitted. "I'm imagining something in black-and-white playing at a drive-in movie theater, and you in the back seat of a two-door, twenty-foot-long Buick with some unsuspecting coed."

"Sam, you're a funny guy. Ever think of stand-up?" Daniels laughed. "But seriously, I think you'd like the book. The protagonist is an ardent fly fisherman."

"I'll take a look," Sam promised. "So, what? Another couple of months?"

"Weeks. I've done some work in the law library. Van Devanter is going to credit some time toward my sentence, I hear." Judge Alec Van Devanter had presided over Daniels' trial due to Bridger's obvious conflict. "Hell, they'll be glad to be rid of my old ass, I think. If nothing else it will save the State the cost of refilling my prescriptions." He offered a tired smile. "So, how is trial prep going?"

"I've got nothing. You think simply playing defense will be enough? Everything they've got is circumstantial."

Daniels sat quietly, considering. "Juries around here take the burden of proof seriously," he said. "I've seen lots of folks acquitted who should've been rung up. But I can't think of any right now where I thought the jury got it wrong when they convicted a guy. Lemme ask you: can you put your client on the stand?"

"No."

"Why not?"

"Because he is a pencil-necked smart aleck. The jury would hate him—hell, I hate him."

"That's no good," Daniels mused. "As I recall, they've got nothing directly tying your client to the drugs or showing that he provided the drugs to that little girl, true?"

"Right."

"But a mountain of circumstantial evidence."

"Right."

"Can you attack the investigation?"

"Not effectively."

"They'll put on the investigators, the medical examiners, and someone from the lab—that about it?"

"I think so. Probably someone from the motel to show he rented the room."

"You've talked with her?"

Sam reflected on the gum-chewing clerk hitting on him. "I probably need to get back to her."

"You should. She might've seen something," Daniels advised. "Anyone else?"

"Everyone else is dead."

"Yeah. To that end, any chance of a plea agreement? You could probably get four to six with a couple of years imposed. Then you wouldn't have to worry about sticking your neck in a noose ethics-wise."

"Not a chance. Gustafson won't do time. Besides, that would blow the deal on the other matter."

"Well, it's always better not to put the defendant on the stand, and given your thoughts on him, you might just have to play a prevent defense on this one."

"Meanwhile, my dumbass client is running around town being a jackass."

"Not a lot you can do," Daniels said. "I'll tell you the same thing I told you when we—you—had the trial with Lucy Beretta: it's not your trial. You tell your client how to act and be done with it. What's he doing?"

"Hanging around the bars, flashing rolls of bills, and maybe dealing."

"Not smart, but if he wants to run around and be a dipstick, so be it. You just be ready to try the case and do the best you can. Use the State's burden against them. Remember, we're not seeking truth; we're seeking justice—an entirely different thing."

Sam rolled his eyes. "I hear Professor Daniels coming."

"Go into this trial and don't forget that while it looks like the State has your client by his neck, as a matter of *fact*, they've got to overcome a huge legal presumption: your client's innocence. Don't let the facts confuse or intimidate you. Do what you can to put some small chinks in the State's factual armor, but don't worry too much about it, because the facts are not the issue." Having finished his lecture, he sat expectantly.

Sam took a deep breath. "I know I'm going to regret this, but what exactly is the issue?"

"Cathy prosecuting?"

"Yeah."

"The issue, then, is whether Cathy can convince twelve ordinary men and women to overlook the gaps in her story. Have you seen the list of jurors?"

"No. Comes out next week."

"That'll be key. You've got to have a couple of hardheads on that jury who will hold the State's feet to the fire. Some of the jurors will want to see your guy fry for the dead girl. You need a couple of strong personalities. One of those right-wing nut jobs or an old, government-hating left-wing hippie would be good," Daniels concluded. "So, what else is going on? You still flirting around with Cathy?"

"Not since her appointment, no."

"You should've moved on her earlier."

"Yeah, well."

"Seeing anyone else?" Daniels asked.

Sam nodded. "I am, actually."

Daniels waited. "Well, how's that going?"

How *was* it going? "Really well, except she's kind of . . . cloying, I guess."

"Like how cloying?"

"Boiling bunnies cloying?"

Daniels laughed briefly, then sobered. "You don't need that."

"I think it comes with the package."

Daniels shook his head. "Then you gotta let her go."

"It's not that bad, really," Sam hedged.

"Need some help? Get an order of protection. Those have a tendency to cool the flames of passion. Even toward a catch like yourself, I'd bet."

"It's not that bad!" Sam protested.

"It will be," Daniels predicted. "Take a look at it; that's what they're for."

"I'll think about it," he promised.

"Think fast. People are crazy."

"Fingers crossed," Sam said. They said their goodbyes and Sam walked down the street to his office, envisioning the perfect jury.

While Sam was seeking Daniels' counsel, Cathy was conducting a roundtable of her team. She was still getting accustomed to being in charge, having quickly determined that trying cases was perhaps the easiest part of her job—human resources, budgeting, public meetings, and training young attorneys was far more challenging. Because her witness list would be brief, she had called in Miller to ensure that as the State's key witness she was well prepared to testify.

While Miller watched impatiently, Cathy rummaged through a stack of files on her desk until she found the one she was looking for. Finally, she looked at Miller. "Detective, we've got the presumption of innocence to overcome. Your testimony will be key."

"I think I've heard that before," Miller said, snapping her omnipresent chewing gum.

Cathy smiled wryly before sobering. "I want to begin by telling you that from everything I've seen, you do good work. I know Buck Lucas is glad to have you."

"Thank you."

"And I'm going to show my cards here. This is a good but not great case."

"I know, but—"

"You've worked hard; you've built the best case you could in the time you had. I just want to review a couple of things with you before trial, like we did before Lucy Beretta's trial."

At the mention of Lucy's name, Miller stiffened. She'd faced a withering cross-examination from Sam Johnstone during that one. "O-Okay."

Cathy saw Miller stiffen. "Remember," she began. "There are only three major rules you need to follow. First rule: listen to the question, then answer the question and shut up." When she saw Miller nod, she continued. "Most witnesses get in trouble either because they lie, they exaggerate, or they can't shut the hell up. So, answer the question and shut up —understand?"

"Yes," Miller said. She'd been through this before.

"Right," Cathy said. "Rule two is the easiest: just tell the truth. Even if you think it will benefit them, even if you think it will blow the case, tell the truth. Do not let Sam catch you in a lie." She leaned forward to emphasize her point. "I can work my way through anything except a lie. A lie—no matter how small—is fatal. You've been in the hot seat before, and you know Sam knows what you are supposed to do, and he'll know what you have and have not done, and what steps you took—or didn't take—during the investigation."

"I remember."

"In this case, he doesn't have a lot—if anything. So, expect him to focus on everything you *haven't* done—steps you didn't take, no matter how far-fetched or unnecessary. He will try and show the jury you missed something. You'll be tempted to try and cover by saying you did something. Just remember he knows the answer to every question he is asking. Don't fudge. If you did it, you did it. If not, own it."

"Understood."

"The third rule is simple, as well: if you don't know, say so. Don't guess, don't speculate, don't exaggerate to look smart or to avoid looking dumb. If you don't know the answer, simply say so. Again, I can sort that out. We can work with that. But if you give it a wild-ass guess, we're stuck with that answer—right or wrong. Understand?"

Miller nodded. "I understand."

"All right, let's do this. I've got a meeting here in a few minutes, but I'm going to bring in Dylan Roberts—he's an experienced prosecutor and a friend of mine who is helping with Grant Lee's case. He and Aiden will go over the questions I'll ask you on direct examination during trial. I want you to know what I'm going to ask. Then they'll ask you some questions we think Sam will ask. I've instructed Dylan to discuss your responses with you and then brief me later. You and I will meet one more time before trial, okay?"

"Okay," Miller agreed.

Cathy called for Roberts and Cates, and when they arrived, she left for her meeting. Roberts then looked to Miller. "Let's get started, shall we?" And for the next hour he observed as Cates walked Miller through her direct examination. Then, just as promised, Roberts conducted a practice cross-examination. At last, he sat back, apparently satisfied. "Detective Miller, you'll do fine. Just remember Cathy's rules."

Miller assured him she would, and when she had departed, Roberts and Cates returned to their respective offices. Cates sent Cathy a message. *I think she'll do fine*, he reported.

Thank you, was all Cathy sent back.

On the Saturday before trial, Sam was in his office reviewing his notes and reflecting on a conversation he had just finished with Gustafson. "Will you agree to do a split?" he had asked. A "split" was a term of a felony sentence —usually a year—to be served in a local jail rather than prison. "I think we could get her to agree."

"Hell no," Gustafson replied. "I told you, I'm not going to do any time. I'm not pleading to anything that has me doing time."

"She's got voters to answer to," Sam explained. "Hayes and his little band aren't gonna be satisfied unless you are in jail."

"They aren't ever going to be satisfied then—are they?"

Sam hoped not. "I can't say," he replied. "But you know what's at stake here and—"

"And you know what's at stake!"

"I'm not the one who could be doing fifty years. The best time to hit up a prosecutor is right before trial—she's been looking at her case, losing sleep, and she now sees all the holes in it."

"Awesome! Then she can drop the charges!"

"She's not going to do that. What she might do is a deal. She might be wobbly, and we should try and hit her up. If we wait until Monday—when the jurors are here—she won't do a deal because it will look like a waste of taxpayer dollars. She'll want to stand firm so she doesn't look weak."

"It is a waste! She can't prove it because I didn't do it."

"Look, I'm certain that if you'll agree to three to five, with a year to serve, she'll do the deal. You do good in jail, we'll petition to bounce you early, and you can get on with your life before next Christmas."

"No."

"Fine. I'll talk with you Monday. And remember: meet me here at eight a.m. Don't be late." When Gustafson had hung up, Sam shrugged. "What the hell," he said. He keyboarded a short message. *My guy says he will do a deal.*

What is it? she replied seconds later.

She was at the office, as well. *He'll plead to felony possession and do a six-month split. Balance suspended. Fines out the wazoo—he's got money.*

No. That isn't going to happen, Sam read. *Rebel Hayes' dad won't buy it.*

He hunted and pecked in response: *You are the county attorney.*

Her answer was brief and to the point. *I know that, but we've got a dead kid here. Hayes and his supporters are calling my office every day.*

Welcome to my world, Sam sent, but he understood. Prosecutors were elected officials. Smart ones knew the value of keeping victims' families happy. *I think you might get a conviction on possession. But you can't directly tie my guy to Rebel's death,* Sam ventured. Careful now. *There is no link between the drugs in his room and the drugs in her system.* If she read between the lines it could reveal his trial strategy, so he took a deep breath and held it before sending the message.

Again, her response was rapid. *Not now that your prior client is dead—conveniently, I might add. But there are lots of folks sitting on death row on the basis of circumstantial evidence.*

She didn't know about the analog issue. *I'm just saying that the connection isn't there,* he replied.

He had the drugs and she died from them. I think a jury will connect the dots, she predicted. *I gotta go. Dylan and I are having a working dinner. Get some rest. You will need it.*

She didn't know. And she didn't know she didn't know. There was a chance. Sam pushed his keyboard aside and took a deep breath, then thought about what she had told him. Dinner?

40

On the fourteenth of November, Sam followed the deputy's instructions and was inside the courthouse a few seconds later. He made his way down the hall to Bridger's courtroom while courthouse security, augmented by contracted off-duty law enforcement, struggled to keep onlookers in line. Sam nodded at Fricke and Frac as he made his way to the courtroom double doors.

At precisely nine a.m., Bridger strode into the courtroom and took his seat at the raised bench. He looked out over the crowd and commanded, "Be seated. District Court for the Twelfth Judicial District is in session, we are on the record. Good morning, ladies and gentlemen!"

"Good morning," the assembled men and women replied unenthusiastically. Many were concerned with not only the time but the money jury service would cost them.

"My name is Walton Bridger. I was appointed sometime back as district judge here in Custer. I grew up on a ranch outside Pinedale, went to the University of Wyoming, and then law school out of state. I spent most of my career in Cheyenne, but my family and I are proud to be a part of the Custer community," he said. His initial jitters had disappeared, and he was warming as he delivered his usual spiel. "Now, most of *you* folks don't act thrilled to be here," he continued. "But jury duty—whether you are selected to serve for this trial or not—fulfills one of the most important obligations one has, and that is to serve as a juror in the trial of one's peer."

He had everyone's attention and took a sip of water before continuing. "This isn't going to be like a movie, or like television—don't expect to be entertained, and don't expect it to be over in an hour. But be ready to be challenged. This is the big leagues of the court system here in Wyoming; cases decided here are complicated and important. In a few minutes, we will start the process of seating a jury. We're going to start by putting twelve jurors in the box. Madam clerk, why don't you go ahead and call the first names?"

Violet Marshall, the county's elected clerk of district court, stood, and with a quaver in her voice, called the twelve names. After the bailiff got them seated, Bridger continued. "Just because you were seated doesn't mean you will be on the jury, and just because you are not seated in the box doesn't mean you are free to go. The process takes time, and at times it can be tedious; but I'm not going to apologize, because this is a tried-and-true method to obtain as even-handed a jury as possible," he concluded, seeing jurors looking around them.

"The case that has been called is the State of Wyoming versus Trent Gustafson. The defendant in this case is the man seated at the defense table wearing the navy-blue suit," Bridger said. Trent flashed a smile at the jurors just as he and Sam had practiced. "Next to him is his attorney, Sam Johnstone," Bridger continued. "Seated at the other table are County Attorney Cathy Schmidt and Mr. Dylan Roberts, who is the county attorney over in Jefferson County. He will be assisting Ms. Schmidt in this matter. They are the lawyers for the State of Wyoming, and they have the burden of convincing those of you eventually chosen for duty that Mr. Gustafson is guilty.

"Mr. Gustafson is charged with felony possession of fentanyl, possession with intent to distribute fentanyl, and drug-induced homicide in the death of Rebel Hayes, a minor. He has entered pleas of not guilty, and as you look at him right now, you are looking at an innocent man. If you are selected, and after jury selection and opening statements, you will hear the testimony and view evidence presented in accordance with Wyoming's rules of procedure and evidence. After you have heard all the evidence, I will instruct you on the law to be applied in this case. You must apply the law I give you to the evidence you heard, and not the law as you wish it was to the evidence you wish you heard. We will talk more about that when the time comes. In the meanwhile, remember: the burden is always on the State's lawyers to show the defendant is guilty beyond a reasonable doubt; he doesn't have to prove a thing.

"Now, let me tell you up front that a reasonable doubt is not a doubt that is fanciful or remotely possible; rather, a reasonable doubt is one that is fair and based on reason and common sense that arises out of some or all of the evidence, or the lack of some evidence, or the sufficiency of the same. Now, some important rules: don't talk about the case with anyone. Don't read or listen to the news or follow the case or discuss it on social media. Don't have or allow contact with any participant or party, or the media, or anyone else who might have an interest in the trial—even about matters having nothing to do with this trial. Okay, that's enough to get started."

Bridger looked over the jury pool to ensure each prospective juror was paying attention. "Now we'll start the formal jury selection process. But first, I'm going to ask some preliminary questions just to make sure everyone is qualified to begin with. Remember: we're not trying to pry into your personal affairs. The sole purpose of my questions is to ensure that we have a fair and qualified jury."

As Bridger spoke, Sam arranged the notes he had on each potential juror. Weeks before trial, Cathy and Sam had been provided with juror questionnaires. Each questionnaire contained biographical information provided by each juror—not only name and address, but occupation, marital status, spouse's name and employment, and the like. Cathy and Sam had each spent considerable time learning each juror's background. As Daniels had once advised Sam, "You hear people talk about profiling as if it is bad. They are full of shit. Knowledge of juror predispositions is crucial to the outcome of any trial; good attorneys conduct lawful and vigorous profiling on each potential juror. You don't want to do that, stay away from trial work." Sam would be looking for people with an ax to grind; Cathy, in turn, would want rule-followers.

After getting a nod from the jurors, Bridger asked the panel several questions dealing with their age, citizenship, general health, criminal history, and the like to establish that each was a qualified juror. When he had completed his questions, he looked to Cathy. "Ms. Schmidt, would the State care to inquire of the panel?"

"We would, Your Honor," Cathy replied. She stood and moved to the podium. She was wearing a charcoal suit with matching heels, making her appear even taller and thinner than usual. Bridger might have tried to differentiate real life from Hollywood, but in Sam's opinion Cathy fit the bill. She quickly introduced herself and the members of her team, then ensured that none of the jurors were well-acquainted with any of the parties. Because Custer was a small town, several of the jurors had heard of the case, and most knew someone on one side or the other. Cathy waded patiently through each situation, ensuring that each juror committed to deciding matters fairly and impartially.

"Can you apply the law as instructed by Judge Bridger even if you personally disagree with the law?"

"Do you agree that Mr. Gustafson is innocent until and unless we as the State show you otherwise?"

"I'm going to propose to you that 'beyond a reasonable doubt' does not mean beyond all doubt. Does anyone have a reaction to that?"

"Can we agree that there might well be some doubt, some possibility that someone else killed the decedent, but that unless the doubt is reasonable, you would have to vote to convict?"

Cathy had done her homework and was a deft, able questioner. Because the rules limited a prosecutor's ability to try the case by posing pointed questions or preconditioning jurors toward a particular verdict, her questions were carefully circumscribed and intended to root out anti-state or anti-police prejudices. Despite the limitations, her questioning took several hours.

As always, some potential jurors were clearly desirous of not being selected and tried to assert they could not be fair. Every judge and experienced attorney had been confronted by similar jurors, and it was quickly determined which were merely inconvenienced and which were truly incapable of being fair and impartial. Most, when put on the spot, expressed they simply didn't want to serve, but would follow and apply the law if selected. Some were afraid to be placed in a position of such responsibility.

A select few held out, insisting they would vote to convict or acquit no matter the evidence, and were dismissed. Finally, just past three p.m., Cathy passed the panel "for cause," meaning she would not seek to dismiss additional jurors for reasons of bias, incompetence, or health.

"Ladies and gentlemen, I think we are all a little tired at this point," Bridger said. "We're going to take a brief recess, and then I'm certain Mr. Johnstone will have some questions for you. But first, please listen to the following." He then spent several minutes repeating his earlier admonitions to jurors to not talk about the case, speculate as to the defendant's guilt, talk to reporters, and the like. When he had finished, he stood.

"All rise!" Marshall commanded. When the judge had departed, the noise level went up immediately.

"Now what?" Gustafson asked over the excited roar.

"Now it's our turn to talk with the panel," Sam explained. "Then we will decide which jurors will remain. I need to take a few minutes to gather my thoughts. Please go with Cassie. We'll talk when I get back."

Sam had been pleasantly surprised with the initial panel. Cathy had managed to bounce a couple potential jurors he favored, but the panel was favorable—for now. He had prepared a long list of questions, but he would "read the room" like a veteran comic and deviate as necessary.

Fortunately, judges usually afforded defense counsel considerable latitude in the questioning of potential jurors. Sam reflected on his pre-trial discussions with Daniels. In discussing this trial, they agreed that for this case, the ideal juror was a male from thirty-five to fifty years old, blue collar, and preferably single or divorced with a minor criminal history. Exceptions would be made for teachers and engineers—engineers because they would take the State's burden seriously, and would rigorously apply the rules of law, and teachers because they habitually sided with defendants. No moms, preachers, coaches, or anyone who had lost a loved one to addiction.

Ultimately, fourteen jurors would be seated. At the end of the trial (assuming all jurors had made it through trial), two would be excused as alternates and the remaining twelve would be the jury to decide the case.

By mandating alternates, Bridger hoped to preclude a mistrial due to something outside his control, such as jurors getting sick or having a family member die.

When Gustafson returned, Sam gestured to him. "Lean in here." When Gustafson did so, Sam whispered, "I want as many men as possible on the jury, but it is important that no matter who I am talking to, you look at them and try to make eye contact. I need to know who you think likes you and who has it in for you."

"Got it."

After Bridger had everyone seated, he looked to Sam. "Does the defense care to inquire of the panel?"

"Yes, Your Honor." Sam walked to the podium, made eye contact with each juror, and introduced himself and Gustafson. As he did so, he noticed that a number of jurors gave only a cursory glance in his client's direction.

Feigning a drink from the water glass he had brought with him, he eyeballed a couple of jurors closely, then placed the glass on the tabletop and asked his first question. "Does anyone here think that if you use or sell drugs you deserve whatever comes your way?"

When no one responded, he continued, "Raise your hand if you think anyone who uses or sells drugs does not deserve a trial—perhaps we can just take them somewhere and dump them over a cliff." When everyone in the panel remained stock-still, he continued, "Well, that's a relief."

A few titters, but nothing more. With a quick look toward Cathy, he asked his next question. "Have any of you ever been in the presence of someone doing something wrong—like using drugs? You, sir." He pointed to a small, middle-aged accountant timidly raising his hand. "Has that happened to you?"

"Many times."

"What did you do?"

"Well, nothing. I was a roadie for a rock and roll band back in the day. They wrote my checks!"

Sam laughed along with everyone else. "So, we can see there is a reason why someone might be in the presence of others using or doing drugs," he said. "And can we all agree that sometimes, people who aren't using or selling drugs can be in the presence of those who are?"

Before anyone could respond, Cathy was on her feet. "Your Honor, bench conference?"

"Of course," Bridger instructed. "Counsel, please approach." Cathy joined Sam at the bench and began to state an objection but was interrupted by Bridger. "Mr. Johnstone, I'll not have this case tried in voir dire."

"I'm only trying to—"

"You know better, Mr. Johnstone. We had this issue during the last trial between the two of you. Get to it, or I'll cut your questioning short."

"Thank you, Your Honor," Sam replied, loud enough for the jury panel to hear. It was an old trick, designed to make the jurors think he'd been validated somehow. For the next hour, he continued probing gently to try and discern which jurors might not be fair to his client. Who had lost a family member to drugs? Who had been the victim of a drug-related crime? Would any juror admit to suffering from addiction? When he had finished, he looked to Bridger and asked if he could have a moment with his client.

"Are there any questions I haven't asked that you think I should have asked?"

"No, Sam," he said. "I can't think of any."

Sam stood and looked at Bridger. "Pass the jury for cause." He'd been able to dump one woman—an older lady who had lost a nephew to drugs and insisted that she wouldn't be able to be fair to Gustafson. Sam was relieved; the judge's decision to dismiss her for cause saved him a peremptory challenge.

"Thank you, Mr. Johnstone," Bridger said. "Ladies and gentlemen, I'm going to excuse all of you while we meet to make final selections. Once again, I caution you, do not discuss the case, don't read any media accounts, and reserve judgment until the conclusion of trial. Bailiff, please escort the panel from the courtroom."

When the potential jurors had departed, the process of jury selection began in earnest. In Bridger's court, each attorney was able to challenge nine potential jurors peremptorily, meaning with no explanation given. This—along with life experience and responses to questionnaires—was where the earlier profiling came to the fore.

Sam had asked Gustafson about the potential jurors before the trial. Now, because his client had been able to watch the men and women who were ultimately selected, Sam asked again, "What do you think? Anyone who needs to go?"

"Doesn't matter," Gustafson replied. "Anyone with half a brain will know I'm innocent."

Years before, he had discovered that a client had come to the realization that he did know a potential juror following voir dire. "Okay, anyone on the panel you know?" Sam asked.

"No."

"In a minute we have to get rid of several of them," Sam explained. "Anyone you feel really good about?"

"The dude in the front row with the motorcycle T-shirt, the gal with the purple hair, and the young guy in the last row."

Sam was pleased. He'd reached the same conclusion. "How about the other way?"

"The two old ladies gotta go, as well as the retired fireman."

Again, Sam agreed with his client. The retired fireman had mentioned the dozens of times he had happened on overdose cases, and the two women had emphasized their disapproval of not only drug dealers but users as well. Cathy would come to the same conclusions as Sam and Gustafson, so the trick would be to keep as many as he could while ridding her of as many jurors as possible who would side with her.

"Who are the alternates?" Gustafson asked at one point.

"Don't know until the end of the trial," Sam said. "There are a lot of ways to do it. Bridger selects the alternates at the end of the trial by random means—that way the alternates don't know and will pay attention, and we as attorneys won't treat them any differently."

After twenty minutes of back-and-forth, the parties had a jury of ten men and four women. "All right," Bridger said. "Let's get the jurors back in here and get them seated."

When the bailiffs had the potential jurors in their seats, Bridger had Violet Marshall call the names of the fourteen men and women selected, then quickly administered oaths to the jury and the bailiff, Fred Ringer. He looked at his watch. "Ladies and gentlemen, that's enough for today. I'm going to let everyone go a little early. We'll get started after we handle some preliminary matters in the morning, so I'm going to have you follow the orders of your bailiff." Looking to Ringer, he continued, "Fred, I'd like to be able to get started at nine, so go ahead and back-plan accordingly. Please conduct the jury to the jury room."

Everyone stood until the jury had departed. With everyone still standing, Bridger looked at Cathy and then Sam. "Anything further we need to discuss?" When each attorney answered in the negative, he nodded approvingly. "Fine," he said. "We will reconvene at nine tomorrow morning."

After speaking with Gustafson—and once again cautioning him to keep quiet—a relatively satisfied Sam returned to his office, did some paperwork, and then, seeing he still had enough time to visit Daniels, did so. Having the retired judge available was reassuring.

"How we lookin'?" Daniels asked as the two sat down.

"Ten bulls, four cows," Sam said, pleased to hear Daniels use the word *we*. "And I think everyone will listen to our side, at least."

"That's promising," Daniels replied. Both men recalled a juror in Sam's first murder trial who openly abhorred Sam and his client. Daniels knew his advice would be ignored but gave it anyway. "Get some rest, Sam. You've done your job; you're ready."

"Thanks, Press. I'll try," Sam promised. "But I wish you were in there with me."

"Me, too," Daniels agreed. He experienced another bout of extended coughing, this one ending with his spitting into the now-omnipresent tissue. "God help me, I love trials."

"That doesn't sound good," Sam observed. "Seen a doc?"

"Go away, Mother."

Despite his concern over Daniels' cough, Sam left the detention center feeling more positive than he had in some time.

41

In his chambers before Tuesday's sunrise, Bridger reviewed a points of law memorandum his law clerk had prepared for him and said a quick prayer of thanks that the case to be tried featured two competent attorneys in Cathy and Sam. Bad lawyering led to more reversals and remands than bad judges ever did. Good lawyers tried clean, well-planned cases that resulted in the judge having little to do with the trial. Evidentiary questions, questions of procedure, and even objections were meticulously planned. Arguments made by good lawyers were characterized by citation to case law and relevant statute. Poor, lazy, or novice lawyers were generally "winging it" and frequently argued, citing "fairness." Whether due to sloth or inexperience, the trial judge was called on frequently to intervene and to rule on innumerable objections and motions that ranged from petty to asinine.

From his perspective, selection of this jury had gone well, and they were starting trial right on his anticipated timeline. Approaching the bench, he recalled his earlier advisals to counsel: avoid middling objections and skip any squabbling over nonmaterial issues.

When all were seated, he addressed the jury. "Welcome back! And now that you are the jury, I am going to give you some instructions to guide you as jurors in this case. Let me begin by telling you that you and I have very different roles in this process. My responsibility is to determine what evidence you can see or hear, and what rules of law apply in this case. Your job is to find from the evidence what the facts are. You alone are the judges of the facts. You will then apply to those facts the law given to you. You must follow that law whether you agree with it or not. And remember, nothing I say or do during the course of the trial is intended to indicate what your verdict should be."

So far, every juror was paying attention. "Now, the evidence from which you will find the facts will come from the testimony of witnesses, the introduction of documents and other things received into the record as exhibits, as well as any facts the lawyers agree or stipulate to, or that I may instruct you to find. Remember that statements, arguments, and questions by lawyer are not evidence. Objections to questions are not evidence. Lawyers have an obligation to their client to make an objection when they believe evidence being offered is or may be improper. You shouldn't be influenced by the objection or by my ruling on it. If it is overruled, you treat the answer just like you would any other. If the objection is sustained, then you don't listen to the question or the response and follow my instructions. Remember as well, you must decide this case solely on the evidence presented here within the four walls of the courtroom. Nothing said or heard outside the courtroom may be considered.

"Most importantly, it will be up to *you* to decide which witnesses to believe, which not to believe, and how much of any witness's testimony to accept or reject. You'll hear from me later regarding techniques for determining the credibility of witnesses. As you all recognize, this is a criminal case. There are three basic rules about a criminal case that you need to understand. First, the defendant is presumed innocent until proven otherwise. Second, the burden of proof is on the government now and always. The defendant never has to prove his innocence or to present any evidence or to testify. Third—and we'll talk more about what this means later—the State must prove Mr. Gustafson's guilt beyond a reasonable doubt."

As Bridger spoke, Sam watched each juror in turn. Each seemed to be following along, especially the little accountant, who was sporting a bowtie this morning. Boredom might set in later, but for now the judge had their collective attention.

"Bear in mind," Bridger continued, "that you must listen to all of the evidence in this matter and the arguments of counsel and my instructions of law before you begin to formulate an opinion regarding the defendant's guilt or innocence. To do otherwise would be an injustice," he concluded, knowing full well that research showed most jurors reached their conclusion long before the trial concluded.

"Now, let's turn to process. Momentarily, the State's attorney will make an opening statement. An opening statement is simply an outline to help you understand the evidence as it comes in. After that, Mr. Johnstone may make an opening statement, or he may reserve to make it at a later time, or he may waive one altogether. Opening statements are neither evidence nor arguments. After the opening statement or statements, Ms. Schmidt will then present the State's witnesses, after which Mr. Johnstone may cross-examine them. Following the State's case, the defense may or may not present witnesses whom the government may then cross-examine. Then, after all the evidence is in, I will instruct you on the law. Finally, after all that, the attorneys will make their closing arguments to summarize and interpret the evidence for you and the case will be given to you for your decision and verdict."

Bridger looked up from his notes. He still had the jury's attention. "Ladies and gentlemen, please listen to counsel as they make their opening statements. Ms. Schmidt?"

Sam watched as Cathy stepped carefully to the podium, arranged a couple pieces of paper in front of her, and took a deep breath. Just as she was taught in a trial advocacy class years prior, she intentionally made eye contact with each member of the jury before she began.

"Good morning, members of the jury. Someone once said that, 'It's all fun and games until somebody gets poked in the eye.' This is a case about drugs. Regarding drugs, it's all fun and games until somebody dies. This case is about death. It's about the death of a young woman at the hands of a drug dealer. That drug dealer," Cathy continued, pointing at Gustafson, "sits before you. His name is Trent Gustafson, and the evidence is going to show that he had in his possession a felony amount of the drug fentanyl, that he intended to and in fact did distribute that drug, and that he made it available to Rebel Hayes—a sweet, free-spirited, seventeen-year-old girl who died as a result."

She waited before continuing, watching as each juror peeked at Gustafson. "Throughout the course of this trial, you are going to hear and see a lot about the science of drugs. But at the end of the day this is a case about people, and two people in particular: Miss Hayes, a seventeen-year-old girl who was just starting her life, and Trent Gustafson, the defendant, a man with few connections to Custer. In fact, you will see evidence and hear testimony that his contacts with Custer existed solely for the purpose of selling drugs to our afflicted men and women." She paused to stare at Gustafson for a moment.

"You will hear evidence from law enforcement officers that in early April, Mr. Gustafson rented a room in a local motel. You will hear testimony that on April tenth, law enforcement were watching him in his room and observed the arrival of Miss Hayes and a man named Clayton Pierce. You will hear that Mr. Gustafson left the motel room some minutes after the arrival of Rebel Hayes and Clayton Pierce, and that law enforcement officers from the county and DCI immediately arrested him on suspicion of possession and distribution of a controlled substance. You will hear that after his arrest, officers searching his room discovered Mr. Pierce in distress, and a deceased young woman. That young woman was Rebel Hayes. You will hear that Clayton Pierce died weeks later from an overdose, as well.

"You will hear that Mr. Gustafson, in the opinion of law enforcement officers, provided the fentanyl that Rebel Hayes ingested just before her death. You will learn that there is forensic evidence showing that there were fentanyl pills in Mr. Gustafson's room, and evidence that the needle in Rebel Hayes' arm was provided by Mr. Gustafson."

Cathy paused to enable jurors to surreptitiously steal another glance at Sam's client. "You will hear testimony from experts at the Wyoming state laboratory that the substance found in the deceased young woman's body was fentanyl. That evidence, combined with the syringe and the fentanyl located in his room, can lead you to one reasonable conclusion only: Mr. Gustafson supplied the fentanyl that resulted in Rebel Hayes' death. A beautiful seventeen-year-old woman, just beginning her life, the daughter of one of our local citizens, died because of Mr. Gustafson's desire to get rich by preying upon the troubled people of this community. At the conclusion of this trial, I will ask you to render a verdict of guilty. I am confident that you will do exactly that," she concluded, and returned to her chair.

"Thank you, Ms. Schmidt," Bridger said. "Mr. Johnstone, is it the defendant's desire to provide an opening statement at this time?"

"It is, Your Honor." Sam moved to the podium, and just as Cathy had, made eye contact with each juror while shuffling some papers. When he was ready, he looked to Bridger and then to Cathy. "My name is Sam Johnstone and I've been an attorney here in town for three years or so. I want to talk a little bit about the case that you are going to hear, of course, but I'm really more interested in talking about your thoughts and actions as jurors."

He was watching the jury closely. A couple of the women—mothers of young children—seemed irritated with his approach already. He would have preferred they not be seated, but they were the lesser of evils, so to speak, so he had struck others. They would bear watching.

"You heard Ms. Schmidt talk about the evidence that you are going to be presented. And I want you to know up front that she will show you what she promised. She will," he repeated. "And you will note that throughout this trial, we will not object to most of the testimony or the exhibits she seeks to introduce for the simple reason that I'm not interested in wasting your time. For the most part, the evidence is what the witnesses will say it is."

Again, he met the eyes of each juror. "Now, if you watch a lot of television, you may find that odd. And I'll tell you straight out that isn't the way they teach it in trial advocacy courses in law school. But this is not television, and this is not a classroom. This is real life, with real people and real freedom at stake. There are rules of discovery, and we have already seen the evidence that's going to be presented and we have a pretty good idea what the witnesses are going to say, so I promise I won't spend my time quibbling about minor points."

He noted a couple of jurors nodding in approval. "The reason I'm not going to do that is because I am confident both as individuals and as a group you will listen, consider what you have heard, and withhold judgment until you have heard *all* of the evidence. Then I know you will make your determination of the facts, and you will apply the law the judge gives you."

He paused for a moment to let that sink in. "And then, ladies and gentlemen, I am confident that you will find yourselves in the same position as I am as I stand here, and that is you will be convinced that the State has failed to prove its case against my client beyond a reasonable doubt."

One of the female jurors had pursed her lips and was looking at her shoes. "As Judge Bridger mentioned, he's going to advise you regarding the law you must apply. I'm not going to get into all of that, except to tell you that you must hold the State to its burden. I've already told you that everything the State will tell you is true. All Trent Gustafson asks is that you apply the law to the evidence—just as the judge will tell you. Because when you do that, you will find the State has failed to prove that my client possessed the drugs, let alone that he intended to distribute them, or that he provided the drugs that killed Rebel Hayes."

Sam took a sip of water. The final part of his statement was key.

"Admit that what they've got is bad," Daniels had counseled. "Then tell 'em it ain't enough. You'll gain credibility with the jury that way, and you'll be set to remind them at closing why you didn't piss and moan along the way."

Sam set the glass down. "I'm not going to tell you there will be *no* evidence that he provided the drugs. I'm not going to tell you that he *couldn't* have provided the drugs. I won't even try and convince you that he *wouldn't* have provided the drugs. What I'm telling you is that at the end of the trial, the State will not have shown beyond a reasonable doubt that Trent Gustafson provided the drugs, because they can't. They can't." He shrugged.

"Listen to the testimony," he continued. "View the exhibits. Then compare that to what in your mind would *prove* my client is guilty beyond a reasonable doubt. The difference between what the State claims evidence is, and what it actually is—that difference, that small difference—is reasonable doubt. The difference between what the State says an exhibit shows and what it actually shows is reasonable doubt. In this case, after all is said and done, you will have reasonable doubt such that you will have to acquit Trent Gustafson of all charges. Ladies and gentlemen, thank you for your attention here today, and thank you very much for participating in this matter."

When Sam had returned to his chair, Bridger nodded approvingly. "Ladies and gentlemen, we're going to take a brief recess. When we return, the State will begin its case."

42

Back in his seat twenty minutes later, Sam took a deep breath as Bridger climbed the steps to the bench. Finally, following months of preparation, thought, effort, and failed negotiations, the State would present its case for the incarceration of Trent Gustafson to twelve local citizens. In the end, the case would come down to Sam's ability to demonstrate and exploit the few gaps in the State's theory, and to convince the jurors that those gaps added up to reasonable doubt.

When he was seated, Bridger looked to Cathy. "Ms. Schmidt, please call the State's first witness."

Cathy moved to the podium. "The State calls Officer Ronald Baker."

Sam leaned forward and wrote, *Difference between what it means and what they say it means equals reasonable doubt* on a yellow legal pad. Gustafson looked at him quizzically, then leaned over and indicated a desire to say something, but Sam quieted his client with a brief glance.

When Baker had been sworn and seated, Cathy began her questioning. "Please state your name for the jury."

"Ronald Baker."

"Mr. Baker, are you employed?" Cathy asked, despite him being in full uniform.

"I am."

"What do you do?"

"I am a patrol officer with the Custer Police Department."

"And how long have you been so employed?"

"A little over three years."

"Are you a post-certified law enforcement officer?"

"I am."

Cathy then led Baker through a brief review of his education and training. "Were you acting in your capacity as a patrol officer on April tenth?"

"Kind of. I'd been detailed to help Detective Miller watch a motel. DCI Agent Polson was there, too."

"Why were you watching the motel?"

"We had been informed the occupant might be selling drugs."

"Was the motel in Custer County?"

"Yes. It was the Horseshoe."

"Did you have a warrant?"

"Detective Miller did."

"Why didn't you just go and knock on the door and arrest the occupant?"

"You'd have to ask Miller."

"Who was the occupant?"

"The defendant, Trent Gustafson, is the one who rented the room."

"Had you ever seen him before?"

"I'm not sure."

"Ultimately, did you make an arrest that night?"

"Well, we actually made two. We arrested the defendant right away, and someone arrested Clayton Pierce, but I think that might've been later. Not sure."

"Who arrested Gustafson?"

"I did."

"Did you obtain identification?"

"I took his wallet out of his pocket, yes."

"And you identified him as—"

"Trenton Gustafson."

"Is the man you identified as Trenton Gustafson here in the courtroom?"

"Yes."

"Can you tell the jury where he is and what he is wearing?"

"He is sitting at the defense table next to Sam Johnstone. He's wearing a gray suit. Brownish hair. The younger guy without readers."

Cathy and everyone else laughed as Sam feigned being offended. By eliciting responses to seemingly innocuous questions, Cathy had established evidence that the events in question occurred on or about the tenth day of April, in Custer County, and that Gustafson was the defendant alleged to have committed the acts. The elements were seemingly obvious, but the process of proving someone guilty was a step-by-step process, and good prosecutors didn't rush through establishing fundamental facts. She would obtain corroborating testimony for these elements from other witnesses, but the remainder of the trial would concern her attempt to prove that Gustafson had knowingly and intentionally possessed fentanyl, that he possessed it with intent to distribute it, and that he had in fact distributed it to Rebel Hayes, who died as a result.

When the laughter died down, Cathy continued. "Did you in fact arrest Mr. Gustafson?"

"I did."

"What were the circumstances?"

"I was positioned at one end of the motel wearing coveralls. Investigator Miller was at the other end—it's one of those old kinds of motels where you drive right up to your door," Baker explained. "Gustafson exited, took one look at her, and headed my way. I closed on him, told him I had a warrant for his arrest."

"Was he arrested without a struggle?"

"Kind of."

"Meaning?"

"He started to run, but I got ahold of him, put him in an arm bar, and placed him against the wall of the motel."

"Then what?"

"I told him he was under arrest and started reading him his rights."

"Did he react?"

"Well..."

"Officer Baker, did he say anything?"

"He told me to kiss his ass—I'm sorry, Your Honor." He looked fearfully in the direction of Bridger, who nodded in acknowledgment.

"Then what?" Cathy asked.

"I cuffed him and put him in the car and went to assist Investigator Miller and DCI Agent Polson."

"And where were they?"

"In the room."

"Did you enter the room?"

"I did when Investigator Miller yelled for me."

"What did she need?"

"My naloxone. It's a, uh, drug to help people who are overdosing."

"Did you give it to her?"

"I did. She tried it on the little girl, but it didn't do any good."

Sam considered objecting regarding Baker's characterization of the decedent, but decided to deal with it on cross. Cathy had been side-eyeing Sam expectantly. "Who was in there, doing what?" she asked.

"Investigator Polson was using naloxone on the male, and Investigator Miller was looking at a female. The male was on a bed, and the female was on the floor on the other side of the bed, near the wall."

"And what happened next?"

"I made a call to dispatch saying we'd need more naloxone, then secured the scene while they worked on the two people."

"And then?"

"Eventually, I took the defendant to jail and had the staff book him, did paperwork, and stuff like that."

Cathy seemed satisfied. "May I have a moment, Your Honor?"

"You may," Bridger replied.

Cathy stepped to the table and conferred with Roberts. "We good?"

"You want to ask straight out if he saw drugs, evidence of drug sales, or evidence Gustafson sold to Rebel?"

She shook her head. "I could, but I know Sam will pound those nails, and I'd really like the jury to hear that a minimum number of times."

"Could take the wind out of his sails," Roberts opined.

"It might, but I think I'll let him bring that up." She looked to Sam. "Tender the witness."

Sam had decided to start out aggressively. "Officer Baker, did you see my client use a controlled substance?"

"N-No, sir."

"Did he appear high on drugs when you arrested him?"

"Not at all."

"Did he have any drugs on him?"

"No."

"How do you know?"

"I searched him on scene, and they searched him again at the jail."

"You didn't see him deal any drugs?"

"No." Baker was looking to Cathy for help.

"And you didn't see him give, convey, sell, or loan any drugs to either Clayton Pierce or Rebel Hayes, did you?"

"No."

"Did you write the affidavit for a search warrant?"

"No."

"So, you're not even sure why you were there?"

"He was suspected of selling drugs."

"To whom?"

"Pardon me?" Baker was again looking to Cathy for help.

"To whom was he selling drugs—allegedly?" Confidential Source No. 1 was Pierce, of course.

"I—I don't know."

Sam smiled at Baker, then at the judge. "Thank you, Your Honor. No more questions." At closing, he would hammer home Baker's inability to provide any evidence of Gustafson's guilt. One down.

Bridger didn't return Sam's smile. "Ms. Schmidt, any redirect?"

"No, sir," she replied tersely.

"Witness may step down," Bridger said, then looked at his watch. Trial judges were professional multi-taskers. "I have another matter to address briefly. Let's take a long lunch today." He again warned the jurors about communication with each other, making up their minds prematurely, and the like. When he left the courtroom, the volume increased.

"I'll meet you in the counsel room," Sam said to Gustafson as he motioned to Cassie. "Go with Cassie and do not—I'm going to say this again, *do not*—talk with anyone on the way."

"Okay, Sam," Gustafson said. "How are we doing?"

Sam ignored him. "Go with Cassie."

Gustafson looked at Sam curiously but did as he was told. "I'll be there in a minute," Sam assured him. When Gustafson was gone, Sam gathered some materials and organized others. As a courtesy, attorneys didn't look at each other's materials, but there was no reason to advertise, either. Cathy was doing the same thing, and each turned toward the space between their tables, almost bumping as they did so.

"Sorry," Sam said.

"No worries," Cathy replied. "I'm calling Punch after lunch, by the way."

"Thank you." Nothing required the State to indicate who was up next, and as an experienced defense attorney, Sam could be presumed to be prepared for all her witnesses. "I appreciate it."

In the counsel room, Sam met briefly with Cassie to make a lunch plan. He then excused her and sat for a moment with Gustafson. Off the little room was a restroom, negating the need to wade through reporters, observers, and others to use a public restroom. "If you need to go, now's the time," he said, and made some notes on his legal pad.

"I'm good," Gustafson said. "I might in a minute, though."

"Fine."

They waited, Sam listening as Gustafson droned on about his accomplishments to date and future plans until Cassie brought their lunch. They ate in silence, Sam writing with one hand and eating with the other. Gustafson was staring at Sam as he wrote on the pad. "Sam, I've told you everything," he said at one point. "I need you to believe in me."

"Give me a minute," Sam said. "I have an idea." He returned to his notes.

Several minutes later, Cassie knocked and opened the door. "It's time."

When she closed the door, Sam looked at Gustafson. "No, I don't need to believe you," he said. "All I have to do is my job. And I will. And when we're done, and if you walk, you will give me what you've got, or—"

Cassie opened the door without knocking. "Sam, Ms. Perry says now!"

"—I will bust your balls."

Cassie's eyes were wide. "Go with her now," Sam directed.

"But I've got to—"

"Missed your chance. Go. Now."

43

As promised, Cathy's first witness that afternoon was Punch. Sam expected straightforward but credible testimony designed to augment Baker's and to foreshadow Miller's, and that was exactly what unfolded. Cathy led the detective through a lengthy recitation of his education, training, and experience, thereby establishing credibility in the jurors' minds. She then had him review his part of the investigation into Gustafson's activities before finally posing questions designed to elicit damaging testimony.

"So, on the date in question you were surveilling his room?"

"Not so much surveilling him as awaiting a good time to arrest him."

"And you were where?"

"In my assigned car, monitoring radio traffic and keeping headquarters apprised of what was going on."

"And the plan was?"

"To grab Gustafson when he emerged from the motel room. We didn't figure he knew Miller, since she's newer, so we had parked an old Buick a couple of rooms down. She would turn the car over occasionally, but we had disabled it so it wouldn't start. Then she'd act like she was on the phone with someone."

"So you thought—"

"He'd either help her or head the other way to the location of his car. Baker was wearing cotton utility clothes, posing as a maintenance worker."

"And what happened?"

Punch then commenced a lengthy explanation of the subsequent events that largely mirrored Baker's, but added his personal observation of drugs in the room, their packaging, along with paraphernalia common to drug sales.

"Do you have an opinion," Cathy began, "based on your observations, training, and experience, whether the amount of fentanyl was consistent with what is normally reserved for personal use?"

"I do."

"What is your opinion?"

This was layperson opinion, which was acceptable under certain circumstances. Sam listened closely.

"I've never seen that much in one place possessed by someone for anything other than sale," he said. "In my experience, that amount was about one hundred to two hundred times what people keep around for personal use."

"So, personal use is generally one or two pills?"

"Objection." Sam stood. "The jury can do the math."

"Overruled," Bridger said. "You may answer."

"Yes," Punch replied.

"Did you observe anything regarding the manner of storage that gave you pause or reason to believe the drugs were for distribution?"

"I did," Punch said, and launched into a long recitation of his training and experience with drug distribution. "For these reasons, I concluded that the defendant was in the business of dealing drugs—fentanyl in particular."

"And the decision was ultimately made to arrest?"

"We'd already made that decision." Punch nodded. "What we saw and found confirmed what we'd been told we'd find."

"Your Honor, a moment?" Cathy asked. When given permission, she consulted briefly with Roberts and then returned to the podium. "No more questions."

Sam was up quickly. He wouldn't get much but would try and act as if he obtained valuable concessions.

"You'd been following and/or investigating my client for some time?"

"Yes."

"Both as a member of the Custer Police Department and as a member of the Wyoming Division of Criminal Investigation?"

"Yes."

"But no decision to arrest was made earlier?"

"That's right."

"Why not?"

"I'm not sure."

"Well, it was because there was insufficient evidence—true?"

"I can't say. Not my decision."

"If it had been your decision, my client would have been arrested a while back—true?"

Cathy was beginning to stand but Punch's reply was out before her objection would do any good.

"Absolutely."

"But someone felt there wasn't enough evidence to arrest?"

"So they say."

"But there's enough now?"

"In my opinion, yeah."

"But no one saw my client give anyone drugs, did they?"

"No," Punch conceded.

"And no one saw my client enter that room with drugs, did they?"

"No."

"And no one saw my client deal any drugs, did they?"

"Not this time," Punch replied.

Sam stood straighter, acting as if he was surprised. "I'm sorry, I've reviewed my client's file—did I miss something? Has he previously been charged with dealing drugs?"

"I'm not sure."

"And you didn't see any direct evidence of a crime, did you?"

"Possession, for sure. I think the drugs in his room with scales and stuff is as good as it gets."

Sam suppressed a smile. He could use that. "But no direct evidence of my client dealing, or dealing to Miss Hayes—true?"

Punch sat quietly. "Not directly, no," he said at last.

"Thank you, Detective. As always, you've been honest and forthright," Sam concluded. "Your witness," he said to Cathy as he returned to his chair. That was as good as it would get. One step at a time.

44

Between witnesses, Sam quickly reviewed the file on the State's medical examiner while studiously ignoring an increasingly uncomfortable Gustafson. When Bridger entered, Sam touched Gustafson's elbow, indicating he should stand.

"Like a damned jack-in-the-box," Gustafson groused.

"Quiet," Sam whispered.

When he was seated, Bridger asked the attorneys about preliminary matters, and when none were voiced, he called for the jury. After the jury members had filed in, he ordered the audience seated and looked to Cathy. "Call the State's next witness."

"Your Honor, the State calls Ronald B. Laws." She turned and faced the rear of the courtroom, causing most observers to turn their heads as well. Court security opened the double doors and a diminutive, frail man entered the courtroom and walked to the bench, stopping in front of Bridger to raise his hand. When the oath had been administered, he seated himself in the witness box and peered through thick glasses at those assembled before finally nodding in Cathy's direction expectantly.

Sam noted that Dr. Laws' lenses were visibly thicker than he had previously observed. "Too bad he's not an eyewitness," he mumbled.

"What's that?" Gustafson asked eagerly.

"Nothing," Sam replied. "Just talking to myself."

Cathy again started slow, for the benefit of both the jury and the witness. "Would you state your name, please, and spell your last name for the record," she requested.

"Ronald B. Laws, M.D. That's L-A-W-S."

"And where do you live, Dr. Laws?"

"I'm assuming you do not want an address?" he asked.

Cathy reddened slightly. He might be losing his vision, but he was as prickly as ever. "City and state will be fine," she said. She then obtained testimony regarding the doctor's background, education, and experience sufficient to have a basis for the more substantive questions she had.

"So, you work with the Custer County Hospital, and you are also the contracted Custer County Medical Examiner?"

"All true."

"What is a medical examiner?"

"In a smaller community, the medical examiner is the physician assigned to the coroner's office part-time. Somewhere like Denver—or even Fort Collins—the medical examiner is a full-time position. The medical examiner heads the office in charge of investigating non-natural deaths—the accidents, suicides, and homicides that take place in a community—and sudden, unexpected deaths, which are deaths where no doctor was in attendance to sign a death certificate. I investigate those cases."

"What is a coroner? We hear that term a lot."

"The coroner is an elected position and does not have to be a licensed physician," Laws replied. "The coroner is responsible for all the things the medical examiner actually does, plus management and administration of the office, answering to the public, and the like."

"You mentioned you perform investigations," Cathy began. "As part of your investigation, do you perform autopsies?"

"Not all the time," Laws said. "But . . . routinely, yes."

"How many autopsies have you performed?" she asked.

"Oh, I would say perhaps one hundred fifty or more," he replied. Laws had a habit of examining his nails. He was looking at them now.

"Have you ever conducted an investigation where the suspected cause of death was a drug overdose?"

"Oh yes."

"Any idea how many times?"

"I would guess dozens."

"And did any of those suspected deaths involve the drug fentanyl?"

"Several. Sadly, it is becoming more common among . . . some people."

Sam made a note to follow up on that.

Cathy now had the background she needed to establish him as an expert in the minds of the jury, and the foundation necessary to begin asking questions specific to this case.

"I want to go back to last April," Cathy continued. "Did you participate in an investigation into the cause of death of Rebel Hayes?"

"Well, *I* conducted one, yes."

Sam suppressed a smile. The doctor's ego was immense.

"Let's talk about *your* investigation, shall we?" she asked, flashing a brief smile. "How did that commence?"

Laws provided a lengthy explanation of his arrival at the crime scene—which he later determined to be the death scene—and his activities there. "My initial impression, then, was that the deceased had died from an overdose," he concluded.

"Did you perform an autopsy on the decedent?" Cathy asked.

"I did," Laws replied.

"And when did you do that?"

"I performed the autopsy on the twelfth day of April."

"Can you tell the jury, in general terms, how an autopsy is conducted?" Cathy walked to the prosecutor's table and got a drink of water while the doctor embarked on what she knew would be a lengthy explanation of the procedure he generally followed. Back at the podium, she asked enough questions to avoid an objection by Sam based on Dr. Laws answering in the form of a narrative. In so doing, she was building the doctor's credibility in the jury's eyes in preparation for his conclusion. When Laws finally took a breath, Cathy posed a more specific question. "Is that the procedure you followed during the autopsy of Rebel Hayes?"

"It is."

"You testified a few moments ago that you are familiar with death by overdose?"

"I did. I am. Death by intoxication is a not-infrequent manner of death for young people, unfortunately."

"You personally went to the location of the decedent's body?"

"Of course."

"And you assumed jurisdiction?"

"Yes."

"And ordered an autopsy?"

"I did. My observations of the decedent—bleeding from the mouth and nose, froth in her mouth, the needle in her arm, a room replete with syringes and crushed powders—was sufficient to convince me that intoxication was a possible cause of death. Per the National Association of Medical Examiners, an autopsy is proper in that type of situation."

"And what next?"

"Well, not next exactly, but before, during, and after, we continue to investigate by looking at things like prescription histories, ensuring we differentiate between medicines on scene for legitimate medical reasons, evidence of illicit drug use, etc."

"And based on your findings, did you order a toxicological examination?"

"Of course. As I stated earlier, my initial observations included evidence of illicit drug use, needle marks, the syringe in the arm, and the bleeding and frothing."

"And did you receive a report from the toxicologist?"

"I did."

"And did the contents comport with your expectations?"

"They did."

"And as a result, did you complete the portions of the death certificate dealing with cause of death, manner of death, and how the injury occurred?"

"I did."

Cathy nodded, then turned to Bridger. "Your Honor, may I approach the witness?"

"You may."

Cathy crossed the well to the witness stand and handed Dr. Laws a single sheet of paper. "Doctor, I'm handing you what has been previously marked as State's Exhibit 14. Please take a moment to review it and let me know when you are ready to answer some questions about it." When Dr. Laws almost immediately nodded, she continued. "What is that?"

"It's a death certificate."

"Did you prepare it?"

"Most of it, yes. I didn't complete the administrative blocks at the top; as you can see, the elected county coroner signed it."

"So, what we might refer to as the substantive portions were completed by you?"

"Yes."

"And you found a cause of death?"

"Yes."

"In your opinion, what was the cause of death?"

"Fentanyl intoxication."

"And the manner of death?"

Sam held his breath. This was key to his defense. If the doctor merely recited what he had put on the death certificate, Sam would have something to work with, but if she elicited an explanation, it could lessen the anticipated impact of Sam's cross-examination.

"Undetermined."

Sam held his breath.

"And how did the fatal injury occur?"

"Illicit drug injection."

"Thank you, Doctor," Cathy said. "No more questions."

Bridger looked at his watch. "Ladies and gentlemen, I think now would be a good time for our afternoon recess. Let's reconvene in fifteen minutes." He then—again—instructed the jury not to talk about the case with anyone and to avoid reaching any conclusions. When the jury was out of earshot, he excused the participants, and left the bench.

Fifteen minutes later, Bridger took the bench and called for the jury. When they were seated, he looked to Sam. "Mr. Johnstone, I expect you have some questions?"

"Just a few." He stepped to the podium and began immediately. "So, Doctor, while you went to the scene, you don't have any first-hand knowledge regarding who, if anyone, gave Rebel Hayes the drugs, do you?" Sam had cross-examined Laws previously. The man was both arrogant and irascible, which made things easy. He simply had to ask a question that could be seen as questioning the doctor's integrity or competence, and he would flare like a gas well. The question had its intended effect.

"Of course not. That's not my job," Laws snapped.

"And you don't know anything about how drugs came to be in that room, what they were doing there, or the like—true?"

"I am not an investigator of that sort."

"I'll take that as a no," Sam said. "You don't know who had the fentanyl in that motel room, do you?"

"Well, I know that young lady used some."

"But you don't know her source, do you?"

"Of course not."

"And you don't know who gave it to her?"

"I just said I don't."

"And you don't know whether she bought it, borrowed it, was gifted it, or anything else about the circumstances of her obtaining it, do you?"

Laws now had his hands clenched in front of himself. "I do not," he said tightly.

"So, you don't have any idea what *my* client's involvement with the drugs was, do you?"

Cathy was on her feet. "Your Honor, I'm going to object as asked and answered. My client has already explained he is not an investigator."

"Mr. Johnstone?"

"I'm just trying to establish the limits and utility—if any—of this witness's testimony, sir."

"Then I think you've done that," Bridger said. "Objection sustained. Move along."

"Thank you," Sam said, and bowed slightly, as if he had been granted a favor. Then he returned his attention to Laws. "Let's turn to your particular area of expertise, then, Doctor. You ordered the toxicology reports?"

"I did."

"And the toxicologist performed their tests using samples that you provided?"

"Yes."

"Who drew the samples?"

"I did."

"From what part or parts of the body?"

"From the right femoral artery."

Sam stood as if perplexed, then shuffled some papers. "You are familiar, of course, with the National Association of Medical Examiners—you've already referenced them."

"I am. In fact, I am in the process of applying for fellowship."

"Congratulations," Sam said. "So, you must be familiar with the position papers they produce."

Laws could smell a trap. "In my areas of emphasis, yes . . . to a degree."

Sam smiled tolerantly as the jury's attention shifted to him. "Are you familiar with NAME's position paper on the investigation, diagnosis, and certification of deaths resulting from drugs?"

"I am," Laws sniffed. "You must know the writers footnoted an article I authored some time back."

"I do," Sam replied. "So, as a prospective fellow for this esteemed organization, what purpose do position papers serve?"

"They provide best practices in selected areas."

"So, recommended actions to take?"

"Yes. Strongly recommended, in fact," Laws said, smiling toward the jury.

"But the membership is free to disregard?"

Laws stared hard at Sam. "That would, of course, be inadvisable. Best practices represent the best medical advice available."

Sam put a finger to his lips as if deep in thought. "So, I guess my question is, why then in this case didn't you draw blood from the femoral artery in the manner recommended?"

Technically, the question lacked foundation and assumed facts not in evidence, but if Cathy objected, Sam would break it down into bite-sized pieces and feed it to Dr. Laws while the jury watched. Laws was on his heels. "Exactly what do you mean?" he asked carefully.

"Can you explain how exactly you drew the samples of blood?"

"By percutaneous puncture."

"You stuck a needle in her femoral artery about here?" Sam asked. He indicated a spot between his upper thigh and abdomen.

"There's a little more to it than that," Laws replied.

"Well, I've been doing some reading and I'm made to understand that how one draws blood can result in differences in everything from the presence of drugs to their concentration. Do you agree?"

Laws was watching Sam closely. Sam's mention of reading had him on high alert. "I do."

"Now, back to your procedure: during the autopsy, you drew blood from the femoral artery?"

"I did."

"Did you massage the leg first?"

"Of course not," Laws answered dismissively. "That can adversely impact the sample."

"Did you clamp the vein prior to sampling in order to preclude the drawing down of blood from the inguinal vein?"

"I don't believe it is necessary," Laws answered.

"Is it best practice?"

"Perhaps," Laws allowed. "But in my experience—"

It was time. "Did you draw samples from both the left and right femoral veins?"

"Again, I did not."

Perfect. "That *is* best practice, is it not?"

"Well, it is, but in my experience—"

"So, you'll admit you didn't comply with best practices in obtaining the blood samples?" Sam asked. He was watching the jury. They were paying attention. The accountant was enraptured.

"Look, it's not like I used jugular vein blood or something—"

"A simple yes or no will suffice," Sam interrupted.

"I admit."

"So, fair to say you varied from best practices in at least two respects . . . so far?"

Laws unclasped his hands and placed them on the dais in front of him, then shook his head in exasperation. "As a physician, I always have the discretion to vary from the norm. That's the art."

Sam nodded as if in agreement. "So, as a physician you did what you thought was best?"

Laws nodded vigorously. "Medically appropriate, yes."

"But contrary to best practices," Sam stated, then stared at Laws without saying anything. The ploy failed.

"Is there a question?" Laws asked.

"Oh, yes. Several, in fact," Sam said quickly. "You also violated best practices when you assigned 'undetermined' as the manner of death, rather than 'accident'—didn't you?"

Laws nearly leapt to his feet. "I certainly did not!"

"Isn't it best practice to attribute an overdose—in the absence of evidence to the contrary—to an 'accident?'"

"Well, that's the recommendation, yes," Laws admitted. "But I wasn't so sure here."

"Meaning?"

"The manner of death could be accidental or . . . otherwise."

"So, you don't think it was an accident?"

"No, it's correct to say I don't *know* her death to be the result of an accidental overdose."

"Isn't it true that NAME's position paper specifically holds that medical examiners should reserve 'undetermined' for cases where evidence supports more than one possible determination—isn't that true?"

"I'm not familiar with the contents of every paper on every subject. How could I be?"

"You testified you were familiar with this one, Doctor. In fact, I recall you telling the jury you were footnoted in it. If you looked at the paper, would that refresh your memory?"

"It might, but—"

"Well here, take a look," Sam said. "I've got it right here."

A witness's memory couldn't be refreshed in this way, and Cathy was right to object. "Objection!"

"Sustained," Bridger intoned. "The witness will return the document to counsel; counsel will return to the podium."

Sam was back at the podium a moment later and looked to Bridger for the go-ahead. When he got the nod, he continued, "I'm going to represent to you that the best practice is to use 'undetermined' only when there is reason to believe there are one or more possibilities. Do you accept that?"

"That is my general recollection, yes."

"Then what are the possibilities aside from accident?"

"Medically speaking?"

"Of course," Sam said. "Medically speaking."

"Suicide, for one. Accident, of course. And then the intentional administration of drugs by another—"

"Murder?"

"Objection," Cathy said. "Witness is not qualified to answer."

"I'll sustain it," Bridger said.

"You're saying the manner of death could result from another person administering the drugs?"

"Yes."

Sam again tapped his lips with a finger as if in thought. "So, you are saying that there was evidence of something other than an accident, are you not?"

Laws faced a conundrum: he could admit he perceived more than one possible manner of death, thereby playing into Sam's hands, or he could say that he merely made a clerical entry, which would support the effort to convict Sam's client but would make him appear like a functionary. While he was thinking it through, Sam pounced. "You believe there is more than one determination as to the manner of death that is possible, don't you?"

"Well, anything is possible," Laws replied, thankful for a painless way out.

"The manner of death might have been an accident; it might have been something else?" Sam said, smiling widely.

"Yes. Or something else."

"And your determination of the manner of death is made on the basis of your medical opinion?"

"Yes."

"To a reasonable degree of medical certainty?"

"Yes."

"So, it is fair to conclude, isn't it, that you cannot say with a reasonable degree of medical certainty the manner of the decedent's death, can you?" Sam concluded. He stood and watched the doctor come to the realization that he had been trapped.

"Well, no. That's not what I'm—"

"And you don't have any first-hand knowledge of the location, use, or intent of the drugs, do you?"

"Asked and answered," Cathy said.

"Sustained," Bridger ruled.

"So, you don't know the manner of death, nor do you know who was involved?"

Cathy was red-faced. "Same objection."

Bridger was flushed, as well. "Sustained. Mr. Johnstone, move along."

Sam was watching Laws, who was clenching and unclenching his fists. "Certainly, Your Honor," Sam said. "Doctor, in Block 7 of the death certificate you listed the presence of several drugs in Rebel's system at the time of her death, didn't you?"

"I did."

"Your Honor, may we approach?" Cathy asked.

"Certainly," Bridger replied. When Sam and Cathy were before him, he looked to her. "What is it?"

"He's improperly impugning the decedent's character," she said.

Bridger looked to Sam. "Counsel?"

"I'm merely questioning his entries on a document already placed in evidence by the State, sir."

Bridger stared at Sam. Neither he nor Cathy had discerned Sam's strategy as of yet. "Overruled, but be careful, Mr. Johnstone. I'll not have it."

Sam returned to the podium and began again when Bridger nodded his readiness. "There were a fair number of drugs in her system, true?"

"Yes."

"I renew my objection. He's impugning her character!" Cathy said, pointing to Sam.

"Not true," Sam countered. "The drugs are listed in her system as contributing to the cause of death. I didn't fill in the blanks—he did. I'm just asking why and—"

"But in so doing—"

"It's collateral!"

The gallery gasped at Sam's raised voice. "Enough!" Bridger boomed. "Overruled. Counsel will cease and desist this bickering immediately!"

Sam bowed slightly toward Bridger. "My apologies, Your Honor." Turning to Laws, he continued, "Do you remember the question?"

Laws had figured it out. "I did list them, yes."

"Tetrahydrocannabinol?"

"Yes."

"That's the active ingredient in marijuana, true?"

"True."

"Cocaine?"

"Yes."

"Methamphetamine?"

"Yes."

"Heroin?"

"Yes."

"You listed these drugs as the cause of death, or as contributing to the cause of death—true?"

There it was. Laws took a deep breath, then attempted to equivocate. "In a technical sense, yes."

Sam smiled indulgently. "So, technically speaking, all of the drugs listed were the cause of—or at least a contributing factor in—Rebel Hayes' death?"

"Well, yes," Laws replied.

Cathy now shared Laws' pallor. "Objection. Misstates the testimony," she argued without conviction.

"Overruled," Bridger said.

With a couple more questions Sam could humiliate the doctor and hammer home the point for the jurors, but a quick scan of their faces convinced him they'd understood. Asking more questions of Laws would be gratuitous. He looked to the little accountant and saw approval. "No more questions, Your Honor," he said. "Tender the witness."

Cathy had already gotten to her feet. "You aren't saying Rebel Hayes didn't die of an overdose?"

"Oh, she certainly did."

"And the cause of that overdose?"

"Fentanyl ingestion."

Cathy nodded as if satisfied, then sat as if she had removed all doubt. It was the best she could do.

Sam considered his options. One more question and he could establish irrefutably that the State couldn't prove that fentanyl alone had killed Rebel—if Laws didn't quibble. On the other hand, if Laws decided to parse the phraseology of his question, he could confuse the issue or take everyone down a rathole that might lessen the impact of the doctor's concessions to this point. It was better to take his argument to the judge alone on a motion for a directed verdict on the drug-induced homicide count. He made eye contact with the judge and shook his head imperceptibly.

Bridger got the signal. "You may step down," he said to Laws. When Laws had cleared the well, Bridger looked around the courtroom. "This appears to be a good time for our evening recess." Turning to the jurors, he again repeated his admonitions before turning them over to the bailiff.

———

"You kicked his ass!" Gustafson said to Sam as soon as the door to the attorney-client conference room closed behind them.

"Settle down," Sam replied. "Long way to go."

"But we're doin' good, right?"

Clients needed encouragement, but their expectations needed to be managed, as well. "We're doing well, yeah. I think we've got the drug-induced homicide claim kicked as a matter of law."

"Then we're winning!"

"Still looking at twenty-seven years."

"For possession?"

"And intent to distribute," Sam reminded him. "But it was a good day."
No reason to get his client wrapped around the axle. Yet. Besides, if
Gustafson was going to come across with the information he'd agreed to
provide, he'd need to be in a good frame of mind.

"Awesome!" Gustafson said, holding a hand aloft in anticipation of Sam
giving him a high-five.

Sam looked away. "It's only one of three counts. But for certain," he
continued, "you'll be in a better position to negotiate if the judge buys my
argument. Most drug offenders don't do significant time for possession,
even with intent, and even if the jury convicts. Cathy Schmidt knows that.
So now might be a good time to plea bargain."

Gustafson looked at Sam suspiciously. "Like what?"

"I think she might accept a plea to possession with minimal jail time.
She's gonna want something. In return she'd drop the intent to distribute.
You might even walk away on probation and be done with it."

"No way, man," Gustafson replied quickly. He shook his head vigorously. "I'd be like a felon and shit."

Sam shrugged. "A free one in short order, in all likelihood—but yeah."

"I ain't agreeing to that."

"Listen up for a second," Sam said. "You get convicted and Bridger
could ring your bell. I mean, it's not common for a guy to go to prison for
possession, but there's a dead girl—"

"I thought we got rid of that one?"

"Technically, yeah. But the judge can't un-know what he knows—and
that's a dead girl on the carpet of your room at a no-tell motel and a
grieving father and his posse in the courtroom every day."

"What about a deferral?"

A deferral resulted when a defendant pleaded guilty but the entry of the
finding of guilt was deferred and the defendant was placed on probation. If
the defendant successfully completed probation, the charge was dismissed.
"Not a chance," Sam replied. "A girl died. Cathy won't offer that up."

Gustafson sat back and tried to look assured. "I'm not talking if I'm not
walking."

"How long did it take you to come up with that line?" Sam sneered. When Gustafson didn't respond, he continued, "Even if you do limited time?"

"Even if." Gustafson nodded self-righteously, sensing an advantage. "So you better be good and get me acquitted on these other charges if you want your boy Ronnie to smell fresh air again."

Sam stood, opened the door, and motioned to Cassie, who had been waiting outside. "Get him to his car, please," he instructed. When they had departed, he sat down and closed his eyes.

Moments later, he made his way into the crowded hallway and was immediately accosted by Penrose. "Sam, what's your assessment of your client's chances to this point?" she asked.

"I think the State is doing the best it can, but I think we've pointed out the holes in its case," Sam replied.

"Will your client testify?"

Sam smiled. "I can only say that for now, we are keeping all options on the table."

"Court records show only a couple of possible witnesses. What's your strategy?"

"I can call witnesses subpoenaed and listed by the State," Sam pointed out. "We have the ability to get the evidence we need for acquittal on the record."

"Your strategy?"

"Get the facts and the law in front of the jury. Trust the process."

"That's it?"

"That's all anyone can do." Sam stepped around Penrose and almost blundered into Cathy. "I'm sorry!" he said.

She grinned. "No sweat." She looked left and right. "Got a minute? I'd like to see you downstairs," she whispered.

Sam looked at his watch. He was hungry and tired, but this had to be done. Maybe he could get a hotdog on his way home. When they had made their way to the basement, Cathy preceded Sam through the locked door. "Come on back," she said. He followed her, trying not to see her as a woman. "Sit," she directed.

Sam recalled prior sessions with her and awaited the expected offer. He considered telling her what Gustafson had said. Better to wait.

"I'm sure you know why you're here. I'm—"

"Gonna jump my bones?"

It was a lame attempt at humor, and she didn't try and make it better than it was. "Hardly. I've got an offer for your man. He pleads to felony possession, and we argue the sentence. I'll move to dismiss drug-induced homicide and possession with intent to distribute, and I'll cap my argument at five years imposed."

No way the judge was going to impose five years, and they both knew it. But this would allow her to save face. It was a decent offer, but his client wouldn't do the deal. "My client won't accept that," Sam replied. When Cathy raised her eyebrows, he continued. "He's convinced he is going to walk."

"He's an idiot."

"I don't deny that."

She nodded quickly. "Talk to him. This is best and final, Sam. I don't have the time or the interest in screwing around. Get it to your client." She stood to her full height, glaring down at Sam.

"Sit," he requested, pointing to her chair. When she had done so, he looked at her for a moment, deciding. "There's more to the story."

"Yeah?"

"Yeah. He says he has information on Ronnie's case." He was watching her closely.

"What's he got?" she asked, then listened closely while Sam explained. "Ronnie did the deed," she said when Sam was finished. "I was there when he coughed up his confession."

"I know, but Gustafson says that he has information—information he will only provide if he walks," Sam explained. Seeing the arched eyebrows, he continued. "I don't know whether he's got the goods or not. But I can't afford to take the chance. How about probation only?"

She chewed her lip. "I can't do it, Sam. I can't in good conscience put your client back out on the street on the basis of something he *might* know and *might* say. This crowd"—she indicated the noise made by Hayes and his supporters outside—"would have my head on a stick."

"Cathy, I need to know if what Gustafson has is good. Paul and Jeannie deserve that," he said. An appeal to a parent on behalf of parents. "If he knows anything, he'll testify to it."

"How do you know?"

"Because if he doesn't, he's a dead man."

"I'll pretend I didn't hear that." She stood and walked to Sam, herding him to the door. "Go and talk with your client. And remember, Counsel: best and final."

45

After meeting with Cathy, Sam had texted Gustafson and ordered him to be in place early Wednesday to discuss the offer. Entering the courthouse, Sam took a deep breath to compose himself and hustled to the small conference room, where Cassie and Gustafson waited. "We've got an offer," he said.

"What's that?" Gustafson asked. "And where you been?"

"Remember I was telling you about a possible deal?" Sam asked hopefully. "Well—"

"I'm not doing a deal. I told you, no walk, no talk!"

"I am bound by the code of ethics to communicate the terms to you," Sam explained. "I need you to listen."

"No."

"The State is offering—"

He looked at his phone like a sulking teen. "I don't care."

"Trent, I have an obligation to bring the offer to you. I don't have a choice," Sam explained. "And if you don't put that damned phone down, I'm going to shove it up—"

"Sam," Cassie said quietly.

"So tell me," Gustafson said, setting his phone on the table and folding his slender arms.

"You plead to possession, and they drop the other counts."

"And?"

"We argue sentence." Sam shrugged. "They cap their ask at—"

Gustafson snorted. "You must think I have shit for brains, dude."

Sam exchanged a look with Cassie, who was shaking her head. "That's the offer, and I think it might be the best and final from her end," Sam said.

"I'm not agreeing to that," Gustafson said. "Sounds like you either win this outright or your boy is going to sit forever."

The little weasel. "How about we look at it as the opening in a negotiation?" Sam suggested. "I think if we counter with a demand they agree to probation only, she might take it. You've got no record; you'll likely get a short stint if any."

Now Gustafson was on his feet. "You haven't been listening, have you? I don't want to do time. I can't do time!"

Maybe he should have thought of that before he started dealing drugs. "I hear you, but you've gotta understand—"

"But nothing! What don't *you* understand?"

Sam was getting hot—as angry as he'd been with anyone since he was counseling Lucy Beretta in this very room some time back. "Fine, you don't want me to counter? I won't counter. But I don't want to hear squat from you when you're doing a quarter, okay?"

"Nobody's gonna give me twenty-five years for possession, Counselor," Gustafson said. "I've been doing some reading. Don't try and blow smoke up my ass."

"You seem pretty sure for a guy reading online articles," Sam observed. "That kind of legal advice is worth what you're paying for it."

Gustafson started to reach for his phone.

"Don't!" Sam ordered. When his client had withdrawn his hand and was sulking anew, Sam explained, "This is not a standing offer. You've got one shot at this. You walk away and you are putting your future in the hands of twelve ordinary citizens."

"No, Sam. I'm putting Ronnie's future in *your* hands. You signed up for this, and that's why I'm paying you the big bucks. It's your job to convince them I'm innocent!"

"But you're not," Sam replied quietly. "In fact, we both know you're guilty as hell and you are directly responsible for that girl's death."

Gustafson's smile didn't reach his eyes. "She made a choice."

"She was seventeen!"

"Old enough."

Cassie pointed at the clock. "Sam, it's time."

Sam continued to stare at his client. This was for Paul and Jeannie. "When and if you walk, you better have the goods."

"Don't threaten me, Sam. I'm not afraid of you."

Sam was watching the skin twitch under Gustafson's eye. "Then you're not as smart as you think you are."

"Sam, it's time," Cassie insisted.

"Let's go," Sam instructed.

With Sam leading the way, they made their way through the small crowd of spectators to the courtroom. Wrangler Hayes and his supporters yielded the way only when Sam stopped to face them. "Mr. Hayes, let us pass."

"This time," Hayes said, and motioned for his followers to allow Sam, Cassie, and Gustafson through to the courtroom. "But there's gonna come a time."

―――――――――

With Gustafson next to him at the defense's desk, Sam scribbled a note to Cathy and placed it face down on her chair. When she and Roberts entered the courtroom and were taking their seats, Cathy saw the note and picked it up. Sam could see her stiffen as she read it. She handed it to Roberts, never looking at Sam.

Gustafson had been watching Cathy. "You were right, Sam. I think that's it," he said. "She's pissed. You don't get me acquitted and Ronnie is going to grow old in a cage, man."

Sam was about to reply when Bridger entered the courtroom. When he and the jury were in place, he called the court to order. "Ms. Schmidt, please call your next witness," Bridger instructed. For the next several hours, Cathy called a series of minor fact witnesses, each of whom testified in detail to their role in the process of twenty-first-century crime scene investigation. Sam could do little to slow the State's momentum—these were the inevitable, harmful facts to which Daniels had alluded. He asked few questions when presented the opportunity to cross-examine each witness, looking instead to the piece of paper upon which he had penned, *Remember what's important.*

For his part, the façade of arrogance and assurance Gustafson had displayed in the conference room was fading fast. "What the hell are you doing?" he hissed when Sam passed on the opportunity to cross-examine a crime scene technician regarding the chain-of-custody for some evidence.

"My job," Sam replied without moving his lips. "Now sit there quietly and smile like it doesn't mean anything, just like I told you."

"But it does!"

"Of course it does," Sam agreed. "If it didn't, she wouldn't put the evidence on."

"Then ask them questions!"

Sam side-eyed his client. "Sit there and shut up. You know how to deal drugs; I know how to try cases."

Gustafson nodded, grabbed a pen and paper, and scrawled, *It's your boy's ass!*

Sam took the paper and—knowing Gustafson was watching—drew a line through the word "boy's" and passed it back to him.

46

Following the afternoon recess, after Bridger recalled the jury, a tense and drawn Cathy stepped to the podium. "Your Honor, the State calls Marcus Leland."

Leland, Sam knew, was a forensic toxicologist. Sam suspected that she knew the gaps in her case as well as he did, so he expected she would ask a few questions to bolster Laws' testimony that Rebel succumbed to a drug overdose. After obtaining information on Leland's education and training, and after having him describe relevant procedural background in this case, she moved to the heart of the matter.

"What is forensic toxicology?"

"Broadly, forensic toxicology is analysis of biological samples to determine if there are any street drugs, prescription drugs, alcohol, or poisons present."

"And in connection with a case like this, what is your deliverable?" Cathy asked.

"Generally, a report detailing what is present and—to some degree—what is not present in the blood and/or urine of the subject."

Cathy was watching the jury to ensure they were following. Sam's questions to Laws had her concerned that the jury might be sniffing along the wrong path. "Did you test the decedent's blood for drugs and alcohol?"

"I did."

"And what did you conclude?"

"She had a variety of drugs and trace amounts of alcohol in her system at the time of her death."

"What did you do with your report?"

"I provided it to Dr. Laws, and to the detective—Miller, I think?" Leland said.

Cathy quickly elicited a comprehensive listing of the drugs in Rebel's system, focusing Leland on the presence, chemical composition, and probable effects of the drugs discovered in her system and their concentrations. "Looking at the drugs and alcohol—and discounting for the moment the presence of fentanyl—were any present in a concentration such that overdose was possible?"

"Not in my opinion," Leland said. "But I'm just a toxicologist."

"But you've seen many cases where the decedent fatally overdosed, true?"

"Yes, and in those cases the levels of drugs aside from fentanyl were generally much, much higher than what we found in the decedent's blood," Leland said.

Cathy nodded. Good enough. "No more questions, Judge. Tender the witness."

Bridger looked at Sam. "Questions from the defense?"

"A few." Sam had the report in his hand and made a point of underlining and highlighting several spots on the first page.

Bridger was getting impatient while watching Sam's obvious ploy. "Mr. Johnstone, do you need a minute?"

"No, Your Honor," Sam said. "We're ready." He stepped to the lectern and looked steadily at the witness, measuring him. "So your testimony was that, generally, your report—the deliverable the State spoke of—will outline what is and is not contained in the decedent's blood and urine. Is that right?"

"Yes."

"You are familiar with the report the State has labeled State's Exhibit 43?"

"Of course," Leland said. "I prepared it." He had been questioned by

Sam in previous trials, and Sam noted the witness already had his arms crossed in a defensive posture.

Sam looked from the report to the jury. "Then you'll be able to answer some questions about it, won't you?"

"I will," Leland answered. Perhaps sensing his response had been impudent, he broke eye contact with Sam and looked to Cathy, who was taking notes.

"In preparing this report, you reported the testing you performed on blood samples, true?"

"True." Leland had a prominent Adam's apple, and it moved significantly as he swallowed.

"But you didn't take the samples, did you?"

"I did not."

"So if some sort of contamination of the sample occurred at the scene, you would have no way of knowing that?"

The Adam's apple bobbed again. "Well, I have no reason to—"

"I'm only asking for your response to my question," Sam interrupted. "True or false: if there was a problem with the collection of a sample, you likely wouldn't know about it?"

Leland was going pale. "Well . . . true," he said.

"And if there was a problem with the sample of some sort, it could affect the results you obtain?"

Another bob of the Adam's apple. "Well . . . yes."

"So, if someone took a sample not in accordance with best practices, it might affect the sample—true?"

"Objection," Cathy said. "Facts not in evidence."

"Your Honor, I think the fact is in evidence, but I'm only asking for his understanding that if sampling is sub-optimal, the process will be less reliable. He's an expert."

Bridger tapped his pencil and thought about it. "I'll allow it. Overruled."

Sam looked to Leland, who squirmed slightly. "Yes, if the sample is bad, the analysis could be flawed. But I have no way—"

"Thank you," Sam interrupted. "Now, according to your report, there were a number of illicit drugs and some alcohol in the decedent's system —true?"

"Yes."

"How much alcohol?"

"Just a trace."

"But some?" Sam asked.

"Yes," Leland replied.

"Let me ask you this: could that alcohol have acted in combination with the fentanyl to kill her?"

"Well, the fentanyl alone probably would have killed her."

"Not my question," Sam replied, shaking his head. "My question was, could the alcohol have contributed to her death?"

Leland looked to the ceiling, thinking. "Only in an overkill way."

"But it could have?" Sam insisted.

"In the same way that getting hit by a train and then run over by a bus could kill a person, yes." Leland smirked.

Sam ignored the sarcasm and the laughter in the courtroom. "Same question regarding the methamphetamine?"

"Yes, it could have added to the already deadly amount of fentanyl."

"How about the heroin? In combination with fentanyl—"

"Yes. That would be a deadly mix in this case."

"Same question regarding the cocaine."

Leland sighed. "Yes, in combination with the fentanyl, cocaine could have contributed to her death, but I still say—"

"Can you explain what the term 'therapeutic level' means?"

"Certainly," Leland replied. "That means the concentration of a drug usually observed when it is being taken as prescribed."

"Thank you. Now, what drugs were present in the decedent's blood in amounts exceeding the therapeutic levels?"

"Well, I guess all of them. There is no therapeutic use for some of them, and there is no evidence she had a prescription for the others."

"And you don't have any idea who supplied the drugs to her, how she got them, or how they were administered, do you?"

"No."

"Could have been her cocaine dealer?"

Cathy was on her feet. "Objection! Assumes facts not in evidence."

"I'll withdraw the question, Your Honor."

"Good," Bridger said. "Jury will disregard. Continue, Mr. Johnstone."

"Just a couple more questions." Sam made a point of looking to the report, then stole a quick glance at the jurors, and noted at least two of them shaking their heads. The bow-tied accountant was clearly appalled by the drugs in Rebel's system. He made a note to emphasize the quantity of drugs in her system when it came time to close. "So, what you are saying is that any of these drugs in combination with the fentanyl could have contributed to Rebel Hayes' death?"

"Objection, Your Honor!" Cathy said. "He is misstating the testimony."

"Sustained," Bridger ruled.

"Thank you," Sam replied. "And you've no first-hand knowledge of who or how—"

"Your Honor!" Cathy pleaded.

Bridger interrupted Cathy. "Mr. Johnstone, that's been asked and answered. Have you another line of questioning?"

Sam stood still, acting as if he might be finished. He shuffled some papers and then looked to Leland. "I do, Your Honor." He paused to allow an audible groan to pass through the gallery, then focused on Leland. He had enough for Bridger to grant a motion to acquit on the drug-induced homicide count; it was time to plant some seeds of doubt in the jurors' minds on the other charges. "You attributed the death of Rebel Hayes to her ingestion of fentanyl, true?"

"Yes."

"What is fentanyl?"

Cathy was again on her feet. "Your Honor, this line of questioning is unnecessary and irrelevant. He is—"

Bridger had a hand up. "Ms. Schmidt. I made clear at the outset my dislike of speaking objections. Cease and desist," he ordered. Turning his attention to Sam, he asked, "Mr. Johnstone? Like counsel, I am growing impatient."

"The relevance will be clear in a couple of questions, Your Honor."

Satisfied, Bridger nodded. "Overruled. Please proceed . . . quickly."

"Thank you, Your Honor," Sam said, bowing slightly. "Mr. Leland, can you talk a little bit about fentanyl and its analogs?"

Leland's eyes shifted to Cathy and then back to Sam before he turned to the jury. "Fentanyl is a synthetic opioid developed as a surgical analgesic—a painkiller. And as with most drugs, there are variants. These variants, as you might imagine, contain different compounds and have different chemical structures, but they all contain a common ingredient, and that is fentanyl."

"And all are controlled substances?"

"Oh, yes. They are all illicit alterations of medically prescribed fentanyl. All are dangerous in untrained hands—some incredibly so."

"What are some of the more common analogs?"

"Acetylfentanyl, carfentanil, alfentanil . . . there are dozens, really," Leland explained.

"All are deadly to some degree?"

"Oh my, yes," Leland replied. "Some are hundreds of times more potent than fentanyl." Warming to his subject, he continued. "Carfentanil is one of the more common analogs; it is one hundred times more potent than fentanyl and ten thousand times more potent than morphine." He looked around the courtroom, basking in the audible gasps.

Sam was watching the jury. A couple of the jurors had leaned forward and were taking notes. He allowed the toxicity of analogs to sink in before posing his next question. "Can standard post-mortem opioid testing identify the presence of specific fentanyl analogs?"

Again, Leland looked to Cathy and then back to Sam. "Well, we can identify the presence of analogs, yes, but—"

"Not my question," Sam began. "I'm asking if standard post-mortem opioid toxicology testing will reveal the presence of fentanyl analogs."

Out of the corner of his eye, Sam could see Cathy and Roberts whispering urgently at the State's table.

"Well, no," Leland admitted. "We don't routinely run tests capable of identifying specific analogs unless we have reason to believe there is a need. The presence of an analog would generally return as positive for fentanyl."

The accountant was leaning forward. "Why not?" Sam asked.

"They're expensive," Leland answered quickly. "We don't have the budget for it."

"So, let me ask this. If you run a traditional test, and there is fentanyl present, it could be because fentanyl was present, or because of the presence of fentanyl in an analog?"

"Yes—or both," Leland added eagerly.

"So, when you performed the toxicological examination on Rebel Hayes' blood, did you test for the presence of analogs?"

Cathy was up at Roberts' urging. "Your Honor, I guess I'm not seeing the relevance here. Mr. Johnstone—"

"Overruled," Bridger said quickly. "You may answer," he said to Leland.

Leland was already shaking his head. "We did not. Specific testing for analogs is not routinely performed."

Sam put a finger to his lips. "No request was made to look for analogs?"

"No, sir."

Sam nodded and pretended to make a note. "So, did your office do confirmatory tests on the drugs found in the motel room?"

"We did."

"In that testing, did you test for the presence of analogs?"

"No."

"Same reasoning?"

"Yes," Leland agreed. "We don't routinely do those tests—too expensive. We want to spend taxpayers' money wisely."

"That's a laudable goal," Sam replied. "We all appreciate that, I'm sure . . . except that in this case, the pills found in the room could have contained a fentanyl analog—true?"

"Well, they could have, but—"

"But we'll never know, will we?"

"Well, we could test—"

"And the opioids in Rebel Hayes' system could have contained a fentanyl analog, true?"

"Well, yes."

"But again, we don't know."

Leland shook his head. "We don't. But we weren't asked to—"

"And did you compare in any way the results of your confirmatory testing of the pills found with the results of the toxicology of the blood of Miss Hayes?"

Leland sat back in the witness chair. "Well . . . not directly."

"Meaning no?"

"As I have explained already, we performed testing on the samples in the room, and samples on the blood drawn by Dr. Laws. Both showed the presence of fentanyl."

"And either or both could have contained an analog, and either or both could have tested positive for fentanyl as the result of the presence of an analog. True?"

"Well, yes."

Cathy was exasperated. "Again, Your Honor, asked and answered."

"Sustained," Bridger said.

"So you cannot say with certainty that the drugs in Rebel Hayes' system at the time of her death were toxicologically—if that's a word—the same as the drugs found in my client's room, can you?"

"Oh, no. I can't say that."

Sam stared at an increasingly uncomfortable Leland for a moment, allowing that to sink in. "Your Honor, I think that's all the questions I have for this witness." He moved to his chair and sat down, ignoring his beaming client. He stole a look at the jury and saw some of them making notes while others fixed doubtful stares on Cathy.

Cathy stood and spent a few minutes trying to rehabilitate Leland. As she did so, it became increasingly clear that Sam's questions had knocked Leland off his feet. She could see the same thing Sam could, and she gave up quickly. "No more questions," she said glumly.

"Thank you, Counsel," Bridger replied. He studied the clock on the wall for a moment, and then, having made his decision, called it a day. "I have a number of other matters that need attending," he explained. "Juveniles in particular," he added, flashing a rare smile.

Sam noted that few members of the jury returned Bridger's smile—a good sign. Judges represented "the system" in the minds of most jurors, no matter how hard they tried to be neutral. Today had been a good day. He half-listened as Bridger gave instructions to the jury.

47

Sam had gotten a fair night's sleep, so it was with a clear head that he pulled a manila folder from a banker's box he kept next to the defendant's table that had his cross-examination notes for Miller. All eyes were on the young detective as she made her way to the witness box and was sworn by Bridger. When she was seated, Cathy began. "Please state your full name for the record."

"Ashley Miller. No middle initial."

"Are you employed?"

"I am a detective for the Custer Police Department."

"How long have you been employed in that capacity?" Cathy asked.

"Maybe eighteen months?"

"What did you do prior?"

Miller's wooden appearance had Cathy concerned, so she re-positioned herself to the side of the lectern, forcing Miller to follow her with her eyes.

"I was a patrol officer with the Casper Police Department."

"And how long did you do that?"

"About ten years."

Cathy moved back behind the lectern, again requiring Miller to move her head. "Any other law enforcement experience?"

"Yes, I was with the military police when I was in the air force."

"Are you a certified law enforcement officer in the state of Wyoming?"

"I am."

"Was your certification current in April of this year?"

"It was."

"You are chief of detectives?"

"That's the title," Miller said, "but there's only two of us."

Cathy waited for the laughter to die down. "What are your duties?"

"I respond to patrol officers' calls and conduct investigations when a serious crime is suspected to have occurred. I also train newer officers in basic investigative techniques."

"Have you investigated a murder case before?"

"I have."

"And have you investigated drug cases?"

"Yes."

"Drug overdoses?"

"Unfortunately."

In asking these questions, Cathy had quickly established foundation, which would provide context for Miller's testimony and establish her bona fides in preparation for later questions seeking her opinion. Not infrequently, attorneys in a hurry failed to establish proper foundation with their investigating officer. In contrast, Cathy was taking her time, and Sam knew the jury would ultimately find Miller persuasive. She now moved to the salient events.

"Did you have a reason to be surveilling a motel where a room was occupied by the defendant on or about the tenth of April?"

"I did."

"How so?"

"We had received information from several confidential sources that Mr. Gustafson was dealing methamphetamine and fentanyl in the area. Our investigation resulted in Judge Downs issuing a warrant for his arrest."

Cathy nodded her approval. "So, on the tenth of April you were doing what?"

"We were watching the room the defendant had rented. Our plan was to arrest him when he left the premises."

"Did anything of significance happen?"

"Well, the decedent and another man—who we later determined to be Clayton Pierce—entered the defendant's room at approximately seven p.m."

"Then what?"

"We had decided that because the defendant wouldn't know me, I would position myself outside his room and act like I had car trouble."

"We?"

"Myself, Punch—er, Detective Polson, and Officer Baker."

"And so what happened?"

"Well, as I said, the decedent and Mr. Pierce entered the room. Approximately ten minutes later the defendant left the room, saw me, headed the other way, and was arrested by Officer Baker."

"I was assaulted by him!" Gustafson said.

"Quiet!" Sam hissed.

"Then what?"

"Then Detective Polson and I entered the room, secured it, and found Mr. Pierce and Miss Hayes."

"And then?" Cathy asked.

"Both were in distress, so we administered naloxone to each."

"Did they respond?"

"Pierce did, and he was ultimately arrested for use and possession."

"And Miss Hayes?"

"She didn't respond despite multiple cartridges of naloxone being administered."

A wail arose from the gallery as Hayes stood. "You killed my daughter!" he yelled, pointing to Gustafson.

"Sit down, Mr. Hayes!" Bridger barked.

Sam stood. "Your Honor, my client would like Mr. Hayes immediately removed from the courtroom—"

"No!" Hayes yelled.

"—Based upon a demonstrated inability to control his emotions. The alternative, of course, is a mistrial," Sam finished.

"Your Honor," Cathy argued. "A bit of indulgence on the court's part seems deserved, here. After all, he's lost a daughter."

"He's interfering with my client's right to a fair trial and—"

"Quiet! All of you!" Bridger cried. "Mr. Hayes, I will give you and your supporters one shot at this. Any more disruptions and I will clear this courtroom!"

Cathy resumed her questioning, focusing on demonstrating that Miller had run a clean and comprehensive investigation culminating in Gustafson's arrest. Miller had improved substantially on the stand since Sam had seen her last; he would need to be careful to avoid alienating jurors. The direct examination was effective and lengthy.

When she finished at last, Bridger looked at his watch. "Ladies and gentlemen, I have some other matters to attend to. I'm going to give you a rather lengthy lunch, and because I expect Mr. Johnstone will have a long list of questions, I think this will likely be our last witness of the day. So again, please recall my earlier admonitions, and follow the bailiff's orders. Fred, please conduct the jury, and have them back here ready to go as of two o'clock."

Two hours later, Sam was at the podium. When invited to cross-examine, he took the measure of Miller. Despite Bridger's prediction, Sam had only a couple of points to make. "Did you arrest my client that night?" he asked.

"I did," Miller replied. "We charged him with possession and possession with intent to distribute."

"Did he have any drugs on him when he was arrested?"

"No."

"No scales, baggies, large amounts of cash, or anything like that?"

"They were all in his room," Miller replied. She licked her lips.

"Nothing on him?"

"No."

"So, you arrested him based on what was in the room?"

"Well, yes—"

"Where Clay Pierce and Rebel Hayes were?"

"Well, yes—but it wasn't their room. It was his."

Probably as well as he could do on that point. "You didn't see my client deal any drugs?"

"No."

"And he didn't admit giving any drugs to Rebel Hayes?"

"No, he lawyered up."

"It's not uncommon for suspects to do that, is it?"

"No, not really."

"So, fair to say you arrested him on the basis of drugs and stuff in his room?"

"That's fair."

"And you didn't immediately charge him with drug-induced homicide, did you?"

"I did not."

"Then what?"

"Well, we finished doing what we needed to do on scene. The next day I attended the autopsy. We sent evidence collected there off to our experts. As information began to come back over the course of the next few days, I made the decision to arrest him for drug-induced homicide."

"Why?"

"Because I came to believe he had provided fentanyl to her and she had died from it."

"Why did you believe that?"

"Well, the presence of the drugs. The manner and cause of her death." Miller looked around the courtroom as if it was obvious.

"You've heard the testimony in the trial to this point?"

"I have."

"So, you've heard the manner of death is in question and that she might have died from something other than my client having given her fentanyl?"

Cathy had seen this coming. "Objection! Misstates the evidence."

"Overruled," Bridger held, then made a note.

"I heard that, yes." Miller glanced at Cathy and then made eye contact with Sam.

When she was looking at him, Sam asked his next question. "If you had known then what you know now—"

Cathy was again on her feet. "Objection. She's not an expert. She can't comment on a hypothetical."

It was a proper objection, and it was time to change subjects. "I'll withdraw," Sam offered. When Bridger merely nodded, he pressed on. "How many people did you question regarding the presence of drugs in my client's room?"

"I'm not sure."

"A few? Dozens? Hundreds?"

"A few."

"During the course of your investigation, did you develop any other suspects?"

"No—well, we arrested Mr. Pierce."

Sam recalled her testimony in a previous trial. "I believe you once told me that you were trained to believe the suspect and to try and find reasons why their story was true, and to then eliminate them—am I remembering that correctly?"

"Yes."

"Can you talk about the steps you took to eliminate my client?" Miller pursed her lips and sat thoughtfully, so Sam continued. "Did you speak with motel staff?"

"Oh, yes. It was his room."

"Did you talk with the housekeeper responsible for his room?"

"Well, no."

"So you don't know that my client didn't rent a room full of drugs, do you?"

Miller shrugged. "Highly unlikely. I mean, Martians could have come down in a spaceship and—"

"But you don't know for a fact that didn't happen, do you?"

"That Martians didn't come down?" Miller asked, playing to the gallery.

Sam smiled tolerantly, as if speaking to a small child. "You don't know for a fact what was in that room at the time my client rented it, do you?"

"No. I can't say he didn't stumble into a room full of drugs." She smirked sarcastically and looked at the jurors.

Sam noted that none returned her smile. He pressed the issue. "Because you didn't check with motel management, did you?"

"No," she admitted. "Not management."

"Or housekeeping?"

"No."

"So you can't say that the materials that contributed to your belief that drugs were being dealt weren't already in the room, can you?"

Her smile disappeared. "I cannot, but his fingerprints were all over it!"

Sam smiled indulgently. "It was his room, wasn't it?"

"Of course, but if, as you're saying, he took over a room full of drugs—"

"I didn't say anything, Detective. I'm merely pointing out what might have happened."

This time Cathy didn't bother to stand. "Objection. He's arguing with the witness."

"Sustained," Bridger ruled quickly.

"No more questions, Your Honor," Sam said. He looked to the jury when he was back in his chair. Most of the jurors met his glance. The bow-tied juror was nodding in appreciation. Doubt had been sown. The degree was in question, of course, but he had gotten his point across.

"Any redirect?" Bridger asked Cathy.

She held up a finger as if to ask for time and consulted with Roberts. "No, Judge," she said at last. She'd gotten what she needed from a relatively inexperienced investigator. Best to leave well enough alone. She could deal with Sam's magically appearing drugs at a later time.

Bridger recessed the court and instructed the jury on the actions they could and could not take. When everyone was gone, Sam gathered his materials and headed for his office. It was going to be a long night.

48

Several hours later, Sam was in his office preparing his closing argument. As usual, he was feeling pessimistic about his client's chances; he was chastising himself for questions not asked, follow-ups not made, and objections not interposed. VA Bob had once told him he was a perfectionist, which Sam took as a compliment until Bob explained what he meant. Accurate, for sure.

The music from his playlist was going, and a favorite by Cody Jinks had just started when the knock came. Because he had purposely walked to the office to avoid parking his truck out front, and thereby alerting clients of his presence, he had expected to work uninterrupted. The knocking continued, so against his better judgment, he answered.

"What do you want?" he asked Gustafson, who was accompanied by two effete-looking man-boys. Sam motioned for Gustafson to enter. "You two wait out here," he directed.

When Gustafson was inside, Sam closed and locked the door behind them and led him down the hall to his office. "Don't get comfortable—I'm working. You haven't answered my question. What do you want?"

"Oh, sorry," Gustafson said. When Gustafson turned to face him, Sam felt himself getting angry. The little bastard was high. "Why are you high?"

"I—I'm not, Sam," Gustafson said, and smiled.

"Don't blow smoke at me. Been there, done that. What do you want?"

"I jus' wanna talk, man. Feelin' like you don't believe and stuff—you know?"

"I know you're wasted, and I know I don't have time for this. We've got closing arguments tomorrow." Sam put his hands on Gustafson and turned him back to the door. "Now get your ass home and sleep it off."

"Sam, you don't understand, man."

Like hell he didn't. Gustafson was just like every defendant in every trial. "I do. I get it. Now try and get home without being seen by the cops, and I'll see you tomorrow. I need to get this done, and I need to get some rest."

"I know, dude. Man, you're doin' such a good job, man. I—"

"And I'll keep working until we're done. Now get out of here," Sam urged.

"You know your buddy's kid, Ronnie? He ain't a bad guy, man. Jus' got mixed up with the wrong peeps, you know?"

Sam knew there was something lamer than a Colorado or Wyoming white guy trying to talk street, but he didn't know what it was. "I know, Trent, I know. Now, go meet your boys and get home."

"How come you never call me Gus, man? All my bros call me Gus."

"Because I'm not your bro. I'm your attorney. And I'm about to toss you out into the hands of your bros if you don't leave."

"I know who killed Kaiden, you know."

"I know."

"And it wasn't Ronnie."

"That's what you keep telling me," Sam said. "And I'm busting my ass to get you off. And if and when I do, you better be able to back up the shit you're talking." As he finished, he guided Gustafson to the door. "Go home," he said as he opened the door and looked outside. Seeing the two pencil-necked young men on the sidewalk, he spoke to them. "Get him home safe and sound," he directed.

A voice from the darkness boomed, "Listen, the soldier boy is barking orders and shit."

Sam recognized the voice and turned to face Damon, who had apparently been lurking in the shadows. "What do you want?"

Damon showed his teeth. "Nothin', man. Just makin' sure you behaving yourself and not makin' any bad decisions." He was now on Sam's step.

"Doing my best. Now, why don't you and Reggie go do whatever you do in the dark and leave me to finish prepping for tomorrow?"

"Just make sure you don't throw my brother under the bus, man. We watchin'."

"Yeah? Well, your ass is gonna be watching from outside." Sam attempted to close the door, but Damon had his foot wedged between the door and the frame. Sam looked at Damon's foot and then at the bigger man. "Officer, I had this big scary man trying to get into my office in the middle of the night. What could I do except shoot his ass?"

Damon's eyes narrowed. "You ain't got the balls." Sam shrugged and began to reach behind his back. "Okay, man," Damon said, holding his hands up. "You got it. But you heard me. And this ain't over."

"I heard you," Sam agreed. "Now, you and your boyfriend there can go back and tell Davonte—your boss—that you saw me and passed the message."

"Yo, he ain't my boss."

"You always say that, but you always seem to be doing what he tells you."

Damon moved his foot, and Sam quickly closed and locked the door.

"Really?" he asked aloud. "I just need a couple hours of uninterrupted time. Just two hours," he said as he marched down the hall to his office, stopping only to get coffee from the small kitchen. He needed to complete the first draft of his closing argument, but the words wouldn't come.

What if Gustafson was full of shit? Or what if he wasn't, but the jury convicted? He stretched, then stood and walked to his office wall and looked at a frame hanging there. It was large, made of rustic, distressed wood, and had five four-by-six photos arranged inside. Veronica Simmons had given framed photos to Sam back when they were seeing each other; she'd taken the photographs at Arlington National Cemetery during their visit after the Olsen case. Each picture showed a grave that held the remains of a soldier who died on his watch. For months, he'd been successful in avoiding thoughts about the men, their wives and families, and wondering what they might be doing today if he had done a better job.

He thought of Veronica and why she left, then thought about having a drink. Ah, yes, the return of old habits. He needed to get to a meeting, and soon. He turned from the framed photographs, wiped at a tear, and blew his nose, then turned out the lights and headed for his apartment.

The argument could wait.

The drive was uneventful and the parking lot surrounding the apartment complex was free of Hayes and his friends. He locked the door behind himself. In his bedroom he emptied his pockets: car and house keys, lip balm, half a tissue, a receipt from that morning's coffee, his old wallet, and a used handkerchief. He placed the items in their customary spots, then unbuckled the holster and hung that on his bedpost. After brushing his teeth and washing his face, he plugged in his phone, turned down the volume, got into bed, and removed his leg. He fell asleep looking at the textured ceiling and thinking about Mickey.

49

On Friday morning, when all but the jury had returned to the courtroom and were seated, Bridger looked at Sam. "Mr. Johnstone, has your client made a decision on whether he wishes to testify?"

Sam sat quietly, saying nothing. Bridger looked impatiently at him and was about to say something more when Gustafson spoke. "He doesn't want me to testify, Judge," he said.

The audience in the courtroom stirred. "Mr. Johnstone, it seems to me this would be a good time for the court to conduct its usual colloquy on the subject. Do you agree?"

"Yes, sir."

Bridger turned to Gustafson. "Mr. Gustafson, let's talk about your decision. You've indicated a desire to testify—is that true?"

"Well, I'm not sure. I want to tell the jury what happened."

"I understand," Bridger began. "The court advises you that you have the absolute right not to testify, and that if you do not testify, no inference of your guilt may be drawn from your being silent and not testifying."

"I understand, Judge. Sam told me. But—"

Bridger held up a hand. "Let me finish. Now, if you do testify, anything you say can be used against you, and you will be cross-examined by the attorneys for the State, just like any other witness. Do you understand that?"

"I do."

"Now, it sounds like you and Mr. Johnstone have discussed your decision. Is that true?"

"It is."

Again, those in the gallery stirred. Bridger looked to Sam, who was staring straight ahead. "Okay, well, is it fair to say that he isn't forcing you to testify?" Bridger asked.

"For sure," Gustafson said. "He told me I'd be better off keeping my mouth shut."

Sam felt dozens of pairs of eyes on him. Bridger looked around the courtroom until it had quieted, then focused on Gustafson. "Do you and Mr. Johnstone need some additional time to discuss your decision?"

"No, it's my decision—right?"

"It is. How would you like to proceed?"

Gustafson looked to Sam, who continued to stare straight ahead, then back to Bridger. "Maybe I do need a minute."

"Of course." Bridger pushed a button that turned off the microphones at the defense table and filled the courtroom with white noise.

"Sam, what do you think?"

"Same as I've been telling you. I think we're in decent shape. If you testify, it's gonna put your freedom at risk."

"But I've been readin' and all those websites say the defendant oughta testify if he can show he didn't do it."

"I already explained that online legal advice—especially when it's free —is usually worth what you pay for it."

Gustafson watched Sam for a few seconds, then leaned over and whispered, "You'd better be right, bro, or poor Ronnie's gonna rot in jail." He looked to Bridger, who turned off the noise and activated the microphones in the courtroom. "I'll waive my right to testify, Judge," Gustafson said.

Bridger looked at Sam, whose expression hadn't changed. The judge had seen a hundred instances where a defendant had insisted on testifying, and while it was usually to their detriment, the final decision was theirs. "Do you understand you have the right to testify?"

"I do."

"Do you waive that right?"

"I do."

"All right. The court will find the defendant has been fully advised of his rights and having been so advised, waives that right after consultation with counsel." Bridger looked pointedly at Cathy. "Shall I call for the jury?"

"Your Honor, a moment?" she asked.

"Of course, Counsel," he said. While Cathy conferenced with Roberts, Bridger looked over the jury instructions. When he looked up, Cathy was standing, prepared to address the court. "Ms. Schmidt?"

"Your Honor, the State has concluded its case-in-chief," she said simply.

Bridger looked around the courtroom to quiet the murmuring, then glanced at his watch before turning his attention to Sam. "I imagine you have something you would like to discuss, Mr. Johnstone—is that correct?"

Sam stood. "Yes, Your Honor."

"Fine," Bridger replied. "Let's take five."

When he was gone, Gustafson asked Sam what was going on. "I'm going to make an argument that for legal reasons the charge of drug-induced homicide shouldn't go to the jury," Sam replied. "Right now, I just need you to walk with me to the conference room. No comments to the press, no stopping to bullshit with friends or fans. None of that."

"Okay, okay, man."

Cathy sat heavily in her chair, picked up a basketball-shaped stress ball, and squeezed hard. "Leland was a crappy witness. Sam hurt us there," she said.

"Only on the drug-induced homicide," Roberts opined. "We're solid on the others."

"So, should we make the offer again?"

"Not unless you are willing to sweeten the pot," Roberts advised. "Otherwise, he's already rejected us and his position has only gotten stronger."

"He's still looking at 27 years."

"He's got no record. Bridger won't—"

"We've got a dead kid."

"I know, but—"

"The pressure's on."

"I know. What are you going to do?"

Mary had worked for the last three District Court judges, as well as the occasional visiting or retired judge. "Your Honor, how is it going?" she asked, hoping for some insight as to the course of the trial or his thoughts regarding the relative merits of each attorney's trial strategy. Other judges always discussed trials with her. It was one of the job's pleasantries. Instead, she was subjected to a litany of complaints regarding his physical health and the inconvenience the trial was imposing upon him.

When he took a breath, she asked again. "So, will you finish today?"

"Perhaps," Bridger replied irritably. "But first, Sam Johnstone is going to argue for acquittal."

"Surely not on all counts?" Mary asked, showing unusual insight.

"I doubt it. I expect he will argue count three for sure. Possession and possession with intent to distribute will go to the jury for sure, and probably drug-induced homicide."

"So the case *will* go to the jury?"

"Absolutely."

"Okay," Mary said. "I'm going to contact our caterers."

After the recess, Bridger looked to Sam expectantly. "Any motions from the defendant?"

Sam stood. "Yes, sir. Defense moves for a judgment of acquittal pursuant to Rule 29 of the Wyoming Rules of Criminal Procedure on count three, drug-induced homicide. We will admit the State has provided sufficient evidence on the other counts for the matters to go to the jury, but on the drug-induced homicide we believe the State has fallen short of what we can all agree is a very low burden. May we be heard?"

"Yes."

"Your Honor, as you know, in order to meet its burden, the State was required to present evidence to show that my client personally delivered a controlled substance to a minor, and that minor died of the use of any amount of that controlled substance." He took a visibly deep breath before continuing. "Your Honor, we contend the State's evidence as presented in its case-in-chief is such that a juror must have a reasonable doubt as to the elements of count three. As a threshold matter, there is no evidence—I say again, no evidence—that my client personally delivered the drug or drugs in question to the decedent. There is evidence that drugs were in his room, and evidence that she used drugs of a similar nature. But there is no evidence directly linking my client to her or her death."

Sam paused to review his outline. "Further, and even if we assume we could link my client to the decedent's use of drugs, the State has not shown beyond a reasonable doubt that the drugs alleged to be in my client's possession—which I am made to understand were fentanyl pills—were the sole cause of the decedent's death. You will recall of course that in *Burrage*, the court held that where—as here—it is alleged that one gave drugs to another resulting in death, it must be shown that the drugs provided were the sole cause of death. The State's own witness would not make that claim with scientific certainty—because he can't. He cannot say that the fentanyl's effects were not enhanced by the presence of the other drugs in her system at the time of her death."

Bridger had steepled his hands in front of him, elbows on the bench with his index fingers pressed against his lips. Sam was uncertain whether the judge's posture was an indication of deep thought or to preclude himself from interrupting. He was about to continue when the undercurrent of distress in the gallery became audible. He turned to see Hayes engaged in fervent, demonstrative conversation with his supporters. "Your Honor—"

"Ladies and gentlemen in the gallery, please be still!" Bridger barked. "You have a right to be here, but it is not one without limits. These are important matters under discussion, and should your actions interfere with our ability to conduct this trial, I will clear the courtroom. I will give no further warnings!" he said. "Mr. Johnstone, please continue."

"Your Honor, there is no direct evidence my client knew that the pills alleged to be in his possession contained fentanyl. Here again, the State missed the mark." This was a weak argument—it strained credulity to assert that a dealer didn't know what he had, so Sam hurriedly moved to his final, and much stronger, point.

"Finally, Your Honor, the State failed to compare the chemical make-up of the drugs alleged to be in possession of my client with those alleged to be the cause of the decedent's death. That alone raises serious doubt. Not some doubt, but serious doubt—doubt sufficient to preclude Your Honor from passing this matter to the jury. We ask, therefore, that you dismiss this count pursuant to Rule 29 of the Wyoming rules of criminal procedure. Thank you."

Bridger nodded approvingly, Sam thought. "Ms. Schmidt, what says the State?"

Cathy was at the podium quickly. "Your Honor, we appreciate Mr. Johnstone's decision not to contest passing counts one and two to the jury. We only wish he had come to the same conclusion regarding count three. He has cited the law on the subject accurately and that is appreciated, as well. Our disagreement lies in his interpretation of that law," she explained. "Mr. Johnstone urges the court to find that in the absence of evidence certain to result in conviction, the court must acquit. But that is not the law. Instead, the law instructs the court to acquit if no reasonable juror could convict."

Sam watched, impressed as always with her command of the law and the facts. This wasn't her first rodeo, and she had clearly anticipated his motion. "The evidence to this point includes evidence that Mr. Gustafson was suspected of dealing drugs; that drugs were found in a room rented by him; that along with the drugs was evidence of an intent to distribute drugs; and that a young woman walked into his room under her own power and died shortly thereafter from the effects of the drug that Mr. Gustafson possessed." She smiled sardonically. "Surely, Your Honor, it would be reasonable for a finder of fact to connect the dots and to find the defendant guilty. That's what happens every day, and it is decidedly *not* unreasonable. The State asks that you deny the motion."

Sam had been watching Bridger nod in agreement during Cathy's argument. "Mr. Johnstone?" Bridger asked.

Sam stood and moved slowly to the podium, trying to decide whether to rebut her argument. No use urinating into the wind. "Your Honor, I believe the defense has made the argument it needs to make."

Bridger waited for Sam to be seated. "I appreciate the arguments made by counsel today. The bottom line is this: I'm going to deny your motion, Mr. Johnstone, and send this matter to the jury for their determination." He then cited the law on the subject and re-hashed Cathy's argument. "In conclusion, the court is going to find that, giving the State every reasonable inference—and allowing jurors to do the same with what looks to me like circumstantial evidence—a reasonable juror could find the defendant provided the drug that killed the decedent. Let the record show you made the Rule 29 motion on count three alone, and that I denied it." His conclusion was quickly followed by cheers from Hayes and his supporters.

Sam was immediately on his feet. "Your Honor, I am again concerned—"

"The jury is not present—" Cathy began.

"Quiet!" Bridger barked. "This is not a football game. Another outburst like that and I will clear the courtroom, and some of you will be looking at jail time."

Sam waited for Bridger to take a breath before continuing. He was about to say something when the sound of sirens outside the courthouse interfered. When the volume had lowered sufficiently, he continued. "Your Honor, respectfully, I do not believe we can wait that long. I'm concerned about those individuals' ability to keep their emotions in check, and I'm concerned that we'll have a mistrial if an outburst occurs with the jury present."

Roberts was on his feet. Sam saw Cathy watching Roberts, mouth agape. "Judge, that's ridiculous. This is a highly emotional case, and the public has a right to see and hear everything—"

Bridger had heard enough. "Sit down!" he yelled. Roberts complied. The courtroom was eerily silent as Bridger hissed, "I'll have no more of this. No more antics in the gallery; no more arguing by counsel; no more anything other than the respectful trial of this case." He looked to Roberts. "Mr. Roberts, please stand." When Roberts had complied, Bridger continued, "I am of a mind to hold you in contempt for characterizing this court's comments as ridiculous. I will give you the opportunity to dissuade me."

"Your Honor, I meant no disrespect—"

"Yet you were disrespectful."

Roberts took a deep breath. "Your Honor, if the court interpreted my remarks—"

"You referred to my ruling as ridiculous. Are you saying that the issue here is *my* interpretation?"

Cathy was on her feet, whispering in Roberts' ear. He nodded and immediately turned his attention to Bridger. "Your Honor, I wish to apologize to the court for my outburst. It was unprofessional and not representative of who I am."

Bridger looked closely at Roberts for a long time before speaking. "I accept your apology, Mr. Roberts. I will suggest that nothing like that should happen again." He stared at Roberts while the attorney sat. When the courtroom was suitably uncomfortable, Bridger declared a recess and stalked from the bench.

———

During the recess, Sam again guided Gustafson to the attorney-client conference room. While he looked at his notes, Gustafson used the men's room.

"What is that guy's problem?" Gustafson asked after exiting.

"He's the judge." Sam shrugged. "He hears the evidence, then hears the arguments, then makes the call."

"But it's bullshit!"

"It's always a longshot," Sam replied. "Every judge wants to allow the case to go to a jury. It takes a real screw-up on the part of the prosecution, or an earlier decision to not put on any evidence, to lose on a Rule 29 motion."

"Then why have it?"

"One more rule in place to protect defendants from bogus charges."

"But these *are* bogus!" Gustafson stressed. Seeing Sam looking at him doubtfully, he sat across the table from his attorney. "So, whattaya think?"

"About what?" Sam asked.

"The whole thing. Am I gonna walk?"

"Couldn't say," Sam replied. "It's never wise to try and anticipate what a jury will decide."

"I better walk, dude, or your boy is going to be behind bars forever."

Sam took a deep breath and slowly counted down from five. "If I were a betting man, I think you're probably going to walk on the drug-induced homicide and the possession with intent, and the jury is going to convict you on the possession," Sam replied at last. "Same as I told you before. You should have done a deal; you maybe could have gotten probation."

Gustafson stiffened. "Maybe you should have done your job better and—"

Sam was on his feet and had Gustafson up against the wall before either man realized what had happened. Months of this little man alternately sneering and threatening him had taken its toll. "You little—"

"Let go of me! Let go of me!" Gustafson cried. Sam let go of Gustafson, but not before shaking him by the front of his shirt, popping a button and loosening his tie. "I'm calling the cops!"

"Do it."

"You'll be in jail for assault!"

Damn, that was stupid. "That was a battery."

"Whatever."

Why did he do stuff like that? "Do what you need to do, but right now, I need you out of my sight. I am sick of your ass."

Gustafson was tucking in his shirt and straightening his tie. "You're sick of me? I'm sick of your self-righteous ass, I'll tell you that. You look down on people like me, just like everyone else."

"No, I can assure you I look down on you alone."

"What?" Gustafson asked, confused. "Well, just remember: I don't walk, and you know what happens. In fact, I might not say anything if I *do* walk."

Sam was again across the room. This time he didn't touch Gustafson, but backed him up against the wall. He ignored the sound of the door opening. "You don't come across, I will kill you."

"Sam!" Cassie barked. "Let him go."

"He can go," Sam said, backing away from his client and turning to face her. "I gotta take a leak. Why don't you escort him back to the courtroom?" Gustafson sprinted out of the room while Cassie stood with the door ajar.

Sam's phone rang; it was a county number. "Would you mind closing that?" he asked, and when she had done so, he answered, "Hello?"

"Sam, it's Punch."

There was a brief, awkward silence. "Punch, what's wrong?"

"They've taken Press Daniels to the hospital."

Oh, God no. Please, no. "What happened?"

"Not sure," Punch said. "I know you're in trial and all, but I wanted you to know."

He couldn't deal with this. "Is he alive?"

"He was when they were transporting him."

"Will you keep me posted?"

"Of course."

Press, I need you. "Thanks. I appreciate it."

50

In the courtroom moments later, Cathy approached Sam. "I heard about Press, Sam," she said. "If you want to move for a continuance, I won't object."

Classy. "Thanks, but I won't need to. I'm not going to call any witnesses. Let's just get this over with."

Her eyes widened briefly in surprise. "Well, if you need something, let me know," she said, and placed a hand on his forearm. "I mean it."

"I'll do it," he said. He observed Roberts watching the two of them with interest. He was about to add his thanks when Violet Marshall called the courtroom to its feet. "All rise!"

After Bridger had instructed all to be seated, he motioned for the attorneys to approach. When Sam, Cathy, and Roberts were in place, Bridger stood and leaned over the bench. "I heard about my predecessor; I'm sorry. I know you were especially close, Mr. Johnstone. Do either of you wish to move for a continuance?"

"No, Your Honor," Cathy and Sam replied simultaneously.

"Okay, back to your places, then."

When the attorneys had returned to their tables, Bridger called for the jury. When everyone was settled, he smiled. "Members of the jury, thank you for your patience. When last we were here, the State concluded its case.

It is now proper for the defendant to have his say if he wishes to do so. Mr. Johnstone, please call the defendant's first witness."

Sam could feel a stirring in the courtroom as jurors and observers alike anticipated what the defense would have to say. "Your Honor, the defense will present no witnesses," he said simply. "We rest." As the words left his mouth, he heard a rustling in the gallery behind him, and turned to see Penrose hurrying from the courtroom.

Bridger's face had colored—he was caught off-guard and stuck between instructing the jurors on a Friday afternoon and thereby risking a capricious verdict, or releasing them for the weekend and risking some sort of complication. He sat quietly, staring at the wall, well aware all eyes were upon him.

"Thank you," he said at last, then turned his attention to the jury. "Ladies and gentlemen, I'm going to apologize for having you running back and forth like eighth graders during a fire drill, but this is the way it works out sometimes. I'm going to release you for the weekend while the attorneys and I are getting some things in order. Your presence is not necessary. So, we'll take a little extra time and I'll see everyone Monday morning at nine sharp. Please heed my prior warnings regarding no discussion of the case and the like. Fred, please conduct the jury."

After the jury and the judge had departed, and while the observers and other participants filed out, Sam spoke quietly with Gustafson, asking him to wait for a moment. Sam began to gather his things and turned to find himself face to face with Cathy. He indicated he wanted to speak with her, and they moved to a corner of the courtroom, out of Gustafson's earshot.

"Taking a big chance," she said.

"You'd have eaten him alive."

"I'm not going to lie; I think I would have. Going to be interesting," she said, eyeing Gustafson.

As she started to turn, Sam touched her arm. "Hey—"

"Yes?"

"I know you said now or never, but that offer . . ."

"I'd consider it," she replied. "Let me know, but once it goes to the jury. . ."

"Understood," he said. After Cathy left, Sam finished packing his materials for the day. He had done what he could do in the face of seemingly overwhelming evidence. The case would soon be in the hands of the jury, which would very likely convict—at least on the possession charge. Sam needed to find a way to get Gustafson to agree to testify if he didn't get any significant time, which was a possibility. A plea agreement with Cathy— one eschewing any jail time—was the surest way.

During the trial, Sam had developed an end-of-day routine with Gustafson. After the judge adjourned for the day, Sam and his client would wait until the courtroom cleared out and then—with the assistance of court security officers—Sam would guide his client through labyrinthine hallways to a first floor exit marked "Staff Only," where Sam would administer his daily briefing to his client: "Stay safe; stay out of the public eye; don't answer any phone calls from unknown callers; stay sober and keep your mouth shut."

"That all?" Gustafson would generally respond, and then climb into the vehicle driven by an associate.

Today, Sam stopped Gustafson inside the courtroom. "Listen," he began as Gustafson eyed him suspiciously. "She says it's not too late. She'll still consider a deal."

"You selling me out?"

"No, but a deal is the only way to ensure that you walk."

"Except that I'll have a record."

"Well, yeah. Small price to pay for—"

"For you, maybe," Gustafson replied. "Besides, if she's considering a deal, she must think the jury's gonna acquit."

"Not necessarily," Sam countered. "But it would ensure she gets something out of it, for sure. Juries are unpredictable."

"Screw that," Gustafson replied. "I'll take my chances with the jury."

"Whatever," Sam replied. He was tired of his client's arrogance. "Go. And behave," he said, closing the staff exit door behind him.

Moments later, he paused at the top of the steps to talk with members of the press when a ruckus arose from the back of the courthouse. Several loud voices were joined by others, followed by the honking of a car's horn. Sam joined the others in racing around the courthouse, where he saw Hayes and his supporters surrounding the car belonging to one of

Gustafson's hangers-on, beating on the hood with fists and signs. Sam watched as the back window was lowered and a bloodied Gustafson flashed a vulgar sign to the group as his driver accelerated quickly from the scene. Fortunately, no one was run over or otherwise injured during the escape.

Penrose had been observing, of course. "Care to comment?" she asked Sam.

"Of course not," he replied.

Hayes ran up to Sam. "You see that?" he asked. "Your client's buddy almost ran over some of my people."

Sam could smell the booze emanating from him. "I didn't see anything other than my client bleeding," he replied quickly. "Mr. Hayes, you are interfering with the course of a trial. I'm going to speak with the judge first thing—"

"You do whatever you want, lawyer-man. I'm going to get justice for my Rebel!"

"Justice is what the jury says it is." Sam put a hand on Hayes' chest to hold him at bay. He was feeling light-headed.

"Don't you touch me!" Hayes protested.

Punch appeared out of nowhere. "Give him some space!" he yelled as he stepped between Hayes and Sam.

"He pushed me!" Hayes claimed, pointing to Sam. "You saw it! Arrest him!"

"Wrangler, I saw the whole thing," Punch assured him. "You crowded him and all he did was push you off. Now, go on and get out of here. You've got no quarrel with him," he said, indicating Sam, who was standing stock-still.

"I sure as hell do! I got a quarrel—"

"Wrangler, go. Now. Or I'm gonna arrest you for breach of peace and interference," Punch said. He stood quietly, meeting the glares of Hayes and his supporters, before placing a protective arm between them and the still-frozen Sam. He now lowered that arm.

"C'mon, Wrangler, let's go," urged a tall man wearing a baseball cap, grabbing Wrangler's shoulder. "Ain't no use in fightin' the cops—yet."

"This ain't over!" Hayes yelled before being collared by the man in the cap and two more beefy companions. "It ain't over!"

"You okay?" Punch asked Sam when the men had departed. Hearing no response, he asked again. "Sam? You with me? You okay?"

Sam relaxed his fists. "Fine," he said at last. "I'm fine. Thanks, man."

"You want me to give you a ride to your office, home, or what?"

"I'm okay. I need to check on Gustafson." He was looking over Punch's shoulder at something in the distance.

"What are you looking at?"

"There." Sam indicated with his chin.

Punch turned and saw Reggie and Damon in the distance, laughing and carrying on. "Sam, don't worry about them. I'll go and talk with them."

"Sure, Punch. No problem," Sam replied. "Listen, I gotta go."

"Go ahead," Punch said. He watched Sam for a long moment as he walked around the courthouse, then turned his attention to Reggie and Damon. As he watched them, they took notice. Each leaned back on the car and folded his sizeable arms.

51

At the hospital, Sam was stopped outside the emergency department by a nurse who was not the poster child for the hospital's wellness program. "How can I help you?" she challenged.

"I'd like to see Judge, er, Preston Daniels?"

She put a pen to a clipboard she was holding and wrote something, then fixed her small eyes on Sam. "So, nothing wrong with you, then?"

"Just visiting a friend."

"So, like, not family?"

Sam was looking at the many chins under her fleshy mouth while he decided how to respond. "No," he said at last. "I'm his lawyer."

"Well, lemme see if he's here. If he is, and you ain't family, we'll have to ask him."

"He's here," Sam assured her. "The police told me."

"Them's the rules. Have a seat." She shrugged, then turned and lumbered off.

Sam sat as instructed, pulled his phone from a pocket, and quickly located a book of prayers he had bookmarked. Eyes closed, he was silently reciting the Serenity Prayer when he felt someone standing in front of him.

"He says he'll see ya," the nurse said. "Five minutes. Doctor's orders.

C'mon." Sam followed her slowly down the hallways until she stopped and pointed into a room. "There. Five minutes."

Daniels was on his back on the narrow hospital bed when Sam entered, mouth slack, bed sheets to his chest, breathing through a device taped to his nose. An IV was affixed to his right arm, administering some sort of clear fluid. His eyes were closed and Sam stood silently, watching Daniels' chest expand and contract with regular but shallow breaths. Something was in his eyes, so he turned and looked out a window, ashamed.

"What the hell's the matter with you?"

Sam turned to face his friend. "I'm just here to check on your sorry ass. What happened?"

"Oh, hell . . . I don't know. One minute I was in the shower; next thing I know I'm in the ER with some doctor lookin' me over."

"What'd he say?"

"She. I couldn't understand a word she said, all of that medical mumbo jumbo they speak."

Despite himself, Sam smiled. "Sounds like a judge I know."

Daniels shook his head, then winced. "No. Too many syllables. But something about my heart, I think," he added, looking at Sam closely. "What's the matter? You got a face like a bulldog chewing a turnip."

Irascible as ever. "Like I said, just checking on you."

"Well, relax," Daniels said. "I'll be fine. Just waiting on that doc to make her rounds. Assuming I'm good, she can send me back to jail." He smiled wryly. "By the way," he added conspiratorially. "She ain't bad. You should find out if she's single."

"I'll pass." Sam laughed.

"You see her, you'll reconsider," Daniels assured Sam. "Hey, what time is it? I gotta get outta here before that big nurse decides to give me a sponge bath."

Sam laughed again. "You wish!"

Daniels gave him a weak smile that didn't reach his eyes. "They ran a bunch of tests. She's supposed to have some results today. Assuming they do, assuming she comes by, and assuming she speaks English and not that doctor-language, we should have some idea what's going on."

"You want me to hang around?"

"No. I want you to go win that trial so you can get back to finishing my will."

Sam nodded obediently. "Okay . . . Well, hopefully it's nothing too serious," he said lamely.

Daniels' eyes were closed when Sam shut the door behind him.

While Sam was talking with Daniels, Cathy, Roberts, and Miller were in Cathy's office at her request. She had called the meeting to discuss the possibility of a last-minute plea agreement. Cathy was behind her desk; Roberts and Miller occupied the small armchairs across from her. She had purposely selected armchairs that were not particularly comfortable—the better to avoid long meetings.

"Sam asked if we might still do a deal," she began. "Wanted to get your thoughts."

"Does that mean he's nervous?" Miller asked. "I'm not a lawyer."

"Not necessarily," Roberts replied. "I doubt he went into this case thinking he'd walk his client on all three counts—that rarely happens. He's probably trying to limit the damage."

"I think that's right," Cathy added. "He's a good attorney—better than good, really. I think he's expecting a mixed result, just like we are. A bird in the hand and all that."

"So why would we do an agreement now?" Miller asked.

"Same thing: certainty," Cathy offered. "If we do a deal, we can get a conviction and have some say in the sentence. Otherwise, we leave it to the jury and then the judge."

"I'm thinking we stand pat," Roberts offered.

Cathy was pleased to hear him use the word "we." She smiled encouragingly.

"Let the jury figure it out," he continued. "You tried a solid case. They've got the evidence, and they'll get the law. If they decide to walk him, so be it—it's not on you. And if Bridger goes light on him, it's not on you, either."

"What if they walk him on all counts?" Cathy asked. "Then we let the opportunity to get at least some time slip through our hands."

"I just don't think that's gonna happen," Roberts opined. "I've watched a lot of juries, and unless this one is fooling me, I think Gustafson is going down—at least on the possession charge. But even if he walks, it's not on you."

Miller snorted. "No one is going to believe the-drugs-were-already-in-the-room story, are they?"

"You underestimate the gullibility of people at your peril," Cathy advised.

"I'm with the detective, here, on this one," Roberts said. "I think they'll convict on possession and acquit on the drug-induced homicide. Could go either way on the possession with intent to distribute." He shrugged. "Just my two cents' worth."

"That's why we're here," Cathy said. She drank from her basketball-shaped coffee cup. "So, let me ask you this: let's say he is convicted only on the possession charge. Is he going to do time? He's got no record. He's young, etcetera."

"I doubt it," Roberts replied frankly. "Lots of pressure on judges to seek to rehabilitate offenders noncustodially."

"But someone died!" Miller said. Seeing the lawyers turn their heads toward her, she made a fist. "Someone's daughter died," she repeated, pounding the fist into a palm. "I'm sorry, but if you're dealing fentanyl and someone dies, there has to be repercussions. He needs to be in prison!"

A perfectly rational, understandable view of the world. "Agreed. But we're not the decisionmakers. Right now, I need your best guess as to what might happen," Cathy said. "I want him doing time; I'm just not sure he'll agree to that."

"But he's guilty as hell!" Miller lamented.

"Not until and unless the jury says so," Roberts reminded her. He looked to Cathy. "I agree with you; you cannot do a deal unless he agrees to do some time."

Miller was on her feet. "This is so much . . . crap!" Seeing the attorneys' reaction, she sat back down. "I'm sorry; I'm no lawyer, but this was a solid bust. My team and I put a lot of time into this one, and it couldn't have been better unless we had video of him handing the drugs to her!"

"Agreed," Cathy said. "Ashley, have faith in the system—it's a good one. Unfortunately, that demands faith in the public."

"I don't trust nobody, let alone a system."

And with what she saw all day, every day, it was no wonder. "I understand," Cathy said. "But Dylan and I have to try and keep the faith." She looked to him. "It's not easy sometimes."

The three of them sat quietly until Cathy stood up. "I'm going to tell Sam Johnstone no deals. We'll just have to wait until Monday to see what the jury has to say."

"And the judge," Miller added.

"One step at a time," Roberts advised her.

52

After a sleepless weekend, Sam was up with the chickens Monday morning and in the office signing paperwork by six-thirty. He arrived at the courthouse at eight-thirty and paced the hallways in front of the courtroom's enormous double doors until Gustafson arrived, whereupon Sam scooped him up and ushered him into the attorney-client conference room.

"What's up?" Gustafson asked. "You look like shit, by the way."

"Thank you," Sam replied. "Real quick: Bridger will make some remarks, then read the instructions—that will take what feels like forever. Then Cathy and I will give closings, then more instructions from the judge. Then it will go to the jury. I need you hanging tight and within ten minutes of this courthouse once the jury starts deliberating—understand?"

"Yes, boss."

"I'm serious," Sam snapped. "If the jury comes back with a question or a verdict and you aren't here, it won't matter what the verdict is, your ass will be in jail."

"Okay, okay. Stop nagging, will you? I'll be here."

"You'd better be," Sam warned.

"I will be!" Gustafson snarled. "And tell you what: this might be the last time you tell me what to do."

"Let's go," Sam said, and opened the door. "Go straight in and sit down."

When all were seated, Bridger called the court to order and spent the better part of an hour reading the instructions the jurors were to follow. It was no judge's favorite task, and Bridger stopped on multiple occasions to drink water. When at last he had finished, he put down the thick sheaf of papers.

"Ladies and gentlemen, you have now heard all of the evidence in this case and you have been given your instructions of law. The final piece of the puzzle will be closing arguments by each side. Again, I remind you that the arguments by counsel are not evidence but are intended to assist you in recollecting the evidence and to guide you in interpreting the evidence. You are not bound by anything the lawyers say. Rather, it is your recollection, understanding, and inferences that are important—not those of Ms. Schmidt or Mr. Johnstone. You will hear first from Ms. Schmidt. You will then hear from Mr. Johnstone, and because the government has the burden of proof, Ms. Schmidt gets the last word. Ms. Schmidt?"

Cathy was up quickly, nodding in acknowledgement to Bridger before turning her attention to the jurors and flashing a brilliant smile. "Ladies and gentlemen, I want to begin by thanking you, not only for your presence throughout this trial, but for your attention. One of the things we do as counsel is to watch jurors closely to ensure they are paying attention to what is going on, and I am happy to say that this jury was attentive through-out. We appreciate that. We know that as participants, cases can be inter-esting at times, and especially where scientific evidence is involved, not so interesting at others. So we appreciate your being here and your listening.

"Now, let's turn to what it is that you as jurors heard over the past few days. Let's talk about what it all means. You heard that the defendant, Trent Gustafson, was long suspected of being a drug dealer in Custer. Law enforcement informed you that they had been tailing and surveilling Mr. Gustafson for months prior to his arrest. Officer Baker, Detective Polson, and Detective Miller all testified to that, and testified that on the night in question they were positioned outside a motel where Mr. Gustafson had purchased a room with cash. You heard that right. The defendant purchased the room. In cash. Not anyone else."

She paused to let that sink in. When she was satisfied the jury under-stood the implication, she continued. "Each witness testified that the defendant initially occupied the room alone before being joined by two persons —a man and a young woman who are now deceased. The seventeen-year-old victim, Rebel Hayes, and a man who would soon overdose, Clayton Pierce. You heard testimony that those two arrived some ten minutes after Mr. Gustafson had entered the room. Don't leave your common sense at the door. Ask yourself, how and why would those two appear so soon after the room was rented. Were they friends? There's no evidence of that. Were they acquaintances? There is no evidence of that, either. The best answer is they had pre-arranged a visit there so that they could purchase drugs from Mr. Gustafson."

She paused to drink water. "In any event, Detective Miller and her team were watching, and she had already decided to arrest Mr. Gustafson whenever he departed the room. So just as planned, when he left his hotel room, she moved. Unfortunately, his arrest was too late, because as you will remember, immediately after effecting the arrest of Mr. Gustafson, Detective Miller and her team entered the motel room only to find Miss Hayes, a beautiful seventeen-year-old girl with a bright future ahead of her, dead with a needle in her arm. You will recall testimony that the needle contained fentanyl. You will recall testimony that the needle had Mr. Gustafson's prints on it."

She pointed to Gustafson. "You'll recall testimony that fentanyl was found in his personal property in his room in a place accessible only by him. I'll say it again: don't leave your common sense at the door. The fentanyl was in his possession; fentanyl was what killed Rebel Hayes; fentanyl was contained in a syringe with his fingerprints on it. Did you have a witness testify to actually seeing Mr. Gustafson hold the drugs or sell them? That'd be nice, of course, but the possible witnesses are dead. They are dead."

She stepped to the side of the podium and looked to Sam long enough that she could be certain the jury would, too. "Momentarily, Sam Johnstone will try and convince you that one plus one does not equal two. Do not allow him to take your eyes off the ball. The question is *not* what could have happened; the question is what happened. The question is *not* what was not done or discovered. Mr. Johnstone will likely spend some time talking about what law enforcement didn't do, what the Wyoming state laboratory didn't do, and what the technicians didn't do. In general, he will do every-thing he can to take your eye off the ball. But while he is talking, remember this: he is not talking as a concerned scientist. He is talking as an advocate; he is attempting to poke holes in the State's story to convince you that what you've seen and heard isn't enough to convict. Do not let him do that.

"Instead, focus on what you know. You know that Mr. Gustafson rented a room and was there alone until Rebel Hayes and Clayton Pierce arrived. You know that they were soon in distress. Miss Hayes died, and Mr. Pierce was saved by law enforcement. You can use your common sense and make reasonable inferences, and if you do that, you'll conclude that the pair went to Mr. Gustafson's motel room to buy drugs and they did so, resulting in her death and his overdose.

"Focus as well on the elements of the crimes and weigh the evidence. And when you do so, you will conclude we have met our burden and have shown beyond a reasonable doubt for every element of each crime that Trent Gustafson is guilty of possessing a controlled substance in a felony amount, that he had an intent to distribute that drug, and that he know-ingly distributed that drug to that little girl and she died as a result. Ladies and gentlemen, you have heard all the evidence that you need to find Mr. Gustafson guilty on each count. Thank you again."

Bridger nodded approvingly in Cathy's direction, then turned his atten-tion to Sam. "Defense may proceed with his closing argument."

There were lawyers who went on ad nauseum during closing argu-ments, leaving everyone in the courtroom exhausted and ill-tempered. Because he'd been in court with Cathy before, he was ready when she finished and moved slowly to the podium, still considering his final argu-ment. While brief, Cathy's argument had been persuasive in Sam's opinion, and from the body language of at least two jurors, in theirs, as well. As a strategic matter, he would focus initially on the two jurors he believed had bought Cathy's line of reasoning.

"Members of the jury, I too wish to thank you for your attentiveness throughout this trial. There's an old adage that says only the hard ones go to trial, and I think this is a case that fits squarely within that old saying. I don't envy you in the task that lies ahead. This is a hard one. But sometimes we need to take a step back. While Ms. Schmidt was talking, I was reminded of a discussion I had when I was a kid with a coach who took me under his wing. We were talking about hunting, and he showed me his favorite rifle. It was a single-shot .280. I remember asking him why he used a single-shot rifle and he replied, 'I only need one.'"

Sam smiled at his own story, and most of the jurors—including the two he was most concerned about—flashed brief smiles before sobering. "As the judge noted, I get only one shot at this—and that's okay, because you've been listening closely and I think that's all I'll need," he said. "Do you all recall how at the start of the trial Ms. Schmidt told you what the evidence would show? Do you remember that? She said the evidence would show this and that, and the witnesses would say this and that—do you remember? I do, and as I look back on last week, what I remember is that the witnesses did testify as she said they would. That doesn't surprise me: she's a fine attorney and I knew her witnesses would be up to snuff. But I don't think the evidence showed what she promised it would, and that's what I want to talk to you about—because the difference between what she said the evidence would show, and what the evidence did show, is what is known as reasonable doubt.

"You saw the evidence. You heard the witnesses. And what you and I both know is that while there is circumstantial evidence that my client possessed the drugs—they were in his room, after all—there is no direct evidence that he had them in his possession. No one testified to him having the drugs. Not Officer Baker. Not Detective Polson. Not Detective Miller. No one testified to the room being drug-free when he rented it. No one testified to him distributing drugs from the room," Sam continued. "Moreover, while there's evidence that someone might have intended to distribute them—a large amount, scales and whatever—there's again no direct evidence that it was my client, because they never looked for anyone else."

Sam could see open skepticism on the face of some jurors; he needed to address that, and quickly. "Oh, there's *some* evidence," he allowed. "There's circumstantial evidence. But is that enough? All we know is that there was fentanyl found in his room, and that his prints were on a syringe found in Rebel Hayes' arm and on bags of drugs in his room. But who is to say that she didn't bring the drugs and offer to sell them to him? He's gotta get it from somewhere."

Sam paused as an audible groan passed through the gallery. "We also know that there are dozens if not hundreds of fentanyl analogs, meaning that—like people—every dose of fentanyl is potentially different from another. Law enforcement could have eliminated the possibility that the fentanyl found in the room and the fentanyl found in her body were different. The laboratory could have reached the same conclusion. But they didn't. And because they didn't, there exists the possibility that the fentanyl that killed the victim was not from the same batch that was in Mr. Gustafson's room. We will simply never know."

As he wound down, he went after the State's jugular. "You were here; you saw and heard the State's investigators' and technicians' inability to answer my questions. 'Did you talk with the front desk?' 'Did you compare the drugs in her system to the drugs allegedly in his possession?'" he asked rhetorically, then waited while the implication of that sank in.

"The State of Wyoming's law enforcement officers did not perform a comprehensive investigation. The State of Wyoming's laboratory technicians did not perform a comprehensive investigation," he added. "Now look, it doesn't matter if they didn't have enough money or enough time, or if they simply forgot or didn't know. What matters is they didn't do a comprehensive job. Accordingly, we are left with doubt regarding the source of the drugs that killed Rebel Hayes. Ladies and gentlemen, thank you for your consideration; thank you for your service. On behalf of Trent Gustafson, I would ask you to undertake a vigorous debate, to consider the evidence, and to apply the facts to the law given to you by Judge Bridger. We believe that if you do so you will have no choice but to acquit Trent Gustafson of all charges. Thank you."

Again, Bridger nodded and then turned his attention to Cathy. "Ms. Schmidt, any rebuttal?"

Cathy was at the podium quickly and delivered a sharp, incisive rebuttal to Sam's remarks, focusing on the jury's need to keep it simple, to focus on the elements required and the evidence they had, and—most importantly —to "not leave your common sense at the door. Finally," she continued, "thank you again for your service in this matter. We ask that you carefully consider what you have seen and heard over the past few days, keeping in mind that absolute, positive, one-hundred-percent scientific certainty is neither the goal nor the standard here. Rather, to convict you must find only that the State has shown these allegations to be true beyond a reasonable doubt. Not beyond *any* doubt, but rather, beyond a *reasonable* doubt. I believe in my heart that the State has met its burden. Please consider what you saw and heard in the context of real life, not some televised courtroom drama. I believe when you have done so, you will find Mr. Gustafson guilty of all charges. Thank you."

———

After the jury had departed, and solely to ensure Gustafson would keep his mouth shut, Sam walked with his client through the mass of reporters and onlookers to the back entrance, where a friend of Gustafson's would see him to Sam's office. "Stay there until you hear from me," he instructed when they got to the door. "No bars, no booze, no drugs. Just—"

Sam was interrupted by Rebel Hayes' father. "Gustafson, you sonuvabitch!" he said as he approached.

"Mr. Hayes, I'm gonna ask you to back off a little bit, okay?" Sam said, feeling the hair on his neck stand on end.

"Yeah, you got that option," Hayes said. "I wish Rebel did—but he killed her!"

"Now, sir, we're here to let a jury figure that out," Sam cautioned. He held up both hands in an effort to keep Hayes from pressing forward. "If they decide that he did, a judge will take care of it."

Despite Sam's efforts, Hayes pressed forward. "You bastard!" he yelled, pointing at Gustafson. "You killed her! You killed my little girl! I'm going to see you rot in hell!"

"That's enough now," Sam said. "Back off. Let's let the jury make a decision."

"What about her? Didn't she have rights? She had a right to life, didn't she?" Hayes asked, edging closer.

Sam could feel the buzzing in his ears that always preceded his involvement in a violent situation.

"And you?" Hayes added accusingly, focusing on Sam. "How do you defend a piece of crap like him?"

"We've already had that discussion. It's my job," Sam responded levelly. "I can defend his rights without condoning anything he may have done."

"That's lawyer-speak," Hayes countered. "You're just as guilty as he is, if you ask me!"

"Mr. Hayes, I'm going to ask you one last time to back off just a little bit. You're in my bubble."

"And whattaya gonna do if I don't?" Hayes asked, leaning forward and balling his fists, his flushed face now so close to Sam's that his booze-soaked breath was evident.

He must have had a bottle with him. Sam was seeing red and about to respond when two court security officers stepped between them.

"Mr. Hayes, how about you back off a little, okay?" said the taller of the two, a woman Sam didn't know. "Mr. Johnstone is trying to get his client out of here."

"His client killed my daughter! What would you do?"

"Well," the officer replied, "I can't tell you I know for sure, but I'm pretty sure you bein' in jail won't help."

"He helps killers!" Hayes continued, pointing to Sam, oblivious to the officer's words. "He uses fancy legal words and tricks to let guilty people go free. Even when the evidence is clear!"

"I hear you, Mr. Hayes. Now, c'mon. Let's go talk for a minute," she said. Having positioned herself between the men, she turned toward Sam. "Mr. Johnstone, if you want to head on out that door"—she pointed with a finger —"Mr. Hayes and I will head that way." She indicated the opposite direction with her thumb.

"Got it," Sam said. He put a hand on Gustafson's back and pushed him out the door.

"Man," Gustafson said when they were outside. "That dude is crazy!"

"He's not crazy," Sam replied. "He's grief-stricken. But that doesn't make him any less dangerous."

"Seems to me it was you he was after," Gustafson observed. "And I gotta tell you, the look on your face. I thought you were gonna—"

"I don't want to talk about—"

"You would have killed him!"

"I just said I don't want to talk about it," Sam scolded. "Something you didn't understand?"

"Well, no, but—"

"You need to get in that car and get to my office and stay there. Lie low. I'll let you know when the jury has a verdict. When you hear from me, you need to get here. No detours. We will enter the courtroom together."

"How long will it be, you think?"

"No idea."

"But you killed 'em in there! They've got to see—"

"Juries do what juries do. From the outside, sometimes it seems like there's no reason, but there always is."

"If you were a betting man?"

"I'm not. Just do what I tell you."

Gustafson watched Sam for a moment, then extended a hand. "Thanks, Sam. You were the right man for the job. When I get acquitted, you and me need to head to Mexico for a few days. I know a remote resort where the sand is hot and the women are—"

"Go," Sam said, indicating the car that had just pulled up. "I'm gonna call Cassie to make sure you are there." When Gustafson had complied and the car was pulling way, Sam added, "Dumbass." He turned and made his way around the courthouse to the front entrance. As he rounded the corner, he saw Hayes in a passing car. From the passenger seat, the grieving man pointed at Sam with a hand mimicking a pistol and pulled the imaginary trigger.

"Nice," Sam grumbled. He mounted the stairs with his head up and on a swivel. "Ain't no discharge on the ground," the cadence went.

53

Hours later, Sam was in his office, reviewing a rental agreement. It had been purchased at a local bookstore for less than fifty bucks and wasn't worth that, as it didn't reflect Wyoming law. Sam had seen the client a year or so prior and had quoted his standard rate for the preparation of an agreement.

"You gotta be kidding me! I could just do my own, right?" the man had asked.

"You could," Sam admitted. "You could also do your own dental work." Sam made a lot of money in civil law matters when people didn't pay for his services upfront, only to have to pay him hundreds per hour to litigate the matter later.

"Well, I ain't paying that," the client had said, and departed with Sam's blessing. Predictably, the deal had gone sour, the man had gotten sued, and Sam was now untying the knots at his hourly rate, which would quickly exceed what he had quoted the man to do the deal properly. It was a common situation.

Sam was making notes when Gustafson knocked and entered. "What's up?" Sam asked.

"How long is it gonna be?" Gustafson whined.

"You sound like a kid asking if we're there yet," Sam replied. He turned from his computer and saw Gustafson sprawled with his legs on the side of a small recliner. "The jury will decide when the jury decides. And get your freakin' legs off my chair."

"Oh, sorry, man. I'm jus' wondering what you think," Gustafson said as he turned in the chair.

"I think it's up to the jury, and I don't know what they'll decide," Sam snapped. "I already told you that."

"What's up with you, man?"

Sam studied Gustafson, whom he suspected had somehow gotten high —probably quaffed a gummy bear laced with THC. Something had changed. Best to ignore it and hope he sobered up by the time the jury came back. "I'm trying to get some work done, and I don't like interruptions, especially when it's a question I can't answer."

"Dude," Gustafson replied. "I'm wonderin' what you *think*, man."

"I don't *think* in the manner you are asking about. I try the case and wait on the jury. Which is what you should do. Now go back to the waiting room and look at your phone or whatever and wait."

"Okay, man. Jus' checking."

"And listen to me: don't go running off on me. Last guy who did that missed his acquittal." When Gustafson snorted, Sam bristled. "I'm serious; your ass needs to be here—"

"You already told me that. I'll be here—"

"Because you and I have business to attend to."

"Only if I'm innocent."

Technically, juries didn't find defendants innocent, but that was a distinction certain to be lost on Gustafson on a good day, let alone in his inebriated condition. "I've done the best I could," Sam reminded him.

"For your friend's sake, I hope it was enough."

The jury deliberated until after eight p.m., after which Bridger sent them home for the evening. Sam in turn had instructed Gustafson to get something to eat and to go home and stay there. Instead, Gustafson had called in his retailers and told them to bring their people to help him celebrate his pending acquittal. By the time they all arrived at the Longbranch, his followers far outnumbered the other patrons, a collection of surly miners and cowboys. He was sitting in a corner booth with a hard-bodied woman on each side of him, enjoying their attention and unconsciously wiping his nose following his most recent visit to the men's room.

"That's some good stuff," the blonde cooed.

"Nothing but the best, baby," he said. He waved Gino over. "A round for the house—whatever they're drinking."

When the applause died down, Gino's eyes narrowed briefly. "Show me the money, there, big spender."

While meeting Gino's stare, Gustafson retrieved his wallet, extracted a thick wad of one-hundred-dollar bills, and handed it to Gino, who thumbed the wad and then looked around the room.

"You got a lot of folks here," he observed. "You got anyone with expensive taste, this won't go far."

"I've got more," Gustafson assured him.

"Your money." Gino shrugged, then turned and walked back to the bar. He pulled the string on a large bell, announcing someone had bought a round.

Gustafson sat back in the booth, then accepted a kiss from the brunette next to him. "These rubes don't realize it's their money. They been buyin' my stuff for years. Like shooting fish in a barrel. Got all these dudes who come to work in this town, leaving their wives and kids behind. Living in campers and hotels, they've got cash and nothing to do but drink and do drugs."

The blonde leaned over and whispered in his ear.

"Yeah, that too," he said. He watched as Gino and his staff poured and served, nodding his acknowledgment of the patrons who raised their glasses in his direction. Thoroughly enjoying the outpouring of appreciation, he scanned the room for familiar faces until his eyes came to rest on a large, brooding man drinking in a corner. In contrast to the others, when Gustafson made eye contact with this man, he stood and approached Gustafson's table.

"I suppose you think congratulations are in order," Hayes said.

"I'm sorry about what happened to your daughter," Gustafson said. "But you were there. You heard the testimony. I didn't have anything to do with your daughter's death. Here, let me buy you a drink," he suggested, signaling Gino.

"I don't want your booze," Hayes said quietly. "I don't want anything from you."

Gustafson raised his arms so the women could move away from him. "What can I do for you?" he asked, looking for some of his men.

Hayes placed both of his large hands on the table and leaned forward so his face was mere inches from Gustafson's. "You can die," he said. "And you will."

"Problem?" Gino asked as he stepped up next to Hayes. "Wrangler, I don't want no trouble in here. This man asked me to get you a drink. What'll you have?"

Hayes straightened and looked at Gino, then at the three men who had quietly surrounded him. "I'll pass," he said. "And you can call off these parasites," he added, indicating Gustafson's friends. "I'm leaving. But you should know that I intend to finish this. You and Sam Johnstone might get that jury to believe your lies, but I saw through them. You're going to pay."

He looked at the front door as Punch and a uniformed officer entered the bar. Punch took a quick look around the room, spotted the potential trouble spot, and with the officer in trail approached Gustafson's table. "Evening. How can I help?"

Gustafson smiled. "Deputy Polson! How good of you to come! You could—"

"My daughter is dead," Hayes said to Punch. "Well, lemme tell you something, *Detective*. This ain't over. This boy killed my Rebel, and I swear he's gonna pay."

Punch's eyes narrowed. He'd decided to ignore Gustafson's obvious bond violation. "Mr. Hayes, let's take a walk. I need to talk to you for a minute," he said. The uniformed officer stepped forward, but backed off when Punch shot him a look. "No need, Officer. Mr. Hayes is going to cooperate with us—aren't you, Wrangler?"

Hayes stared levelly at Gustafson for a moment, then looked at Punch. Tears welled in his eyes and his shoulders sagged. "It ain't right! He killed my kid!"

"Come on over here with me," Punch said softly. "Let's talk. I'm buying."

He watched Hayes closely for signs of compliance, and when at last Hayes took a step in his direction, he placed a hand on the grieving man's shoulder. "Officer Jones, get us a table, would you? And Gino, how about a couple of beers?"

"On the house," Gino said.

"Another round, Gino. For the house!" Gustafson added.

For a minute or so, the bar was subdued, but as Gino and his staff began to pour and serve, the noise returned to its prior level. The women returned and Gustafson tried to relax, but Hayes had gotten under his skin. "Let's get out of here," he said after a few minutes. "That dude is crazy, and I'm not so sure the law in this town is gonna do anything about it. Bunch of freakin' losers. All of 'em."

Across town, Cathy was cranky and irritable. The trial behind her, she'd called a meeting to talk about the Lee matter, but the conversation quickly turned to the Gustafson trial. She had tried a straightforward, clean case. She'd gotten the evidence she wanted viewed admitted, and the testimony she wanted heard in front of the jury. She felt that the jury had more than enough to convict on all counts—to include the disputed count three—but as expected, Sam had found the small gaps in the evidence and exploited them. Prosecutors accept the cases that need to be tried, and generally only the toughest go to trial. Thus, they also accept the ulcers, high blood pressure, anxiety, alcoholism, and sleepless nights that came with the job.

"They have to convict, right?" Miller asked. "How could they acquit?"

"A couple of things," Roberts opined. "Juries hold the State to its burden, and they think every case is like TV."

"But the evidence—"

"Was there, of course. But jurors sometimes want more than we can deliver. Good defense attorneys take advantage of that."

"Huh," Miller said. She sat back and drank from a small can of caffeine-laced liquid. "I've heard nothing but good things about Sam Johnstone. But to take on a guy like that—well, the money must be good, huh?"

Cathy stood and walked to her window. She'd given Roberts the background on Sam's decision to take the case.

"Johnstone can't possibly get involved in that," Roberts had observed. "That's about as clear a case of conflict of duty as you'll see."

"I'll leave the ethical decisions in his hands," she had replied. "I'm trying to get a verdict."

"So what now?" Miller asked.

"Now we wait," Cathy said. She retained doubts; the idea that Gustafson had any real information seemed unlikely. She caught her reflection in the window and didn't like what she saw. She needed some sun and some exercise. Maybe she and Kayla needed some time away. Kayla was sleeping fitfully, of late. She'd been to see her father recently and—as usual—had come home singing the praises of his new girlfriend. "She's young and pretty and likes me!"

She thought of Sam and her decision to take on the county attorney position, thereby cutting that cord. She turned to see Roberts watching her. He winked.

"Let's talk about Lee, shall we?"

54

At ten o'clock Tuesday morning, Bridger was in his chair with a foot on the desk, polishing a newer pair of dress boots. They were cognac, full-leather, laced, and had cost him a small fortune. But they were sharp and drew compliments, and that was important to him. When Mary knocked, he dropped a foot to the floor.

"Enter," he commanded.

"Your Honor, the jury has a question."

"Of course they do," Bridger replied sourly. "Did they write it down?"

"Yes."

"Okay, have the bailiff bring me the writing, and then contact counsel and have them meet me here in chambers."

"Yes, sir."

Several minutes later, there was a tentative knock on his door frame. "Your Honor?" It was Fred. Bridger didn't care for most people, but he liked Fred. A retired law enforcement officer, he'd been in-country during Vietnam's Tet Offensive and had a Purple Heart and recurring nightmares for his trouble. Upon redeployment, he'd endured the cold stares (at best) and denunciations (at worst) for decades until it became popular to support the military again. After several years as a law enforcement officer, he had retired and now served as a part-time bailiff during jury trials.

"Come on in, Fred," Bridger said, reaching for the folded piece of legal paper in the older man's hand. He read: *Can we find that he did not have possession of the drugs, but that he did provide them to the girl? Alternatively, can we find he possessed the drugs, but did not provide them to the girl? Or do we have to find both the same?*

"Thanks, Fred. I've got it. We'll see you in the courtroom soon."

They were straightforward questions, and he began to draft a response. He was finishing up when Mary informed him Sam, Gustafson, Cathy, Roberts, and Cates were present. "Have them come in," he said. When they were seated, he handed each attorney a copy of the questions he had received from the jurors. When each had read them and looked up, he continued. "Seems pretty straightforward. How do you want to handle this?"

"I'd suggest we simply say that the jury can make findings independent of each other," Sam offered.

Cathy and Roberts had their heads together. "Why don't we just answer the questions?" Cathy asked.

"Because that would almost tell the jury how to vote," Sam argued. "I think we draw a clean line if we just tell them they can decide each issue independent of the others."

Bridger was with Sam on this one. It appeared the jury was leaning toward a conviction on something—or at least discussing the possibility. From the tone of the questions, it was unlikely the jury was going to acquit Gustafson on all counts. Best to break the instruction down as cleanly as possible, because Gustafson would almost certainly fire Sam and appeal if he was convicted. "Ms. Schmidt?"

"Your Honor, I just think as a general matter, the less we say, the better."

"Judge, the jury is clearly confused," Sam said quickly. "I think we have an obligation to instruct them so they don't convict my client because of a misunderstanding."

"There's plenty of evidence on all counts, Your Honor," Cathy shot back.

"But—" Sam began, before stopping when Bridger held up a hand.

"Here's what I've drafted in response," he said, handing each a copy of his proposed response. "Thoughts?"

Sam read: *You as jurors must look to each count and determine if the State has met its burden of proof on each, without considering whether the State met its burden on any other count.* "I like it," he opined. "Answers the question and doesn't guide them."

Cathy shrugged. "No objection," she said.

"Well, let's get in there and provide the jurors a response," Bridger directed.

When all were assembled moments later, he read the jurors the response. As usual, several jurors were clearly nonplussed, expecting a more complete response. Jurors always did. But for good and valid reasons they were expected to simply follow instructions in deliberations. After sending them back to deliberate, he looked at his watch.

Sam had returned to his office and was pouring hot water over a bag of Japanese green tea when he got the call from Mary. "They've reached a verdict, Sam. Judge says be here in fifteen minutes."

"Got it," he replied to Mary. He switched lines and told Cassie to tell Gustafson to meet him in court in ten minutes. "And tell him not to be late."

As Sam approached the courthouse, he scanned the crowd for threats and unconsciously felt for the revolver. He groaned when he realized he had left it on his desk. Briefly, he thought about returning to his office, but a glance at his watch convinced him he didn't have time. Approaching the steps unarmed, he scanned his surroundings with a purpose, performing the same readiness drill he had for decades: know, locate, and observe.

The most obvious threat was Hayes and his cohorts, who were watching him closely from the top of the courthouse steps to the east side of the entrance. To the west of the doors, Damon and Reggie stood with their backs against the courthouse, arms folded. Sam met their stares and then shifted his glance to the distance between himself and the columns, then himself and the planters along the steps, and then between himself and the double doors. Three-quarters of the way up the stairs he saw a short, bearded man he had seen somewhere before. He seemed out of place at a courthouse, wearing oversized camouflage pants and a black, long-sleeve T-shirt with a motorcycle brand emblazoned upon it. They made brief eye contact before the little man looked away.

Damon and Reggie pushed themselves away from the wall at the same time the volume of voices in front of the courthouse increased a notch. Sam stopped, turned, and watched as his client stepped out of a long black SUV. Seeing Sam, he was taking the dozen or so steps two at a time while Sam waited for him halfway up. Gustafson was approximately ten feet from Sam when he heard the first of several gunshots and watched his client fold forward in slow motion. Sam ignored the pink mist and the tugging at his sleeve and caught his client as the young drug dealer collapsed into his arms.

He rolled onto Gustafson protectively, lifting his head only briefly to scan for the shooter. Most of the onlookers—to include Hayes and his supporters—had either frozen in place or dropped to their stomachs. On the steps above, Damon and Reggie had drawn weapons and were brandishing them. Only the small man was moving.

"There!" Sam pointed with a blood-covered hand. "There's your shooter!"

The buzzing in Sam's ears, combined with the noise from the crowd, made it impossible for him to hear anything. He carefully rolled his client onto his back lengthwise on a stair and placed his briefcase under the young man's head.

"Gus! Can you hear me?" he thought he shouted. "You're gonna be okay! Stay with me!"

"You're . . . fired. Effective now," Gustafson replied weakly. "I—I didn't . . ."

Sam searched Gustafson's eyes for clues, then shook him roughly. "What? You didn't what?"

Gustafson met Sam's stare. "You . . . lose," he said. He closed his eyes.

Sam spoke earnestly. "Listen to me, you shitweasel. I know what you are. I know the pain you caused. I know the lives you ruined. I took this case only because you told me you had information that could help a friend's kid that I wasn't going to get any other way. Now, I did my part. You're going to live, and you're going to do yours, or I will take off this leg of mine and beat you to death with it."

"Let him go!" It was a court security officer. "Sam! Let him go!"

With that, Sam released his client's arm and stood unsteadily, aware of gunshots in the distance.

"Sam! You're bleeding!" another security officer said. "Sit down. I'll get someone to help you."

55

The Custer National Bank had been formed just after the turn of the nineteenth century by three brothers named Clark who had moved west from Missouri to avoid federal usury charges. As the homesteaders and railroad came west, there was a need for capital to build and trade, and the brothers—using family money made in large part by selling substandard foodstuffs to the Union Army—started bank operations in the back of a wagon before constructing one of the first buildings in town.

When the first oil boom hit in the 1920s, the brothers funded sometimes risky oil exploration efforts in return for a share of the revenues and royalties, and when a number of those ventures succeeded the bank flourished to the point where it survived the Great Depression and World War Two largely intact. Throughout the post-war period, the bank floundered along, loaning money to ranchers on the strength of mortgages bought and sold, until the 1970s brought the discovery of vast coal deposits, starting a second boom that lasted another quarter century. Just about the time those dollars began to wane, coal-bed methane sparked yet another boom—this one sufficient in scope to enable growth to the point where Custer could survive on its own.

Through it all, the Clark brothers bought and sold assets, loaned and borrowed money, and survived crises man-made and otherwise. Now, well into the twenty-first century, the goal was to remain viable in the face of more convenient options such as online banking and digital currencies.

Thus, the continued provision of safety deposit boxes. Quaint but profitable.

Two days after the shooting, Sam entered the bank and got in line, looking alternately at his watch and out the large windows. He was aware of the stares but not surprised. He'd spent the prior two evenings in the emergency department; apparently the shooter—the little man in the camo pants—had winged Sam before running away and being critically wounded in a shoot-out with the Custer PD. According to Punch, Gustafson, Sam, and the female police officer who brought down the shooter were the only casualties, and the officer was expected to make a full recovery. He had assured Sam that he had a couple of men guarding the shooter's room, and he himself was hoping to get an audience with the man as soon as—and if—he awakened.

"We'll find out who did this, Sam," Punch had assured him. "I promise."

Now, standing in line wearing sweats and a sling, Sam was weary, feeling the effects of the prescription painkillers, and was about to ask for help when he was approached by a middle-aged man wearing a coat and tie.

"I'm Sean O'Hanlon," the man said. "My tellers are saying you might need some assistance?"

"Sam Johnstone," Sam said, accepting the outstretched hand. "I need to get into a safety deposit box."

"You bet," O'Hanlon replied. "Follow me. You know the number?"

"I don't," Sam replied. "Sorry."

"Give me just a minute."

After O'Hanlon departed, Sam paced for a few minutes, then sat and read part of a hunting magazine. He was about to get up when O'Hanlon appeared at the other end of the lobby and waved to Sam. As Sam approached, O'Hanlon's brow furrowed. "You opened this one with that Gustafson fellow, right?"

"Yes." Sam shrugged. "Is that an issue?"

"He the guy that got killed?"

"Yeah."

"You didn't have a dual key provision, did you?"

"Not that I'm aware of."

"Then it shouldn't be an issue. Wait here while I check." O'Hanlon slipped through the door and closed it behind him, presumably to check a record of some sort. A scant moment later he opened the door and indicated Sam should enter. "We're good," he said brightly. "Could I see your key?"

Sam handed him the key. O'Hanlon looked at it, went to a nearby wall, and withdrew the metal box from its frame. "Is there anything else I can do?"

"I don't think so."

"Will you be long?"

"Depends," Sam replied. He quickly inserted the key, turned it, and opened the top, then slammed it shut. The little bastard. "Thank you," Sam said. "I do have a question."

"Yes?"

"Can you tell me when that box was last accessed?"

"Of course," O'Hanlon said. "I just looked at the registration materials online, and I happened to notice it was accessed at four p.m. Monday."

"Thank you," Sam said tightly as he removed the key from the lock. "You can close the account."

"I think it will take two signatures to do that." O'Hanlon was shaking his head sorrowfully. "We'll have to have that man's estate probated."

"Whatever," Sam replied.

"Mr. Johnstone . . . I just want you to know that we're all real glad that . . . well, that you made it."

"Thanks," Sam said. He tossed O'Hanlon the key and left the vault.

56

Sam was attempting to sign pleadings, but the sling was effectively preventing him from doing so. "Damn it!" he finally yelled in frustration. He was anticipating Cassie's scolding when she buzzed him.

"Sam?"

"I'm sorry!" he barked. "It's just that this damned sling—"

"It's that lady from Bozeman," Cassie interrupted. "I think it's bad news."

What else? "Okay. I'll take it in here," Sam said. "Patch her through."

"Okay, Sam. I hope everything is okay," Cassie said, knowing it was not.

"Me, too," he replied, also knowing it was not. He looked idly at the brief he had prepared for the argument in front of Judge Bridger. When the phone rang, he took a deep breath before answering. "Hello?"

"Is this Mr. Johnstone?"

"It is."

"This is Linda Dillon from the hospice facility here in Bozeman. We've spoken before."

Yes, they had. "Good morning," Sam said. "How can I help you?"

"It's—it's your father. There's no easy way to say this, but he passed away this morning. It was peaceful. I don't think he felt a lot of pain," she said. When Sam didn't respond, she continued. "I just felt like you should know."

There was a buzzing in Sam's ears. Was it a bad connection? "Thank you for your consideration," he said. "We weren't close, but I want you to know how much I appreciate the care you gave him and the time that you have taken to keep me informed."

"You are very kind," she said. "It seems to me that he was kind as well. It's a shame that the two of you didn't get along. Did you get a chance to call him?"

"No," Sam admitted. "I—I've been kind of busy." It was a lame excuse. He knew it; she knew it. He had missed his shot.

"Well," she said. "I'm sure he understood."

Sam was ready to hang up when she stopped him. "What would you like us to do now?"

"What do you mean?" Sam asked.

"With his remains?"

"Oh . . . I guess I never thought of that. Did he say anything?"

"No, not to me."

Sam had never given it any thought. "Is there a cemetery in Bozeman with a section for paupers?"

"Well, yes, but why?" she asked. "Your father had money. Let me ask you this: would you like us to put him in the veterans section?"

"Is he eligible?" Sam seemed to recall his mother mentioning his father's service once.

"Well, we think so. Our records show that he served honorably. Did you get the package we sent?" Linda asked.

Sam was silent, trying to remember his mother's words.

Linda was waiting patiently, but finally asked, "Would you prefer the veterans portion of the cemetery?"

"Yeah, I think so," Sam said, rubbing at his eyes. "I've really got to get to court," he lied. "Is there anything else?"

· · ·

"Well, just the package." When Sam didn't respond, Linda asked again. "Did you get the package we sent?"

"I don't know," Sam said. Truthfully, he hadn't checked. Cassie had been harassing him about going through his mail, but he hadn't gotten to it. "I'll ask my secretary."

"Well, keep an eye out. It sounds like you are going to be surprised."

"I'll do it. Thanks again." He hung up the phone and sat back in his chair. Could this day possibly get any worse? When the knock at his door came, he wiped at his eyes and turned to his computer. "Yes?" he said over his shoulder.

"Is everything okay, Sam?" Cassie asked.

"Well, no, not really. My father passed away this morning, I guess."

"I'm so sorry," she said. "I know the two of you weren't close, but still. Is there anything I can do?"

Sam pretended to keyboard. "Look for a package from Bozeman. Supposedly it has some stuff in it for me."

"It's been in the conference room for two weeks."

He could tell she was standing in the doorway, unsure what to do. "You've got a caller waiting."

"I've got to get this done," he lied. "Close it behind you, please."

"You might want to take this one."

"Who is it?"

"Grant Lee."

Criminy. "Close the door," he said, then picked up his phone. "This is Sam."

"Mr. Johnstone, this is Grant Lee."

"Sam will be fine," Sam said. "What's up?"

"I'm in deep trouble. Don't know if you saw, but Cathy Schmidt thinks I killed that woman!"

"You did."

"Well, yeah—but it was self-defense!"

"I hear you. There's a provision for that," Sam said. "Of course, it involves you showing up with your lawyer and pleading that."

"That's why I'm calling you!"

"No dice. I'm conflicted—you know that."

"It's never bothered you before."

"Wow. You really know how to persuade a guy," Sam snarked. "Let's say I'm a born-again ethical attorney and call it good."

"Mr. J—Sam . . . I need help."

"Don't we all."

"I'm serious. If you don't help me, I'll—"

"I'm sorry, Grant, but right now I'm too busy, and as I mentioned, I've got a conflict."

"I need you to believe me! I need your help!"

"I'm sorry," Sam said. He hung up slowly, then stood, walked to the window, and looked outside, dreading the November wind.

57

The pitch was right down the middle of the plate. Sam shifted his weight from his back foot, took a short stride with his front, and swung. He saw the ball off the bat, dropped the bat, and sprinted toward first base until he heard the first base coach holler, "Sam! Slow down! It's out of here!"

His heart pounding in pure joy, he rounded the bases, accepting his third base coach's congratulations between third base and home plate.

He touched the plate with one foot, turned to the dugout, and jogged toward his teammates, enjoying their smiles. En route, he snuck a look to where his father had been sitting with a skinny blonde woman only moments before. Their seats were empty. He accepted more congratulations as he made his way through the dugout—in high school, balls leaving the park were rare, after all. He found his cap and glove and walked to the end of the dugout, exulting in one of the game's—and of sports'—greatest individual accomplishments. A home run.

He took a deep breath, drank water from a paper cup given to him by one of the team's benchwarmers, and then stood. Turning to face the back of the dugout, he looked through the broken wood slats and saw his father in the parking lot, making out with the skinny blonde like two eighth graders at their first dance.

"You missed it! You missed my first home run!" he yelled in disgust.

His father didn't respond, focused as he was on the barfly in his arms. The pounding coming from the bleachers was all he could hear. "Sam! Sam!"

Were they cheering for him?

"Sam! Sam!"

He turned from the dugout and saw the door to his bedroom. He was soaking wet, sitting on his bed in the small apartment. It had been yet another dream. He struggled up on one foot and hopped over to the side of his bed while the pounding continued, strapped on the artificial leg, and moved as quickly as possible to the front door, from whence the pounding emanated. Without thinking, he ripped the door open. "What?" he demanded.

"Sam!" Bill said. "I was about to call the cops! What the hell are you doing? You're yelling and raising hell, and scaring the hell out of Mrs. Hamilton. She called me and asked me to come over."

"I—I'm sorry, Bill," Sam replied, breathing heavily in an attempt to catch his breath. Seeing Mrs. Hamilton behind Bill, he began an apology. "Ma'am, I am so sorry, I—"

"You need help, young man!" the old woman interrupted. "How many times is this? You're waking peaceful people up in the middle of the night! Scaring old women like myself and such!"

"I know, and I'm sorry. I'm seeing a counselor—"

"Well, good for you. But my patience is wearing thin," she said as she marched off.

When she was gone, Bill offered a wry grin. "I'm sorry, Sam. She doesn't understand."

"No, Bill. I'm sorry for disturbing all of you."

Bill studied Sam for a moment. "You need a roommate. A woman, unless—you're not gay, are you? Not that it would matter," he lied.

"No, Bill, I'm not gay," Sam said. "And no woman wants to be around me right now."

"I dunno," Bill said. "You're a decent-looking guy; good job. Hell, I got a sister over in Grand Junction what—"

"Bill, thanks for checking on me, and thanks for not calling the cops. I appreciate it," Sam said, trying to close the door.

"Okay, well, you take care of yourself, Sam. And get some help."

Sam closed the door, only then realizing he'd answered it in his boxers, his artificial leg exposed. "At least they'll know I'm not faking it."

58

On a sunny morning in early December, Sam was a thousand miles from Custer, admiring the dawn sun shining on the face of the Catalina Mountains, just north of Tucson, Arizona. Days earlier he'd gotten an email from an old Army buddy, a man he'd met in Ranger School at what used to be called Fort Benning and served with in Afghanistan. Rob Gray was now a defense contractor based near Los Angeles and was managing a project near Flagstaff. Sam looked at his calendar and—having no court scheduled that week—accepted on the spot. Hours later, he hopped in his truck and made the eighteen-hour drive from Custer to a resort on the north side of Tucson in one sitting, surviving on beef jerky and gas station coffee. The windshield time had been good for his morale; he'd passed the hours listening to Jon Pardi, Midland, and Cody Jinks and thinking about everything except his clients' problems. He hadn't seen Rob since his medical evacuation from Afghanistan but recognized the walk as Rob crossed the parking lot to meet him.

"Dude, it's been a while," Rob said as they hugged. "Look at that piece of shit." He eyed Sam's truck. "You drove that all the way?"

"I did," Sam replied with a smile. "Thanks for the invite. I need this."

"What's with the sling?" Rob asked, eyeing Sam's arm.

"Got a little banged up."

"I didn't realize being a lawyer was so tough." Rob laughed. "Surprised you made it in that thing."

"That's my fishing ride."

"Oh, man." Rob laughed again. "You still chasing those little fish?"

"I like the places where little fish live."

"Yeah, well, I'll take three hours and eighteen holes any day," Rob said. "You play? This place has two spectacular courses . . . of course, I guess with that, you're out."

"Haven't played in years—since I left D.C."

"Well, we've got a lot of catching up to do," Rob said. "Here." He offered Sam a beer.

"No, thanks," Sam said. "On the wagon right now."

Rob looked quizzically at Sam—they'd downed a lot of booze together. "You okay?"

"Fine."

"Well, more for me. Give me that," he said, reaching for the old duffle bag that served as Sam's luggage.

"I've got it," Sam said.

"You sure?" Rob looked pointedly at Sam's legs. "How's the leg?"

"Rob, I lost five of my men," Sam said, shouldering the bag. "How bad could it be?"

"Wasn't your fault." Rob shook his head. "Intel was bad—as always, right? What were you going to do? Coulda been any of us."

Sam snuck a glance at his old friend as they began to walk toward the resort. Rob's face was flushed, and he'd put on some weight. "Where are we going?" Sam asked.

"Just up this way. We have adjoining suites. Share a deck, the whole bit."

"I meant to registration—I got a room."

"You *had* a room. I cancelled your registration," Rob said. When Sam began to protest, he raised a hand to stop him. "It's all on the company. I got it okayed, you being a hero and all. Besides, Beth—she's my girlfriend—insisted. She's heard a lot about you."

Somewhere along the line, Sam had heard of Rob's divorce from his wife Tana. Rumor was that it had been especially ugly. "Rob, I don't know, man. I'm kind of monastic, really, and you two probably need your privacy."

"Sam, we live together; we will leave you alone." Seeing Sam's hesitation, he continued. "It's not gonna be weird. I promise."

Sam relented. "You mean it's not going to be like that night in Fayetteville when you and that stripper climbed naked onto the roof of that hotel with a five iron, a bucket of balls, and a bottle of scotch?"

"Christ, I forgot about her. She was something else—quiet, here's Beth," Rob said as the door to the luxurious suite opened. "Sam, I'd like you to meet Bethany. Beth, this is Sam."

She was, as Sam had expected, beautiful—and a near clone of Rob's ex. She was intelligent, charming, and a good cook as well, Sam would find. She'd done the shopping before his arrival and seemed to enjoy cooking for the three of them, a glass of merlot at the ready. Each evening, Sam and Rob would sit on the suite's kitchen barstools and swap tales while she prepared dinner. Beth, who owned a boutique clothing store in some Los Angeles suburb Sam had never heard of, listened closely, alternately amused and horrified as the men shared stories of youthful, drunken, testosterone-fueled shenanigans.

"Oh, my gosh!" she said one evening. "The two of you were such trouble."

"We were, I suppose," Sam agreed. He was drinking green tea, occasionally augmented with coffee or diet cola. Rob was pounding craft beers. Most evenings, that was how it went: Rob drinking heavily, Sam content to stick with non-alcoholic beverages and trying not to count Rob's drinks.

One afternoon, when Rob had started early and passed out on the couch just after lunch, Sam and Beth decided to take a short hike into the Catalinas. For three hours they talked and hiked. Beth was well-conditioned and strong, and on occasion she helped an increasingly frustrated Sam navigate the boulder-strewn trail they had chosen. When at last they had reached a lookout, they filled their lungs with crisp, clean air and drank water from bottles he had loaded in a small backpack. She watched silently while Sam adjusted the socket on his prosthesis.

"Damned thing is bugging me," he said. "This isn't what they are for."

"You are amazing."

He turned his head to look at her. She had removed a baseball hat she had borrowed from Rob. He watched while she smoothed her hair and replaced the cap. The dark sunglasses she wore obscured her eyes. "What are you talking about?" he asked.

"You, Sam. What you've been through. What you've overcome. The fact that you are here."

He quickly erased the visions of explosions, PTSD episodes, lost jobs, and ruined relationships that came to mind. "You don't know me very well."

"I don't," she agreed. "But Rob says you are a good man, and I haven't seen anything to show me he is wrong."

"He saw a lot of the same stuff." Sam looked at her for a long moment, not knowing what else to say. It was always that way. "Maybe we ought to head back down," he said, changing the subject. "Down is always harder for me than up."

On the way down, she helped on a couple of occasions as he attempted to navigate particularly difficult spots in what passed for the trail. Twice, he felt as if her hand lingered longer than necessary.

A couple of nights later, Rob was again asleep on the couch early, snoring softly. They had shared a few war stories and a morose Sam was standing on the deck drinking ice water and wondering if his wound could be infected by a dip in the hot tub when he heard the sliding glass door open and close and felt Beth's footsteps on the deck. In a break from the norm, she had been drinking heavily with Rob that evening. She swirled a glass of sangria from a pitcher she'd made earlier, then traced a long finger in the condensation on the glass.

"I think he is drinking too much," she said, placing the glass on the rail between them. "I think he is struggling."

"I can see that," Sam agreed, nodding slowly. He had tried not to notice, but Rob's drinking was prodigious. "He's trying to forget, I suspect."

"What can I do?" she asked.

"Not a lot. Make your feelings known. Don't enable him. He'll either figure it out, or he won't."

"He ignores me." When Sam didn't respond, she pulled a piece of an orange from the glass, bit off the fruit, and tossed the rind off the deck, then brushed a loose strand of blonde hair from her eyes. "Surely he knows I'm unhappy."

"Not necessarily. When we're in what I call the 'active alcoholic vortex,' we don't really see anything," Sam explained. "The booze has a hold on us, and it substitutes for emotion, judgment, and empathy. We're either drinking or thinking about drinking—anything to keep us from thinking about the real issues out there."

"That's terrible," she said, replacing the glass on the railing.

"It is," he said. He was thinking about PTSD- and booze-fired shit-shows in his past when he noticed she had turned so that she was facing him directly. "He's very jealous of you, you know," she said.

"I doubt it," he countered. "I lost men."

"Not that. Your . . . sobriety." She picked up her glass and swirled the contents but didn't drink. "How did you stop?"

"I asked for help," Sam said. "But it took a while."

"He's afraid to ask," she said. "Afraid of what people will say. Afraid for his new career. Says no one can understand."

"Perfectly normal," Sam said. "Reasonable, even."

"So how do I—"

He thought he saw a tear making its way down her cheek before she brushed at it with a well-tanned shoulder. "You don't," he said. "Beth, I'd advise you to figure out whether you can live with it or not. Then tell him and see what happens. It's up to him to make the change."

"Because he won't change until he's ready, right?" She looked at him with deep blue eyes, anticipating his agreement. She moved closer, and was now well inside his bubble.

He shook his head. "I don't know anyone who was *ready* to change. People go to treatment or otherwise stop drinking because they are in trouble. Either they are court-ordered, or their wife and family are on their ass, or they are sick and tired of being sick and tired. People seek help when the pain gets unbearable—no one is ever really *ready*."

"What a terrible thing."

He shrugged. "Addiction is a bitch."

"Did—did you lose someone because of your drinking?" she asked, studying him closely.

"In part, yeah," he said, shaking ice from his glass into his mouth. Veronica had hounded him about his boozing at times before she walked out. "But I have other issues."

"You're a hero," she said.

"I did my part is all," Sam said. "And so did Rob."

He could smell her perfume and the wine on her breath. She was too close, and he felt his heart pounding. He turned from her and leaned into the deck rail and looked out over the desert. The acacia and saguaro were pungent, and he was trying to focus on their smell and think about anything to take his mind off her presence when she broke the silence.

"I'm thankful for men like you," she said. Out of the corner of his eye, he could see her watching him. A few seconds later, having apparently made up her mind, she moved close to him and put her head on his shoulder.

He shivered. "Beth—"

"Don't worry," she said. "You're safe."

"It's not that," he said, wondering how Rob could ignore a woman like this. Then, remembering his own history, he knew exactly how. "You're lonely and drunk and he's my friend and—"

"Sam, I just need to be close to a man for a bit." She put an arm around him, and he could smell her hair and the lotion he'd watched her apply earlier that evening.

He took a deep breath and looked at the stars. They stood together for a long time. At some point, she suggested they try the hot tub. *In another life.* He declined, and she remained uncomfortably close to him until his phone rang. It was after midnight and the number was Punch's. This couldn't be good.

"I need to take this," he said quickly. He stepped away from Beth, knowing she was watching him. "Hello?"

He couldn't say he was surprised.

When he rang off and turned toward her, Beth was watching him, concerned. "What is it, Sam? Is everything okay?"

"A guy just died," Sam replied. "He wanted me to help him. I refused. Sounds like he put a gun in his mouth."

She embraced him again. "Oh my God! You poor thing! What can I do?"

"Nothing," Sam said. "You've been . . . very kind." He tried to pull away. "I'm tired, Beth. Long drive tomorrow." She hugged him a little too long before they parted. "He was an ass."

"Who?"

"The guy who died. But damn it, I should have done something, said something. . ." He sighed heavily. "Good night, Beth." He walked into his room and closed the glass door behind himself. He was lying on his back, staring at the ceiling and listening to Jelly Roll, trying to think of anything other than booze or drugs, when an hour later the door to his suite opened.

Still later, he started his truck and drove north, drinking coffee, listening to a playlist, hating himself, and trying not to re-live yet another poor decision.

59

According to the radio reports Sam heard on his way into town, the shooter had been life-flighted to Denver and had hung on for a couple of days before he died. Between that and Lee's offing himself, Sam wasn't entirely surprised to see Punch's car outside his apartment as he pulled into the parking lot. "You're like a buzzard," Sam remarked as he exited his truck and painfully shouldered the old duffle bag.

"That's better than what a lot of people call me," Punch said truthfully. "Need some help?"

"No. Come on in. I didn't know you were coming or I'da laid out some Christmas cookies."

Punch smiled wanly and briefly. "Sam, I was sorry to hear about your dad." Seeing Sam's surprise, he explained. "Cassie told me. While you were gone, I stopped in, and she told me that you'd gotten a package from some hospice outfit in Bozeman. Between your dad, you and your client getting shot, the whole deal with Ronnie, Judge Daniels, and now Lee, she's worried about you. Your life's kind of a shit-sandwich of late."

"Thanks for pointing that out," Sam said. "We weren't tight. Any of us," he added. "And I'd appreciate it if you spare me any pseudo-psychological bullshit."

"Actually, I was gonna invite you for dinner with me and Rhonda,"

Punch replied. "Not sure those gas station hotdogs are doin' you any favors."

"Thank you, Doctor," Sam said sarcastically.

"Ouch," Punch replied. He took a seat at the small dining table in Sam's kitchen. "Did I mention that hurt people . . . hurt people?"

"Sorry. I don't mean to be a dick." Sam stood and walked to his refrigerator, opened the door, looked in, and closed it. "How's the judge?"

"Not sure. The good news is, I haven't heard anything bad. I'm sure he's barking at the nurses and doctors—he can't be much of a patient. Like putting a sweater on a cat."

No news was good news. Sam smiled. "I'd offer you something to drink—"

"No need," Punch said. "Can't stay long. Just need to ask you a couple of questions."

"About?"

"First, how come you keep that bottle of beer in your fridge?" Punch asked, pointing.

"As a reminder. And if it's ever gone, I will be too."

"Interesting approach." Punch looked at his watch. "Cassie says you spoke with Lee the other day."

"Cassie talks too much. They find him here?"

"No. Back east somewhere."

"Then what's your interest?"

"Just doing the cop thing, trying to help out another guy."

"All I know is he called and wanted help," Sam explained. "And I said no."

"That's what I heard."

"Then why are you busting my—"

"Just checkin'," Punch interrupted. "Trent Gustafson."

"Yeah?"

"You ever seen that guy who shot him? And you?"

Sam thought about seeing the man earlier at the VA. "No, I don't think so . . . Maybe. I'm not sure. Could have."

"I'll put that down as a solid 'unknown,'" Punch said. He looked up from his notepad. "Gustafson have any enemies you know about?"

"How many people live in Custer?"

Punch snorted. "Right. Anyone in particular?"

"Well, you know as well as I do there are a lot of people in jail doing time who covered for him," Sam said. "And there's others who, if they thought he was gonna testify, well, it wouldn't do them any favors."

"Like Davonte Blair?" When Sam looked steadily at his kitchen wall but didn't respond, Punch nodded. "Some of Davonte's family members have been around—I'm sure you've seen them?" Sam nodded. "Disregarding any possible involvement with your former client, any reason to believe they might have been involved?"

"None that I'm aware of," Sam replied. "The shooter . . . he never said anything?"

"Nope," Punch said. "By the way . . . they said he's from D.C."

"Who?"

"The guy who shot your client."

"Yeah . . . so?"

"So . . . did you know him? Before, I mean."

"No," Sam replied. "Why, what are you thinking?"

Punch shrugged. "Well, it wasn't much of a secret that you weren't fond of your client—"

Sam looked down at Punch. "You're the one who encouraged me to represent him! And there's the little matter of me getting shot, too."

"Yeah, I know, but there's a complication beyond that."

"What's that?"

"The shooter. He didn't die of his wounds," Punch began. "Doc Laws says the docs in Denver are telling him he mighta been poisoned while he was in the hospital. In Denver."

"Punch, are you shitting me?" Sam said. "Your theory is that I had a guy shoot my client, and then I went to Denver and offed the shooter?"

"I wouldn't call it a theory, as much as I'd say I'm examining all possibilities." Punch made another note and then stood, as well. "People tell me things. Me? Id'a never thought of it. But I hear things and I start thinking that, well, maybe he got shot by accident. Of course, if you'd tell me—"

"I was in Tucson. Spent some time with a friend." And his girl.

"How'd you get there?"

"I drove."

"Through Denver?" Punch asked. When Sam didn't answer, he pressed on. "Come back the same way? Sam, I just need someone to vouch for your whereabouts. I mean, I personally don't suspect you, of course, but I've got folks whispering in my ear and lots of interest in this one, so if you could tell me—"

Don't insult me. "I don't know, because I don't know when the shooter got offed, now do I?"

Punch smiled. "You're no dummy. But just for shits and giggles, can anyone vouch for your whereabouts from the night before last to early yesterday—say from around eleven p.m. to around four a.m.?"

She could, but would she? And did she really need to? "I'm not sure."

"I'm just trying to eliminate everybody," Punch explained. "You gonna make this hard?"

"Just legal," Sam said. "And that's all I'm going to say right now," he added, gesturing to the door.

"This witness," Punch said as he grabbed the handle. "You'll give me a name?"

"Soon as you name the 'people' you keep referring to."

"Now you know that can't happen."

Sam knew, but he didn't like it. "If I have to, when I have to."

"Sam, it might be easier if—"

"It wouldn't be," Sam interrupted. He could smell the perfume and tanning lotion and could taste the sangria. "Trust me."

Punch watched Sam for a long minute, then rendered a faux salute before leaving Sam's apartment and walking to his unmarked car. Sam turned the locks, unconsciously felt for his revolver, then returned to his small kitchen.

60

Cassie had delivered the box to his apartment while Sam was out of town. Earlier he had retrieved it and placed it on a chair in his kitchen, awaiting the right moment to open it. Occasionally, he would sneak a peek, but until just now he had avoided the temptation. The return address was from Bozeman's hospice center, and a neat feminine hand had inscribed Sam's name on the address label.

He was feeling less sorry for himself tonight. His discussion with Linda Dillon at the hospice center had him feeling guilty before he ever left Custer, and events in Tucson had him questioning everything, so on the drive back he had called his sponsor and confessed to screwing his buddy's girlfriend. He'd done the reading and prayer suggested and was feeling better about yet another bad decision. Earlier tonight he'd had a pizza delivered. He ate half, tasting none of it, and had to move the longneck bottle of beer to make room for the leftovers. "Evening, soldier," he said.

Finished cleaning up, he returned his gaze to the box and made his decision. Using a large kitchen knife, he cut several layers of tape from the box and carefully pried apart the flaps at the top. With one hand, he moved things around as he performed a quick perusal of the contents. At the top was an inch of yellowing papers of various sizes and stocks. Below that were newspaper clippings covering various aspects of Sam's life: athletic achievements, high school graduation, his commissioning as a lieutenant, a copy of a news article written about his being wounded, a program from his law school graduation. How in the world did Les locate and obtain all that?

Below those were a few dusty framed certificates and diplomas. Still lower in the box were several plastic cases that Sam recognized immediately as those that held military medals. He began with the papers. Thumbing rapidly through them, he found a copy of the marriage certificate between Les and Sam's mother, as well as a faded copy of his own birth certificate. Further down, he located Les' diploma from basic training and a certificate commemorating his graduation from airborne school. The medals included a Bronze Star and a Purple Heart. He removed those and found a shoulder patch from the 173rd Airborne Division. At the bottom of the box was a set of dog tags and a sealed envelope. On the outside of the envelope Sam recognized his father's handwriting. It read, *To be opened only if I don't get back.*

Sam sat back in his chair and took a deep breath. Everything he thought about his father had been contextualized in an instant.

There was little doubt about it: given the medals, ribbons, and the patch, Les was a hero. Damn it, he or Sam's mother should have said something! Given Les' failure to discuss his service, and his mother barely mentioning Les' time in uniform, Sam had always assumed his father had essentially "been there and fogged a mirror." But had he known, he might have better understood the absences, the awkward silences, the inability to get close—especially after his own service.

He was looking at his reflection in the television's black screen when his phone rang. He was tempted not to answer, but he paid a small fortune every month for an answering service. It could be important. Without checking the number, he answered, "Hello?"

"Are you alone?" Mickey asked.

"I am," he said.

"Can I come in?"

"What? Where are you?"

"I'm outside." When he didn't reply, she pressed the issue. "So are you going to let me in, or what?"

An hour later he donned his leg and the sling, rolled out of bed, and walked to his bathroom—what a realtor would grandly term the "master bath" in the tiny residence. He stopped short upon seeing his reflection in the mirror. He was getting pale and paunchy. He slapped his stomach with both hands and vowed for the umpteenth time to start getting in shape.

Minutes later, he made his way quietly to the kitchen and stood in the darkness, staring at the refrigerator until he made his decision.

What the hell.

He retrieved the lone bottle of beer, walked the few feet to the small living area, and sat heavily in his worn recliner. How many nights had he spent in this chair?

He held the bottle in both hands and closed his eyes, enjoying the feel of the cold glass. How many bottles like this, in how many places? Four continents, from tiki bars to honkytonks, from English and Irish pubs to Mediterranean and Gulf of Thailand waterfronts. The music, the women, the good times. Truth be told, he'd taken more out of booze than it had ever taken out of him. Way more. Maybe he had overreacted.

Besides, everyone had their limits. Gustafson, Lee, his dad—people around him were dropping like flies, not to mention the new scar. A couple of beers never hurt anyone. His sponsor might not understand—screw him. But VA Bob—he'd cut a guy some slack. Eighteen months sober; that was enough to show he had a handle on it.

He put a hand to the bottle top and tightened his grip. *If it's ever gone, I will be too.*

"Sam?"

COURSE OF CONDUCT

For one small-town lawyer, the defense of a client could be his undoing at the hands of another...

In the latest twist of fate, defense attorney Sam Johnstone confronts a formidable challenge: defending a renowned surgeon accused of domestic battery against her estranged husband, who happens to be a local attorney. This seemingly straightforward misdemeanor case spirals into a complex murder trial, where Sam must show his client acted in self-defense. But the courtroom isn't his only battleground.

Sam finds himself in a difficult situation when a former lover, obsessed with him, directs threatening attention towards him and his client. He faces a tough choice: striving for success in the courtroom or focusing on safety outside of it.

**Get your copy today at
severnriverbooks.com**

ABOUT THE AUTHOR

Wall Street Journal bestselling author James Chandler spent his formative years in the western United States. When he wasn't catching fish or footballs, he was roaming centerfield and trying to hit the breaking pitch. After a mediocre college baseball career, he exchanged jersey No. 7 for camouflage issued by the United States Army, which he wore around the globe and with great pride for twenty years. Since law school, he has favored dark suits and a steerhide briefcase. When he isn't working or writing, he'll likely have a fly rod, shotgun or rifle in hand. He and his wife are blessed with two wonderful adult daughters.

Sign up for James Chandler's newsletter at
severnriverbooks.com